# LUCKY GIRL SUMMER

## MORGAN ELIZABETH

*To the ones who make their own luck.*

# PLAYLIST

Wood - Taylor Swift
    Dancing in the Dark - Bruce Springsteen
    Ring My Bell - Anita Ward
    Bed Chem - Sabrina Carpenter
    Don't Stop Me Now - Queen
    Lucky - Jason Mraz and Colbie Callait
    Delicate - Taylor Swift
    Dive - Olivia Dean
    Luck Be a Lady - Frank Sinatra
    If It Makes You Happy - Sheryl Crow
    Whim - Hailey Williams

# A NOTE FROM MORGAN

Dear Reader,

I've always been a very superstitious person.

I knock on wood, I wish at 11:11, I see my lucky numbers every-where I go, and most importantly, I fully believe in lucky girl syndrome. There's something so magical about believing that in the end, everything will. work out for you because that's what the world wants for you. I keep a running list in my phone's notes section called "Good things are always happening to me!" and add to it anytime something happens, big or small.

Since I introduced June in Tourist Trap, I knew she was going to be a lucky girl. I loved the idea of writing someone who is so blissfully optimistic that nothing can touch her. Loses her job? Ehh, it was for the best. Accidentally has a one-night stand with her new boss? I mean, at least she has a job? But there was no way I could have known just how much I'd have writing this book. In a way, I feel like June's burnout and journey to find joy in creativity are things I felt while writing this.

Writing this book, I giggled.

I kicked my feet.

I had full blow butterflies.

I tried something new, and I won't lie: I think I absolutely SLAYED it, which is hard for me to admit because I have a very hard time complimenting myself.

But the truth is, this book is all me. It's a love letter to my own optimism, though sometimes hidden in sarcasm, the way I attempt to see the best in the world as a whole, and my love for all things silly and goofy and colorful and unserious. I said that Tourist Trap was my love letter to the Jersey Shore, a place I love and cherish, and this continues it but adds to it. my own love for whimsy.

All that to say, I love June and Graham, and I hope you do too.

That being said, as with all stories, this one touches on a few things that you should know about, such as parental abandonment and mild neglect, and it wouldn't be a Morgan Elizabeth book without a healthy use of the word "fuck" or a healthy dose of people fucking. As always, please use your best judgment, and remember that reading is always supposed to be our safe space!

I love you to the moon and to Saturn,

Morgan

# ONE

# June

"Give me a sign," I groan, dropping my head to the steering wheel of my old clunker of a car. Instantly, the air conditioning cuts out.

I guess, in theory, that could be considered a sign.

My head tips to look at the drooping headlining on the roof, but my focus is directed beyond it toward whatever higher power is in control of my life. "I meant more regarding my career path, but thank you, I suppose."

My stomach growls, reminding me I barely ate half of my lunch today. I need some kind of sustenance before I make huge, life-altering choices, and everyone knows nothing eases big decisions like a soft pretzel and a fountain soda from a convenience store.

With a sigh, I roll down my windows and leave the parking lot. After my snack, I'll head home to make a pros and cons list to choose between taking the sure-thing job versus taking an entire year off.

Reason number one on the pro side: it's a job that pays actual money and is in the field for which I went to school.

Unfortunately, the first con is that *I secretly hate teaching*.

The school board has decided to reduce the number of fifth-grade classes in our small town. Since I was the most recent hire, I'm the first to go. My boss was able to pull some strings and has found a position at a school district an hour away if I want it, but it would mean uprooting my entire life for a career I don't even know if I enjoy anymore.

Alternatively, I could wait out the next school year until one of the other teachers retires, but that would mean being effectively unemployed for an entire year.

Either way, I will not be working at Seaside Point Elementary next year.

Even worse, I've been given barely any time to make my decision: Mrs. Jones needs an answer by tomorrow afternoon.

If I were presented with this choice one year ago, I would have instantly chosen the responsible, logical option: the guaranteed position, financial security, and the opportunity to continue teaching.

But over the last year, the job I spent my entire life believing was meant for me has begun to feel anything but. Burnout has zapped every last ounce of joy from my days, leaving me exhausted and uninspired. It's why I've been weighing the scarier option of taking a hiatus and seeing what else I might want to do with my life.

The mere concept sends a dart of nervous optimism through me, though guilt and panic come rolling in almost immediately after. What on earth *could* I even do other than teach? It's all I've ever known, and people in my life have given up a lot to make sure I could follow that dream.

*But was it really ever* your *dream?* a voice in my head asks, a voice that's been getting louder and louder each day. My anxiety rises as I park, but I push it down, reminding myself of my plan.

Fountain soda, pretzel, home, *then* total meltdown.

I don't bother to roll the windows up as I pull the key from the ignition and step outside. This is Seaside Point in the off-season, and with my A/C out, I'd rather my car not get any stuffier. As I enter the store, I wave at Connie, the cashier whose kids I used to babysit in high school, then head to the back. There, I grab the largest cup on offer, fill it with ice, and soda. Next, I carefully pick out my pretzel, choosing a double since carbs are a beloved coping mechanism of mine, before heading to the end of the surprisingly long line at the cash register. It seems everyone needed a midday pick-me-up. I'm forcing my mind to bask in these few moments of peace before I head home and failing miserably when a man steps behind me, arguing with someone on his phone.

"If you can't meet those deadlines, I'm happy to find another contractor, Carl," he says, and my interest is piqued. Carl is my brother's biggest business rival in town and a huge asshole. "No, that wasn't a threat; it was simply a statement." I widen my eyes at the tone, fighting back an entertained smirk. "The work you've done is shoddy at best, as I pointed out on Thursday. That has not been rectified as of this morning. I have a month until we need to open, and you're the number one thing holding me up." He pauses, and I try to sneak a glance at the man.

I'm a bit shocked when I don't recognize him: Seaside Point is a very small town, and while it gets packed from late June to early September, outside of those times, it's incredibly rare to see someone you don't know. He's tall and severe-looking, dressed in a well-fitted, white button-down shirt with the first two buttons undone. His hair is dark brown with a bit of a wave to it, combed back neatly, though a few pieces are unkempt in a way that tells me he's been running his hand through it often. There's a thin layer of scruff on his face that's a bit beyond five o'clock shadow, as if he purposely shaves it close, but not all the way. He's clearly good-looking, even if his cold eyes make him seem more like a robot than a human.

I bet if he smiled, he would be absolutely stunning.

He continues arguing with Carl, ending the call with a fierce threat: "If I don't have a firm plan by tomorrow morning, I'm canceling our contract and moving on." He hangs up, grumbling to himself and furiously tapping at his phone. For a moment, I contemplate minding my own business, but I've never been good at that. Instead, I reach into my bag, pull out my wallet, and grab a card for Grant's business.

"I wasn't trying to eavesdrop." I start, turning and offering the card to him. "But I overheard your struggles dealing with Carl. If you're looking for a new contractor, Taylor Contracting is the best in town. Tell them June sent you, and they'll fit you in right away." My eyes drift from his face to his hand, where he's holding a hot cup of coffee and a protein bar. He looks from me to my hand, and for a moment, I think he's going to ignore me, but then he takes the card, inspecting it before sliding it into his wallet.

"Thank you," he says with a hint of hesitation, and I smile.

"You're not from here, I see."

"No. Just here for work."

"Well, Grant is the best. And if you are looking for the best coffee, you have to go to Seaside Coffee. They just got their seasonal coconut syrup back, and it's the best thing ever. She has food, too. Breakfast sandwiches, bagels, and pastries. They run out quick, but the chocolate frosted donuts with the rainbow sprinkles could genuinely cure any ailment."

He stares at me for another long moment, as if unsure of what to do or say, before he nods again.

"I'll keep that in mind," he says, then tips his chin toward the cashier. I turn to Connie, who is now waiting to ring me up.

"Sorry," I say with a cringe, as always, putting my foot in my mouth by recommending the hot stranger shop elsewhere. She shakes her head and gives me a kind smile.

"No, that's where I get my coffee, too." She grabs my purchases, including the bag of candy I added on impulse, and starts to ring me up. As she does, my eyes drift down to where the scratch-off tickets sit below the counter.

As I take in the brightly colored rolls, bittersweet memories flood me. Sunday mornings with my grandfather, waking up early to get bagels, then going next door to the small convenience store. We'd separate once we walked in, and I'd pick out a strawberry milk for myself and an orange juice for Grant while Grandpa made himself a coffee. He'd be waiting for me at the counter, the giant brown bag in hand filled with still-warm bagels, and he'd let me choose which scratch-offs he'd get. With thirty dollars to spend, I'd carefully choose which ones intrigued me, themed ones for Mother's Day or the holidays, a crossword puzzle, or some kind of tic-tac-toe.

*Trust your gut*, he'd tell me, *it will never steer you wrong*. I would meticulously point out each one until we had a big stack. When we got home, we'd have breakfast, then sit at the table and make a mess of silver flecks, scratching at the cards with pennies Grandma would hand Grandpa, Grant, and me. Sometimes, we'd win big, a couple of hundred dollars that would make for a new toy or a fancy dinner, and sometimes they were all losers, but I always cherished those lazy mornings, believing in luck and chance.

I remember then, something else I had long forgotten—how Grandpa also used to make decisions with lottery tickets, saying his lucky stars were guiding him. Some people use coins, ask friends, or make a pros-and-cons list, like I'm planning to, but not my grandfather. He was a dreamer of the highest regard and believed the universe would always guide him where he needed to be.

I idolized that about him, the way he just trusted in things he couldn't see. He passed down that dreamer attitude to his daughter, my mom, and because of it, she was never around long enough to take on the responsibility of raising us. Even though that mindset saddled him with two kids long past his prime, he never made it seem like a bad thing. Instead, he always told me the universe was guiding me along, reminded me to trust in the process, and believe it would all work out in the end.

Maybe I should try putting this decision in the hands of the universe, let someone else decide for me. There's an old overstock ticket from St. Patrick's Day, lucky icons littering it, my grandpa's favorite holiday for obvious reasons, and it feels like a sign.

A horseshoe, just like the one I keep in my entryway, facing up to catch any good luck that could possibly come my way.

A ladybug, the first and only tattoo I ever got, hidden on my hip so my grandparents couldn't see it.

A four-leaf clover, like the ones I've spent hours and hours searching for my entire life.

I asked for a sign, didn't I? Maybe this is it.

*I am so lucky, and everything works out for me,* runs through my mind unbidden. I have the saying hanging as a print in my apartment, reminding me to *believe* that I have Lucky Girl Syndrome, even when it sometimes feels like the complete opposite. Without a second thought, I point to the ticket beneath the glass. "Can I also get one of those?"

Connie smiles and moves to get me one, and I smile over my shoulder at the man. "Sorry, I don't mean to hold you up." He gives me a noncommittal look and a wave of his hand as I pay for my small haul.

After, I shift down the counter out of the way to scratch my lottery ticket. I can't wait to do this at home, not when it feels like my future hangs in the balance. I guess, in a way, it does:

If I win, I decide I'll take the hiatus and see what happens.

If I lose, I'll accept the out-of-town position. Either way, I'm leaving here having made up my mind.

"Shit," I mumble, as I dig through my bag, already hitting my first hiccup. I turn to the man who is now checking out at the register. "Do you happen to have a coin I could borrow?" His stoic, uninterested look transforms into confusion, and I expand. "For my scratch off." He stares, unspeaking once more, before moving to his pocket and pulling out a penny. "How lucky!" I exclaim as he hands it to me. "Thank you so much! I never have change anymore. Everything is credit." He nods, the very edges of his lips just barely tipping up, and even though he's not actually smiling, I see my guess confirmed: he's *hot.*

Like, really hot.

So much so, in fact, I think his hotness short-circuits my brain, making me ramble.

"If I win, I'm going to quit my job," I inform him as if he asked.

"I don't know if a scratch off is great for life advice."

"I'm not taking life advice from a lottery ticket. I'm taking life advice from the universe," I say as if that's any better. He looks at me as if I have completely lost it, lifting an eyebrow at me.

"Do you have a backup?"

I let out a laugh and shake my head.

"No. But I'm lucky. Everything always works out for me."

"Everything?"

"Everything always works out the way the universe intends," I correct, and he narrows his eyes at me, but despite everything, I believe that to be true. It hasn't been foolproof, but when I look back at hiccups in my life, everything has genuinely always worked out. I was crushed when I got into my number-one pick college but didn't get the scholarships I was counting on, but it meant I went to a state school on a full ride, where I met my best friend, Claire.

There's also how Claire met and began dating Paul, the absolute worst person on earth, but after they broke up, she ended up living with his brother, Miles. Now they're madly in love, and she lives in my hometown, where I get to see her all the time.

Or the time I desperately wanted tickets for an outdoor festival but missed the presale. It ended up raining the entire weekend, and no one got refunds.

It always works out. Everything happens for a reason, even if it seems like, in the moment, that nothing is going right. It's what I've had to tell myself most of my life in order to make it through without losing my mind, and I won't be stopping anytime soon.

"That sounds like how people justify things not working out for them," the stranger says, not buying it.

"A little positivity never hurt anyone," I tell him as I begin scratching at the small ticket. My heart races as I reveal different icons.

One acorn.

One ladybug.

One rabbit's foot.

One four-leaf clover.

None of them is my lucky icon, which is a horseshoe.

Maybe I'm meant to take the safe option after all. Disappointment fills me, surprising me with its intensity. But when I scratch the last icon, I squeal as the corner of it is revealed. Quickly, I scratch the rest off to be sure.

"Ahhh!" I yell once it's fully cleared, jumping up and down. "Oh my god!" The man watches me attentively as I celebrate, an entertained eyebrow lifted.

"Did you win?"

"Yes!" I shout, waving the lottery ticket in his face. "Look!"

"A hundred bucks," he confirms, with a nod. "Will that cover your bills enough for you to quit your job?" I stare at the ticket again, a wide grin on my face, my chest light as I shake my head.

"No. Not at all. But I'm going to do it anyway. It's a sign. Everything is going to work for me." When I speak the words aloud, I believe them, each one settling into my chest and a sense of peace washing over me as I make my decision.

"Because you're lucky," he says.

"Exactly." He grabs his things and moves to step away, but I stop him. "Thank you," I say, the penny in the palm of my hand. He looks at it, then at me, before shaking his head.

"Keep it. It might be lucky." He walks out before I can say anything else, and I turn to Connie, who is grinning at me.

"You're a nut, girl."

"I know," I say with a laugh. We chat for a bit as she cashes out my lottery ticket, and with one hundred dollars I didn't have before in my pocket, I'm feeling a bit more confident about the choice I think I was always going to make.

I'm terrified, but it's the right decision—somehow, I know that in my bones.

When I get into my car, the air conditioning starts up without a problem, and I decide it's another sign that I'm moving in the right direction. Somehow, some way, everything is going to work out for me, because I am lucky and *everything* works out for me.

# TWO

The entire drive back to my place, I force my mind to stay on a positive track. Anytime it veers off, I remind myself that the universe has made my decision for me, and I'm sticking with it. It's not *me* making irrational, off-the-cuff life choices: it's the universe.

*I am so lucky, and everything works out for me.*

The second I walk through the front door of my shitty apartment, I set my bag down and bring my laptop to the kitchen. Without giving myself another moment to overthink, I send off an email, accepting being laid off for a year and thus taking the leap into the unknown. With each word I type, a bit of the tension leaves my chest, signaling I'm maybe-probably making the right choice.

Finally, I hit send, slam my laptop shut, take a deep breath, let it go, and stare at the wall for a minute.

I did it.

Thursday will be my last day of teaching for over a year.

I quit my job, in a way.

Relief washes over me as I realize it means *I won't have to be a teacher for a year.* Quickly on its heels, panic surges in.

*I just quit my job.*

I quit my job with absolutely no safety net. I might have savings and low overhead, but I *do* have bills to pay.

*I just quit my job.*

In a rush, I reopen my computer, trying to see if the unsend feature is still active, only to see Mrs. Jones has already replied with a cheery, "Great, thank you so much for understanding! Excited for you to come back to Seaside Point Elementary next fall!"

I just quit my *fucking* job.

Then, I do what every girl on the verge of a meltdown does: I call my best friends.

In less than thirty minutes, Claire and Lainey are at my place, Lainey having asked her dad to cover for the night at the bar the second she heard the panic in my voice. They sit on my couch while I pace, running my hands through my hair over and over as I tell them everything that happened in the last three hours. When I get through telling them how I sent an email quitting my job without even thinking it through, I finally stop and look at them with wide eyes.

"So, now I'm freaking out." My throat is tight, on the verge of tears that I've been barely keeping at bay.

They just stare at me, Claire looking intrigued, Lainey looking shocked. I expect utter chaos to erupt, a mix of *what-the-hell-were-you-thinking* and *why-didn't-you-call-us?* I expect them to be shocked and panicked, the way I feel right now, maybe even disappointed, which I fear most of all, but instead, they...smile.

"June, this is the luckiest thing that has ever happened to you," Claire says after a moment.

"Claire, I just lost my job," I remind her, flopping into the old, beat-up armchair across from her that was my grandma's. It has small specks of paint on the left arm from when she used to paint, and a few more on the right from my own art projects. Even though it doesn't fit in with my decor at all, I'll keep it until it's falling apart. Both of my grandparents passed almost six years ago, barely two months in between them, and I still cling to the small things I have left of them.

In response to my accusation, Lainey sighs and rolls her eyes.

"Let's not be dramatic, you didn't lose your job. You were laid off and given the opportunity to take an alternative job if you wanted." She's always the logical one of the three of us and the most likely to quickly sift through any bullshit.

"Yeah, a job in another town an hour away. I couldn't just completely upheave my life like that," I say, draping an arm over my eyes in defeat.

"You could have and would have if you loved teaching. But the mere fact that you aren't even thinking of that as a viable option tells me everything I need to know. I, for one, am relieved you're taking a break." My brows furrow, not understanding. Her face goes soft before she lands her next blow. "June, you've been so burnt out it's scary."

My tongue dips out to wet my suddenly dry lips, unable to argue her point because she's right: I am burnt out. Part of that is because that's the reality of being a public elementary school teacher, but in my gut, I've known for a long time that that burnout wasn't just the reality of teaching.

It was something more. Something that no amount of summers off would repair. If I really think about it and am honest with myself, I've needed a break for a while.

"I love you, June, like a sister, but you're not happy," Claire adds, her voice gentle, but her words still strike me directly in my chest, knocking the breath out of me. "For as long as I've known you, you told me you wanted to be a teacher, but do you *really*? Did you really want to be a teacher all your life, or did you just fall into it, and everybody convinced you that's where you should be?" I glare at her, despising the kernels of truth in her words. Everyone tells you that having best friends who know you is so great, but they conveniently leave out how they will absolutely call you out on your bullshit when you don't want to hear it.

"I hate that you found your dream life," I grumble instead of acknowledging her truth. A year ago, Claire came to Seaside Point to work as a lifeguard as her one last hurrah of chaos and freedom before she forced herself to, in her words, get a big girl job. Thankfully, while she was here, she fell in love with my brother's best friend, who also happened to be her ex's older brother, and fell into her dream job of managing the Recreation Department.

"And I hate that you haven't found yours," she says, that same softness in her words. "I want you to have it too, June. You, more than anyone else, deserve to live your dream life."

"You're the kindest, sweetest person I know. It kills me to see you not enjoying every day, but pretending you are for everyone else's benefit," Lainey agrees.

I contemplate denying their words, but where would that even get me?

"How long have you guys known?" I ask instead. I've held the truth in for so long, and as I admit it in this small way, a weight leaves my chest. Lainey lifts a shoulder in response and gives me a sad smile.

"A while. You wear every emotion on your face, and we're your best friends. We can tell when you're lying, even if the person you're lying to is yourself."

"You never said anything," I say, picking some imaginary lint off the yoga pants I changed into while I waited for the girls to get here.

"You wouldn't have wanted to hear it. It's like when I was dating Paul," Claire explains. My nose scrunches up because her ex-boyfriend was the absolute worst. "And it wasn't the right time. You wouldn't have changed anything. It would have just stressed you out more, knowing we knew you were miserable, especially if you had nothing pushing you to make a change. But now you do." There's a gentle smile on her face now, like she's trying to keep her excitement at bay. "This is the perfect solution, June, and you know it. You can spend the next year doing...anything."

"And if you find yourself missing teaching, desperate to get back, you'll have a position waiting for you next fall," Lainey adds, speaking the logic I've been telling myself aloud. "But this way, you can make sure that's the case. It would be terrible to spend your entire life doing something just because it's the safe option." I know what they're saying is the truth: it's how I sold myself on this decision after all, but it doesn't make this any easier in the present.

"What am I even going to do for the next year? As sunshine and rainbows as you both are being about this, I need a job. I have bills to pay."

"Of course. Get a job. Pay your bills. But now, you have the opportunity and, most importantly, the time and energy, to do whatever you want. Something different and exciting, something that makes you happy," Claire says.

"I thought I *was* doing what I wanted to do. How the hell do I know what will make me happy?"

Claire and Lainey look at each other, an assessing look passing between them before Claire nods softly and Lainey turns to me. Her face is firm now, and I know in my gut I'm not going to like whatever they've just silently communicated.

"You could try to sell your paintings," she says, and I groan, closing my eyes and shaking my head. "Oh, come on. The whole reason you haven't been doing it is that you don't have enough time. Now you have time to do it. You're an amazing artist, June, and—"

I cut her off, having heard this argument a dozen times.

"I love the confidence, but that's not a career. Art doesn't pay the bills," I say with a laugh, shaking my head. It's a lesson I watched play out over and over through my childhood, and a lesson I refuse to learn firsthand.

Art is a hobby.

Art is a stress reliever.

Art is not a career. Art is not something you can rely on, and surely not something that can support a family when the time comes.

"Not when you refuse to try and make it pay the bills," Claire says. She's been the most adamant about encouraging me to start a small shop and list my paintings. Over winter break last year, she even went so far as to help me set one up, but I chickened out before I could even go live. I allowed myself toget wrapped back up in school and after-school obligations, lesson plans, and grading papers, so I never touched it again.

"Claire..." I start, but her eyes are fierce on me,

"If you never try to sell them, you're right: you will never pay the bills. This is the perfect way to test something. You've got a year to see if you can make something happen, make it so you wake up every morning excited to go to work. I know in my heart you could make something of it, but you're the person who needs convincing. Is that how you would want your students to be? Deeply logical and practical, and never living for their dreams?"

My gut twists, knowing the answer, but...

"It's not that easy."

"It could be, June," Lainey adds, and I get the distinct feeling they've talked about this before. "You're talented, you're just too scared to end up like your parents, something that we all know would *never happen,* if only because Grant would never let it." Her words bring a dread-filled reminder that soon, I'll have to tell my brother the news, but I push that away quickly. I have enough to focus on right now. "But the truth is, if you never try, you'll never know."

There's silence as they stare at me, and all of their words swirl around me, making me dizzy. Claire must see the brewing panic on my face, because she shifts, sitting up and reaching for my hands, and giving me a smile. "We can table the art discussion for later, because you've got a lot going on, but here's what I *do* want you to promise us. I want you to give in to your inner woo-woo girl and let the universe guide you along. Say yes to crazy ideas and opportunities that fall into your lap, take advantage of all of the luck the universe sends your way. You're always saying you're so lucky, and everything works out for you—apply that tenfold this summer."

The suggestion alone makes my pulse jump, but not with nerves this time.

With excitement.

"Instead of lucky girl syndrome, live out your lucky girl summer," Lainey adds.

"My lucky girl summer," I say, rolling the idea around in my mind and finding that it intrigues me. Hell, I just made a huge life decision on an impulse based on a lottery ticket because I *believed* that it would lead me in the right direction. Why can't I apply that theory to the entire summer? I stare at them, then take in a deep breath and nod, speaking on another impulse and praying it won't lead me astray.

"Okay. Deal."

"Woo!" Claire yells, throwing her hands in the air as if I just agreed to go skydiving instead of just living my life to its fullest.

"Now I just have to figure out how to tell Grant I quit my job," I say with a sigh. The mere thought of disappointing my older brother and telling him I purposely got laid off sends me into a cold sweat. He's always been responsible and was the loudest voice encouraging me to go to school to become a teacher. He gave up so much in his own life for me, staying home in Seaside Point to help raise me as our grandparents got older, and I've always felt I owed him everything.

What will he say when I tell him I threw away everything he did for me, even if it's only temporary?

"I don't get it, June. Why are you *scared* of your brother?" Lainey asks, a hint of irritation in the words.

"I think you're the only one *not* scared of him, Lainey," Claire says low.

"That's because I have common sense. What the hell is he gonna do, glare you to death?" Lainey asks. I lift a shoulder.

"Yeah. And tell me he's disappointed in me."

"A killing blow," Claire says solemnly, but Lainey rolls her eyes.

"He'll get over it," she says. "And if not, you can just send him my way. I'll set him straight."

"And just how will you do *that*, Lainey?" Claire asks, a smile on her lips. My childhood best friend rolls her eyes at my college best friend, and I'm reminded once again just how lucky I am that these two get along so well, so we can be the perfect little friend group.

"Shut up, Claire. Now, I'm starving. What do we want for take-out? My treat." And even though it's clearly a diversion to change the topic, we allow it before deciding on Chinese. We spend the rest of the evening eating, laughing, and watching trash TV. When they leave, I go about my nighttime routine before sitting in my bed with my laptop and opening up job sites. I'll have to revamp my resume, but tonight, I just want to see what my options might be. I scroll for a while, finding a few interesting things and adding them to my favorites before making a list of small businesses on the boardwalk that might need help this summer.

And then, with a pounding heart, I find myself opening up the shop Claire helped me make months ago. My hands shake as I look at the three listings we put up, my eyes drifting to the corner of my room to the stack of canvases that could use new homes. What if they're right, and I should use this opportunity to...try? And if it fails miserably, I'd be secure in the knowledge that come next fall, I have a job waiting for me.

After a moment, though, I shake my head, close my computer, and wipe the idea from my mind.

I don't have time to think about a hobby, not when I need a real job as soon as possible. Still, as I drift off to sleep, I can't help but wonder if it would really be that terrible to try both.

# THREE

## June

"Why are you coming with me again?" Grant asks on Friday morning as I slide into the terribly oversized truck I constantly make fun of. It might make sense for him, since he owns a small contracting company and does a lot of the work himself with his small crew, but I am his little sister, which means it's my job to constantly make his life more difficult.

"It's take your sister to work day. Duh."

He glares at me. "That's absolutely not a real thing."

"Like you would know. You never even remember when Halloween is."

"Why would I? I don't have kids," Grant says.

Every year, I bring two bags of candy to his house on the thirtieth, knowing damn well he is not going to have any for the next day. Since he lives on a cul-de-sac in the suburbs, he always gets a ton of kids coming to his house. If it weren't for me, he'd probably be a big target on Mischief Night.

"Because it's the same day each year!" I argue, and the very edges of his lips tip up, signaling he's purposely trying to irritate me. I sigh and shake my head. "What I'm saying is, you don't know holidays, so why would you know if Take Your Sister to Work Day isn't real?"

"Because I have two brain cells and I've known you your whole life. I know when you're bullshitting me to avoid talking about something that you're reluctant to address." Unfortunately, he had more to do with raising me than our parents did. This often meant sifting out untruths and lies—not that I did that too often—but if anyone can read me like a book, it's my older brother. "So, tell me why you're really here?" An anxious flutter twists in my stomach as I force myself to sound casual.

"I just wanted to see what it would be like working for you," I say, focusing on my nails and avoiding his gaze. I spent last night painting them a pretty pale pink to distract myself while filling out job applications, all the while dreading having this conversation with Grant.

"Why would you want to do that?" he asks, rightfully confused since physical labor and I have never been friends.

"In case I want to work with you."

He starts to creep through the parking lot, moving forward as he gives me a puzzled look.

"Why?"

I bite my lip instead of meeting his eyes. "Because I quit my job, and I'll need a backup soon."

He slams on the brakes, making me test the crash resistance of his seatbelt.

"Jesus, Grant," I grumble, rubbing at my neck where the strap rubbed it.

"What did you just say?" He turns in his seat to face me.

"Okay, so, I didn't quit." I roll my lips into my mouth. "Technically, I've been laid off. But only for a year," I add, trying to sound upbeat. "They needed to reduce the number of teachers, and I'm the newest addition. I'll get my position back when Mrs. Evans retires. I could have gone to Bridgeville to teach, but I chose to be laid off and come back next fall." Might as well just rip the Band-Aid off all at once.

"June. Why would you choose to quit instead of taking the other job? That's reckless, and you know that."

"I didn't quit. I was laid off," I say, my voice low and childish sounding even to my own ears.

"Laid off, quit, whatever. June. What were you thinking?"

*I was thinking that each morning I woke up dreading the hours ahead, and I couldn't live like that forever.* But saying that out loud would trigger exactly the kind of alarm I'm trying to avoid. Better to keep that to myself—at least for now.

Or concern him more than how alarmed he already looks.

"I just wanted a change," I say. Wrong answer.

"Then dye your hair!" he says, throwing his hands in the air. "Get a tattoo! You don't just up and quit your job. I can't believe this, June. What are you going to do? You're just throwing everything you worked for all away?"

"It's just a year," I mumble, doubting myself.

"What will you do for that year?" he asks.

"I don't know. I just...I saw the chance to catch my breath, and I took it. Some days..." My words trail off as I stare out the window, pressing my forehead against the cool glass. Nerves pull tightly at my stomach. "Sometimes, I don't know if I want to be a teacher anymore," I admit, the confession escaping before I can stop it, my voice trembling.

"What do you mean you aren't sure if you want to be a teacher anymore?" Grant's voice is sharp with surprise, and anxiety floods my chest. I chew my lip, my hands growing clammy in my lap as I fight the urge to shrink away.

I knew this wouldn't go over well.

Grant gave up so much to support my dreams, and he's always been the most responsible person I know. How could I ever explain that, even after getting everything I wanted, I sometimes feel lost? I force a smile, even though my cheeks ache from the effort.

"No, I mean...I don't mean that I don't want to be a teacher. I just think it will be fun to try something new for a bit. I've only ever worked with kids; I've never tried anything else. I love teaching. I'm young—why not take the opportunity to try something new?"

He continues to stare at me, though the tight look of concern starts to fade, and relief moves through me.

"So what's your plan?" he asks. "You're obviously not going to start putting up drywall with me, and you're not going to run off to California to become some hippie artist."

That's what our parents did, after all. They're hippies and while they were always happy, Grant and I were the ones who suffered. They never had real jobs, refusing to work for The Man, and instead always had odd jobs that barely kept them fed and in art supplies. Soon after Grant was born, they dumped him on Grandma and Grandpa to watch while they chased their dreams. For a while, I think everyone thought they'd actually do it—land some big gig and then fly Grant out to be with them—but when I came along, and it was more of the same, I think our grandparents and Grant both became a bit jaded. It's why Grant has always pushed both of us toward the most practical jobs, with him running a contracting business and sending me to school to be a teacher.

Normal, respectable jobs with consistent income and reliable hours.

I lift a shoulder, leaning into my regular happy-go-lucky attitude. Despite the fact that I don't have a job, the mere fact that the worst of this conversation is over has my spirits lifting.

"I don't know. I just...I'm going to figure it out, because I'm very lucky—things always seem to work out for me," I say, trying to exude confidence.

"Jobs don't just fall into your lap, June."

"They could," I say. He rolls his eyes and shakes his head, but we're turning into the lot for Surf, the luxury beach club that was built a few years ago and sold over the winter to Daydream resorts and Grant's newest contract. They're creating a new line of their luxury day resorts, and this is the first location. Apparently, Claire's older sister, Sutton, encouraged her boss, the VP of Operations for the large luxury chain, and his girlfriend to spend a week vacationing here, and they fell in love with the area.

As soon as he puts the truck into park, I open my door, eager to get out of this jail cell.

"June," he says, looking at me, and my entire body stills. "We're not done with this conversation. We have to figure out what you're going to do."

"I've got it covered, Grant. I'm lucky; it will all work out. It always does." It's what I've been telling myself all week, desperately trying to believe it myself, but I force myself to sound convincing enough for Grant. He lets out a deep sigh and shakes his head.

"What am I going to do with you, June Bug?"

"Love me eternally. Unfortunately, you're my big brother, and that's your only option." He sighs and looks up at the roof of his truck as if looking for some peace he might find up there, and while he's distracted, I hop out of the car and toward the entrance. A door slams behind me, and the locks bleep before Grant is taking long strides beside me.

"I've gotta see what the guys are doing. You stay here since those shoes aren't great for a construction zone," he says, looking at my feet, which are in a pair of sandals. "Don't think construction is really in your future."

"Excuse me, I would rock a pair of steel-toed boots," I say, and he rolls his eyes.

"Just stay in the business area, okay? Don't get into trouble," he says, walking me through the front door.

Stepping in, I take it in. The place looks totally different from the last time I was here, taking shots with Claire and Lainey on the night Claire fell into Miles' arms, literally. It's wild to think that was barely a year ago, considering it feels like it was an entire lifetime ago. In place of the dark nightclub vibe it boasted then, it's bright, open, and fittingly beachy, with a small stand at the front where I assume someone will check guests in and a dining area right beyond it. I follow him through a hidden door to the left of the entrance and into a much less interesting area with a few desks and offices, white walls, and fluorescent lighting. Grant wanders off with one last reminder to behave before I move through the space, too nosy not to inspect. I'm wandering around the office area, which looks almost clinical compared to the beauty area for customers and clients, when a door opens to an office. On instinct, my head turns to it, and I see a familiar face.

"Hey, June!" Sutton Donovan says, walking out of an office and scanning the room, smiling when she sees me there. "I didn't realize you were my next interview!" Her light blonde hair is tucked behind her ears, and she's wearing a pretty purple dress and sneakers, somehow looking both effortlessly cool and businesslike.

"Sutton! Hey! What are you doing here?" I ask, stepping toward her.

"My boss sent me here to help out at the beginning of this project," she says with a roll of here eys. Sutton is Claire's older sister and works for Daydream Resorts. "Come on, come on! I am in desperate need of a coffee, and we can chat in the break room. You're perfect for this job, kind of a shoo-in." My brows furrow, and I look over my shoulder, confused and wondering if maybe she's speaking to someone else, but I'm the only one in the room.

"Job?" I ask, hesitantly.

"Yeah, honestly, it's so easy, mostly making sure everyone leaves Julian alone so he can handle the important stuff. Making sure his calendar is sorted, deadlines for permits and whatnot are going well, that kind of thing." She leads me into a break room, pours herself a coffee, and offers me one, though I shake my head, still totally lost. Finally, Sutton sits on the edge of a table, an iPad in her hands.

"The rest of the candidates were okay, but they didn't have the personality required to handle a job like this. You'd be perfect. Hell, if you can wrangle a group of fifth graders, you can handle this easily." Claire must have given her an update on my current jobless status, something that doesn't bother me, since I like Sutton and always have. "Plus, your brother is the contractor on this, and the person you'll be working to keep him on target. I can't think of anyone better."

"I, um," I say, biting my lip and looking around. "Do you have my resume?" I know I applied for a dozen jobs the other day, but I don't remember filling out one for...whatever this position is. She shrugs a shoulder and grins.

"Something happened to the docs, so they accidentally got deleted." My eyes widen. "Don't tell Graham, okay? I can't figure out for the life of me how to undo it, and he'd never let me live it down. I'm so lucky you were one of the candidates because I already know your qualifications." I should tell her that I'm not here for an interview and I will, but what could learning about this position Sutton seems to think I'd be perfect for hurt? I did say I was going to try harder to say yes to opportunities, didn't I?

"Can you, um...can you remind me what the job is for?" She nods eagerly, then turns the iPad toward me, an email on the screen.

"This is the position, and I've highlighted what I've been approved to offer the final candidate." My eyes narrow at the screen, trying to take in everything at once, but failing miserably as my eyes move right to the highlighted section.

The salary is double that of my teaching job, which, granted, isn't that hard, but if I kept this job even for a year, I would be able to set myself up and add more padding to my savings. Even if I went back to teaching, I would have so much less stress. And if I didn't...I'd have a buffer if I wanted to try anything else.

The job itself, Coordinating Assistant to the project manager, seems like a relatively straightforward position and one I could absolutely do. Maintain the manager's meeting schedule, sift through applications, stay on top of township deadlines, identify and reach out to influencers for promotional opportunities, and manage any remaining tasks related to the opening and operation of Daytrip, the new offshoot of Daydream Resorts.

Excitement brews in my belly, just a bit, because it actually sounds like a fun position. Still, I can't take advantage of my friend this way. Sighing, I hand the tablet back to her. "Sutton, I don't want to get you into trouble. I'm almost positive I didn't apply for this. I do need a job, but I really don't want you to get in trouble for offering a job to someone and—" She cuts me off with a wave of her hand.

"Look, I know you, I trust you, and I have shit to do. You'd be helping me out, really. I could stop looking and focus on what I have to do. It would be so easy to train you. Plus, you know everything about this town. Whatever hiccups we're bound to hit, you'd know the best way around them. You're probably more qualified for this job than I am."

"I don't know about that," I say with a laugh.

"I do. Now, will you please take this job so I can stop interviewing people?"

"Don't you have an interview, like, right now?"

"No show," she says with a shrug, as if it's a non-issue. "But you came instead. Kind of feels like it was meant to be, doesn't it?"

It does, actually. In fact, the kismet of it all feels exactly like what I promised Claire and Lainey. I promised myself I would view this as my lucky summer, and if an opportunity like this just falls into my lap...it has to be the universe giving me a sign, right?

Right.

"Uh, well...in that case...sure. Yeah. Why not?" I say with a wide smile, feeling a bit crazed and reckless, but excitement running in my veins all the same. Sutton grins.

"Yay! Amazing—I'll send over your paperwork tonight. I'll text you for your email. Could you come in on Monday for your first day? I know it's soon, but we're neck deep in opening day tasks, and I'm heading to Hudson City at noon to help Rowan with something for the Bali location." She starts tapping at the table as if checking her schedule or sending an email, already busy on her next task.

"I, uh..." I bite my lip, a sudden nervousness taking over the momentary excitement, but then I spot Grant talking to someone in the background, and my resolve strengthens.

I don't want him to worry about, once again, having to step in to help me. He's done more than enough by now.

"Yeah. That's totally fine."

"Yay!" Sutton says, clapping, then standing to pull me into a huge hug.

"What's going on here?" Grant says, taking off his hat and flipping it around, looking at Sutton and me with confusion. I expect him to remind me he told me to stay in one place and out of trouble, but I speak before he can lecture me.

"I just got a job," I say with a winning smile.

He looks at me, rightfully confused. "What?"

"Sutton just offered me a job here at Daytrip. Assist the project manager who has been running this thing. Pays pretty well, normal weekday hours, a desk job."

"With insurance!" Sutton adds, and I nod, smiling wider.

"And with insurance." He looks at me again for a long moment before shaking his head, a smile on his lips as he puts a shoulder around my arms, pulling me in for a side hug.

"Only you could literally have a job fall into your lap," he says.

"It's what happens when you're lucky," I say, genuinely feeling it to my bones, because I am *so* lucky, and everything is working out for me.

# FOUR

# June

I float on air through the weekend, secure in the fact that I made the right choice. How could I believe anything different when everything is working out perfectly? Sure, I may have changed my entire career path, but before I even had one full day unemployed, I had a new job.

On Saturday, I head to the Seabreeze to celebrate with Claire. Sunday, I spend the day cleaning my apartment and getting myself ready for my first day of work. By four, I'm out of things to do and eager to fill up my time to fend off any first-day jitters. On the table sits a half-finished piece I started months ago, but haven't touched it since; I pick it up and consider working on it. For a moment, Claire's words about selling my work run through my mind, but I push the thought aside.

Instead, I head down to the boardwalk, resolving to enjoy the warm early summer night, maybe read a book. But once I settle into a bench, I don't find myself opening the book I brought or peacefully watching the ocean. I don't even find myself mindlessly scrolling social media. Instead, I open up the sketch pad I also brought and doodle what I see: the crests of the waves, a seashell in the sand, a seagull grabbing a dropped French fry. After a while, my attention is pulled back to reality when a voice rises beside me, a man sitting one bench away.

"I don't care what you have to do, we agreed that the furniture would be delivered in two weeks, and if that's not adhered to, you're in breach of contract," he says, voice firm and angry and just a bit familiar. I force myself not to be nosy and look over at him, instead, keeping my eyes on the pad in my hands. I pretend to sketch as he talks about contracts and terms; I assume he must be a lawyer in town for the convention this week. I sit there for another minute, the man moving on, his voice low and growly and clearly irritated, before I finally give in to the urge to glance over.

That's when I realize the voice was somewhat familiar because I've run into this man before.

It's the man I met in the convenience store. I fight every urge to swipe my fingers against my pocket where I've been carrying the penny he gave me, and instead, grab my phone, opening my group chat with Lainey and June.

The hot guy is here.

On the boardwalk near Surf. He's HERE.

C: What?

The hot guy from the convenience store is here! I came here to draw, and he sat on the bench next to me. He's on his phone.

C: Sounds like your lucky stars are lining up again.

L: What are the chances of that happening?

C: TALK TO HIM!

C: FUCK HIM

Claire!

C: Come on, the universe put him in your path again. It's a sign you need to get laid.

That's not how the universe works.

C: It could, though!

Lainey, tell Claire that's the dumbest idea ever.

L: Talk to him, absolutely. Fuck him, maybe if he doesn't seem like a serial killer or like he's married.

You two have officially lost it. I'm not going to fuck a stranger.

C: You promised you'd take every opportunity the universe gave you. This feels like an opportunity the universe is giving you.

C: I'll give you my parking spot at the Seabreeze for a month if you say hi to him.

God damn it, that's a good deal.

C: You don't even have to fuck him. Just see where things go!

I don't think Miles would be okay with that

C: Well, Miles didn't win it, so he can suck my dick

The conversation continues, Claire and Lainey going back and forth, but the stranger has ended his call, and despite my denial, I can't help but feel they might have the tiniest bit of truth. I mean, what are the possibilities of bumping into the same man twice? There are two dozen benches along this stretch of boardwalk: he could have sat anywhere, and he sat right there.

If I don't say hi, I'll probably wonder what would have happened forever. My mind made up, I take in a deep breath, trying to seem as casual as humanly possible as I turn my head again, pretending to spot him for the first time.

"Oh my God, it's you!" I say in a gasp that sounds fake even to me. His head shifts, and something dances in his eyes. "You're the guy from the convenience store, right? You gave me a penny?" He stares at me for a long moment, assessing, and I think maybe he won't speak at all before finally, he does.

"You knew it was me the whole time," he states, and my eyes widen, the shock this time genuine.

"What?"

"You looked at me a handful of times; then you texted about it. You knew I was here."

I blink twice before deciding the correct path is total denial.

"I don't know what you're talking about." He lifts a single thick eyebrow at me, and I crumple, smiling. "Okay, I may or may not have been watching you. I was just shocked it was you. What are the chances, you know?"

I stand, gather my bag, and slide the sketch book inside. Then, I walk the ten feet to his bench and sit beside him, leaving about two feet of space between us.

"Yeah, sure. Feel free to sit next to me." His words are deadpan as he gestures toward me, and I grin.

"I'm June," I say, putting a hand out to him. He looks at it a second longer than polite before his own large hand comes out, engulfing mine and shaking it cordially.

"Graham." His thumb brushes over my knuckles lightly before he releases my hand. "So did you do it?"

"Do it?" I ask, confused.

"Quit your job."

"Ah, yes. I did."

"How do you feel?" he asks, leaning back and crossing his arms on his chest. His white button-down stretches across broad shoulders in a way I most definitely do *not* notice.

"I... I don't know," I admit with a laugh.

The setting sun plays across his features: a thin layer of scruff that doesn't look unkempt on him, his hair mussed by the wind off the water, his green eyes reflecting the colors of the water.

"I actually start my new job tomorrow, so we'll see if I deeply regret it or not." I let out a sigh, that nervous energy creeping. "But I really don't want to talk about work. I feel like this is all anyone wants to talk to me about, and it's making me a bit bonkers."

"Fair enough," he says.

"What were you yelling about?" I ask.

"Work. But I don't really want to talk about work, either."

"Fair enough," I say with a laugh.

After a while, we fall into a silence. It's not uncomfortable, but it's there, lingering between us. I think of Claire and Lainey, my phone still buzzing in my pocket, before I gather the nerve to speak once more.

"Do you want to get a drink with me?"

"A drink?"

"Yes. Liquid that you imbibe? Sometimes alcoholic, often an excuse to extend the time you're spending with someone?"

Then it happens: the edges of his lips tip up in the barest hint of a smile. It's handsome, even if the whisper of the expression looks a bit unnatural on his face.

"You want to spend time with me?"

"I'm sorry; that's weird, right? Ignore me. I'm just gonna—" I start with a laugh, shaking my head and standing as I prepare to leave.

Before I can walk away, he stands up too. He reaches out and wraps his hand gently around my wrist, pulling me closer. I have to look up at him as he shifts his arm to wrap around my waist. It should be strange to be touched by a stranger, but instead, my body relaxes, and it feels surprisingly natural.

As if this was meant to be. I've always believed in luck and fate, but standing in Graham's arms, I can't imagine *not* thinking that the universe has guided me along so I would end up right here.

"It's not weird. I've been trying to think of a way to casually get you to spend more time with me."

"Oh," I say the words in the barest whisper.

"There's a good bar at my hotel. Let's get a drink. See where things go," he murmurs.

"Where are you staying?"

"The Sunrise," he says, naming the very expensive hotel on the boardwalk. It's not far from here, maybe a quarter mile down, and has both normal rooms and small townhomes that can be rented long-term. I've heard that the entire place is absolutely stunning, though despite living here my entire life, I've never had a reason to enter the building.

Until, possibly, now.

"Big baller," I say with a smile and a raised eyebrow.

"My work put me up in it," he says with a nonchalant lift of his shoulder. "So? What do you say?" His fingers on my waist graze the bare skin where my tee meets my shorts, and I shiver. "I really don't want to end our night here."

I weigh his offer, biting my lip even though I know I'm going to say yes.

"Okay," I say. "But full disclosure, I'm telling my friends I'm with you, and they have my location." He nods but doesn't let me go. "Women's safety, and all."

"I'd be worried if you didn't," he says. I smile at him, wide and genuine, before he finally lets me go. "Take your time."

I tap out a quick text to my group chat, then slide my phone into my bag, ignoring the suddenly blasts of texts.

"Let's go."

One drink turns to two, and through them both, we sit close in the dimly lit bar, chatting low, and I thoroughly enjoy myself. We talk about absolutely nothing, my telling him a bit about Seaside Point, and him sharing the most minuscule details about himself, but each one feels like a prize, some snippet about his life that I earned. True to his word, we stay away from talking about work, though I learn the basics about him.

Not long after the second drink is gone, he gets the check, paying without giving me the time to offer, and then leading me out of the bar with a hand on my lower back. With each step, a strange and unexpected disappointment fills me, knowing our night is ending.

"Well," I say when we stand in the luxurious lobby, biting my lip. "It was very nice bumping into you again."

"Seemed very lucky," he murmurs, voice low and rolling through me warm and hot. He's standing close, not touching me, though my skin feels hyperalert, anticipating the lightest graze.

"I told you, I'm a very lucky person."

He looks at me, eyes dropping to my lips as he steps closer. My heart pounds with the small movement and is almost beating out of my chest with his next words.

"I would very much like for you to come upstairs with me," he murmurs, and my breathing stops. "You don't have to, of course. No pressure at all. Only if you'd like, otherwise, thank you for a drink with a gorgeous woman."

The invite hangs in the air between us, tempting and nerve-racking.

Claire and Lainey's promise to me rings through my mind: to take advantage of all the opportunities the universe sends our way.

Well, this is an opportunity, right?

"Yeah," I say, breathy and dazed. "Let's go up."

His eyes go hot with promise, and that heat curls in my belly before he tips his chin to me.

"Text your friends," he says, and I look at him, confused, before it registers. Another tip of his lips. "Women's safety and all."

He's hot, and he's *funny,* too, in that crazy way I find him far too attractive. It can be off-putting for some men, the dry, brusque kind of humor, but on him it's not. It just fits his personality perfectly.

I'm heading up to the hot guy's hotel room.

C: WHAT?

L: What's his name and room number?

"What's your name. And room number?" I ask, looking up at him. I expect him to balk, but he doesn't, instead giving me both quickly.

"Graham Hawthorne. Room 372."

I nod, type in the information, and *I will give you guys all the details in the morning. Talk to you then.* I hit send. Before they even get the chance to respond, I silence my phone and slide it into my bag, taking in a deep breath. My hands are nearly shaking with nervous energy, and I bite my lip before smiling wide at Graham. "Done."

"Let's go," he says, gesturing toward the elevator bank, and as we walk, he settles his hand on my lower back, sending more anticipatory heat through me. I haven't even kissed this man, and I am somehow absolutely *desperate* for him.

Thankfully, he settles that issue the moment we move into the elevator, pulling my chest into his, one hand sliding down to grab my ass as he looks over my shoulder. He presses a button for his floor, then steps, moving both of us until my back is pressed to the cold metal of the elevator. I gasp with the movement, but it's swallowed quickly as his lips fall to mine before the elevator doors even close.

That's when I learn I was right. This man can *kiss.*

It's not tentative or soft or sweet, not the first kiss of a man trying to make a lasting impression. It's the kiss of a desperate man, filled with want and need and lust and everything I absolutely needed him to give me in this moment. He's tall, and I have to tip my head back a bit to deepen the kiss, my tongue dipping out to run over his bottom lip. He groans into the kiss, his hand tightening on my ass and his other hand sliding into my hair, holding me tighter. My hands move to his neck, holding him close as his lips part, as his own tongue comes out to slide into my mouth.

When the elevator dings, he pulls back, a bit disoriented, which I'm contented to see—at least it's not just me. He glances up to confirm the floor as the doors slide open, then steps away from me, twining his fingers with mine as he tugs me out of the elevator and down a hall. We're silent as he pulls out his keycard and as we walk into what I realize is one of the townhouse-style apartments. He locks the door behind us, then continues to pull me through and up a flight of stairs until we're at a bedroom, a giant bed in the center with large windows overlooking the ocean. I don't have time to take in anything else because the next thing I know, my back is to a wall, pinned there by his hard body.

"You're so fucking hot," he groans before crashing his lips to mine. It's filled with aching desire, as if whatever neutral mask he normally wears is completely fractured now that he has me alone. His hand is moving beneath the shirt I'm wearing, large, warm hands moving along bare skin of my waist.

"I want you," I murmur, my head dropping to press kisses on his neck as his hands move to tug my shirt up. I've never been so brazen, so honest with a man, much less one I just met. I've never even *kissed* a man I barely knew, much less agreed to go up to a hotel room with him. In college, Claire and I would go out, party, and have fun, but I never fooled around; I enjoyed commitment far too much to be into playing the field.

But right here, right now, with Graham's fingers digging into my hips, with his hard body pressed against mine, I can't think of anything I want more in this world than to be with him.

My tee is over my head and tossed to the floor, and I toe off my sneakers as his lips return to mine. His hands make quick work of my bra before gliding down to my hips, then to my ass, gripping and lifting me so I have no choice but to wrap my legs around his waist.

He presses into me, his hardness settling between my legs, grinding as his lips graze down my neck. I moan, my head falling to the side to give him more access as my hips move with a mind of their own, seeking more friction. He chuckles low in my neck, and for a fleeting moment, I'm disappointed can't see the entertained look I'm sure is there.

"Needy?"

"Very," I groan, trying to pull his face to mine for a kiss. He acquiesces, and I catch the very hint of a smile before his lips are on mine again. My nipples are hard, and the friction of his dress shirt against them is exquisite torture. When he steps back from the wall, cradling me in his arms, my belly flips, and my center tightens as he steps toward the bed. After a moment, he tosses me onto it, then tugs down my shorts and underwear until I'm lying on his bed, fully naked, while he stands over me, fully dressed.

"God, you're fucking gorgeous," he groans. "Knees up, spread. Show me what you're going to give me."

*Holy fucking shit.*

I never thought a demand like that, much less a man telling me I'm going to give him something, would be hot, but with the burning look in his eyes, there's no other option. I do as he asks, planting my feet in the bed and spreading my legs, my pussy on display for him. When his eyes lock there, his fingers fumble on the button as he lets in a ragged breath, and suddenly, I realize I'm into it not because he has the power right now, but because I do.

I can't think of anything more powerful or erotic than knowing that the mere *look* of me turns him on so much that he can barely work a button. It makes me feel brave and sexy and wanted in a way I've never experienced before, and my hand trails between my legs, parting my center and sliding over my clit.

"Yeah, just like that. Play while I get undressed. Give me a show," he murmurs, and I moan. I fight to keep my eyes open despite the pleasure, because I want to watch him undress, see the impact watching me has on him. I slide a finger inside of myself, gathering wet beefore pulling it out and circling my clit. All the while, his eyes watch with rapt attention. It takes a minute or two for him to unbutton his shirt, take off his tee, his belt, and finally his pants and boxer briefs. The entire time, I play with myself, eyes locked on Graham. When he's finally undressed, he goes into a drawer and grabs a condom, tossing it onto the bed before he moves to his knees at the edge of the bed. Then, he wraps his hands around my hips firmly and tugs me to the end of the bed. I let out a small squeal, but it melts into a loud moan when, without warning, his tongue flattens along my center, licking me from entrance to clit, where he sucks hard. I let out a loud shout of pleasure, already teetering on the edge from playing with myself.

His fingers slide into me, and I moan, my hips shifting as his tongue and lips move on my clit, sucking and licking. He pulls back and gives me a heated look. "That's it, baby, that's it, June. Take what you need from me. Come on my face and my fingers so I can fuck you out of my system."

I blink at his words, realizing that just like me, he's been thinking about our brief, momentary interaction for the last week. Something about that makes the moment fire hotter, and my hand moves down, taking in his wavy hair between my fingers, and tugging him back down to my pussy. He groans at my brazen move, and I moan louder when it vibrates agains against my clit.

I ride his face then, lost in the feeling of his fingers deep inside of me, stretching me, his mouth on my center, giving me everything I need. I could do this all day, teeter on this near-painful ledge, and I know somewhere in the deep recesses of my mind, when this man is long gone and this night is just a memory, it will keep me warm at night. That's the thought that has my hand pressing his face into me a bit further, getting a rougher touch and a deep thrust of his fingers before I shatter.

I come, moaning his name, my fingers twining in his hair as I arch my back. He goes into me, the vibrations extending my release even as I come down from my high.

"My turn," I mumble when he pulls back, sitting on his heels and giving me an approving look. I'm dazed, and my legs are shaky. "Let me suck you off." The sound that leaves his lips is part moan, part regretful laugh, a sound that makes my pussy tighten despite the recent hard orgasm.

"No need," he says.

"I know. But I want to." I move to my legs but nearly fall, seeing as they're still wobbly.

"Next time," he mumbles, pushing me back gently until I'm lying on my back, and he climbs up until his body is hovering over mine. His lips press to the sensitive spot between my neck and my jaw, and my breath hitches. "Next time you can suck me off, okay, lady luck?"

lady luck.

That's hot.

I don't bother to tell him there won't be a next time. Not with him only in town for a conference, and with me living in Seaside Point. Instead, as I stay in the moment, fully living whatever exciting new experience the universe has decided to gift me with, Graham rolls a condom over his thick cock.

He lines himself up with my entrance, pressing kisses along the bare skin on my neck as he goes, and by the time he's made it to my lips, I've completely forgotten about anything but him and the way I feel in this moment.

# FIVE

# June

I wake up in an unfamiliar bed, something heavy lying over my chest. Blinking at the white ceiling, I attempt to remember where I am and how I got here. When I shift, the weight on my chest tightens, pulling me back into a hard chest.

Looking down my body, I note I'm in a T-shirt that is not mine, and when I look over my shoulder, I realize the chest I'm being pulled into is bare, and the face is that of Graham Hawthorne, the man I met in a convenience store and then on the boardwalk. The man I went home with last night, and who fucked me twice before we both passed out.

I had a one-night stand with a man I barely knew, something so wildly out of character for me, it's almost comical. Strangely enough, I don't feel the panic I might expect in this situation. Instead, I feel at ease.

Warmth and calm and—

My eyes meet the clock on his bedside table.

6:30

*Six-thirty.* On Monday morning.

Oh, fuck.

No, no, no.

My body jolts up—or tries to, at least, but his arm turns into an iron vise. Last night, I was enamored as his muscles flexed while he brought me more pleasure than I could imagine, but right now, his strength is a bad thing. I slap at his arm frantically.

"I gotta go. Shit, shit, shit." Relief moves through me as his arm releases me. Graham wakes slowly, blinking as I roll out of the bed, nearly falling in my haste, but I catch myself before I hit my head on the bedside table. I do *not* have time to cover up a giant bruise. At this rate, I barely have time to get home, take the world's fastest shower, and get ready for my first day of work.

"What's going on?" he asks, blinking.

"I have to go. I have to go to work. It's my first day!" I look around for my shoe. "Shit! Where the hell are my shoes!"

"I set them against the wall," he murmurs, sleep coating the words, and my *god,* in another world, I would love to see how long it takes for that tone to wear off, to find out if he's less grumpy and domineering this early in the morning. Instead, I give him an appreciative wave and run in that direction, grabbing my shoes as I go. My shorts are beside them, and I sigh in relief, sliding them on, followed by my sandals before moving back to Graham.

I bend to where he's now sitting up in the bed, hair a mess, face creased with sleep, and I press my lips to his, hard and fast. One last moment to remember this magical night by. "Last night was great, really. But I have to go," I say, then stand.

"You're leaving?" he asks, still groggy, and I shake my head, sliding my top, bra, and underwear into the bag, deciding I will be stealing his white tee as a souvenir.

"I have to. Thanks for a great night. Later, Graham," I say, then I'm making my way through his place until I'm out the door and nearly running down the hall. When I'm safely closed into the elevator, I let out a girly squeal, a happy, giddy sound, before pulling out my phone. There are a dozen texts from Claire and Lainey, asking me what happened, each one getting more ridiculous. Instead of reading them, I decide to call Claire to tell her I'm alive and well. She picks up as I'm walking out the front door of the hotel. My apartment is about half a mile away; if I book it, I can make it there in about five minutes while I give her the fastest rundown of my night possible.

I make it to my apartment in record time, and forty-five minutes later, I've showered, fixed my hair, and done my makeup with fifteen minutes before I need to be out the door and on my way. I'd planned to pick out my clothes last night before bed, but now I'm staring into my closet with utter panic. Unfortunately, my wardrobe very much screams *fifth-grade teacher who loves color,* not executive assistant at a luxury beach resort. As my anxiety stacks within me, my phone rings from my dresser, and I let out a breath of relief before answering Lainey's call.

"Thank god you called, I'm freaking out," I say, hearing the frantic tone of my voice despite trying to push it down.

"Well, hello to you, too," she laugh. I'm surprised she's awake, since she works late as a bartender at her dad's bar, but knowing Lainey, she set an alarm to call me before work. "Is this freakout because you had your first one-night stand or because it's your first day?" I brush off the first half and focus on what's important.

"What does someone wear to be an executive assistant to a hotel project manager?" I ask in a whine.

"Okay, a new job freak out," she says, and I can almost hear her little nod, locking in to help me out. "Wear something simple, but still you. You're not going to work at a Fortune 500 corporate headquarters. You're going to work at a beach club in Seaside Point that hasn't even opened yet." I take a deep breath and let her words slide through me, relieving some of the tension. My eyes drift over my options in my small closet before I form an opinion.

"Cardigan, a white tee, and a skirt?" I ask, biting my lip.

"Perfect. The pink cardigan with red hearts. It's—"

"It's lucky," I say with a breath, tugging it off the hanger and tossing it on my bed. I set her up on speaker while I get the tee and a loose, black knee-length skirt, then start getting dressed.

"So now that we've conquered the outfit, how was last night?"

"It was amazing, spectacular, and I promise to tell you all about it later, but right now, I need to get ready. I have ten minutes until I have to leave."

"Fine," Lainey says, but there's no irritation in the word. "Then, how do we feel about your first day at your new job?" she asks. Her voice is smooth and calming. I take in another deep breath, letting it reach the bottom of my lungs before letting it out. In the classroom, I would tell the kids to picture all their bad feelings coming out with the exhale. I take my own advice, and as I inhale again, I feel marginally better.

"I... don't know," I admit. "I've never had a job that wasn't working with kids, so I'm not sure what to expect," I say, having realized this fully just yesterday.

"You're working for a man, so you're basically still working with children." I let out a small laugh, the action easing me further. "But also, not working with kids is exactly why this is the perfect choice for you," she says. "You started working with kids while you were still a kid yourself. You kept it up because everyone told you it was what you were meant to do. You never gave yourself any room to try anything else." Her words hit right on the spot that I've been contemplating for months myself.

I started babysitting at age twelve, around the same time I realized Grant wasn't going to college. It wasn't because he wasn't crazy-smart. It wasn't because he hadn't earned any scholarships that would have more than covered the tuition. It was because he didn't want to leave me behind in Seaside Point with only our quickly aging grandparents to care for me. His sacrifice required one of my own. Instead of joining clubs and hanging with friends after school, I started working to earn my keep.

By fourteen, I had people telling me how good I was with kids. *A natural.*

At sixteen, I started tutoring on the side, helping elementary and middle school kids with math and reading for extra money, and had parents and teachers alike telling me I *had* to be a teacher.

By eighteen, I had chosen education as my major.

By twenty-four, I had my master's in education. I was offered a fifth-grade teaching position in my small hometown and began settling into the life everyone had always imagined I'd have.

I liked it well enough.

But I never loved it. It didn't feel like the one thing I was *meant to be doing*. More and more often, just thinking about doing it forever made me feel suffocated.

"You never gave yourself the freedom to be anything but what everyone told you you should be. This is the complete opposite, so it's perfect. Who knows? You might love it, and if you do, that's amazing. If you hate it and you realize you desperately miss working with kids, perfect: you've got a job waiting for you. But we all know that you went into teaching because it was the obvious, safe choice."

"No, it wasn't," I lie.

"June, I've known you since kindergarten. You can't give me stupid lies like that and expect me not to question them." My face pinches as I pick out a pair of socks, slipping on a pair with cute little ruffles at the top. Sneakers should be okay—I only have dressier shoes for going out, not for work—but Sutton wore sneakers on Friday, which reassures me. "All that to say, I hope you have a great time, but I hope you give this a real shot. I know it's scary, but trying something new is good for you."

I almost bring up how she's always worked at the family bar she grew up in, but I rein myself in. That's an unnecessary low blow, stemming from my own insecurities. Instead, I move to my jewelry box, searching for earrings that might fit a corporate environment.

"I appreciate you, and I told you guys I would try to be braver. But I can only handle so many new things at one time," I say.

"I know," she says as I pull out a pair of earrings with a pearl stud and a dangling gold bow. Cute, but discreet, I think. "And I'm so proud of you, really. You're going to have the best first day ever." I let out a little laugh and shake my head.

"I haven't even met my new boss yet. I wouldn't hold your breath."

"It's your lucky girl summer, right?" I roll my eyes, regretting agreeing to their scheme. "Part of being lucky is recognizing luck for what it is and accepting what the universe brings you."

"Since when are you the queen of manifesting?"

"Since I've been friends with you, allowing you to force your woo-woo stuff down all of our throats." I let out a laugh, shaking my head as she continues. "Now, go, get to work and have the best day ever, okay? Call me after work?"

"Okay, Lainey. Thanks for talking me off a ledge," I say. My chest does feel a bit lighter after chatting with her.

"Anytime. Love you!"

"Love you more," I say, then click off and finish getting ready.

# SIX

# June

"Cute earrings!" Sutton says when she meets me in Daytrip's entryway.

"Thanks! I wasn't sure of the dress code, so I hope—" She waves a hand, cutting me off and shaking her head.

"There is none. The staff wears uniforms, but you won't be customer-facing. As long as you look presentable in case you meet or speak to someone, you're good." I glance at her outfit—a cute top, jeans, and sneakers like mine—and let out a relieved breath. "You'll get the handbook today, but what you have on is perfect," she says, moving into the lobby and through the hidden door of the business suite.

"Like you saw Friday, back here is where the staff break room and the offices are." She gestures toward a large desk tucked into a corner before an office, and I nod, taking in the brightly lit space again. The fluorescent lights are just as blinding. The entire place is still clinical and cold, especially compared to the rest of the building. "That's the project manager's office. You can put your things down on your desk, and then I'll introduce you to him." She rolls her eyes, and my stomach tightens. "He's a giant grump, but don't let him get to you." I lift an eyebrow, unsure of how to take that. "But you're used to dealing with Grant and Miles, so I know you can handle it."

Unease settles in my gut, but I keep a smile plastered on my face as I move to the black chair behind the desk and set my bag down.

"I'm gonna go warn him we're coming in. His door is always closed because he likes to keep to himself, so I want to make sure he's not on a call. You just wait here." Sutton moves his door, knocking and not waiting for anyone to welcome her in before moving to the doorknob. "Graham cracker," she calls in a teasing tone as she opens the door and dips her head into the office. A deep groan leaves the room, irritation twined into the sound. Sutton lets out an entertained laugh.

"I told you to stop calling me that," the man grumbles low. The voice tickles something in my mind, the vaguest hint of familiarity that I can't quite pinpoint, but it's gone just as soon as it comes.

"Stop being a stick up your ass douche, and I will." Another unhappy sound filters out as I bite my lip, both entertained and increasingly nervous. Sutton looks over her shoulder. "Once I'm gone, you need to keep up the effort of trying to get him to become less of a robot," she tells me. I lift an eyebrow. "He's boring and grumpy and has no friends."

"Jesus, Sutton," my alleged new boss grumbles. "When do you go back to Rowan again?"

"Whenever I want, so be nice to me, or I'll be here every day for the foreseeable future." The man doesn't speak again, and a pleased smile spreads on Sutton's face at his silence. "Exactly. Now, can I introduce you to your new assistant?" He must nod, because he doesn't speak; instead, Sutton steps to the side, holding the door open for me, tipping her head to the side in a gesture for me to come over. I take in a deep breath and wipe my suddenly sweaty hands down my skirt before moving closer as Sutton steps inside the office.

"Graham, June Taylor. June, this is Graham Hawthorne," I step in the door behind her and plaster the most pleasant smile I can muster across my now incredibly panicked face. *Please no,* I think. *Please,*

*please no. This is supposed to be my* lucky *summer, and this would very much* not *be lucky.* But any semblance of hope I was clinging to is long gone when I spot the man sitting behind the desk before me.

Because I've met him before, just last week in a convenience store.

I gave him a business card, and he gave me a penny.

I spent most of last night getting fucked into the mattress by him.

Slowly, I put pieces together and realize he must have used the card, since Grant got the job here, which led me to come on Friday and get a job.

The universe is truly fucked for this one.

I do my best to put on a happy face, convincing myself I simply need to move forward with a positive attitude, and everything will be *just fine.* Right?

Right.

"Uh, hi," I say, a small apprehensive smile tugging at my lips, "Wow. Small world, huh?"

"You two know each other?" Sutton asks, curiously looking from Graham to me and back again. I shake my head.

"No, no, not really, we bumped into each other once last week. Talked for a minute." I leave out how I spent most of last night with him inside me, but something tells me Sutton can smell the lie. Graham's face on the other hand is blank in a way I don't know how to decode.

"*You're* my new executive assistant?" he asks. There's a hint of disdain in his tone that has my back straightening.

"Yes, I..." I fight the all-consuming urge to bite my lip. "I guess I am." A beat passes, and I stand awkwardly, unsure of what to do. He's looking at me as if he would rather anyone else be standing before him. His disapproving silence builds the uncomfortable tension in the room before he speaks again.

Any hope that things could be normal or copacetic melt away with his words.

"How do I know that you're not going to scratch off a lottery ticket and quit? I can't have flaky staff here when we're in the middle of opening and launching this brand."

"Graham!" Sutton says in a gasp. I should also be annoyed or irritated, but his tone flips some kind of switch, a challenge in it that helps me feel not so out of my depths.

I've seen this challenging face a dozen times on children trying to put me to the test to see if I'm going to back down. I stretch my shoulders and tip my chin before answering.

"Well, for one, I didn't quit; I was laid off."

His eyes narrow. "You said you quit."

"Sorry, I didn't realize I was having a job interview in a convenience store. Next time, I'll be sure to share *all* my life details. Do you think my home address is necessary?" Sutton snorts out an entertained noise, but I don't shift my gaze from the man before me, who continues to glare back at me.

"Oh, this is going to be perfect," Sutton murmurs to herself.

"You were laid off: what was your old job?" Graham asks, ignoring Sutton.

"Fifth-grade teacher. I got laid off because they were reducing the number of classes: it had nothing to do with my skills, qualifications, or work ethic." He nods, then looks me over, and once again, I feel inadequate. I know Sutton said this outfit was fine, but the man is sitting in business attire, a button-up shirt and dress pants, from what I can see. He's not wearing a tie, which is a relief, but still, he's far more dressed up than I am.

"What makes you think you're qualified for this job?" he asks, sitting back and crossing his arms over his broad chest. "This isn't playing with kids all day or teaching letters. This is managing deadlines, employees, and handling the minutiae of the day-to-day of the business, so I can make sure it succeeds. I have a lot to prove with this concept, and I can't have someone coming in here because she wants to play Business Barbie."

*Nothing*, I don't say, even if it's the first thing that comes to my mind. He's right: I'm not *specifically* qualified for this position.

But I refuse to admit weakness. That's what this man *wants* me to do. It's written clear as day across his face: he wants me to back down, to give in, to apologize and walk away with my tail between my legs, but he doesn't know me at all.

He surely doesn't know that there are two things I have always hated: one is making decisions.

The other is people underestimating me or questioning my abilities.

"As a teacher, I am required to balance multiple deadlines and objectives each day, as well as work with many different personalities and learning styles. It's my job to ensure the entire class can collaborate and maintain a happy and positive environment. I often work closely with other teachers, administrators, and parents to ensure my students excel individually. If you replaced *student* with the different lines of your business or tasks you're juggling, you'd see that having a teacher on staff might be the wisest decision you've made. I am also a lifelong Seaside Point resident, making me qualified to handle the unique and sometimes frustrating ways of this small town. If you want to be so stuck up as to think only someone with a business degree could do this job, you can just say that, but I am more than qualified for this job." I take in a deep breath, the adrenaline waning once my mini monologue is over, nerves settling in alongside reality.

I'm screwed.

Not only am I not going to get this job, which, if I'm being honest, I kind of sold *myself* on, but I'm going to let down Sutton, who asked me to make her look good.

I'm a terrible friend.

I'm un-hirable.

I'm—

"Fine," he says, cutting off my internal meltdown. He's now looking at me in a way that *almost* resembles approval, despite the irritation still written across his face.

"Fine?" I ask hesitantly, unsure whether I heard him correctly. He nods.

"Fine. You're hired."

Sutton sighs, and when I turn to her, she's rolling her eyes and shaking her head. "She was already hired, Graham."

"Not by me." His attention moves back to me. "Now, you're hired by me, but I expect full professionalism and for you to take the initiative with your position. It's not rocket science, and I don't have time to show you how to do every single aspect."

I nod. "Of course not. I wouldn't expect you to. I'm very resourceful."

A blush burns on my cheeks, and he watches me in a way I'm not sure I like, completely exposed to his assessing gaze, before he turns to his computer. An awkward moment passes, and during that time, I look to Sutton, unsure of what to do. She rolls her eyes, clearly exasperated by his antics.

"Now, are we done? I have to make a call," he says, reaching for the phone sitting on his desk.

"God, you're so pompous," Sutton says, but turns anyway, heading back out to the door. Unsure of what to do, I nod toward Graham.

"Thank you, Mr. Hawthorne. I look forward to working with you." His eyes leave his screen to meet mine, and there's the slightest softening of his features, the tiniest tip of his lips, a reminder of the man I spent my night with last night, before it's gone again, replaced by that cold demeanor.

Despite all common sense, something in me desperately wants to know what he'd look like if he smiled for real.

"Close the door on your way out," he says in dismissal.

With a nod, I turn on my heel, quietly leaving and clicking the door behind me. It's not until I hear Sutton laugh that the tension begins to leave my body, though it's quickly replaced by something worse: panic.

"What the hell was that?" Sutton says in an excited whisper. "You made him *smile*. He does not smile, like at all."

"If that was a smile, then the bar must be in hell. That was a grimace at best," I say with a roll of my eyes, trying to ignore the way my pulse is still pounding in my throat.

"For Graham, that's basically a beaming grin. Do you guys like, have something? Did you guys hook up?"

I give her wide eyes and bite my lip, looking toward Graham's door.

Graham.

*Graham.*

This is supposed to be my lucky summer, and this might just be the least lucky thing that has *ever* happened to me.

My wide eyes trigger wide eyes of Sutton's in response, which shift from me to the door and back again before she wraps her fingers around my wrist, dragging me to a storage closet, flicking the light on, and staring at me with her hands on her hips. She doesn't look angry, which is good, I suppose.

"Okay, *spill.*"

I groan, turning away from her and hitting my head against the wall. A roll of paper towels falls, hitting me on my head and rolling to the ground.

"We hooked up last night," I grumble.

"No way," she says in disbelief, and I throw my hands up.

"It was a last-minute thing!" Quickly, I tell her about bumping into him and the lottery ticket and how I didn't see him after that until I sat beside him on the bench.

"So that means..." she says, understanding moving over her face before a huge smile splits it. "Oh, my god, this is perfect."

"It very much is *not*," I say. "Did you see the way he looked at me? He hates me."

"He didn't hate you last night, it sounds like."

"Sutton! That was...that was different." I bite my lip. "I'm sure there's some kind of rule—"

"There isn't; this is hospitality. If there were a rule about fraternizing, everyone would get fired. And even if there was, that was before you worked here. You're golden. And really, June, you're perfect—you're exactly what he needs." I stare at her, confused, and she adds, "As an assistant. Just don't let his bad attitude push you away, okay? He was the same with me when I first came here for Rowan, and the second I stopped being scared of him and started biting back, he stopped being a dick. If anyone can turn his shit attitude around, it's you."

"Bite back," I say, taking in her advice and mulling it over, because at the end of the day, I really do need this job. I already disappointed Grant enough; I can't imagine what kind of face he would make when I told him I quit two jobs within a week of each other. "So, he's like a surly kid who needs to be stood up to?"

She grins. "Exactly. See? I knew you were perfect for this job."

I smile at her and some of that unease leaves my chest.

Because a surly kid, I can handle. He can act like a surly five-year-old who thinks he can one-up the grown-up in the room: if there was one thing I am good at, it's cheering my way through even the most glum of people.

Sutton spends the next three hours setting me up in the system and giving me access to a full folder of videos that give me step-by-step instructions on how to do just about everything I'll need to do while working here. It's a relief, because it means I probably won't have to bug anyone too much to do my job. Next, she gives me a list of the tasks she's been working on to gear up to the grand opening, all of which seem relatively simple.

*Contact local news and papers to inquire about ad placement and whether they would be interested in covering the grand opening at the beginning of next month.*

*Sorting through applications for different positions.*

*Ask the recreation department about lifeguard permitting and requirements.*

*Call the township about the liquor license.*

*Check in with Taylor Contracting and get an update on final timelines.*

"Okay, do you think you're good to take over for now? I have to head up to Hudson City..." She checks her watch and curses. "Ten minutes ago, but I'll be back later this week."

"Oh my god, I'm so sorry, I—"

"No, no, Rowan is used to my being late. I'm never on time for anything. I like to keep him on his toes."

I shake my head and laugh.

"How have you not been fired?"

"Because I'm amazing at my job, and he'd be lost without me," she says with a lift of her shoulder. "Anyway, there are donuts in the break room, though I wouldn't be surprised if your brother's guys have already demolished them all."

I give her a big hug and a thank you before waving her off, and we agree to meet at the end of the week at the Seabreeze for drinks and to give her updates on how the week went before she's out the door.

I spend approximately three minutes panicking about what the hell I just got myself into, then take a deep breath, get to work, watch a few how-to videos, and get a few small things done. In my inbox, I already have four emails from Graham, asking me to handle different tasks, and I write them down on my to-do list before deciding to refill my water bottle in the break room.

Graham is in there, steadfastly ignoring me as he makes a coffee. I wave, and he looks right through me, but I brush it off, opening the box of donuts. As Sutton predicted, the box is nearly empty, but there's one of my favorites left: a chocolate-frosted donut with rainbow sprinkles.

See? Everything works out for me.

Even if I feel completely out of my depth.

Taking in a deep breath, I view it as a sign to be brave and address the elephant in the room. But when I shift my gaze to Graham, he's already grabbed his coffee and is halfway out the door before I can say anything at all.

By the end of the day, I've finished all the onboarding information that was sent to me, gotten relatively familiar with where everything is, and completed two of the six tasks he assigned me. At four-thirty, I finally get the nerve to knock on Graham's door.

"Yes?" his deep voice calls through the heavy door. Despite my better judgment, it sends a shiver through me. I try to shake it off quickly before opening the door and stepping in just a bit.

"I, um. I'm gonna head out for the day, if that's okay?" I ask, fighting the desire to bite my lip. He looks at the corner of his screen and his brow furrows as if he's confused, though he still doesn't look in my direction.

"Aren't you out of here at four?"

"Yes."

"Then why are you still here?"

My shoulders straighten.

"I wanted to get a few things done, and I wasn't sure about the system or structure for the workday. Usually, on your first day, your boss would walk you through the expectations, but I'm on my own with this."

"You're an adult, so I didn't think I would need to hold your hand. In the future, you can leave at four without stopping in here," he says, tone bored.

I glare at him, letting out a deep sigh and putting my hands on my hips.

"Is this going to be an issue?" I snap, not taking the time to actually think about what I'm about to say. Finally, he looks away from his computer, and his eyes land on me reluctantly. It's almost as if he's been doing everything in his power to avoid looking at me. In the unforgiving fluorescent lighting of an office, his glare is harsher, more frustrated, less patient. I wonder for a moment if that's some kind of workplace persona he puts on. Sure, he was a bit quiet and stern last night, but nothing like this.

Then again, maybe that's just because the woman who ran out of his room after a one-night stand is his new assistant.

"An issue?"

"Yes. Is my working here going to be an issue? I get that Sutton hired me, and you were unaware of those details, but you seem incredibly irritated that I'm here."

"Don't think so highly of yourself, Ms. Taylor—I have no opinion on your working here, so long as you get your job done. We had a night together, and that is all. We are not here to be friends: we're here to be coworkers. If my attitude is too rough for your delicate sensibilities, please let me know, and we can talk about whether you're a good fit for this position. As for me, I won't have an issue with you. Is this going to be an issue for *you*?"

It's a clear challenge, and with the way he's looking at me as if already assuming I'm going to back down, I know there's no way in hell I can do anything but step up to it. I've worked in the public elementary school system for years. If he thinks some corporate paper-pushing is going to break me, he has another think coming.

So I give him a wide, fake smile. "No, it won't be a problem at all. See you tomorrow, Graham. Have a great night."

Then I leave. I fight the urge to look back until I'm all the way out of his office, finally braving the tiniest glimpse back.

When I catch his eyes still on me, his jaw tight and his gaze burning, I know I won this battle.

I smile the entire drive home.

# SEVEN

# June

The next day, I show up at eight on the dot, waving as I pass Decker in the main room. Deck works as the gym teacher at Seaside Point Elementary during the school year, and each summer works on Grant's crew. If I were to guess, I'd say he's assigned to the Daytrip job to keep an eye on me as I start my new job. Once at my desk, I log in and check my email, where four messages from my boss already sit. His door was closed when I came in, and occasionally his voice mumbles through the thin wall. When I head into the breakroom to grab a coffee and a donut (again, my lucky day—there's a chocolate frosted), I see him for the first time of the day.

I'm stirring creamer into my cup when he walks in, eyes cast down and a coffee cup in his hand, but he stumbles when he catches sight of me. Something passes over his face, so momentary that I don't get to dissect it before his neutral mask is back in place. Not for the first time, that urge to see what happens when he's truly knocked off his feet, what happens when he lets his true emotions shine through, surges through me.

I don't give in to that urge, instead choosing to remain neutral as I give him a small wave and a smile.

Normal. I can act normal, right? Just...smile, wave, and get my job done.

He gives me one of those small, cordial but annoyed nods before he busies himself with his own drink. It's not until I'm headed for the door that his voice calls from behind me.

"What are you wearing?" he asks. When I turn, his eyes scan me, not with interest, but confusion, as if he can't make sense of what he's seeing. Today I'm in jeans, a colorful pastel top, and pink sneakers. I went a bit bolder with my earrings, a pair of red hearts that I normally wear on Valentine's Day, but when I saw them in my jewelry box, they made me smile. It looks similar to what I've seen Sutton wear, so I thought it would be fine, but maybe I was wrong.

"I'm sorry," I say, trying not to feel self-conscious with a man like Graham Hawthorne. Something tells me that with this man, being confident in my choices is half of the battle. "Is this outside of the dress code? Sutton told me that there wasn't really one, so long as I looked put together."

"No, no. It's just...very colorful."

"I'm a very colorful person." Tipping my head a bit to the side, I give him a once-over, the same way he gave me, and his body stiffens just a bit. "Is color not allowed?"

Eventually, he sighs. "It's not really professional."

I cross my arms, recalling Sutton's reassurance.

*Don't back down to his surly attitude.*

*Don't give in to his taunting.*

*Bite back.*

"Says who?"

"Says who?" he parrots, confused.

"Yes. Who says colors aren't professional?" His jaw tightens before he looks past me, and somehow, someway, I know this is a win for me.

"No one, I suppose. Just...make sure you look put together, okay? People will come in here, and you'll be the first person they meet. You'll set the tone for any meetings I have."

"Well, then I'd better make sure I'm as fun, inviting, and happy as possible, shouldn't I?" I ask with a teasing tone. "You know, since meeting you usually drains people's energy."

His scowl deepens, and I suppress a small smile at the fact that I'm getting a reaction out of him.

"Make sure you get those applications for the GM on my desk by four, okay?"

A win glows within me.

"Already done. They're in your inbox, but if you'd like me to print them, just let me know. I'm working on sorting through the waitstaff applications now." When his face shifts in confusion, I continue. "I should have *those* on your desk by four."

"Great. Thank you," he says through a tight jaw, before turning his back to me to finish making his coffee. Despite his brush off, I find myself smiling as I return to my desk, knowing somehow I won that battle.

June 1, Graham o.

At noon, my stomach grumbles, signaling it's time for my lunch. Sutton told me that as long as no appointments are scheduled and I get my work done, I can take a lunch break of up to an hour whenever I wish. The sun is shining today, and since I'm now working an office job, I'm eager to spend as much time as I can outside, and I've decided the deck behind the main building over the beach is the perfect choice. Before I go, I take in a deep breath and knock on Graham's door.

I can't spend the next however long I work here pretending this person doesn't exist. Last night, I decided the best course of action was to pretend the other night never happened. I'm just here as a new hire to a semi–grumpy man whom I need to win over.

"Yeah?" he calls, and I open the door, poking my head in. A stack of papers is laid out before him, and he doesn't lift his head to greet me.

"Hey, Graham, I'm headed out to the deck for some fresh air and to take my lunch. Want to come with me?" I ask. He just stares at me. "Lunch. Do you want to have it with me?"

"Lunch?" he asks, clearly deeply confused as to what I'm talking about.

"Yes, lunch. A meal you eat midday? Sandwiches, salads, and soup are the norm. I bought my own, though if you didn't bring anything, I can easily wait and order something in for you. I'm going to eat outside. It's a gorgeous day, and it seems ridiculous to spend the entirety of it inside."

"You want to have lunch with me?" I nod. "Why would you want to have lunch with me?" he asks, genuinely confused.

I tip my head to the side, a smile tipping the edges of my lips.

"So we can get to know one another," I say, and his frown deepens further. "I've decided we have a blank slate. I know nothing about you; you know nothing about me."

"I know plenty about you," he says, his voice smooth and alluring, and my breath catches in my chest. His own face goes blank, as if he didn't mean to say that. I force myself to forget the things I know about him, like the fact that he has a filthy mouth or that he has an impressive cock and very much knows how to use it.

I fail miserably, but I hope that it doesn't show on my face. Instead, I clear my throat and give him a cheery smile.

"Yes, well, blank slate, remember? That's why I wanted to have lunch with you. To get to know you."

"Why would we do that?"

"That's what friends do."

He shakes his head, almost as if that's unfeasible.

"We're not friends. We're coworkers."

I smile, happy to be on this stubborn footing. Stubborn, I can handle.

"We're not friends *yet*. That's the point of the *get-to-know-one-another thing*. That way, we can be friends *and* coworkers."

He bites back a grimace, and for a moment, I think it's at the idea of being friends with me, but I change my mind when he speaks again.

"That's not necessary. I'm here to turn this place around, not to make friends."

"You can do both," I suggest, with a small laugh. "The two are not mutually exclusive, you know. We're going to be spending a lot of time together; might as well be friends."

"I'm good," he says, skepticism written across his face. "Thank you for the offer, though."

I stare at him for a long moment before speaking. "You're good?"

"Yeah. I'm good. I don't really do friends."

"You don't...you don't do friends." He stares at me instead of answering. "Do you *have friends*?"

His jaw tightens.

"Not that it matters, but I have contacts, and I have acquaintances. Calling people friends is sugar coating the fact that in my life, relationships are networking opportunities."

My jaw goes slack.

"Did you just say relationships are just networking opportunities?"

He lets out a deep sigh, one laced with irritation.

"What else would they be?"

"People to spend your time with? People to have fun with? People to celebrate accomplishments with?" Something hits me, and my eyes widen. "Have you ever been in love?" His brow furrows deeper, a wordless answer. "Oh, buddy, we're going to make you live. You know, it's actually so lucky that you found me."

"I feel like we have different definitions of luck," he grumbles, but I barely notice the dig.

Instead, ideas move through my mind, tumbling over and over

before I make my decision and speak it aloud. "I'm gonna win you over."

"You're what?" he asks, lifting one thick eyebrow.

"We're going to be friends, Graham. By the end of the summer, I'm going to be your first real friend."

"Good luck with that," he says with a snort.

I tip my head, giving him a genuine, wide smile. "Haven't you heard? I'm the luckiest girl in the world."

And then I get another one of those rare, increasingly coveted by me micro-smiles, and my chest lightens. I walk off with an extra pep in my step before I eat on the deck. I pull out a sketchbook and doodle as I eat. I spend my break zoning out and drawing the tiniest corner of a mouth, over and over.

It isn't until I'm almost done with my lunch that I realize it's the corners of Graham's mouth I'm drawing.

# EIGHT

# GRAHAM

It's been years since I felt a spark of satisfaction in my day-to-day life. I've been busting my ass for years now, climbing the corporate ladder, always pining for a promotion that will be bigger and better and more impressive, something that would make me feel like I'd made it finally, only to find each accomplishment falling flat and feeling empty.

But when June threatened to become friends with me, the dim world I didn't realize I'd been shuffling through numbly shone just a bit brighter.

# NINE

At the end of the day, I send off one last email with a satisfied sigh. I've only been here two days, but oddly, I'm enjoying myself. It's not groundbreaking work. If I did it every day forever, I might go crazy, but I like the variety—it's a fun job.

And I have to admit, even to myself, that every time I think about returning to teaching next fall, dread curls in my stomach. With that in mind, I push the feeling aside, gather my things, sling my bag over my shoulder, and walk to Graham's office to knock on the frame.

"I'm heading out for the night."

He looks at me and sighs, a sound deep with exhaustion.

"I told you you don't have to announce your departure, June."

"Some of us have manners, Graham."

He glares at me, and I glare back before he sighs.

"Goodnight, June. Thank you for your work today. I will see you tomorrow. Happy?" Warmth sparks in my chest at his acquiescence, no matter how begrudging.

"Radiant. Bye, Graham!" I say, and then, not wanting to push my luck, wave and walk out the door.

I am *so* going to win him over.

I'm still smiling over that as I move down the boardwalk to the large recreation building where I'm meeting Claire.

"Hey, June!" she says when I walk in, pulling me in for a big hug. "I just have a few more things to do if you don't mind."

Last summer, Claire came down to Seaside Point to work as a lifeguard and fit in so well that Maggie, the former Director of Recreation, offered to train her to take her place. Over the last year, it's become increasingly obvious that it was the right choice, with Claire raising more money for the programs than ever before and getting the entire town involved.

"No, you're fine," I say, looking at the piles of papers—probably a mix of lifeguard applications and notes for the summer festival she runs. I sit, taking in the view of the beach and ocean, and after a moment, she finishes writing and turns to me, expectant.

"Okay, tell me everything!" She tried calling yesterday for details about my first day, but my mind was too twisted up, and I needed to sort through my thoughts alone. Instead, I texted her, saying I was exhausted and would give her the full breakdown at dinner. "Since you've avoided the topic, I'm guessing it went badly. I'll have to yell at Sutton, since she promised me it'd be a great fit." I sigh and rub my face.

"It is, I'm sure. The work is simple and interesting enough. Right now, I'm working on combing through applications for different jobs for my boss." She nods, waiting for me to drop the *but* she senses is coming. I take in a deep breath, preparing myself for the chaos that's about to break through. "*But*, my boss is the hot guy from the convenience store," I blurt out.

There's a moment of silence before she blinks twice.

"I'm sorry?"

"Graham, my new boss, is the guy who lent me a penny for the scratch off that made me quit my job."

"Which means..." Her eyes are wide as the concept sinks in.

"Which means I had a one-night stand with my boss the day before I started working with him. It also means because of our unusual meeting, he thinks I'm some flaky woman who quit her job on a whim based on a scratch-off result."

Silence fills the room before Claire bursts out laughing.

"It's not funny!" I whine, letting my head fall to the counter with a resounding thud.

Her hand comes to pat my back in the fakest show of support I've ever experienced, laughter still in her voice when she speaks.

"You're right, it's not funny. It's hilarious." I just groan into the table. "Okay, so he's obviously hot, and you have a crush on him—"

I sit up quickly and glare at her. "I do not–"

"Babe, you specifically called him *the hot guy from the convenience store*. A crush is kind of a given."

"You can think someone is hot without having a crush on them," I grumble, and she tilts her head, looking at me with a raised brow.

"*I* can, yes, but *you* can not. You're June, my sweet, optimistic best friend. You don't call people "hot" and not have at least a teeny-tiny crush on them. Not to mention the entire fact that you had a one-night stand with him, a night you *still* haven't given me all the details about. But we can sift through your delusion later. How was the rest of the day?" I glare at her, trying to decide if it's worth it to argue my point, then sigh, my shoulders slouching a bit with defeat, knowing it is not, in fact, worth it.

"I think he hates me."

"Hate you? How could anyone hate you? You're June. That's like hating rainbows or butterflies." I shrug, not knowing, because I have always prided myself on being likable. Maybe that's why I'm so determined to make him be friends with me. "Is he... is he being mean to you? Is he giving you a hard time because you two—"

"No," I say quickly, because for some strange reason I don't look at too closely, I don't want Claire to have the wrong idea about him. "He just... he seems to be both irritated and confused by everything I do. He told me my outfit was too colorful today."

She leans back, looking over what I'm wearing, and shrugs. "Looks like a normal June outfit to me."

"Well, he's very boring—I've only ever seen him in black and white clothes, his office is completely undecorated—so I think any color shocks him, to be fair. I told him I need bright colors to offset his gloom. He wasn't impressed." Claire lets out a loud laugh.

"I bet he wasn't. Maybe he's in love with you," she says. I roll my eyes at her dramatics, but nods as if it's a logical concept. "Being annoyed and grumpy with me was the number one sign Miles was completely obsessed and in love with me. I know we shouldn't encourage the whole 'he's mean because he likes you,' thing, but sometimes there's truth there. Boys are stupid, simple creatures who don't know how to process real emotions. Maybe he's grumpy because he's in love with you and doesn't know what to do."

"Yeah, I don't think that's the case here," I laugh. "Miles was in love with you long before last summer. The man was holding seashells in his pocket for you for years."

"Well, when we find out in six years that he's been doing something unhinged for you all along, I don't want to hear about it."

"I wouldn't hold your breath. I threatened to be friends with him, and he looked like I told him I was going to blow up the building."

Claire tips her head, brows furrowing. "How does one threaten to be friends with someone?"

"I asked him why he didn't like me, and he said it wasn't personal, that there was no reason for a relationship beyond work." A small smile tips on my lips, remembering the look of confusion and shock on Graham's face. "So I told him we'd be friends by summer's end."

"What did he say to that?" Claire asks, crossing her arms on her chest, looking fully entertained.

"*Good luck with that,*" I repeat in a gruff voice, and she tips her head back, a deep laugh falling from her lips.

"So, he has no idea who he's dealing with, does he?" she asks, and I lift a shoulder, a similar humor bubbling in my chest.

"What's so funny, you two?" Maggie says as she comes in, sliding her sunglasses to her head. She brushes sand from her shins before hugging me from behind as I sit in the chair. "Good to see you, Junie

B." I smile over my shoulder at her, a familiar warmth spreading in my chest, tinged with grief. It was a name my grandmother used to call me as a kid because I was obsessed with the Junie B. Jones books. Maggie was a good friend of my grandparents before they passed, since they were both active in the rec department for years, with Grandma teaching art classes and Grandpa stepping in to coach any team that needed someone. Somewhere along the way, Maggie started to call me that, as well.

"June got a new job, and her boss doesn't believe in making friends," Claire explains to her mentor.

"And he hired June?" Maggie asks, raising an eyebrow.

"Technically, Sutton hired me." She nods as if it all makes sense, and I guess in a way, it does.

"How is it going over there? Sorry to hear about them cutting back on classes. They should have canned Cece Stevens, not you." I bite back an agreement, a grimace crossing my face at the mention of my personal and slightly irrational nemesis.

"It happens. All's well that ends well." Maggie looks me over in a way I know from experience can't mean anything good.

"You know, I'm glad you're here. I've been meaning to seek you out."

"Oh?" I ask, unsure. If Maggie is seeking me out, either there's an issue with a kid, she needs Grant to fix something, or...

"The town council is accepting bids for the new mural at the entrance to town." My eyes widen. There's a large wall on the overpass before the only road in and out, and the town's been discussing adding a mural to brighten up the space for years. I'm surprised they finally agreed on anything. "Proposals are due by July's end, but Chet is hiding it—buried under website red tape—so his daughter will get it if no other proposals come in." Chet Stevens, the town's zoning administrator, is on the town council and is constantly making everyone in Seaside Point miserable. He's passed that trait down to his kids, Carl, who owns Grant's rival contracting company, and Cece Stevens. Cece is two years older than me and a spoiled rich girl who has taken pride in making me miserable ever since Joey Gooding took me to prom her senior year instead of her. We previously had to work together often, since she's also a fifth-grade teacher, and I'm sure my layoff made her day.

"Oh, fuck that chick," Claire murmurs, knowing all too well about my dislike of her, even though Claire didn't grow up in Seaside Point. Even if I haven't whined about Cece many times before, she would know her solely based on her interactions with the Stevens family.

"You *have* to put in a bid, June!" Claire says, turning to me, her face beaming.

Was this a setup? Something Claire and Maggie had talked about and planned ahead of time? It feels like an ambush.

"Oh, I don't know," I say with a small laugh and a shake of my head. "I don't feel very qualified for that."

"And Cecelia is?" Maggie asks, raising her eyebrows to her forehead. "That girl couldn't paint a straight line if she had a ruler." I bite back a laugh, but Claire doesn't, the sound filling the office.

"That's not kind—"

"*She's* not kind, so I don't have to be kind to her," Maggie says. "You really should submit a proposal, June. You're talented, like your grandmother and your mom. It's what Connie would have wanted, you leaving your mark on this town." My chest aches at her words, and Claire senses my weakness and uses it to push her agenda further.

"This kind of sounds like one of those lucky opportunities you're supposed to take hold of this summer, doesn't it?" she says with a smug look on her face. "The universe is dropping something exciting right in your lap."

I glare at her.

"I agreed I'd take chances that came to me," I remind her. I do *not* remind her that the last time I followed that logic, I ended up fucking my new boss, who may or may not hate me now.

"Yeah. And Maggie is bringing it to you. Voila, it came to you."

I roll my eyes.

"This isn't falling into my lap. It's you and Maggie *placing* it into my lap and pretending it's a lucky moment. I haven't even set up my online shop, Claire. Maybe we start small instead of jumping right into making huge proposals I'd have to present to the entire town." She lifts an eyebrow, narrowing her eyes at me.

"Okay, so we start smaller," she says. Maggie leans on a wall, crossing her arms on her chest and watching us go back and forth, clearly entertained. "Where are we with finishing your shop?" I tighten my jaw, but that's answer enough. Claire throws her hands in the air, exasperated. "Why do you keep putting it off? It used to be that you didn't have time, but school's out, and now you're working a normal nine to five."

*Because I am absolutely terrified,* I don't tell her.

"I just want to get myself acclimated to this new job before I add on another layer of stress." Her brows furrow, and I know she's about to ask me why it would be stressful, but I don't feel like explaining the complicated feelings that arise every time I try to finish my shop and put it live. Instead, I tell a white lie. "Next week. I'll finish setting it up and make it live next week, okay?" She narrows her eyes at me, but must see something on my face, the fact that I don't want to dig into this too much more, because she sighs, relaxes, and smiles at me.

"Okay. But I'm going to bug you about it next week."

"Wouldn't be you if you didn't," I say with a sigh, relieved that at the very least, I have another week to think of an excuse.

"I want the shop information once it's up!" Maggie adds, and I roll my eyes.

"If you order, I'll refund you. Tell me what you want, and it's yours."

"Tell me how much and I'll buy it," she says, glaring at me.

"Maggie," I say.

"June," she counters, and a small stare down begins.

"Okay, I know you both, and I know you two can do this all night, but I'm starving and need to eat. Let's go, June. Maggie, once it's up, I'll give you the link."

Maggie smiles, and I roll my eyes, but drop the arguments. Claire is right: we would be here all night if I didn't.

We say goodbye to Maggie before heading to dinner at a taco place right off the boardwalk. We chat and laugh long past when our food is gone before I take her home. I'm grateful that she doesn't bring up the shop or the mural again, instead grilling me about my night with Graham, which somehow feels more preferable than talking about my art.

When I get home, I shower and get myself ready for tomorrow, but instead of settling into my couch for an hour of trash TV before I go to bed, I find myself drifting toward the small corner in my apartment where my art supplies are set up. I put on some relaxing music and start doodling in a sketchbook. As I do, all my thoughts, nerves, fears, and worries evaporate until, as always happens when I create, I'm almost weightless, lost to my art.

I sit like this for well over an hour before a yawn leaves my lips, pulling me back into the real world.

That's when I realize I've been sketching out what could be a mural, with faint lines reading "Welcome to Seaside Point" in the corner and outlines for different iconic landmarks around town dotted around.

It's cute and fun and, thanks to the colored pencils I used, bright and colorful.

It's a love letter to the town I've never wanted to leave, I wonder if maybe I *should* try and submit a proposal. It would drive me crazy to see a mural every day that stupid Cece Stevens made, knowing damn well that she only got the job because her daddy tipped the scales in her favor. But what would happen if I threw my hat in and it wasn't good enough?

*It's what Connie would have wanted*, Maggie said, words that struck me right in my heart because I know she's right.

My grandmother, Connie, *would* have wanted me to pursue art.

In fact, during the lessons she gave me, she would always ooh and awe, tell me I was going to be a famous artist one day, but I also saw what happened when you let that go to your head, when you let yourself believe that a creative career was your destiny at any cost.

And with that reminder, I close my sketchbook and get myself ready for bed, but even as I lie there, my mind can't stop thinking about what would happen if I really were brave enough to give my dreams a shot.

# TEN

# June

I wear an even brighter shirt to work the next day, pairing it with a colorful pair of pants and a stack of jangling bracelets. Even I know I look like a rainbow, but it looks cute together, and that's all that matters. To further my cause of bringing some sunshine and joy to Graham's life, I grab the box of decorations to brighten up my workspace with a grin. When I get to Daytrip, it's twenty before eight, and Graham is already closed in his office.

I get to work with Blu-Tack and tape, unpacking my box, and ten minutes later Graham steps out of his office. He jolts back when he sees me, confusion and shock on his face for a moment before it's hidden back behind his neutral mask.

"What are you doing?" he asks as I add a row of colorful felt balls to the front of my desk. They used to decorate my bulletin board at school, and now they look hilariously out of place in this boring office, a Band-Aid on the wound of a glum world.

Once they're secured, I stand, putting my hands on my hips and giving him a wide, innocent grin. "I'm decorating."

He lifts an eyebrow at me. "Decorating?" The single word drips with disdain. I have to fight back a laugh at his tone.

"Yes. I can't spend all of my days in this boring, corporate America hellscape. This place is doom and gloom. We agreed I need to be a bright ray of sunshine to offset your storm cloud."

His jaw tightens, and joy bubbles in my chest, knowing I'm getting under his skin. I don't know why I love bothering him so much when, normally, I like to make people feel safe and comfortable, but something about Graham makes me want to get a reaction out of him at any cost.

"Agreed is a very strong term for you saying something and me being in the room while you say it."

I let out a small laugh then, because he might be grumpy and stern, but he's also funny.

"Po-tay-to, po-tah-to," I quip. "If I am going to keep my incredibly chipper personality, I need to be in a place that doesn't look like a padded cell."

"I don't pay you to decorate your space, Ms. Taylor. I pay you to get your job done, which you conveniently are not doing."

Some of that happy glow fades out with his words.

"*You* don't pay me at all, Mr. Hawthorne," I say, irritation in my voice. "Daydream Resorts pays me, and if we're really being nitpicky, no one has paid me yet because I haven't gotten my first paycheck." His eyes narrow on me. "But *no one* is paying me to decorate my workspace, because I'm not on the clock. I came in early to decorate. I'm not on until..." I look at my watch and grin at him, forcing it to wash away the irritation I was feeling. "Eight more minutes."

His look morphs to one of confusion. "You came in early to decorate your workspace?"

I bat my lashes at him, giving him a tight, fake smile.

"I wouldn't want to make you think I was wasting company time. That might give you the wrong impression of my work ethic."

He blinks at me a few times before shaking his head, a hand lifting to rub at the back of his neck.

I've frazzled him, I realize. The shock looks good on him, and it makes me want to do it more.

"Oh. Well, I suppose that's fine."

"So gracious of you." He watches me with that same, strange confusion as I reach into my box, pulling out a small vase and then placing a few fake flowers inside. Dead flowers aren't very cheerful, and the chance of my remembering to replace them as they get droopy is slim to none. I fight the urge to look at him again, instead pretending to fluff up the petals. He doesn't seem to be able to fight rising to my bait, though.

"Are you always this stubborn?" he asks finally.

I turn to him, smiling with a raised eyebrow.

"Are you always this uptight?"

"Excuse me?"

"Oh, sorry, I thought we were asking questions with obvious answers."

It happens then.

His lips tip a bit more, still not a smile but the closest I've come to one yet, a light moving into his eyes as if he's enjoying this back-and-forth as much as I am.

With the way my heart skips a beat each time it happens, I wonder if my desire to make him smile for real is more dangerous than fun, but I can't find it in me to care.

"Just...don't go too crazy with it," he says reluctantly, and I give him a mock salute.

"Aye aye, captain," I say, then go back to my decorating. After a moment, he sighs and walks toward the break room. I finish up with the flowers, then sit down and clock in. The whole time, I don't bother to hide the huge smile on my face.

"Hey, Graham," I say, dipping my head into Graham's office at the end of the day.

His door was closed most of the afternoon, his day packed with meetings. If this is what his days normally look like at a new location, I can almost understand why he wouldn't take advantage of making friends while working. If he's only in one place long enough to get it set up and running before moving to the next one, there simply can't be much *time* for making relationships. Unfortunately for him, my empathy doesn't make me more accepting of that fact; instead, it makes me want to try harder. By the time he's done in Seaside Point, I'm determined to make Graham Hawthorne realize having friends can be a good thing.

"I'm heading out," I say. "I sent over my top three contenders for the GM position from the ones you picked, and once you approve them, I'll set up interviews. If you're okay with it, I can handle the waitstaff interviews, but you'll have to be in on the GM interviews, since you know what's needed. Let me know how you'd like me to go about fitting those in your schedule, and I can make some calls tomorrow, schedule some interviews for next week."

He stares at me for long moments, then nods almost begrudgingly.

"Thank you, June. I appreciate it."

I bite back a smile, but nod before taking a step back.

"It's my job," I say, preparing to head out, but his voice stops me.

"Also." I pause, looking at him expectantly. He closes his eyes and takes in a breath as if he's not looking forward to what he has to say next. My stomach turns, worrying that I must have messed something up, but it melts away the second he starts to speak. "If you want to decorate your space, you don't have to come in early to do so. You're highly efficient at your job and have excellent time-management skills. A few minutes here and there to make your space more comfortable is no problem."

I blink at him once before my jaw drops a bit as I pretend to stumble, putting a hand to my chest and leaning on the doorway for support. He looks at me with concern, but I speak before he can question me.

"Was that a compliment?"

"I'm sorry?"

"I think you just complimented me," I say with wide eyes.

"No, I didn't," he says quickly, but I shake my head.

"Yes, you did. You said I'm competent at my job. That's a compliment, Graham."

I close my eyes and smile to myself.

"What are you doing?" he asks, sounding incredibly exasperated. It makes me smile wider.

"Savoring the moment. A compliment is step one on our friendship journey, you know."

I push aside the fact that he *definitely* complimented me plenty the night before I started working here. I open one eye at him, taking in his face, which looks as confused and annoyed as I had pictured. "This came much sooner than I anticipated."

He rolls his eyes and shakes his head at me, but I can see the light of entertainment on his face.

"You're a pain. Has anyone ever told you that?"

"Every day of my life," I say with a smile. "Later, Graham."

"Have a good night, June."

On Friday, I pop my head inside Graham's office midday.

"Want to grab lunch? I'm calling in take-out since it's disgusting out." The gloomy, rainy weather means I won't get to eat outside in the sun, so ordering in from my favorite local lunch spot was a needed treat. He stares at me for a moment, and I think he might just take my offer before he shakes his head.

"No, I'm good. Thank you, though."

"One day," I say with a smile.

"Not likely," he replies low.

"I'm very perseverant, Graham. I'm going to wear you down one of these days."

He glares at me, and I wave, turning back to my desk, but as I leave, I hear him mumble under his breath, *"That's what I'm afraid of,"* and I know I am definitely getting closer.

By the time my lunch is almost over, I'm getting terribly antsy. I've come to realize that while I enjoy this new job, I need something to break the monotony of sitting all day. I'm used to being on my feet, teaching, physically and mentally exhausting myself, and not doing that has left me jittery by the end of the day. Normally, getting outside for my lunch helps, but since it's pouring rain today, I have to get creative. With ten minutes left in my break, I do what I always used to do in my classroom on a rainy day when the kids needed to let out a bit of excess energy: pull up a random music video, hit play, and start dancing out my wiggles.

"What are you doing?" a deep voice asks halfway through my song. I look over my shoulder at him and see he's watching me, leaning in the doorway of his office with something akin to alarm on his face.

"I'm dancing," I say, explaining the obvious. He blinks at me as I continue to move in place, shaking out my arms and legs.

"I see that," he says slowly, brows furrowing deeper. "*Why* are you dancing in the middle of the office?"

"I'm doing a brain break. I used to do it with the kids. Every so often, you've got to get up and move your body, get the wiggles out. Keeps you on your toes and your energy high, especially on a gloomy day like this." I reach out to him. "Want to join?" He looks at my outstretched hand and shakes his head, a small scowl on his lips.

"I don't think that would be... appropriate," he says

"Friends dance together."

"Too bad we're not friends."

"So you keep saying," I say. I continue to move, trying not to show my surprise or feel self-conscious as he stays leaned in the doorway, arms crossed over his chest, watching me, though that second part is becoming more difficult by the moment.

"What's the sound?" he asks after a bit.

"Music. Graham. It's music. Happy sounds that people listen to instead of sitting in boring silence." I bite back a smile when he glares at me. The tiniest things annoy him to no end, and like the little sister I am, I can't help but want desperately to get under his skin. "It's "Ring My Bell" by Anita Ward. It's supposed to be lucky. I saw somewhere that they almost banned it from casinos, because when they played it, everyone started winning. I don't actually know if that's true: I couldn't find any respectable resource on it, but it couldn't hurt." I'm panting now, my breathing growing ragged as I move and talk simultaneously, but when the edges of his lips tip in that almost, not quite smile, my heart rate increases tenfold. "Is it bothering you?" I ask, moving in a circle. "I can bring headphones in tomorrow, or do it in the break room." He stares at me for a moment, then, to my surprise, he shakes his head.

"No. It's not bothering me," he says as the song ends, and I stop moving.

"Because you like me?" I ask. "And you want to see me happy?"

He rolls his eyes before turning back into his office and closing the door behind him without another word.

With his retreat and my song over, I sit in my seat, feeling a bunch better—sometimes you just need to get the wiggles out.

And, maybe, to get a hint of a smile from your grouchy boss.

# ELEVEN

# GRAHAM

When June leaves the office for the evening, once again stopping to say goodbye despite my telling her it's unnecessary, I'm definitely not watching her.

That would be strange and inappropriate.

I just so happen to need to fill my water bottle right after she leaves, and I just so *happen* to catch her walking out the side door toward the parking lot, past the small grassy spot along the sidewalk. Then I *just so happen* to see her drop her things and fall to the ground.

Without thinking, I leave my water bottle on the counter and hurry outside, heart pounding.

"Are you okay?" I call, the summer heat cutting through my shirt. Her head snaps back, brow furrowed.

"Where did you come from?"

"Inside. Are you okay?" I repeat, approaching as she stays on the ground. Maybe she twisted her ankle or something?

"Am I... okay?"

Maybe she got a headache that is actually a brain bleed, and she can't understand what I'm saying?

"You fell and didn't get up."

She tilts her head, confused, but her look quickly turns satisfied.

"Did you...were you watching me?"

"What? No. I went to get a drink, and then from the window I saw you drop to the ground and assumed something had happened to you. It would have been irresponsible not to check on you."

"I didn't *drop to the ground,*" she says with an eye roll. "I paused, saw a clover patch, and then knelt down." I don't argue because I've learned June is inherently obstinate and would argue about it until sunset. "I was looking for four-leaf clovers," she explains.

"Why?" I ask.

She lifts a shoulder. "A little extra luck. I've never found one, so if I see a patch, I like to stop and check."

"I thought you were naturally lucky?"

Instead of getting annoyed by the accusation, she grins wider. "One can always use a bit more." Finally, she stands, then hefts her bag up over her shoulder. As she does, the handle grazes her ear, and she sucks in a sharp breath. She freezes, putting her hand to her lobe and looking around. "Shit."

"What's wrong?" I ask, too quickly to sound uninterested.

"I lost my earring."

She kneels once more, looking around while I stand frozen in confusion. She pats the ground, moving the grass, but after a moment, she shrugs and stands with a sigh. "I'm never going to find it in this dim light. I can try tomorrow. Thankfully, it wasn't anything precious or expensive."

She reaches down to grab a fluffy white dandelion. She plucks it, closes her eyes, then purses her full pink lips and blows, sending the seeds scattering on the wind.

"There." She drops the stem and wipes her hands on her skirt, giving me a small smile.

"Are you okay? What was that?" Maybe she *did* have a brain bleed.

She looks at me like I'm the one who has lost it.

"I made a wish on a dandelion. Sending my hopes up into the universe."

"You made a wish about your earring?"

She winks at me. The woman *winks*. "Can't tell you, silly. That's the rule about wishes."

She watches me for a moment before a joy-filled sunshine smile fills her face. "So you came out here because you thought I was hurt, huh?"

"It would be irresponsible to watch you fall to the ground and ignore it," I say, though the excuse is flimsy even to me.

"Only five days in, and I'm making headway."

"What?"

"Friends notice if something is wrong, Graham. We're getting closer to friends."

"Good night, Ms. Taylor," I say with a roll of my eyes, my default around her. She brings out a childish side of me I've never experienced, and it's one of the many reasons she unsettles me.

"I know I'm getting under your skin when you go back to Ms.Taylor," she says, somehow able to read me like a book.

"Go home, June," I say, opening the door and walking in without looking back, though her laugh follows me.

I definitely don't watch her drive away, either.

Something catches the light as I walk up the walkway to the side door of Daytrip on Monday, making me hesitate before stepping back to squint into the grassy area. After a moment, my mouth drops in awe when I recognize my earring, resting atop the grass, glinting in the early morning sun. I grin widely, my chest warm with a familiar jolt of luck-filled excitement. Quickly, I grab the earring and make my way inside.

"Graham!" I call out. "Graham! Where are you? You'll never believe this!"

"My office!" Graham yells in return, his voice low and distracted.

"Look what I found!" I say. His head lifts as I enter his office and approach his desk. Once I'm beside him, I open my hand to reveal my earring sitting in my palm. He looks at it with a furrowed brow.

"Is that your earring?"

"Yes! Isn't that wild!"

"Where was it?" he asks.

"In the grass. The light hit it just right as I was walking in." I smile at the small piece of jewelry. I wasn't too bummed about losing it, since it wasn't anything precious, more costume jewelry than anything, but I'm happy I have the set complete once more. "I told you it would come back to me," I say lightly. He stares at me, reading my face for a long moment in a way that makes me feel exposed and strangely breathless before he nods.

He gives a small, begrudging smile. "I guess you did."

"Everything works out for me," I say with a smile. "Though I'm shocked I didn't see it before now."

"Maybe you just needed some time for your luck to work its magic," he says with a shrug, as if he's buying into my rambling about luck and being meant to be and everything working out for me. I mean, with the way things just seem to be lining up for me, I would think it's hard *not* to believe.

"I guess." I look at the metal in my hand once more and smile before sliding it into my pocket. "I'm gonna go make myself a coffee—do you want anything?"

He shakes his head as I assumed he would, then I nod, and I make my way to the breakroom to get the day started. But my day feels a bit shinier, knowing that, once again, my luck has shown I'm on the right path.

On Tuesday, Graham let out a loud, angry curse from his office. Normally, I leave him alone unless he calls me in or needs something specific, but with the ire in his tone, I can't ignore it. Peeking my head in his office, his eyes are locked on the screen of his computer, a hand running through his thick hair.

"Everything okay in here?" I ask, trying to insert some cheer into my tone.

"No, everything is fucked. This entire project is cursed."

I tilt my head to the side and step fully inside.

"You're going to have to expand on that one, bud."

I know it must be bad when my gentle teasing doesn't even get me a glare.

"Our permitting is apparently invalid, and because of that, the zoning administrator won't send the building inspector or approve our opening date. You know, the date we have plastered on absolutely everything?" He runs a hand through his hair once more, making it stick up at odd angles before he rubs both hands over his face. I have the sudden urge to run my own fingers through the locks, to smooth them and try to calm him down. When his hands drop to the desk, his head falls back, tipping toward the ceiling as he closes his eyes and takes a deep breath. Like this, it's impossible to ignore how exhausted he looks. I wonder how late he stays each night, or if he takes the weekends off at all. He's here before I arrive every morning and still working away when I leave. He looks like he could use a full night's rest and a long weekend off, though I doubt he'd appreciate that suggestion.

Instead, I need to help solve the problem at hand and take some of the weight off his shoulders.

"The permitting is invalid?" This is confusing because Grant is always on top of permits. But a moment later, I remember this wasn't originally Grant's project. "Fucking Chet," I mutter.

"I don't know who is to blame, but I do know that no one has answered a single one of my calls this morning. Not the zoning administrator, not the inspectors, not even Grant."

"Grant's down in Ashford and gets spotty service there," I say mindlessly, considering the predicament we're in and the best way to solve it as quickly as possible. Both because it's my job, and because I want to have some small hand in erasing that haunted look from Graham's face. "How long has this been happening?"

"A few days," he says, begrudgingly, but when I lift an eyebrow, he sighs and expands. "I got an email on Thursday from the building inspector, saying he was waiting on the zoning administrator to schedule his coming out."

"Why didn't you tell me? I could have helped."

"Because I should be able to handle this on my own. It's my whole job. I've managed projects in big cities with much higher stakes." A flash of embarrassment blooms on his face, clear as day, and I soften. He values doing his job well, and from what Sutton says, he's really good at it. I can see how he would walk into Seaside Point and think everything will be simpler because it's a small town. "I called on Thursday and got the runaround, and then I was promised an update on Monday, but got nothing yesterday. The building inspector just emailed me to say that the permits are missing and that he can't do an inspection without them. I've tried calling the zoning administrator three times already, and he isn't answering."

*And he won't.* I don't say as much, since that won't help his stress levels, but if I know Chet, and he's going to drag this out as long as possible as retribution for Graham working with Taylor Contracting instead of his son's company.

"Have you tried calling his assistant, Maryanne?" I ask.

"Twice, and she also gave me the runaround."

"Were you mean to her?"

"What?"

"Were you mean? Did you scare her by being all...you? If you did, you just said goodbye to your one line of communication to Chet until he deigns to call you back." His jaw goes tight, which gives me his answer before he even speaks.

"I was professional," he says, his voice curt. "I don't see why niceties should matter. This is business, not a political race. I don't need to make friends with everyone."

I roll my eyes.

"That might be true in other towns, but now you're in Seaside Point. You need people to like you here if you want to get anything done without a huge headache. Your all-work-no-play, friends-are-just-networking-opportunities mindset isn't going to work. You need to be friendly." He gives me a blank expression, and I let out a deep sigh, shaking my head. "Thank God you have me. Can I see the original permits?"

Step one in fixing this mess is making sure we actually have our ducks in a row. While I never worked for my brother in any official capacity, I have helped a couple of times when he was super busy in the summer and needed someone to help keep him organized, including occasionally bringing his paperwork to City Hall to file it on his behalf. Graham nods, handing me the papers, and immediately, I relax, seeing that my hopes were right. Carl Stevens' firm may have been listed as the insured and licensed contractor on the project, but Daydream Resorts' legal team filed the actual permits.

Reaching over to his desk, I grab whatever other papers I'll need, sifting through and trying to ignore the way my arm brushes over his chest before grabbing a manila folder and sliding them inside. Leaving his office, I grab my tote bag from my desk, slide the documents inside, and sling it over my shoulder. Finally, I turn to my boss, who followed me out into the hallway. "Come on. We're going on a field trip," I say.

"A field trip?"

"Today's going to be a good day, even if I have to make it so. Let's go, Graham." I head out the door without another word, but he follows me, jogging to catch up after he grabs his phone and wallet, so I call it a win.

Since it's a gorgeous day out, parking is always abysmal outside City Hall, and I thought Graham could probably use a cool down, I decided walking was in order. At some point, Graham rolled up the cuffs of his white business shirt, revealing his impeccably toned forearms, bringing his formal business vibes down a notch and, unfortunately for me, his hot factor up one hundred percent. I've always been a forearm girl, and his are perfect specimens: perfectly dotted with dark hair, veined and muscled in a way that desperately makes me want to know what they look like when he makes a fist. I was a bit distracted during my night with him, and my *god*, I'm now filled with regret. The only thing that stops me from completely ogling and drooling over them the entire walk over is knowing I'm on a mission. Once we reach the entrance, I lead us through the front doors. Graham stops at the directory, but I keep walking.

"Come on, Graham, follow me," I say, tipping my head in the direction I'm headed.

"How do you know where to go?"

"I've lived in town my whole life," I say, leading the way. "And the fifth graders come here on a field trip every year." He nods, seeming to trust me, but when the elevator doors open, and I press level three instead of two—where the zoning office is—he gives me another puzzled look.

"It says the building administration department is on the second floor," he says. "Shouldn't we—"

"Trust me," I say, looking at him with a small smile. "I know what I'm doing." Behind my back, I cross my fingers, because while I have an *idea* of what I'm doing, nothing is foolproof. I'm kind of moving on a wish and a prayer, if I'm being honest. When he eventually nods and lets out a tense breath, a thrill moves through me, feeling like I won something as fragile as Graham's trust.

I'm still thrumming with that feeling when the elevator dings and I lead us toward my destination. My steps slow as we approach the Mayor's office, and Graham looks at me, confused. "June, this is the mayor," he says in a low voice. "We need the—" I turn to him, my stern look in place.

"I know you're like, a genius businessman who can flip a business in six months, but small-town politics is my domain. Let me handle this," I say in a fierce whisper, and his eyes widen like he didn't expect that.

"I just—" he starts, but just then, ten feet ahead of us, a man steps out of an office. My heart pounds as I realize somehow, some way, my plan is falling into place, luck on my side once again.

"Oh, my goodness, Mayor Mosely, I didn't expect to see you here!" I say a bit too loudly as I walk faster toward his office. His steps falter, and he turns to look at me before smiling wide.

"We're outside his office, June," Graham mumbles, thankfully low enough so only I can hear, and I elbow him, hard, but keep a smile plastered on my face. If he doesn't stop, he's going to ruin this.

"Well, if it isn't June Taylor," Mayor Mosely says with a friendly tone. "What a pleasure to see you."

"You too!"

"Let me guess, you're here about the mural? You'd be the perfect candidate," he says. I give him a tight smile and shake my head. I wonder if maybe Claire and Maggie mentioned it to him, too, hoping they could get the mayor on their side to guilt me into applying, which leads me to worry about what other ears they've been whispering into.

"No, no, not that. I'm actually here for work." I turn my body, bringing Graham into the small circle we've created in the hallway, "This is my boss, Graham Hawthorne. He's the project manager at Daytrip."

"Oh, Maggie did tell me you were working over there!" Well, that confirms one theory. "How exciting. Great to meet you, Mr. Hawthorne. We're so excited that Daydream chose our little town to settle into." He reaches out and shakes Graham's hand.

"We're happy to be here. I believe June has already reached out to you about a ribbon cutting?" Mayor Mosely nods excitedly.

"Yes, Fran has it in my calendar. So what brings you over to city hall today?" I speak before Graham does.

"We're actually hoping that Chet would talk to us about a permitting issue, but silly me, I forgot *you're* on the third floor, and building admin is the *second*." Graham lets out a small cough, and once again, I elbow him in the side.

"A permitting issue?" Mayor Mosely says, ignorant of our silent argument, brows furrowing. "I thought that was all already figured out." I nod, biting my lip, trying to seem solemn and not smile smugly that things are going exactly as planned.

"Yes, well, originally, Daytrip was using a different contractor, but things weren't working out, so they ended up working with Taylor Contracting. There seems to have been a mix-up with the permits and who filed them. Grant says everything is in line on his end, and Daydream Resorts' legal team filed the permits themselves, but you know how paperwork can be." I give a girly shrug, trying to sound upbeat and unaccusing, and the mayor nods. "Anyway, I came here hoping it's something that will be an easy fix." I lift my fingers and cross them. "I find it's always better to have these kinds of conversations in person so there's less back and forth. Plus, I wanted Graham to meet our great little town's diligent public servants." Mayor Mosely nods eagerly.

"Oh, of course! The best in the great state of New Jersey! You know, I believe Chet is in the office today. I was just talking to him this morning. Let me bring you right to him! We don't want there to be any hang-ups with that opening day: I already have my big scissors ready!"

*Hook, line, and sinker.* I smile at Graham as we follow Mayor Mosely to the second floor.

A few minutes later, the three of us are standing in Chet's office, Chet trying to maintain a neutral face, but it's clear he's annoyed with me if the lasers he's shooting in my way are anything to go by.

"As I'm sure you know, we're so excited that Daydream chose our town for this new venture, and we really want things to move smoothly. It seems that they changed contractors, and there was a mix-up with the permitting," Mayor Mosely explains to Chet, clearly oblivious to the turmoil in the room. "Can you make sure that they have an inspector out there next week to keep the opening day? I'm going to be attending the ribbon cutting."

Chet's jaw goes tight before he tries to explain.

"Well, you see, the issue is the permits were filed by the initial contracting company," Chet starts, and I don't miss how he leaves out that it was his *son's* company. "And the company retracted them when they were removed from the build, so—"

I lift a hand, a pleasant smile on my face.

"Actually," I say, pulling out the folder I brought and showing Chet the permitting paperwork. "Daydream Resorts filed personally, *not* Stevens Contracting, which would mean that if his firm did not complete the work, there was no reason even to report that. The permits were the sole responsibility of Daydream to confirm, complete, and have inspected." I pull out a few more papers and place them on his desk, fighting the urge to slap them down. "And these are the reports of the work having a projected completion date of next Tuesday. I'm *sure* that now that you have these in front of you, you'll be able to schedule the building inspector to come out and perform the final inspection. Right?"

Chet's face gets a bit red, and I let a full grin take over my face.

"I suppose," he says through gritted teeth.

"Great, perfect! I've got a meeting in ten, but June, make sure you tell Fran what time you want me there on opening day!" Mayor Mosely says.

"Of course. It was so great seeing you!" I say with a cheery wave. He bids everyone a happy goodbye before leaving, and the second he's out of sight, whatever threads of pleasantness that were on Chet's face die out, leaving an angry, irritated one in their place.

"I don't know what kind of game you're playing, but—" he starts, voice menacing. Graham opens his mouth to speak, but I beat him, knowing arguing will get us nowhere.

"I'm just doing my job, like you are supposed to be doing. Your job does not include playing favorites or aiding your son when he throws a temper tantrum because he was unable to complete a job to the agreed-upon timeline or expected quality."

"Pulling the mayor into this was low, and you know it," Chet says low.

"It was simply a lovely coincidence," I say, batting my eyes. "I can't help that he's determined to keep Daydream Resorts in Seaside Point, knowing that it will benefit the community with the amount of tourists it will bring in to our small town." He opens his mouth to argue, but I continue. "Now, I will say Mayor Mosely looked completely thrown back that there would be an issue with permitting, something we both know is a common problem in town anytime your son gets fired, which, again, we know isn't uncommon. Seems to me like you've kept this little scheme of yours under wraps. I happen to know a lot of people in town are increasingly tired of you favoring your son's work, and I've heard murmurings of them wanting to bring it up at a city council meeting."

Chet's head snaps up, his jaw going tight.

"Are you threatening me?"

I smile and shake my head.

"No, not at all. I'm just stating facts."

Graham makes a noise, and I wonder if he recognizes the statement as the words he used to his son in the convenience store when I first met him. Chet looks from me to Graham and back again, his jaw going tight.

"Now, if you would just sign the confirmation of the opening day, then reach out to the inspector to get him out to Daytrip next week—I'm thinking Tuesday will work best for us—we can be on our way. Here, I brought you a pen," I say, handing him a Daytrip pen. He glares at it before grabbing one of his own instead and signing the opening day confirmation paper.

"I'll call Tom later today," he grumbles, naming the inspector, before handing me the paper. I know inherently that the call will not be made today, but before I can say anything, Graham speaks.

"You'll be calling him right now," he insists, his hand moving to my lower back and warming the skin there. "We can wait."

"That's not—" Chet starts.

"No need to do the back and forth to figure out days and times that would work. Call him right now, and we can compare calendars easily." Graham's face is scary-hard, making me realize that the ire he gives to me is nothing but superficial grouchiness. Warmth from where his hand still lies on my lower back filters through my blood, settling in my belly as I realize this man has never actually disliked me.

Not if this is how he treats people he *genuinely* dislikes.

"He might be out to lunch," Chet argues.

"Never hurts to try," I say with a cheery tone. After a moment of staring us down, he sighs, then reaches for his phone. In five minutes, we have a scheduled appointment for Tom to come out to Daytrip to approve the electrical, structural, and plumbing work. Since the fire marshal already approved us, as long as that goes okay, which, knowing Grant and his quality work, it will, we'll be just fine to open up on time.

"Later, Maryanne!" I say to Tom's assistant, a sweet older lady, with a smile and a wave as we head out, mission accomplished. "By the way, I'm sorry about Graham if he was being a bit rude. He was stressed, and he's generally a pretty grumpy guy as it is. Don't take it personally, I haven't fully broken him into the ways of Seaside Point yet."

She gives me a wide grin, though Graham lets out an exasperated sigh from behind me.

"No problem at all," she says with a wave of her hand, then lowers her voice. "I know how dealing with Mr. Stevens can be. It's nice to meet you formally, Mr. Hawthrone." Graham nods, then puts a hand out to her.

"You, as well. I appreciate your quick forgiveness, but I am sorry for snapping at you."

"Already forgotten. Now you two have a great day—go enjoy the sunshine for me."

"Will do. Bye, Maryanne!" I say with a wave, leaving the office with Graham on my heels before stepping out into the bright summer sun.

# THIRTEEN

# June

"How did you do that?" Graham asks, stopping and turning to me once we're on the sidewalk, astonishment written clear across his face.

"Do what?" I ask, sliding my sunglasses down from my hair and onto my nose.

"I've been in board rooms with powerful CEOs, and most would have shit their pants, sitting in front of you while you tore them a new asshole in the most polite and condescending way possible."

I smile wide, preening at the compliment.

"I was a fifth-grade teacher. Everyone knows teachers are much more badass than any CEO out there."

"You handled that in less than an hour."

I lift my shoulder halfheartedly, suddenly shy.

"That's less personal talent and more experience with living in a small town. It's not some big city, where you have a ton of hoops to jump through. You just have to know who to talk to and how to get your way. Chet is an asshole with entitled asshole kids. When they don't get their way, they throw hissy fits, and because of his position, he's able to make their tantrums everyone's problem. I don't like that, so any opportunity I can get to take him down a peg, I take."

"Well, I guess I should be lucky you're on my team," he mumbles, looking at the papers again in a bit of a daze. I take them, slide them back into the manila folder I brought, then put them into my bag.

"The luckiest," I agree. We stand outside the building for another moment, me looking at him and smiling, him looking down at me contemplatively.

"Do you want to get lunch?" he asks after a moment, and my entire body stills.

"Lunch?"

"Yeah. Midday meal, sandwiches, salads," he says, an echo of my own words.

I nudge his shoulder, watching his lips tip up more than ever before. He's *teasing me*. He still isn't smiling, something I'm not fully sure he knows how to do, but I think I might spot the beginnings of a *dimple*.

"Oh. My. God," I murmur, looking around dramatically, trying not to give in to the Graham-induced daze.

Today has really messed with my head, between the almost smile, the forearm porn, and his hand on my waist. Or maybe it's that he and I are spending time together outside of the office for the first time. Either way, my outburst works as planned, his eyebrows furrowing. I grin, basking in his confusion. I like confusing Graham. Something tells me that very few people can get him off kilter, and being one of the few who can feels special.

"What's wrong?"

"I just... It's happening!" I say. "We're one step closer to friends!"

He rolls his eyes and lifts a hand as if to fend me off. "Okay, if you're going to make it weird—"

"No, no. No take-backs. Come on, let's go. There's a good place around the corner."

I grab his arm and lead him toward the small lunch place without another word. When we get there, I greet April, the hostess, and introduce her to Graham.

"Table for two?" I ask, glancing inside. It's packed, which isn't a surprise since it's a popular lunch spot, but I was hopeful they'd be able to fit us in.

"Inside or out? Out is open, but inside is about a fifteen-minute wait." Graham answers for me.

"Outside. Are you okay with that?"

"As long as you are. I need to get my vitamin D. It's what gives me my sunny disposition."

April grabs two menus and leads us to a table.

"You need more vitamin D? I think you're sunny enough," Graham says as we walk.

"That sounded like another compliment, Mr. Hawthorne. Be careful, I think it might become a habit for you."

"It wasn't a compliment," he says quickly with a shake of his head, pulling out a chair for me to sit in.

"Sure it wasn't," I tease, then accept the menu from April. Graham sits, then takes his own menu, and we call into a. comfortable silence as we look them over.

After a moment, Rachel comes over with a pad to take out an order.

"Hey, June! How are you? I didn't expect to see you here," she says with a wide grin.

"Hey, Rach! We had to get some permits at city hall, and I'm determined to show Graham here some of Seaside Point's hidden gems. How's Jonah?" I ask of her son.

"Oh, he's great, working with Claire again this summer as a junior lifeguard. Probably yapping her ear off," she says with an eye roll and a smile.

"She loves it," I say, because she does.

"Well, we're lucky to have her in town," she agrees before looking to Graham and me. "Do you two know what you want, or do you need another minute?" We both agree that we're good to order, and

Rach takes it down. I reach for a tortilla chip in the basket at the center of the table after she walks off, but Graham stares at me skeptically.

"Do you know *everyone* in this town?" he asks after a moment. I smile and shake my head.

"Not everyone, but close. I grew up here, as did my parents and grandparents. Add in working in the school, and it's almost inevitable."

"Did you ever leave, or have you always lived here?"

"I went to college in-state, so I technically left Seaside Point then, but I missed it like crazy and came back a lot of weekends. Sometimes I'm embarrassed that I never tried anywhere else, but most of the time I wonder why anyone would ever want to leave. I have everything I could ever want in this little town."

He's looking down at the basket of chips, lost in his thoughts, though I can't decide if it's in a good or bad way.

"I can see that," he says finally, and I smile, relieved. I don't know why I want Graham to like Seaside Point, but I do. "It's a good place. Good mix of a getaway and a small town you'd want to settle down in, I imagine. You can't say that about a lot of places: it's usually one or the other." Pleasure blooms in my heart at the idea of this grumpy man enjoying my favorite place on earth, especially when he's seemingly been everywhere. "I bet it was nice growing up somewhere like this."

"What about you? Where did you grow up?"

"Everywhere and nowhere," he says, and I remain quiet, eager to hear anything he's willing to share with me about himself. "We moved a lot. I was rarely in the same school for more than two years."

"That had to be rough," I say low.

In another world where my grandparents didn't take us in, that could have been Grant and me, moving around from town to town, living our parents' nomadic lifestyle as they tried to make something of their art dreams.

"I guess, but it taught me a lot. How to read people, how to choose and make friends quickly, and how to climb the social ladder. No matter what school I was in, I always made my way into the popular crowd. I think it helped me get where I am now. If I hadn't learned those skills so young, I probably wouldn't have the job I have. I've used those skills to network, to make quick relationships, and build connections."

"Ahh, I suppose that explains your villain origin story of seeing friendships as networking. So, you've been doing it ever since?" He lifts a shoulder, grabbing a chip and chewing it thoughtfully.

"I guess, in a way. My job is making sure new locations open smoothly, become profitable, and run efficiently from the start, so I'm often moving from one location to the next."

"So how does Seaside Point stack up? Is it exciting because it's your first time being the head of a project, or a disappointment because it's not a huge, full resort?" There's momentary flash on his face confirming my theory that he wasn't happy to be assigned Seaside Point. It's gone almost as soon as it came, replaced with something new, more contemplative. It's almost as if that was his reaction when he was first given the job, but now, after some time, he's changed his view.

"It's..." His eyes drift to me, gaze locking with mine in a way that has the world pausing, the other diners' voices dulling. Emotion crosses his face, a mixture of sincerity and honesty, erasing the normally cold and distant look. Warmth that has nothing to do with the beating sun moves through me. For a moment, he's the man who chatted with me in a dimly lit bar, the one who I was completely enthralled by. "It's grown on me." The words hang in the air between us, and my mind starts to run with them, making stories that don't belong in a workplace relationship. After a moment, he looks off into the distance, making me feel silly for romanticizing a single *look*. "It's just not what I expected. I'm used to full resorts, ones that are a kind of ecosystem in and of themselves, where I only have to focus on the inner workings."

"You had to have known, though, that was what you were getting when you came here."

He nods. "I did."

"So why accept it? If it wasn't what you wanted, why take the job? Sutton told me you're hot shit at Daydream. I bet if you had told them you wanted something bigger and better, you'd have gotten it."

His gaze moves back to me, and he lifts an eyebrow.

"Are you talking to Sutton about me?"

A blush burns on my cheeks, but I brush it off, lift a nonchalant shoulder. "She may have given me some intel to figure out how to deal with your surly attitude."

"Was it helpful?"

"She told me not to back down, and I'd be just fine."

He's quiet for a moment before I get another one of those near-invisible lip tilts and an unexpected answer to my earlier question.

"I accepted the job because I needed a challenge," he says, that spark of entertainment melting away, replaced with something different, a burnout or a complacency that I am far too familiar with. He goes silent, and for a bit, I think that's all I'm going to get. It's more than I expected, if I'm being honest, so I'm willing to take it, but then he expands. "I'd been going through the motions for a while, trying to build a career, to get each new promotion. The only person who rose in the Daydream Resorts ranks faster than me and at a younger age is Rowan, and he's part robot." I know that much from Sutton. "But I kept getting these promotions that I was aiming for, kept setting goals and hitting each one, and every time it felt...hollow. I kept wanting more, thinking it would make that feeling go away, but nothing seemed to work." The words sound like a confession of sorts, and if it were anyone else, I'd reach out and hold his hand. "I know it sounds stuck-up and very first-world problems of me, wanting a more impressive, high-paying, high-powered job because nothing makes me feel satisfied," he says, with a humorless laugh, shaking his head. "I probably sound like such a jackass."

I give in to the urge then, reaching over and placing my hand over his. His eyes lift, and I shake my head when we meet. "No, you don't. I get it," I say, hesitant.

"You don't have to say that, I know it sounds out there, to be bored with doing well."

"No, no. I do. I get it." I lick my lips, my pulse pounding, suddenly nervous. "They gave me the option to transfer to another school, keep teaching next school year, and I didn't take it, even though it was the safe choice. The smart choice. I think... I think I was looking for a way out for a while. I was unhappy and unfulfilled. It's weird to say you don't love your job when it's teaching kids and, in a way, shaping the future. Especially when your whole life, you were told that's what you would be best at. I went to school for years, working to be a teacher, only to realize..." I look off, taking in a deep breath before giving Graham a confession I've never said to anyone else, whispered so low that if his hand didn't shift to squeeze mine tighter, I'd think he couldn't hear me. "I don't like it. Teaching made me miserable, and then the guilt of hating it made me even *more* miserable. I ignored it for a while, but by the end of this year, I was so tired. I was burnt out in a way I'd never experienced." I take a deep breath, laying another confession out on the table. "But since I left, I haven't felt tired at all. So I get it. I get doing something that makes no sense at all just to see if it might make you feel alive. Sometimes you just have to be brave and take a leap of faith and trust that the universe will catch you."

"I think you're the bravest person I know, June," he says, squeezing my hand once more and making my heart leap.

"I quit my job, I didn't run into a burning building," I say, trying to break the tension. It doesn't: instead, he continues to stare at me.

"Bravery comes in all different forms. Trusting your gut might be the most crucial one."

His words settle into me, sinking deep and reminding me that I promised to do that this summer: trust my gut, take leaps of faith, take opportunities that are presented to me. I think about all of the ways I haven't been brave lately, all the things I've been too scared to do. I want to tell him that he has the wrong idea, that I'm not that girl, to set him straight, but before I can refute his claim that I'm brave, our lunch comes, and we fall into a silence that I readily accept as possibly the biggest sign of my cowardice of all.

"Compliments like that definitely creep into friend territory," I say with a small smile, desperate to change the topic. His face stays stoic as he watches me for long moments before opening his mouth to speak. But before he can, Rachel is back to check in on us, breaking the moment.

I wonder for the rest of the day, though, what he was going to say.

# FOURTEEN

# GRAHAM

I don't want to be friends with June Taylor, because friends would never be enough.

Hiring her was the unluckiest thing that has ever happened to me.

Still, I can't find it in me to regret it.

The next day, Graham isn't in the office and won't be until later in the day. According to the email that hit my inbox at ten p.m. last night, he's up north in Hudson City for a meeting with Rowan and the Daydream team. With him gone, I find the morning dragging, an uncomfortable boredom weighing me down. It's strange to think that even though we spend most of the day completely separated, I've come to expect, and, in some way, enjoy Graham's companionship during the workday. By the time lunch rolls around, I'm desperate for a change of scenery. Grant and the guys are on the deck, finishing up some things before next week's inspection, so while I want to sit out there and enjoy my lunch, I know I would just be in the way.

Instead, on my lunch break, I grab the towel I keep in the trunk of my car. Weighing my options, I think about going onto the beach, but realize the sand is bound to be wet from last night's rain and cold. Instead, I walk to the side of the building, carefully lay my towel out on a dry patch of sidewalk, and sit down to eat. I stretch out my hand and idly move it through the grassy clover patch next to me, half-looking for a four-leaf clover as my break ticks away.

After a while, a voice calls from behind me, making me jump in alarm. I quickly pull out one of my earbuds and turn to see Graham standing over me with a disapproving expression.

"Oh my god, you scared the crap out of me," I say, rubbing at my chest where my heart is pounding.

"I've been standing here for two minutes," he accuses.

"I was listening to music. I didn't hear you."

"That's incredibly unsafe. You should always be aware of your surroundings."

I roll my eyes at his dramatics.

"This is Seaside Point on a Wednesday before the season starts, and my brother's on the deck with half a dozen men who treat me like I'm their little sister who needs protecting. This might be the safest place I could be, aware of my surroundings or not."

He crosses his arms, clearly irritated with my nonchalance. I smile. "But you have a good point; next time, I'll leave one earbud out." He stares a long moment as if assessing the validity of my promise before nodding in approval at whatever he finds.

"What are you doing out here?" I ask, looking at him and really seeing him now. He's in the same white shirt and black pants as always, but he's holding a brown bag.

"I got back a little bit ago, figured I'd have lunch. Mind if I come join you?" I stare at him with wide eyes.

"Join me?" I ask, completely dazed by this unexpected turn.

"For lunch," he clarifies.

"Outside?" Despite my confusion, I shift, gathering my things to one side of the towel so he can sit down, trying to ignore how my heart is now pounding harder for a new reason.

"You said vitamin D might help with my attitude," he says, taking a sandwich out of the bag after he sits on the towel.

He looks so out of place, all business-man hot sitting on an oversized rainbow beach towel. For a moment, I wonder if he owns any casual clothes, if he's ever gone to the beach for anything other than work, and, most dangerous of all, what he would look like in swim trunks, laid out in the sand, sweaty and—

*This is your boss, June. Get it together*, I remind myself, but it doesn't seem to help in the least.

"I... I guess I did," I say, still stunned. "Didn't expect you'd actually consider what I said, though."

"Figure it couldn't hurt, just this once." He tips his scruff-covered chin toward my hand, still in the grass. "Are you still looking for clovers?"

I nod.

"Could always use a little bit more luck," I say, happy for the distraction as I divert my gaze to the grass. "I've decided to make this my luckiest summer possible, and I'm taking any extra help I can get."

"How's that going for you?" he asks, and when I look over at him, I note the question is genuine.

"Well, I got this job."

"So, bad," he says, and I let out a small laugh at his unexpected joke. There's a twinkle in his eyes, though his lips don't shift into that tiny hint of a smile that I'm becoming addicted to.

"I wouldn't say that. I've been enjoying working here so far," I say.

"I'm glad you're here," he says after a moment, then quickly adds, as if realizing his mistake, "Because you're really good at your job. You saved the day yesterday."

I let him have that one, mostly because he's now moving his hands through the grass as well, and it distracts me thoroughly. He has nice hands: long, thick fingers, short, neat nails. The way they flex as they move feels like my own personal catnip, and—

Nope, nope, nope. We are *not* doing this. Needing to distract myself, I blurt, "What are you doing?"

"Looking for four-leaf clovers," he states, as if it's obvious.

I stare at him for a moment in confusion. "Don't you have something more grown-up and boring to do?"

"Absolutely," he replies simply. "I was out of the office all morning. I'm sure my inbox is a disaster." Again, my traitorous heart beats a bit faster.

"But you're out here with me?"

He looks around as if assessing the validity before shrugging once more.

"Looks like it."

I stare at him for a moment, his attention back on the grass as he inspects a clover with a torn leaf so it *almost* looks like it had four leaves. With a moment of hesitation, I do the same, biting my lip as I move my hand through the clovers, though I'm not even looking anymore.

This is weird, right? I mean, just last week, he could barely look at me without grimacing and was telling me that my little lucky quirks were ridiculous. And now he's sitting out here in his work clothes, brushing through the grass, looking for a four-leaf clover with me.

I should just enjoy it, bask in the moment, and accept that I'm getting just a bit closer to winning Graham over.

But being me means overthinking every second, unable to simply let anything good just be.

"This is too weird. I can't do this," I say.

He looks up at me with a questioning look. "Are you done looking for clovers?"

"No," I say, shaking my head. "I can't sit here knowing basically nothing about you."

His brows furrow. "I don't see how knowing anything about me impacts your ability to sit beside me."

"Because it's uncomfortable! What if you're a serial killer? I'm pretty sure if a serial killer finds a four-leaf clover, it's counterproductive."

His head tips just a bit as he looks me over. I think he might say something about my not being worried about that when I went to his hotel room with him, but it seems we're both on the same page of pretending that never happened.

"How would getting to know me clarify whether or not I'm a

serial killer? From my understanding, they're great at hiding their motives. That's kind of the whole point, isn't it?"

He has a great point, though I'll never admit it.

"I'm a great judge of character," I lie, because I'm actually a *terrible* judge of character, not that I'll be telling him that. I'm overly trusting, which, in my life, has been fine since I've always had Lainey and Grant, both of whom are so skeptical of everyone on God's green earth, that it outweighs my own lack of skepticism.

"What do you want to know?" he asks, shifting his position so he's sitting upright and leaning back on his hands. My chest tightens, partly from how his shirt stretches across his chest and partly from surprise that he's actually *going along with this game.*

"Want to know?" I repeat, fumbling for another chip and trying to act casual while my attention jumps between the food and him.

"Yeah. What do you want to know?"

I hesitate, unsure, since I didn't actually think he'd go along with it, but...

"What's...what's your favorite color?" I ask, feeling like I already know the answer. It has to be black, or white, or some other very boring, very basic color that fits his personality.

"Blue," he says quickly, shocking me.

"Blue?"

"Yeah. Blue."

"Huh." I sit there, staring at him for long moments.

"Why do you look surprised?"

"Because you only wear black and white, and your office is beige. I expected something boring, not an actual good option." I study him. "What kind of blue?" I expect him to brush me off, but once again, he takes it seriously.

"Like..." He closes his eyes. The sun casts shadows on the sharp lines of his face, softening them as he lets out a breath. I wish I could paint it, capture the moment of peace forever, but it's gone just as quickly as it came. "Summer sky blue. The bright kind that means warm days and—" He opens his eyes and stares at me. "What? Why are you looking at me like that?" I blink and shake my head.

"Nothing," I say, shaking my head, trying to find my grip on reality, to knock myself from this strange dreamland I keep falling into. "I just didn't expect you'd have such a good answer. That's my favorite color too. More like a robin's egg blue, though."

"You wear a lot of blue. It looks nice on you," he says. I freeze, caught off guard by the compliment, unsure how to react or what to say next, when he continues. "Okay, my turn."

"Your turn?"

"Do only you get to ask things?" he asks.

"I...I guess not," I say, confused because I didn't think he'd actually go for this in the first place. I didn't exactly think through the rules, but I suppose fair is fair. "Okay, ask away."

"Favorite movie?" he asks.

"*Sixteen Candles*," I answer without hesitation.

He pauses, looking thoughtful as if he's trying to remember which film it is.

"The one where they forget her birthday?"

I nod and blush. "It happened to me once. My parents are kind of all over the place, wanderers, hippies, that kind of thing, so they left Grant and me with my grandparents."

"Is your birthday not in June? You'd think it would be easy for them to remember," he asks.

"No, late August." He looks as confused as everyone else does when they learn my name and subsequent birthday. "My parents are hippies and never really made much sense. Anyway, they forgot my birthday, which wasn't a surprise because they were out in Utah or Washington or something on a retreat. My grandparents forgot too, because they were pretty old by then, and my brother is a boy, so he just...inherently forgot. I didn't want to make a big deal out of it because I've never liked to make a big fuss about things that are just for me. But a week later, my grandma remembered, and she was so upset. Anyway, every year after that, we watched that movie together on what she deemed to be my second birthday, a week after my real birthday. Until she died, I'd get two presents every year, one on my real birthday, the other on my second birthday." I smile at the sweet memory, one that could have been negative, with the burn of a forgotten milestone, yet became anything but.

"Sounds... nice, strangely enough. I don't think I ever got more than a card with ten bucks in it from my grandparents as a kid."

"They were the best. They raised us and were the coolest, kindest people I've ever met," I say with a smile. I open my mouth to ask another question, but my phone buzzes beside me, stealing my attention. I groan aloud when I read the message on my screen. "Dammit."

"Boyfriend?" Graham asks quickly. "I mean, you don't have to share, I just..." I lift an eyebrow at him as a tiny hint of a blush burns across his cheeks. I smile, but put him out of his misery instead of teasing him more.

"I don't have a boyfriend. Something I hope you already knew or at least assumed because... well..." Now it's my turn for a blush to burn on my cheeks. Instead of digging myself a deeper hole, I shake my head and change the subject. "No, it's just my friend bugging me about something," I say with a sigh, deciding to ignore Claire's text until after work.

"I thought that was the whole point of friends? That's what you've been doing to me, isn't it?"

"Is that you agreeing that we're friends?" I ask with a lifted brow.

"Probably not. I feel like if we were friends, you'd be sharing whatever's bothering you," he challenges, one I feel compelled to rise to, but am not sure if I should. I mull on it as we sit in silence for a bit, and I reach into the bag and grab the last few of my chips. Their loud crunch silences my thoughts enough to build the courage to speak again, turning to him fully as I do.

"My friends are trying to convince me to open up a business. I've always pushed it aside, since teaching took up so much of my time, but now that I'm *not* teaching, they're pushing harder." I don't know why I'm telling Graham this, but as I do, a weight lifts from my shoulders. Maybe this is what I need: an unbiased, logical source to confirm that Claire and Lainey's idea is silly.

"Oh? Maybe I could help. You know, businesses are kind of my thing," he says, settling in, and I shake my head quickly, clarifying.

"Not, like, a real one. Just a little... side thing."

"Every business is a real business," he says.

"That's not something I would have thought you'd say."

He lifts a shoulder. "It's the truth. Anyone brave enough to put themselves out there, to try and build something out of nothing, whether it be a huge corporation or something small, is impressive. So what's yours?"

"Art," I admit on a sigh. "Paintings, mostly. My friends want me to start selling them."

"Are you any good?" he asks, and I lift a shoulder. "Show me."

It's a demand, one I should argue, but instead I find myself grabbing my phone, scrolling through until I find the photos I took to upload to the shop. He accepts the device, and my heart pounds as he swipes through, assessing each one slowly and methodically. After what feels like an eternity, he lifts his head to look at me, nothing but pure awe and sincerity written across his face.

"These are...wow. June, these are amazing." A blush creeps down my cheeks and over my neck, and I bite my lip. "Did you ever take classes?" He turns back to my phone, swiping again, pausing on one and zooming in a bit, taking in the small details of a wave curling, about to crash on the shore.

"Not formally," I say, hating the attention being on me like this. "My grandma gave me lessons."

"Was she a teacher, too?"

"Not exactly," I say, and this time, my lips tip with a small smile. He lifts his head from my phone and looks at me quizically. "She taught art at the senior center and at the jail," I explain, and his eyes widen. "It was funny, this cute little old lady going into the county jail, teaching the basics once a week, but she loved it. She loved teaching, and she told me that everyone deserves to have some beauty in their life, even if they have to make it themselves. That's what art was to her: a bit of joy you make yourself and get to keep." He stares at me for long moments, setting my phone onto the towel before he finally speaks.

"Explains you, I suppose."

"How so?" He leans back onto his hands again, but his face has gone soft in a way I've never had the pleasure of seeing. Part of me is glad I haven't, because it would only make the seemingly constant warring feelings in my chest even more confusing. When he speaks, I expect him to mention that I am a teacher, but he surprises me.

"I've never met anyone who takes low points and sees them as opportunities, constantly looking the bright side, determined to make the best of everything. It's admirable. I've never met anyone who tries to bring more beauty into the world, even though you've been shown time and time again that it can be anything but."

I smile softly.

"I get that from her, too. She was a firm believer that everything happened for a reason, but whether it was good or bad depended solely on how you responded to it, whether you saw it as a curse or an opportunity. She used to say that even if you can't see them, you have to chase the rainbows, to keep going through the storm until you hit the sunshine. There's always something better waiting for you; you just have to look for it." He stares at me for long moments, reading me in a way I don't think anyone ever has before.

"Okay, Miss Optimism, so what's the holdup? I know a dozen people who would pay good money to have original art like this in their homes."

I bite my lip, and for some reason, I find myself sharing more with him.

"Art is...complicated in my family. My parents went off to pursue it. They were always chasing some dream, and most of the time, my brother and I didn't fit into that vision; our grandparents had to raise us because of it. I'm very logical in that regard because of that. I know art is fun and cool and admirable, but I also am aware that the number of people who actually manage to make a living from it is so microscopic, it's not a reliable form of work." I expect him to agree, but he surprises me by shaking his head fervently.

"Not anymore. Maybe in the nineties and early thousands, but these days, with anyone able to make a website and use free marketing tactics on social media? It's much more attainable." He tips his chin to where I'm still playing with the clovers absentmindedly. "You're always trying to collect luck," he says, the change of subject feeling abrupt. "What's the point of being lucky if you're never going to use it? Who knows? You could get lucky, get your piece into the right hands, and your business could blow up."

My pulse picks up with his words.

If even straight and narrow, logical Graham, who definitely wouldn't sugarcoat something to make me feel better, thinks I should go for it, what's stopping me? I run my hand over the grass, contemplating how to reply to his question, but before I can formulate a response, I spot something, and my hand pauses. I shift my fingers again and gasp.

Quickly, I move to my knees, bend over the grassy area, and gently spread the blades apart with my hands, looking more closely. "Oh my god!" I shout, then glance over my shoulder at him. He's looking at me, panic-stricken, and if I weren't so excited, it would be funny.

"What? What's wrong?"

"A four-leaf clover! I found a four-leaf clover!" My eyes go wide as I look at him, anxiousness setting in. "What do I do now? Is it bad luck to pull it out?" Graham looks at me, confused as ever. "I've never found one! I don't know the procedure!"

"I think you just pull it out gently," he says, his voice calm and a bit entertained.

I take in a deep breath, nod, and do as he instructed. A moment later, I have a full, bright green four-leaf clover in the palm of my hand, the roots coming out with it easily.

"I can't believe it. I found one!" I look at him with a wide grin, one I couldn't dim if I tried. I know I must look out of my mind, but I can't find it in me to care. "You know, I think you might be good luck, Graham."

He gives me that soft look once more, and I think I might like seeing this more than the tiny hints of a smile I've been chasing.

"What are you going to do with this newfound luck?" he asks, and I take in a deep breath, the clover still in my hand.

"I think I'm going to be brave. Hit go on my shop. See what happens," I say, letting the words fall from my lips before I can second-guess them. "I mean, this has to be a sign, right? Why else, after a lifetime of looking, would I find a four-leaf clover right when I'm talking to you about my art and starting a business?"

"Agreed. You should do it," he says, the words sincere before he looks at his watch and sighs. "Unfortunately, I should probably get inside. I've got some catching up to do."

"Thanks for having lunch with me," I say, standing and gathering my garbage with one hand, holding my precious clover in the other, my hands still shaking a bit with the adrenaline from finding it. He gently shakes out the towel and folds it before we make our way inside.

"Anytime," he says. "It wasn't a miserable way to spend a meal."

"Anytime, huh? Don't tempt me, Graham. I'll hold you to it," I say with a smile.

"I'm sure you will," he says, then sets the towel on my desk and walks into his office, leaving me with my thoughts and my clover.

That night, I go home and stare at the shop, fully built and ready to go live the way it's sat for about a week.

I stare at it.

And I stare at it.

I move through the pages, making sure everything is perfect, trying to find any reason to procrastinate hitting the go button, but to my horror, I can't find one.

Not a *one.*

And as I sit there, a voice speaks in my mind.

It's not Claire, telling me to just go for it.

It's not Lainey, telling me that it's what I've always wanted.

It's not Maggie, Mayor Mosely, or anyone else telling me I'm talented and should make a go of art as a career.

Instead, it's Graham, asking me what I'm so scared of—asking me why I'm so determined to find luck if I'm never going to use it. My eyes drift to the book whose pages I'm pressing the four-leaf clover in.

I'd never tell him, but he's right.

*That's* the thought that has me taking in a deep breath and hitting *go live.*

Then I close my laptop before I can second-guess myself and put it into the universe's hands.

# GRAHAM

Last night, when I spent three hours searching for a four-leaf clover, then transplanting the entire plant to where she might find it, I thought I had officially lost my mind.

But today, when she got that happy look on her face and saw it as a sign to follow her dream, I knew it was worth it

# SEVENTEEN

# June

I'm following up with influencers about attending the grand opening in exchange for promoting the resort two days later when my phone pings from beside me. It's a strange, new sound, suspiciously like an old cash register drawer opening. I stare at the new notification on the screen and hesitantly reach for the phone.

Then my breathing hitches.

Excitement, nervousness, and hope surge through me all at once, swirling together and bubbling up in my chest, the emotions desperate for an escape. Everything comes out in a loud, unexpected shriek.

Then I stand, the happiness almost making me dizzy, and I can't help but jump and dance on my way to Graham's office, eager to share my news.

"OH, MY GOD!" I shout. "OHMIGODOHMIGOD!" When I enter his office, he's looking at me nervously, but I can't help it—this is the most exciting thing that has happened to me, possibly ever. "Graham! Graham, it happened! I can't believe it! Oh, my god, I think I'm going to pass out."

"June, what the hell?" His brows furrow as he stands and moves toward me, that nervous look transforming into panic. "Are you okay? Is everything okay?" I turn my phone toward him, only a few feet between us as he stares at my screen, trying to make sense of what's displayed there. "I got a sale! My first sale!"

On the heels of my announcement comes the second reward of the day: the closest thing to a full smile I've seen, the ends of his lips tipping up more than ever before, his eyes lighting up with unadulterated pride. The surprise of seeing Graham's reaction fills me with a new rush of emotions, confirming my suspicion that if he ever fully smiled, he'd be the hottest thing on the planet.

"Congrats, June," he says, pulling me from my reverie. His voice is low, and in the whirlwind of endorphins, I do the only thing that feels right in this moment.

I throw my arms around his neck, hugging him.

"I sold a painting!" I say, pressing my cheek to his chest as I squeeze him tight, desperate for somewhere to put all this overwhelming joy. "I sold a painting!" His arms hover at my sides—then, after a heartbeat, finally settle around my waist, his posture softening along with the smile at the corners of his lips. "Can you believe it? I sold a painting, Graham!" I tip my head back so I can see his face change, too, both of us swept up in this surprise.

"Of course I can believe it, June. You're incredibly talented."

I stare at him for a moment, my pulse still pounding.

"It was because of you, you know," I say.

My voice feels thick, like my heart is swelling in my throat, and an unexpected urge to cry wells up alongside gratitude. As I speak, Graham's brows knit together, and something I can't quite name flickers across his face, but it's gone before I can read it.

"Me?"

"You helped me find the four-leaf clover. That's why I made the shop live. You're lucky. And now I have an order! I'm a paid artist!" My voice gets squeaky with the excitement. He shakes his head. His hand lifts and pushes my hair back, the backs of his fingers grazing my cheek. My breath stops. "It's really the luckiest thing that's ever happened to me," I murmur, though I don't know what I'm talking about anymore: the clover or the sale or maybe something different altogether.

"You don't get it still, do you?" he asks, voice softer than I've ever heard it.

"Get what?"

"*You* are the lucky one, June. You're lucky and wildly talented. A four-leaf clover had nothing to do with it." A strange, out-of-character shyness sweeps over me at his words, my face burning as I roll my eyes to hide the sudden intensity of my feelings as well as my reaction to them.

"Sure," I say with a laugh. His hand moves again, touching below my chin, and tipping it up until I'm forced to look at him once more. The world stills as he looks down at me, sincerity in his warm eyes. When he speaks, his voice is low and soft, gentle in a way I've never thought possible from him.

"You believe in everyone else, but not yourself. A shame, if you ask me." My breath hitches, and he's staring at me again, something soft and filled with wonder on his face.

For a moment, I think he might lean down.

For a moment, I think he might kiss me.

And for a moment, I hope with everything in me that he *does*. It would fuck up everything, but really, things are already so twisted, what would it matter? I hold my breath silently, wishing for it, and I think he might actually lower his head just a bit toward me, before—

"Well, well, well, if this doesn't look cozy," a familiar voice says, smugness in the words, and instantly, Graham lets go of my chin, stepping away as if burned. I think I catch the tiniest blush on his cheeks, but the scruff of his face hides it. He looks away, avoiding my eyes. I turn to the intruder, smiling.

"Oh, my god, Sutton!" I say, excitedly. I force myself to sound happy, to feel that eagerness to tell someone else the good news I felt earlier, and to forget the strange things I'd been feeling just moments before.

Strange things I'd been feeling about my *boss*.

My god, could I be a bigger idiot? He doesn't even want to be my friend, and here I am, thinking he was about to kiss me. I really *am* delusional.

"I sold a painting! I opened my shop two days ago, and I already got a sale today! Can you believe it!?" I ask, jumping up and down as that remembered joy floods my system.

"Ahh!" Suton yells, grabbing my hands and jumping with me before pulling me into a tight hug, exactly as I tried to do with Graham.

See?

Completely normal.

Or at least, that's what I tell myself to settle the embarrassment still lingering after attacking Graham like that.

"We *have* to celebrate," Sutton demands once we stop.

"Yes," I agree, because even if I didn't want to celebrate, I know once Claire finds out, she's going to insist. "The Seabreeze! I think Lainey's working tonight, we'll get the crew all together."

"Yes, perfect," Sutton agrees, sliding her phone out of her pocket, probably to text Claire to have her invite everyone. I turn to Graham.

"Graham, you have to come!" I say. "It's a local's bar. Kind of a dive, but a good time. Come celebrate with us!"

He shakes his head as soon as I say *bar*. "No, thank you."

I let out a sigh.

"Come on, it would be good to meet everyone! You've been here for *how long* and haven't done anything?"

He lifts an eyebrow, and for a moment, I think he's going to tell me he very much *has* done something, but the look is gone quickly, melting back into neutrality.

"I don't need to meet anyone. I'm here for work."

I roll my eyes.

"Ah, yes, hold on, let me translate it into corporate asshole for you." I put a hand to my mouth and clear my throat dramatically. "It would be a fabulous networking opportunity, and a chance to do some integration with the local habitat."

"Local habitat?" he asks. Sutton watches the back-and-forth like a ping-pong match.

"Yeah, maybe that was more Steve Irwin than Don Draper." It happens again, the subtle tip of his lips, and it makes me smile wider. I am *so* getting through to him. I decide to use the last tool in my arsenal, the one that has never let me down. My eyes go wide, and my lips pout. "Pleaseeee?" I whine. "Please, please, please? It would make me the happiest girl in the whole wide world, and I'll leave you alone about being boring and lonely and grumpy for, like, at least a week." I think we both know I can't promise forever.

He looks at me, assessing. My heart lifts with hope, nearly bursting, when he closes his eyes and sighs.

"Will you stop making that face if I say yes?"

The face gets them every time.

"YES!" I shout, and again, I get that tiny, infinitesimal smile. My heart soars when I see it.

"Fine. Just let me know when and where. But only for a bit," he says in warning, but I'm barely listening, jumping and clapping.

"Of course! Oh my god, you're the best! You're going to have so much fun and meet everyone! You already know Deck and Grant, but Claire and Lainey, and Benny and Miles and—"

"You're not actually selling this," he says, and I grin wider.

"Too late, you already said yes."

"That actually worked," Sutton says in awe, and when I turn to her, her eyes are wide. "If I didn't watch it happen, I wouldn't have believed it."

"It works every time. It's my secret weapon," I say with a shrug of my shoulder.

"Yeah, I can see it worked great on Graham," she says, her smile turning knowing. "Maybe that's because—"

"Why are you here, anyway?" Graham asks, cutting off whatever she was going to say with a glare. Whatever thread of entertainment that was on his face moment ago is wiped clean, but for some reason, that makes Sutton smile wider.

"I came to see if June wanted to grab lunch and make sure you weren't making her too miserable. I've confirmed the latter," she says, giving a look to Graham that has some kind of meaning I don't understand, before turning to me. "Is your lunch coming up?" I check my watch and nod.

"I was planning to take it in about thirty minutes."

"Perfect, I'll wait. We can celebrate and yap about how to get you even more sales. Now that you're up and running, you can't fend me off."

I roll my eyes, but it's half-hearted. Sutton is great with social media and has offered to help me build a brand more times than I can count.

Excitement bubbles in my chest where the thought of running social media used to fill me with dread. If I got a sale without even talking about it, maybe promoting it would go even better? I don't actually know what I'm doing or how this works, but maybe, just maybe, Claire and Lainey and even Graham were right: maybe I could make something real of this? My mind moves to the mural bid, getting the idea before deciding I've been plenty brave enough for now. That's something Next Week June can contemplate.

"Go," he says, ushering us out of his office. "Go on your lunch now. Get Sutton out of here."

"Want to come?" I ask, a bit hopeful.

"Not this time. Thanks, though," Graham says.

"You sure?"

"Yeah. You're already forcing me to go out tonight, so I have to do some things to leave the office on time. Go on. Don't worry about your lunch running over: you've more than earned it."

And then Sutton and I go to a deli where she asks me a dozen questions about my art and my business. Still, the entire time, I can only think about the fact that, tonight, Graham is coming to the Seabreeze, and he almost smiled, and most importantly, of the way he looked at me when I hugged him.

# EIGHTEEN

# June

"You should really just move down here," Claire says, smiling at Sutton as we sit at the bar. "Then you wouldn't have to do the back and forth nonstop just to see your favorite sister in the whole wide world."

"Uh uh uh!" Sutton says, eyes going wide and shaking a finger at her sister. "No. No way, don't you say that."

"What? I *am* your favorite sister. We all know that, Sutton. It's okay to admit it," she says, reaching over to pat her sister's hand.

"You can't make me choose. If Sloane found out, I'd be screwed." Sloane is the oldest of the Donovan sisters and definitely the most intimidating.

"Oh, she would totally kill you in your sleep for the mere disrespect," Claire says, a happy smile on her lips, completely unfazed. "But she just moved to the middle of nowhere, so really, she can't even blame you for wanting to live at the beach instead of the woods."

"I am very much *not* a middle-of-nowhere kind of girl," Sutton agrees reluctantly with a nod. "I need Wawas and coffee shops and a variety of grocery store options within ten miles."

"And that's why moving to be close to your *favorite sister* is the right choice. I can name four grocery stores that take ten minutes or less to drive to."

Sutton glares, but instead of arguing, she smiles and turns to me.

Well, *that* can't be good.

"Let's stop talking about this and instead talk about how when I came into the office today," she starts, and my stomach drops. I thought it was strange Sutton didn't ask me about Graham when we had lunch together, considering she is a Donovan and thus inherently nosy, but I should have known she was saving it. "June was clinging to her hot boss, and it looked like I had interrupted something."

The blissful calm before the storm lasts a mere moment before Claire breaks it with a shriek.

"*What?!*" Her eyes go wide as she turns to me, then to her sister, aghast. "Why am I only hearing this now? I spent all afternoon with you!" Lainey stands behind the bar, an eyebrow lifted as she dries a glass, quiet but fully entertained.

"Because I wanted to get the full experience of watching all of your reactions," Sutton says as if it's the obvious answer. "And with the panicked look on June's face, I know I made the right choice."

"You were clinging to your boss?" Lainey asks, the edges of her lips tipping up.

"I knew this was going to happen! I *told* you that you had a crush on him! I *told* you there was no way you could separate things!" Claire says, slapping her hands on the bar top.

She doesn't look accusatory, more gleeful than anything. I nervously glance around the bar. It isn't terribly quiet. Miles and Grant are in the corner chatting, and I do *not* need my brother hearing this.

"Everyone has a crush on Graham. Have you seen him?" Sutton asks, and a bolt of something far too close to jealousy cracks through me. I stuff *that* down, deciding to dissect it later. Or, even better, never.

"I wasn't clinging to him," I say. Sutton raises an eyebrow, and I roll my eyes. "Not in the way Sutton is implying. I had just gotten the notification for my first sale, and he was the only person around, so I was excited and hugged him." The excuse feels hollow, though I stick to it.

"And then you two just gazed longingly into each other's eyes?" Sutton asks, her perfectly shaped eyebrow lifting with challenge.

"No!" I say, shaking my head. "That's not what happened."

"Sure, it wasn't." Sutton takes a sip of her drink, watching me over the rim of her glass with a smile in her eyes. I desperately fight the urge to rise to the bait. Maybe if I grey rock her, it will be less of an interesting topic and—

"You should fuck him again," Claire says, sending that theory out the window.

"Totally," Sutton agrees before I can argue, nodding. "He's super-hot."

"I desperately need to lay eyes on this man, the way you both keep talking about him," Lainey says, and Claire nods emphatically.

"Somehow, June convinced him to come in so that he might be here tonight," Sutton promises.

"Yes," Lainey says, pumping her fist. When I glare at her, she slides a drink toward me, which I accept even though my lifelong best friend is clearly betraying me. I'm going home with her tonight for a sleepover, and since she lives in the small apartment behind the bar, I'm okay to drink as much as I want.

"I highly doubt he's *actually* going to come in," I say after a moment.

"Oh, he's going to. Trust me. I saw the way he looked at you," Sutton says, and I glare at her.

"Be serious. The man can barely stand me. I'm working on getting him to accept that having friends is a required human experience. He's never even smiled. In fact, I'm not sure he even has the correct muscles to do so. He's the grumpiest person on earth. I don't foresee him coming to a dive bar just because I gave him puppy dog eyes."

"You gave him puppy dog eyes?" Lainey asks, entertainment spreading across her face.

I roll my eyes.

"It's my signature move. I just wanted him to come out. He's super stressed with the opening," I say.

"What other signature moves of yours has he seen?" Claire says, and I shoot her a glare.

"All I'm saying is you guys are reading far too much into things. Yes, we hooked up once before I formally worked for him. That was all. We haven't ever talked about it since, and he's barely shown the tiniest interest in being *coworkers*, much less friends or anything beyond that," I say, though if I'm being honest, that feels like a lie.

"Maybe he's just grumpy because he's totally, irrevocably in love with you, but it's against the rules to date you, so he's secretly angry that he has to watch you from afar, knowing he's never going to get you." We all look at Lainey, who wears a dreamy face as she rubs a cloth over an already dry glass. When she realizes no one is responding, she blinks, then shrugs as if that was a normal response. "What? It could happen."

The silence lingers for a moment before Claire leans into me, still watching our friend.

"That was weird, right?" Claire says in a stage whisper.

"Definitely," I say, narrowing my eyes at my childhood best friend.

"Oh, shut up," Lainey says with a roll of her eyes. "Everyone knows forbidden romance is the hottest trope out there. I mean, *I want her so badly, but I can't have her, so now I'm going to be an asshole so I can keep my distance?* Elite."

I want to say something, to ask questions that I'm not sure if I want the answers to, especially not with my brother on the other side of the bar, glaring at her the way he always does, but before I can think of what to say, Sutton speaks.

"As...highly in-depth and definitely not at all from personal experience as that was," she says, side-eyeing Lainey. "That's not the case here. Daydream doesn't have a non-fraternization rule. No one would be in trouble for starting something. The hotel industry is inherently horny, and everyone is always hooking up, so if they were to enact that rule, it would be more of a headache than it's worth."

With her words, thoughts I didn't realize I had locked away came to the surface of my mind, taunting and teasing me with possibilities.

"Look at her." Claire nudges Sutton and points at me. "She's contemplating it. She's so into him."

"I'm not! He's my *boss*!" I deny.

"You can keep telling yourself that. All I'm saying is if Graham Hawthorne looked at me the way he looked at you today, I would be *all* over that. Have you seen his forearms?" Sutton says.

I have, of course, seen those forearms, though I don't need Sutton to know that. Or that I've daydreamed about them.

"Why don't *you* fuck him if you're so into him?" I ask, an edge I can't hold back in my voice.

"Ooh, testy," Sutton says, a smile in her tone. "Unfortunately, Graham and I would be terribly incompatible. He's too dominant for me. We'd be in a stalemate nonstop. If he ever tried to tell me what to do in bed, it would be an immediate turn off." Unbidden, the memory of Graham telling *me* what to do in bed runs through my mind, and heat moves through me.

*Oh, I am so fucked.*

Reaching for my drink, I take a long gulp to cool myself down.

"Something tells me June didn't have the same issues," Claire says with a knowing look.

"Oh my god, please drop it," I groan, dropping my head onto the bar, and the girls all laugh at my misery.

"Hey, ladies," Decker asks, eyes on Sutton. Her face screws up in irritation, but he just smiles wider, something I file away for later inspection. "What's so funny over here?" Panic moves through me because while we're all friendly with him, he's also friends with the guys and works with my brother, and I don't think Deck could keep a secret if it would save his life.

"I just got my period today," Sutton says deadpan.

"Got it, my condolences, I'll be over there if you need me," Decker says, lifting his hands and turning around to the guys as fast as he came over. I let out a little laugh, but Sutton groans.

"God, I thought he'd never leave," she says, annoyed as she watches his retreat.

"He was there for a total of two seconds," Claire says.

"Exactly," Sutton says, and her sister lets out a loud laugh before shaking her head and turning to me, probably to continue this miserable conversation. I open my mouth to try and end it once and for all, but before I can, Claire speaks.

"Oh my god," she whispers. I follow her gaze to the front door of the bar and see a familiar form filling the doorway, an apprehensive look on his face as he scans the room before him.

Graham.

Graham is here.

And for once, he's not in completely formal work closed, instead swapping out his button-down and dress pants for a white tee and a pair of tan shorts.

He still looks out of place here, but also not, with his scruff and his hair a bit more mussed than normal, as if his hands have been going through it over and over. Somehow the tee makes his shoulders look even broader, and his shorts show off his thick calves, dusted with dark hair. I suddenly wish he were wearing the kind of slutty inseam shorts Miles favors, because even if I've told myself otherwise, I've been dying to see them again. The way his dress pants hug them is a complete and total tease.

And while I love forearm porn, I am a complete *whore* for a man's thigh.

"Oh my *god*," Lainey says, eyes wide.

"Please tell me that's him," Claire murmurs, and I lift my hand, smiling at him as he scans the room.

"Yes. Don't be weird," I say through my smile.

"Oh, June. You have to fuck him again," Claire says, nearly whining. "That's such a wasted opportunity." I give her a hard glare, all joking melting off my face and replaced with panic as I point at her.

"Do not. None of that. He is my boss, and I know we like to be silly, but he is my *boss*. Do not make this weird, Claire," I say through gritted teeth. Her eyes are wide, and Lainey bites her lip to fight back a laugh. "Promise me."

"I promise," she says, lifting her hands, lifting her hands in deference.

"You too," I say, turning to Sutton. I don't bother to ask Lainey, since I know she will behave. It's the Donovan sisters I have to worry about.

"Okay, okay, I promise, I won't make it weird." Relief moves through me. "Tonight," she adds.

Graham is almost to us, and I don't have the energy or time to continue to argue with her, so I just roll my eyes and shrug before turning to Graham, excitement and irritation playing in my nerves as I slide off the stool.

"Graham! You're here! I didn't think you'd actually come." I stand before him awkwardly, unsure of how to greet him. I'm a hugger, but I'm not sure if that's appropriate, and honestly, I don't know if more contact is the best idea.

"You told me to," he says, looking around.

"Well, I'm glad you're here."

The guys are moving toward us, Grant and Decker probably recognizing him. Hopefully, that will make the girls behave a bit as well. "Let me introduce you to everyone!" I say, clapping as a new wave of excitement rolls through me. "Oh, this is so fun! My work friend is meeting my life friends!

"I think that is against every aspect of work-life balance," Graham mutters.

"Work-life balance is only needed if you have both of them. You don't have a life, so you don't need the balance," I say.

Sutton lets out a loud laugh, and for a moment, I panic that I may have gone too far, but then the edges of his lips tip up, telling me I *probably* won't be fired Monday. I decide to move along with introductions to be safe. "You know Grant and Decker, because they've been working around Daytrip."

"Hey, man, sorry about the permitting drama. Glad to hear it got ironed out," Grant says, shaking Graham's hand, then pulling him in to pat his back. I have to bite back a laugh when I see how uncomfortable and unsure Graham is with the common greeting.

"You know Sutton, and this is her sister and one of my best friends, Claire," I say, and Claire gives him a well-behaved little wave. "And this is my other best friend, Lainey. Her dad owns the bar."

"How's it going? What are you having?" Lainey asks. Graham looks uncomfortable.

"Oh, I don't know if—"

'You have to have a drink, Graham," Sutton says. "Or I'll tell Rowan you have no life, and he'll go all Annette on you, locking you out of the system on the weekends." I look at them both with furrowed brows.

"Is that... is that a real threat?" I ask because Graham looks both deeply annoyed and a bit nervous. Sutton nods.

"Rowan is a workaholic. Or was, maybe? He met Josie—oh my god, June, you'd love her, she's so cool and the biggest badass. She's like, an undercover spy," Sutton says.

"I don't think you're supposed to tell people that," Graham advises, but she just rolls her eyes.

"No one here is a filthy-rich scumbag who is cheating on his wife or on his taxes or selling trade secrets. Not really the kind of people the Mavens usually target." My interest is piqued, but she keeps chattering on, and I file it away to ask about another time. "Anyway, she was on assignment at a Daydream property—someone was trying to sabotage it; it was a whole thing—and then Rowan was there, and they fell in love, and now he actually takes vacations and time off. But before that, Annette—she's the CEO—kept threatening to lock him out if he didn't take a vacation. I'm pretty sure she would have done it, too, because Annette's a badass, too. Thankfully, she didn't have to because Rowan got a life."

"Except, the one vacation he went on, he came to Seaside Point and found Surf and decided to buy it, so wasn't that working?" Graham counters.

"I don't get paid enough to figure out that kind of math, so I don't know. But I *do* know he has a soft spot for overworked people, and if I tell him that's you, he'll get all worried. So have a drink."

"I don't—" Graham starts.

"Rum and Coke, then," Sutton says, turning to Lainey. "Everyone loves a rum and Coke.":

"I don't," Decker says, and Sutton looks him over.

"Sure you don't, big boy," she says, patting his cheek. He goes a bit starry-eyed, then blinks out of the daze she seemed to have put him in.

"What does that even mean?" he asks, a goofy smile on his lips.

"I bet you'd love to know," she says, and they start bickering back and forth as they tend to do. With Sutton distracted, I turn fully to Graham, still a bit awed at seeing him out of his work clothes and here in a small-town dive bar.

"Thanks for coming," I say. "I know it's a lot, very out of your comfort zone. But it's good for you to get to know everybody. It really *is* good networking." His thick brows furrow, and he shakes his head.

"I'm not here for networking, June. I came to celebrate you." Butterflies move in my chest, but I push them away, giving him a playful smile.

"Watch out, Graham. I might think we're officially friends. Celebrating one another's accomplishments is definitely friend territory."

Before he can respond, Lainey slides a drink over to him, and he takes it with an appreciative nod. Grant and Miles start talking to him about properties and projects, and soon Claire begs Lainey to turn on the music. Decker and Sutton pull me into their argument, asking me to take sides, and it turns into another normal night at the

Seabreeze, but this time with Graham in the mix, fitting perfectly into our little group.

At some point, Claire pushes the tables back, making a space for us to dance, and a couple of other patrons come to join us. I check in with Graham often, but he's nursing his drink with Grant and Miles, chatting and seeming to enjoy himself genuinely. I should have known they'd all get along; they all have the same low-key attitude.

Almost two hours after Graham arrives, a slow song starts, one of my favorite old Atlas Oaks songs, and Claire instantly moves over to the group of guys to grab her boyfriend.

"Come on, bud, let's go," she says, grabbing his hand and tugging, though his work-booted feet stay planted in place.

"Claire–"

"Either dance with me or I'm finding someone else who will," she threatens. Miles rolls his eyes, looking at the ceiling before taking in a deep breath, but he doesn't argue any further; instead, he sets his beer on the counter and moves toward the center of the room with his girlfriend.

"I think Graham needs to dance, too," Sutton says, a twinkle I don't like in her eye, but I've had two drinks, and the buzz numbs out some of my common sense.

"I don't think—" Graham says, shaking his head negatively, but I put my hands up, excitedly.

"Yes! It's part of the full Seabreeze experience!"

He lifts a brow at me, and through his refusal is entertainment. He's not *fully* against the idea.

"Getting forced into dancing is part of the experience?"

"Honestly? Kind of," Decker says, with a shrug. Graham sighs, looking from me to the door.

"I was about to head out. I have a lot of—"

"You can leave after you're done dancing with me," I say, deciding that's the obvious answer.

"I'm dancing with *you*?" he asks, lifting an eyebrow.

I blame the alcohol on the short spark of disappointment that moves through me at his shock.

"Oh, uh, no, you can dance with Sutton, if you want. Or Lainey."

I look around, but don't see her behind the bar; instead, Benny is serving Maggie on the other side of the bar. Graham looks at me, his face assessing me in a way I don't necessarily like, before he shakes his head and sets his empty glass on the bar top beside Miles' beer.

"No, no, I'll dance with you," he says, and my stupid, traitorous heart skips a beat. "But I really do have to leave after; I've got a ton to do still."

"Of course," I say, biting back a victorious smile as we walk toward the center of the room. Once there, we stand before one another awkwardly before I say a mental *fuck it*, then move and rest my wrists on his shoulders, our chests touching. In response, his hands move, resting on my waist in the most polite way possible before we awkwardly begin to sway. Tension builds, and not the fun kind, and after a few moments of silence, I shake my head.

I don't want to force him into this if he's genuinely opposed.

"You don't have to do this," I whisper after a moment, making to step back and relieve him from his duty. "I can walk you out—"

"No," he says, his voice firm as his hands slide over my body to my hips, pulling me in tight, keeping me from stepping away. "I want to be here, June. I'm just not sure about the protocol. This is all new to me."

I lick my lips and swallow.

"You want to dance with me?" I ask, a whisper. He pulls me in tighter, and he looks down at me in a way I want to imprint in my mind forever. The bar is dim, and my friends move and laugh and dance around us, but I'm a bubble, just me and Graham.

Instead of answering, he asks another question. "Friends dance, right?" he murmurs, his hand lifting to push my hair back behind my shoulders, then gliding soft from my shoulder to my hip. Each inch he touches makes my pulse beat faster.

"Are we friends?" I ask against my better judgment. My voice sounds breathy even to my own ears. Despite the music and the people laughing and chatting all around, he still hears me, his attention locked on only me.

"I wouldn't come to a dive bar and spend two hours having small talk with people I don't know for just anyone," he says. It sounds like a confession instead of a statement.

"I need you to say it out loud," I say, and despite the emotional turmoil in my chest, I'm beaming up at him. He rolls his eyes and sighs, his warm breath coasting along my collarbones, exposed in the tank top I changed into before heading here, and a chill runs through me.

"You're a real pain in the ass. Has anyone ever told you that?" he asks, and I nod.

"Yes, every day of my life. Now say it, Hawthorne."

He watches me for another moment as we sway.

"Yes, June. We're friends. Okay? You win." I squeal with excitement, my arms tightening around his neck in a hug. When I pull back, a smirk is on his lips, the tiny hint of a dimple returning.

"Does that make me your best friend? Since I'm your only friend?" I say, unable to stop myself.

"I give an inch, you take a mile, huh?" he asks, and I go to agree, but I'm distracted by what happens next.

I get a smile.

Not the small tipping of his lips and the dancing of his eyes I've gotten before, but a true, genuine, wide grin. And I was right: he has *dimples*. Not just one, but two perfect dimples I desperately want to rub my thumb over. The man has fucking *dimples*. The entire picture is so terribly handsome, beauty in its most natural form, that it feels criminal that he constantly hides it from the world.

Right then, I set a new goal: to make those full, joy-filled smiles the rule, not the exception.

And in my heart, I know I'm going to succeed. It is my lucky summer after all.

"He smiles," I shout, throwing one arm in the air, almost giddy with joy. I expect him to hide it when I call him out, but I'm pleasantly surprised when he shakes his head, grinning a bit wider before pulling me in tighter.

"You're a nut," he murmurs through the smile.

"You'll get used to it."

He stares at me for a moment longer than necessary before shaking his head, that smile still there but somehow softer now. Sweeter.

"I don't think anyone could ever get used to you, June Taylor."

# NINETEEN

Despite my best efforts, I spent the entire weekend thinking about that smile.

Every free moment, I plot ways to see it again—schemes, jokes, surprises for him.

I even paint it on Saturday after getting home from Lainey's, determined to capture it on canvas before the memory of that gift fades—and in case he never shares it again.

That's what it felt like, after all.

A gift from Graham. It came tied in a bow, wholly unexpected but even more cherished, alongside him, stopping in the Seabreeze just to celebrate me and the unexpected dance. The feel of his arms around me, holding me tighter in an effort to reassure me when I thought he didn't want to be there, the way his fingers tightened just a bit when he smiled, as if he was truly smiling with his whole body, as if, for a moment, his entire being felt that moment of joy.

I want to see it again.

Again and again, in an addictive way, in a way that feels dangerous and wholly natural at the same time.

Unfortunately, I don't get the time to try over the next few days.

While my first two weeks at Daytrip were relatively calm, it seems that with only three weeks until opening day, the heat is on, and both Graham's and my schedules are packed. On Monday, I spend the entire day on calls or reviewing the checklist with Grant to ensure everything is ready for the inspection the following day, while Graham conducts some of the GM interviews. We barely cross paths, and when we do, it's just to ask a clarifying question and keep rolling.

Tuesday is inspection day. My stomach is in knots all morning; Graham is grumpier than usual, and the whole day is tense. We pass, thankfully, but our week doesn't ease up. Instead, we begin moving in. I stay late helping Grant, Decker, and the team bring out deck and beach furniture, arranging it per Graham's sketch.

Wednesday, I conduct first-round interviews for club servers and staff, staying until nearly five-thirty at which point Graham, of all people, insists I leave. At home, I pack art for shipping and paint while I eat dinner.

Workdays feel like teaching again: busy all day, then more work at home. But instead of feeling drained, I am motivated. I tell myself it's because it's new and special, but I know it's because I love it.

That said, on Thursday, I'm dragging. I'm sitting in Graham's office and going over the different media outlets I've contacted and confirmed when a third yawn leaves my lips.

"I'm sorry," I say, embarrassed. "I was up late last night painting. I should have gone to bed at a normal hour, but I got lost in it, and the next thing I knew, it was way past my bedtime."

Graham frowns, "Probably doesn't help that you've stayed late every day this week."

"Excuse me, you don't really have a leg to stand on," I say, glaring—though I yawn again, softening the effect.

"Okay, get up," Graham says, coming around the desk. "We're going for a walk."

He offers his hand; I hesitate.

"A walk?"

"Yes. A walk. You said vitamin D helps your sunny disposition. I think you need it. Let's go."

I give him an unsure look but take his hand.

"I don't think we have time—" I start, but he shakes his head, pulling me up. He doesn't step back as he does. Only inches separate us, my breath catching as he stands over me, soft concern on his face. He lifts a hand toward my loose hair, then stops abruptly and steps away.

"I don't have the time for you to burn yourself out. Now come on. Let's get some fresh air. You haven't even been outside for your lunch break this week." He stresses at me like he expects me to argue, but this is an opportunity I can refuse.

"Okay. Let's go," I say with a shrug, pulling a small smirk from him before I head out to grab my phone and a bag. He's slowly stepping out of his office as I turn back to him, sunglasses in hand, when I stop.

Because Graham is *undressing* before me.

Maybe I really do need sleep, because this has to be some kind of wild figment of my overtired mind.

"What are you doing?" I ask.

"It's hot out. I don't want to sweat through a dress shirt." I nod as if that's logical, but really, I'm panicking because all my mind can do is focus on the way his fingers move on the tiny buttons of his shirt, revealing a tight white T-shirt beneath.

He might not spend much time with friends, but I'm pretty sure he spends whatever free time he has in the gym, doing who knows what, because the muscles I felt beneath my fingers in the dim lighting of his hotel and have caught glimpses of beneath his dress shirts are much more obvious beneath the white tee, stretching around his biceps and cut tight on his torso, tucked into his pants.

I shake my head, blinking twice before forcing myself to look away and not take in the way his muscles move under that T-shirt. Instead, I pull my phone out and tap at the screen aimlessly, seeing nothing, but at least I'm not staring at Graham.

"Ready?" he asks. When I look up at him, he's staring at me curiously. I smile at him, turning my go-to charm on and covering up any discomfort with friendliness before nodding and making my way to the exit.

It's a five-minute walk to Seaside Coffee, and Graham was right to take his dress shirt off: it's the hottest day of the season by far, and I'm sweating. I'm grateful I'm wearing a tank top dress and I left my cardigan in the office, and even more grateful when Graham holds the door to the coffee shop open for me and the cool air hits my heated skin.

"June! What a pleasant surprise!" Miles' mom says, waving at me as I slide my sunglasses onto my head. Mrs. Miller has owned the coffee shop for as long as I can remember, and considering her son is my brother's best friend, I've spent a lot of time around her over the years.

"Hi, Mrs. Miller! We needed a midday pick-me-up. This is Graham Hawthorne, my boss over at Daytrip," I say, gesturing toward Graham as we approach the counter.

"It's a pleasure to meet you," he says, all gentlemanly.

"Yes! It's nice to have a name for the face," she grins.

"You've met?" I ask, confused.

"Oh, Graham here has been—" She hesitates, her eyes shifting to Graham, then continues, her momentary confusion clearing. "Coming in for coffee often." When I look at my boss, his face is neutral, leaving me even more confused.

"You told me it was the best in town," Graham says with a half-hearted shrug, though I don't miss the slight blush burning over his cheeks. I suppose it could be from the heat, but I'm not sold on that theory.

"It is," I say. "Mrs. Miller roasts the beans in-house."

"Really?" he asks, seeming genuinely intrigued. "Where do you do that?"

"The back of the store is a lot bigger than it looks," Mrs. Miller says, and Graham's face turns intrigued.

"Would you have the capacity for more?"

"More?"

"More roasting."

"I, uh...perhaps. I suppose I don't have them going every day of the week, currently, just a few times as needed."

"While Daytrip is a beach club, Daydream Resorts would like to become a staple in the community, not just a business getting in the way. I'd be interested in seeing if you'd be willing to sell us beans."

"Oh, wow, I mean, yeah, they would be...that would be amazing," Mrs. Miller says, flustered.

"We're looking to stock our gift shop with high-quality items, and I think featuring local businesses would be the perfect way for us to highlight the rich Seaside Point community. Is there any chance you could get us, say, twenty-five units by next Friday? That would be to start, though I'm sure we'd need regular restocks. I'd have to check if we've secured someone, but maybe even serving Seaside Coffee at our restaurant and cafe, if that's something you're interested in?"

"Yes. Definitely. That would be... well, that would be fantastic."

My heart warms at the look of genuine joy and excitement on Mrs. Miller's face.

"I'll have June reach out about your pricing this afternoon." He looks around and tips his chin toward a display of handcrafted mugs. "Do you make the mugs as well?" Mrs. Miller shakes her head.

"No, I wholesaled them from Joanne Reeman. She's also a local; she might be interested in selling for your gift shop as well, though."

Graham nods, lifting one of the mugs and inspecting the bottom where Joanne's logo is stamped.

"Beautiful. I'd love to have as many local businesses featured as possible." Suddenly, I see the vision, and I absolutely adore it. I wonder if he's been sitting on this idea or if it just came to him. "June here is always waxing poetic about how much she loves this town, and it makes me want to make sure all of the visitors get to experience it, as well."

He looks at me, something so sincere on his face, and my chest warms.

"Well, if there's anyone you want in your corner when you're opening a business in town, it would be June. She's the best Seaside Point has to offer."

"I'm very lucky to have her," Graham says, stepping back to the register and looking directly at me. There's a second, a lingering moment where I don't quite believe he means just as his employee. I'm pulled from my messy, ridiculous thoughts, thankfully, when Mrs. Miller speaks again.

"Your regular, June?"

"Yes, please. I gotta enjoy it while I can," I say with a sigh. Mrs. Miller gets a coconut syrup every May, and it's my favorite flavor she carries. Unfortunately, it's only a temporary one, and by the end of September, it's long gone.

"Did I not tell you yet?" she asks. "My distributor has announced they're making that a year-long option, so it won't be disappearing come September."

I gasp, pure excitement in the sound. "No way."

She shrugs, tapping my order into the register as the price appears on the paypad.

"God, this really is my lucky summer," I say, leaning on the counter and trying to pay. Graham puts a hand on my hip before I can, and hands his card to Mrs. Miller.

"Two of those," he says. "And two rainbow sprinkled donuts."

'You have *those,* too?" I ask, with wide eyes, trying to ignore the way Graham's hand burns on my hip. I can feel every finger through the thin fabric of my sundress, and it's terribly distracting.

"I've been trying to keep them in stock just for you," she says with a wink, not at me, but at Graham. I look at him, increasingly confused by this visit, but Graham just shrugs as if he doesn't understand, either. Mrs. Miller has also been a bit of a character, so I just brush it off. A moment later, she hands us the white pastry bag with donuts, then takes Graham's card before we're instructed to step aside while

Mrs. Miller takes another customer's order, and we wait for our coffees.

"I think I want to do more of that," he says, and I look at him with wide eyes.

"More of...?" My mind is still on that simple touch, the idiot I am.

I quickly learn that Graham's is strictly on business.

"Working with local businesses, seeing if we can wholesale from them and carry their products in the gift shop. I was about to place a wholesale order for gift shop items, but maybe it's better to be more niche. Benefit the local economy, create community, like you keep telling me is important...make it obvious that we're not just here for the season, but here to actually benefit the town as a whole."

I stare at him in awe. It seems my weeks of ranting and raving and gushing over the town that I love so much are paying off.

"That's genius, Graham."

"You're the one always telling me how amazing but small this town is. If we want this place to work long-term, it can't just be for tourists; we need support from the town year-round." I nod, agreeing. "Let's spend the afternoon looking around. Do you know any places that would be good candidates?" I blink at him before hesitantly nodding.

"I mean, yeah, but—"

"Great. Show me around, June. Introduce me to your favorite place on earth."

There's something about the way he says it, like he not only understands that Seaside Point is genuinely my favorite place on earth, but also wants to give me the gift of sharing that with him.

I can't help it.

I move to my tiptoes, wrap my arms around his neck, and hug him tight.

"Oh my god, this is going to be so fun!" I say, cheer dripping into the words. He just stares at me before giving me my second-ever Graham smile and wrapping an arm around my waist to return the hold.

We walk the entire boardwalk.

I show him the candy shop where my grandmother used to get saltwater taffy, and we leave with a giant bag.

I point out the bagel shop Grandpa used to take me to every Sunday.

I show him the best arcade, and the one that's a total scam.

I show him the little store that makes statues out of shells.

I show him the only sweatshirt place I actually recommend, the one that isn't just overpriced tourist crap.

I show him the store where they shine up beach diamonds and make all kinds of jewelry.

I show him the candle store, the one that makes the mugs Mrs. Miller showed us, and the shop that has art prints.

"Yours should be up there," he says low, tipping his chin to a wall that says *local artists*. I push at his shoulder and roll my eyes before bringing him to our next stop.

"What about these?" Graham asks as we walk through a gift shop. I've been making a list of items that would work in the gift shop to try and find local creators or sellers to reach out to over the next few days, but when he points to a cage of hermit crabs, I can't help but laugh. "They're kind of terrifying."

He bends a bit, looking into the chicken wire with a dozen sets of little claws latched onto them with a look of disgust. I can't blame him, since they aren't exactly cute. Not that I would ever tell Claire th at.

"They're hermit crabs. Claire has nine of them, now." His head lifts, looking at me with confusion and a bit of horror.

"She has nine of those terrifying things? On purpose?"

"They're rescues. It started as six, but she added three more this spring."

"How does one rescue a hermit crab?" he asks almost reluctantly, and I smile, wide, remembering it well, since I was her lookout the day she stole Big Gina and crew last summer.

"She stole them."

"Why...why would she steal hermit crabs?"

"They were being mistreated. It's actually super unethical to sell hermit crabs the way they do, and they're deceptively hard to keep alive. The majority end up dying, hence the rescue mission. So, if you sell them at the shop, there's a good chance Claire is going to want to rescue those."

"And by rescue..." We both move out of the shop and down the boardwalk, headed back toward Daytrip.

"Steal. She would steal them, and I'd help her because it would be fun."

He looks at me, blinking once, but I just smile sweetly.

"I don't think you're supposed to tell your boss that."

"We're friends right now, not boss and employee," I remind him with a gently hip check and a smile. When he doesn't argue my claim, bliss explodes in my chest, but it quickly deflates when a familiar face comes into view.

"Fuck," I mumble.

"What?"

"My arch-nemesis," I explain. A small laugh leaves his lips, and I don't even have time to bask in the beauty of it because I'm too busy focusing on stupid fucking Cecelia Stevens, the biggest bitch to grace Seaside Point.

I pride myself on being a girl's girl, but sometimes, a girl is just a bitch who hates other girls. When that happens, I then have free rein to hate her, and I hate Cecelia. Her family and mine have a long history of animosity that started when her father tried to date my mom, and my mom chose my dad instead. I don't know why he's so mad about that, since they would never have worked together, but it's a long, deep-seated legacy of hate that has continued between the Stevens and Taylor kids.

"Where?" He looks across the way, but I tug at his arm.

"Stop, don't look!" But my luck must be hiding, because Cece spots us instantly, a smug smile spreading on her face as she makes her way over to us, an extra sway to her steps. "Oh, god, she's coming our way."

"Who is?" Graham says, looking around in confusion, because he might be a business genius, but he's still a boy.

"The bottle blonde, I say through gritted teeth. "She's my number one enemy; her family and mine have despised one another since the dawn of time. Her dad is the one who tried to cancel your permits, and you fired her brother," I say.

"Ahh, so we hate her."

Some sick part of me greatly enjoys the *we* in that statement.

"So much," I agree.

"Why is she coming over this way?" he asks. I bite back a groan, instead putting a sweet smile on my lips and looking up at Graham as if I don't even notice her.

"Because she's a bitch, and I hate her, and she wants to rub salt in whatever wound she can find. Can we head back to the office as naturally as humanly possible, so it doesn't look like I'm trying to avoid her?"

"I—" he starts, but my hopeful naivete is long gone when my name is called in that annoying, squawky voice.

"June? June Taylor? Is that you?" I tighten my jaw and sigh, turning toward the voice and giving her a tight, fake smile. "It is!"

"Cece," I say, not able to have any real excitement in my voice. "How are you?"

"Oh, I'm just great! You know, summer off, getting to get my tan on." She waves her hand down her stupidly perfect body, a bikini top holding in the perfect boobs her dad bought her as an eighteenth birthday present. In a moment, her face goes a bit mean, and a small smile spreads on her lips. "So sorry you were fired, June," she says, not a single ounce of apology in the words. "I hear you've got a little art side hustle going, though. How fun!"

For as long as I can remember, she has always been able to find and grind all my sore spots with perfect accuracy. Normally, I can brush it off, but right now, I'm tired, and I'm hot, and I'm in front of Graham, who I want to think I'm cool and fun and likable, not some loser who got fired and is now selling silly little art projects to keep the lights on.

Kill me now.

Kill me right fucking now.

"You know, I've gotten into art myself. I'm going to be doing the mural this fall," she says with a grin, and even though I've nearly written off bidding on it, I can't help but tip my head.

"I heard it was a bid process? Did they change that?"

She gives me a coy look and waves her hand.

"Oh, well, my daddy said that my entry is the most impressive, so I'm basically a shoo-in. Why, were you thinking about entering?"

"I haven't decided," I say through tight teeth. She lifts a careless shoulder, probably sensing she already hit her target and can move on, knowing she ruined my day.

"Well, I was just about to go get a tan, but I saw you and your friend and thought I'd say hi." Her rude tone softens to something sickly sweet, and she leans in, touching Graham's forearm, eyes eating up every inch of him. It takes everything in me not to push her away, and not to question where the hell that came from. "Aren't you going to introduce us?" she asks.

I don't want to introduce them. I don't want to give Cece any kind of in, any kind of upper hand. She seems like she would be his type—put together, gorgeous, sure of herself, and I know he would be her type—hot, wealthy, powerful.

"This is Graham. Graham, this is Cece—"

"Stevens," she says, putting a hand out to Graham. He stares at it for a long moment before eventually taking it and shaking stiffly. Cece bats her eyelashes at him. "I haven't seen you around. We don't get many new faces in Seaside Point. I'd love to take you around, help you get to know our great town. How do you know our June?"

But even though some part of me sees Graham as *mine*, I know that it's me being silly, so I give her a tight smile and start to answer.

"This is my—"

"Her boyfriend," Graham startles me by saying.

"*You're* dating *June*?" she asks, unable to hide her shock. I force myself to remain neutral, to now show shock at Graham's words or irritation at Cece's insinuation.

"Found the most gorgeous woman in Seaside Point, had to do whatever I could to make her mine," he says, a smug smirk on his lips.

It's not one of the radiant smiles I've seen, something that gives me strange relief since I wouldn't want to share that with Cece. Instead, this one is all sex appeal and cocky attitude. His actions punctuate it, his hand moving to my hip and wrapping to my waist, tugging me into his side and pressing his lips to my hair.

"June would *never* date a tourist," Cece says with a shake of her head. "She hates them."

That's not *completely* true, but I don't get the opportunity to correct her before Graham is speaking.

"Good thing I'm not a tourist then, huh? My lady luck here sold me on this place," he says.

The words roll off his lips so easily, I almost buy them myself.

*My lady luck.*

God, what I'd give to have him call me that for real.

Despite common sense, I find myself melting into his side, soaking it in. He smells good, musky and woodsy, expensive cologne mixed with sweat from walking in the heat for the past hour. I wish I could bottle it up, save it for a day when I'm feeling lonely.

"Hmm," Cece says, breaking into my messy thoughts.

"Well, I hope you have a great day. Great meeting you," Graham says, staring her down, and pulling me closer into him until my hand has to move to his chest to catch myself. I let it rest there, feeling the hard muscles against my forehead, and even his hot chest can't distract me from my misery.

"I'm so screwed," I whisper. "She totally didn't buy it, and now she's going to tell everyone that I'm a big fat loser who needs her hot boss to pretend he's my boyfriend to not let the mean girl make fun of me."

A smile crosses Graham's face, the real one, and even though it is magnificent, I elbow him. A wide grin spreads across his lips, showing me the dimple I find myself doing everything in my power to see. "It's not funny!" I say, but there's a smile in my words. He pulls me in closer.

"It's a little funny," he mutters. Then he pulls me into him fully, his hand settling on my lower back, pulling me chest to chest with him as his other hand slowly tips my chin up.

"What are you doing?" I ask, whispering, my back to Cece.

"She's still watching us. I'm selling it," he says. Before I can ask what he means, his lips are on mine. A gasp leaves my lips, but he holds me closer. On instinct, my free hand moves up to his shoulder, the other gripping the fabric of his tee, clinging onto him. His lips move along mine, his kiss soft and sweet and just as good as I convinced myself it was that first night.

Except better, because it's relaxed and casual, as if we do it every single day. His hand is on my waist, his other cupping my chin to position me where he wants me.

It's the best kiss I've ever had in my life.

He pulls back, then looks over my shoulder, checking to see if our ruse worked, but my mind is in the clouds. "She's still there. Across the street, watching," he says, then leans his head down again, kissing me deeper this time. His fingers delve into my hair, and without thinking, my hands move to his neck, resting there and pulling my body tighter. We kiss and kiss and kiss, and even though I know I will be terribly confused and unsure later, even though with my complex emotions about Graham, I should be keeping my distance, I can't find it in me to care right now.

It's the best kiss I've ever had in my life, even if it is all fake.

Just my luck.

After long moments, Graham pulls away, looking over his

shoulder and resting his forehead against mine. My chest is heaving, though I try to hide how much that kiss impacted me. "She's gone," he says.

"Thank you," I murmur, my breathing heavy.

"That's what friends do, right?" he asks, a small tip of his lips as we separate, but I can't even revel in the fact that he called us friends.

Because for me, nothing about that kiss felt friendly.

Not in the least.

Looking over toward where Graham said he saw Cece, I spy the tiniest dot of her hot-pink bikini, barely visible from here. I wonder if she might have started running. If she stopped on the street corner just a minute ago, I can't imagine she would have gotten that far otherwise.

"What was she talking about?" he asked, distracting me from my pondering. "A mural?" It's like a bucket of ice water on my body, and I sigh, then I start moving toward the office.

"The town is accepting bids for a big mural in town." I roll my eyes, irritation filling me at the reminder. "Cece's dad is on the town council, so she's kind of got it on lock, so there's no point in anyone else applying."

"So because she's a spoiled brat, you're not even going to bid?"

I lift a shoulder, keeping my eyes straight ahead. "I'm unqualified, and I don't know how to put together a proposal, and in the end, it would be for nothing. Chet is just going to manipulate it so that Cece gets the mural." He's silent as we walk, and after a bit, I look at him to see he's watching me, confusion on his face.

"All that luck and you're not even going to try?"

I scrunch my nose.

"Why do I feel like you keep using that against me?"

He lifts a shoulder. "You force me to be social and accept you as a friend; I force you to take chances. It's worked out pretty well for us so far, don't you think?"

I can't argue, and he knows it. He bumps his shoulder into mine.

"So?

"So what?"

"So are you going to do it?" I scrunch my nose, and he continues. "Oh, come on, June. You have to. No one loves this town like you, and you're talented. Even the Mayor thinks you're going to apply."

I forgot he was there when that happened.

"I don't know..." I say, biting my lip, but he's looking at me like he genuinely believes in me, like he'll be disappointed if I say no. I wonder if this is Graham's own version of pleading puppy dog eyes. I groan. "I'll... I'll work on the sketch tonight," I agree, defeat in the words, and he smiles wide, nothing like the fake look he gave Cece. This one is all mine, all because of what I did. "No promises, though."

"Of course not," he says with a small smile. "But you'll work on a sketch tonight?"

I nod.

"Yeah. I'll see if anything feels...natural," I say, not telling him I already have a concept I love or that I have commissions to work on or how I should be making more canvases for my shop.

Still, that night, like promised, I paint.

I paint for hours, feeling energized and inspired.

But when I paint, it's not smiles or shorelines or even a mural concept that I work on.

It's hands and lips and hooded eyes that I can't seem to get out of my mind. The promise of something I can't have, and suddenly, it feels like the unluckiest thing of all.

TWENTY

# June

After our afternoon together, things go back to normal, and by back to normal, I mean I do everything in my power not to think about our kiss again, do my job, and make a friend out of Graham Hawthorne.

*Just* a friend.

That's all we are, and all we'll ever be, and I am *so totally fine* with that.

Really. I am.

On Friday, Graham approaches my desk midday. I hardly notice him standing there until he speaks, startling me. "You ready to go?"

"Go?"

"Lunch. The tables have turned. Now I need to make sure you get your mandated outdoor time instead of letting you work until you burn out," he says. My heart flutters at his words. I consciously push the feeling down, look at him, bite my lip, and smile before turning back to my screen.

"Yeah, I'm just finishing up this application. Give me a sec," I say.

"Application?" he asks, his voice suddenly guarded. I grin widely at him.

"Not for a job, don't you worry, you're stuck with me still. I'm trying to win concert tickets. There's a festival in Wildwood next weekend, and Atlas Oaks is playing. I missed out on the Great War to buy tickets, and resale is like a billion dollars. But there are a bunch of contests to win, so I figured it wouldn't hurt to try my luck"

"What's the name of the festival? I can try and see if I know anyone and get you tickets."

"Okay, moneybags," I say with a smile.

"It's not about money, it's about connections. I network, remember?"

He smiles at me, and I do everything in my power not to melt. I get that smile more and more lately, and every time it sparks a flutter of joy under my ribs. If I were wiser, maybe I'd slow down and question it, try to sift through whether it means danger. But I'm not, so I don't.

"Ah, yes, your steadfast desire to be the most boring man around and have no friends. How's that going for you? Heard Decker invited you to poker night." He makes a strange face, and I burst out with a laugh.

"Yeah, he invited me, though I'm sure it was just to be nice."

"They do a lot just to be nice, but inviting someone to poker night is not one of them. I know people who have been trying to get an invite for years and never have. If he invited you, he likes you. They want you to be their friend." He looks at me with skepticism. "Now, if they invited you to be on their team for trivia night, they'd be doing it to use you for your big brain."

"Trivia night?"

"That's in three more weeks, and I will, in fact, be dragging you because you do, in fact, have a big brain, and I will do anything to beat Grant." He lifts an eyebrow at me. "Decker will try to say that you need to be on his team because it's boys versus girls, but I claimed you first, so that trumps everything."

"Nothing you say makes sense," he says, but his lips twitch. "But you don't have to be doing all of this." He waves his hand at my computer screen. "I have connections, June. I can just *get* you tickets if you want."

"No! That's not as fun! I'm lucky. I believe I will absolutely win these tickets on my own." He stares are my as if I've lost it, and I sigh. "It's not a live or die thing, and it's fun to try. I also have connections: Claire's sister-in-law's best friend is married to the guitarist of Atlas Oaks. If I wanted, I could easily get a ticket."

"Then why not do that instead of jumping through these hoops?"

I glare at him.

"You don't get it."

"I really don't."

"I want to win them. This is my lucky girl summer, and I like that I'm so lucky and everything works out for me. If I'm meant to have these tickets, they will come to me. If I'm not, then the universe is pushing me elsewhere."

He stares at me, looking like he wants to tell me I've completely and totally lost it, but after a moment, he sighs, shakes his head, and shrugs a shoulder before pulling out his phone.

"Fine, what's the website?"

"What?"

"The website to win. I'll fill it out with my email."

"Really?" I ask, my face splitting with a grin.

"Yeah. What would it hurt?" he asks with a lift of his shoulder, his phone at the ready for the website.

"It's for two tickets. You have to take me if you win," I say, a wide grin on my lips. He shakes his head and rolls his eyes.

"If I win, you can have both of them," he states as if that's obvious, but I gasp and shake my head.

"No way! If you win, you get the tickets. Fair is fair. You just have to take me with you." I narrow my eyes at him.

"Fine," he grumbles after a moment.

"And when I win, I'll take you."

"You really don't have to—"

"That might just be how the luck works. I'm not going to tempt fate, Graham." Before he can continue his argument, I spot something on his cheek. "Stay still," I say, voice low as if I have to be quiet or it will vanish.

"What?"

"Stay still, my god, do you ever do as you're told?" I murmur.

"Ironic, coming from you," he grumbles, but does as I ask all the same.

I can't help but smile to myself as I gently brush the eyelash from his cheek. This back-and-forth banter happens more often now. I take it as a sign he's growing more comfortable and friendly with me.

Though the spark that moves through me as I brush my pointer finger across his cheek, my body just inches from his, is the furthest thing from friendly I could fathom.

"Make a wish," I whisper as I lift my finger, an eyelash on the very tip.

"A wish?"

I smile, looking from him to my finger and back before explaining.

"It's what you do if there's an eyelash on your face. Blow it and make a wish," I say. He looks at me, and I expect him to brush me off, but instead, his lips purse gently, the image also going straight to my belly in a way it probably shouldn't, before a gentle breath coasts along my finger and my cheek, sending a shiver through me.

Oh, I am so screwed.

I kind of hope we don't win those tickets, because how on earth would I act normally for hours on end with Graham outside of work?

"I wished you would get those tickets," he says after a moment, his voice hoarse.

"God, Graham, you're so bad at this," I say with a forced laugh, stepping away and shaking my head, needing to put space between us. I reach for my lunch, then my phone, so we can eat outside together. "You're not supposed to share your wish."

"Oh, yeah, I forgot," he says with a laugh, following me out, but the ghost of his breath on my skin lingers for the rest of the day.

# TWENTY-ONE

# GRAHAM

When I arrive at my hotel, I toss my things on the couch and head straight to my laptop. Then, I do what I've done every day since June Taylor first walked into Daytrip.

Whatever I can to make her every whim come true.

I spend hours finding every contest for tickets to the festival she mentioned, inputting her information for each entry, then mine just in case, and then for each of the fifteen burner accounts I've created on the Daydream server, which I've redirected to her email.

Is it ethical?

Absolutely not.

When IT inevitably catches wind of it, will I have to explain it to them?

Absolutely.

Do I care?

Not in the least.

The only thing I can seem to care about these days is whether or not June gets her way, and in this case, I want her to get those tickets.

Most of the contests close tonight or tomorrow, so if by Wednesday she hasn't heard anything, I'll have to take a different approach to make her hopes come true. I have a few feelers out to friends to see if I can get tickets for the festival and stage it as if she's won them, but that's my last line of defense. In my perfect world, June would win the tickets through the contest she showed me, and believe that, once again, her luck is making everything work out.

It's sick and twisted, but I love nothing more than the little smile that lights up her face when she thinks something has worked out for her. The way her eyes light up with excitement anytime something lucky happens to her, the way she looks at me with those wide, joy-filled, summer sky blue eyes, eager to share the news of her latest windfall with me.

It's why I haven't been able to stop myself from making it happen at every turn.

The first day I met her, despite my miles-long to-do list, she was the only thing I could think of for the rest of the night. The next morning, I spent nearly two hours at the coffee shop she recommended, hoping she would stroll in and I could bump into her, talk to her, prove to myself that just like every other person I've met, this obsession was fleeting and surface-level.

I did the same thing every morning for a week, and by Friday, I was ready to throw in the towel, to return to sanity, to try and forget the woman who had ruled my thoughts for nearly a week.

Then she walked into Daytrip that afternoon, and something snapped in me. I caught the tiniest glimpse of her on the security camera I had up to keep an eye on for the new contractor coming in to give me a progress update.

It felt like fate, like the kind of luck or universal push she's always going on about.

Giving her the job was an impulse, a desire to learn a little bit more about the woman who had consumed my thoughts. I needed to know if she really was sunshine personified or if it was fake, some perfectly crafted act I couldn't quite understand.

I convinced myself it was logical. She needed a job, and Sutton had work for Rowan, so she couldn't be here forever. I needed someone who lived in the area to help me out.

"Sutton," I said, the words coming out harsher than anticipated.

"Yes?" she asked.

"There is a woman who just walked into the building. She needs a job." Her face scrunched up, part confused and part irritated, as seems to be her way with me. Rowan had sent her to keep an eye on the place and fill in gaps for me, since I didn't have an assistant of my own. He offered to let me hire one time and again, but I kept turning him down, wanting to prove I could manage this job on my own.

Until right now.

"I'm sorry?" she asked, rightfully confused.

"A woman is coming into the back room in a few minutes with the head of Taylor Contracting. I want you to offer her a job."

She continued to stare at me, lost and a bit concerned. I scrubbed a hand over my face.

"Offer...offer a stranger a job?"

I knew it sounded completely ridiculous. I knew that it was so far out of the realm of common sense. I knew all of these things, but it felt like some kind of sign from a power I didn't realize I believed in until just then. Luck, or the universe, or fate, I didn't know, nor did I care. I just knew I hadn't been able to focus on work for five days after a mere five-minute interaction, and now she was here in my business, and I needed her out of my system.

"Yes. An assistant position. I'll need someone to help out once the resort opens, and you have to go back to your real job."

Her brows furrowed, but if there was one thing that I'd learned from my weeks of working with Sutton Donovan, it was that she loved chaos and she loved a scheme.

She smiled knowingly, then shrugged. "Okay." She grabbed her tablet, tapped a few times to find what she was looking for, and then turned it to me. "This was my position when I started, and is what Rowan has approved for you if you ever wanted an assistant of your *own. Does this look right?" I barely even looked before nodding. "All right, I'm on it," she said, then headed out of my office.*

*I got absolutely nothing done in the next thirty minutes, staring at the door and waiting for her to return. When she did, there was a wide, pleased grin on her lips.*

*"Done. She's going to be perfect for you."*

Every day since then, I have wondered whether she meant she was perfect for the job of my assistant or if Sutton knew something I didn't.

That night I went home on time, not staying in the office late for once, because I finally had a name, a means of finding out more about her.

June Taylor. Fifth-grade teacher at Seaside Elementary.

Went to a state school on a full-ride scholarship.

Won the senior art fair in high school with the most incredible self-portrait I've ever seen. There was a smiling picture in the town paper of her beside it, and like the creep I am, I downloaded it. I've stared at it more than I would like to admit since that day. If it wouldn't have tipped me into stalker territory, I would have printed and framed it, but thankfully, I'm not that far gone.

Yet.

Unfortunately, having her name didn't ease my obsession. It only fueled it. I spent the entire weekend trying to find out anything and everything I could about her, and each new snippet made me more interested, more enamored with the woman.

Then, in another stroke of fate, we found each other once more, the night before she was to start working for me. Try as I might, I couldn't find it in me to be responsible, to walk away, or, at the very least, to tell her she would be my new assistant.

I'd convinced myself that one night would get her out of my system, cure me of this incessant need to learn more about her.

I was wrong. So terribly wrong, because when I woke up the next morning, my body cocooned around her warm one, I knew I would never wake happier ever again.

I also know there was no universe where I could have her.

Even if we weren't complete opposites, wanting different things from life, even if she didn't deserve someone just as sunny and bright as her, I'd tricked her. I'd lied by omission, and things like that never stay hidden for long. The mere thought of seeing that betrayal written on her face was enough to take my secret to the grave.

It's why I set the tone that very first day, acting rude and cold and putting a wall between us.

Even then, I knew in my bones if I let it happen, June Taylor would become my everything in a way I couldn't undo.

I thought being a broody asshole would push her away. A bright, beautiful speck of sunshine like her surely wouldn't want to deal with an asshole who brushed her off, who threw away her attempts at kindness and friendship, but what I didn't understand in my weekend of stalking her was that June Taylor is the most stubborn person I've ever encountered. She didn't see my brush-off as a warning; she saw it as a challenge.

My need to make magic happen for her didn't end with getting her a job.

No, it was simply the start. On her first day, I'd gone to Seaside Coffee early, getting two dozen donuts, including four chocolate frosted with sprinkles. I told myself it had nothing to do with it being her first day, and when that assurance felt hollow, I told myself it would be the first and last time.

Even then, everything I was doing was to make June happy.

I was making my coffee and pretending I wasn't watching when she spotted them. That was when I realized the happy little smile that plays on her lips when a stroke of luck happens wasn't a fluke, something that only happened because she was excited to win a lottery ticket. She didn't jump that time, didn't squeal or cheer, but the light was there, a light that, despite her constant chipper attitude, isn't always shining.

I think that was the moment I fell, the moment there was no coming back from.

After, all I wanted to do was make all of her wishes come true.

That's why I kept going to Seaside Coffee and selling them out of chocolate-frosted donuts with sprinkles so I could make sure she has one in the break room.

That's why I found her earring and placed it where she would find it.

It's why I spent hours searching for four-leaf clovers, digging them up, and replanting them where she sometimes sits along the side of the building.

That's why I found and invested in the company that makes the coffee syrup she likes, so they'd make it year-round.

I bought her first art piece, not just because it was stunning and I wanted a piece of her forever, even after I've left this small town, but because I wanted her to believe the universe was pushing her toward building that dream.

And it's why I'm trying to win her concert tickets.

I want June to have all the luck in the world, even if I have to manufacture it.

# TWENTY-TWO

# GRAHAM

"I can't believe how quickly this place went from a construction zone to a full-blown resort," June says as we walk around the deck area on Tuesday. This morning, the GM and a few other employees came in for onboarding and paperwork with June before she put them to work cleaning up and setting up parts of the resort. They'll be in each day until opening, putting the finishing touches on before opening day next week. While we originally hoped to be open for the Fourth of July weekend, the construction and permitting delays mean we're looking at the Friday after.

It's strange, having people other than just June here, and if I'm being honest, I already miss the peace and intimacy of just the two of us.

"These last weeks always are the most transformative," I agree. It's coming along nicely, the exact vision Rowan and I had when he first brought me here to show me the location. Luxury, but more attainable than the large-scale resorts the company has throughout the world. The perfect way to spend the day at the Jersey shore in utter luxury.

"I checked the weather, and next weekend is now in the ten-day outlook—so far, so good. No rain in the forecast, knock on wood," she says, grinning at me as she turns to the wall behind her and raps her knuckles against it. She turns back to me, that goofy look she gets when she gives in to one of her superstitions on her face. Something behind her catches my eye, distracting me, though. She takes the hesitation as confusion and smiles wider. "Oh, come on, I'm sure you've heard of knocking on wood, I—" she starts, but I'm barely listening, instead stepping to her and wrapping my hand around her wrist.

"June!" I pull her into my chest and out of the way of the falling umbrella that was leaning on the wall. It seems her knocking had the opposite effect of her lucky intentions, making it fall right where she was standing. The heavy umbrella lands on the floor with a loud clatter. My heart is pounding as I stare where it fell, then to her face, her own eyes wide. "It almost fell right on your head," I explain unnecessarily. Her hands are resting on my chest, her own breath heavy as the arm I have around her waist slackens just a bit, the adrenaline easing my system now that she's out of harm's way.

She looks at me, eyes still wide with shock. "Good thing you were here," she whispers.

"Yeah. Good thing." Her breath brushes my lips, and mine catches as I realize I'm still holding her and her hand is resting on my chest, our bodies pressed together. She's wearing a thin sundress, and the warmth of her skin burns through the flimsy fabric, warming my palm where it rests on her hip. There's a heat in her eyes that I know must be reflected in mine, especially when her eyes dip for just a moment to my lips, then back. She looks at me as if asking me to do it, to say fuck it and kiss her.

And I could.

I could kiss her.

It would be simple.

The last time was phenomenal, something I did because I wanted to, but sold it as if I was doing her a favor. Really, I was hoping it would bring a moment of clarity, that it would sate my obsession with her. Just like with every other moment with June Taylor, I thought that a taste would be enough.

And just like every other time with her, I found that not even remotely the case.

Before I can make that reckless choice, her phone pings, bringing me back into reality. My body goes stiff with realization, and I step back, hesitating just long enough to make sure she's okay before clearing my throat.

"Close call," I say awkwardly. She stares at me for another moment before giving me a tight nod, then pulls out her phone to check the new message. In a moment, the disappointment I'm ignoring melts, her eyes go wide, and her head snaps to me with pure, unadulterated excitement written across her expressive face.

"Oh my god!" she shouts. After experiencing this a few times, I know not to panic, though my already heightened senses don't make that easy.

"Yes?" I ask.

"I won!" I furrow my brows, confused, brain still muddled from having her so close. "You must be my lucky charm!" she shouts. "I won the tickets! Oh my god!" She starts jumping up and down, warmth flooding through me at the realization of what happened. "Graham, I won the tickets!"

'That's great, June," I say, smiling as I watch that now familiar and addictive emotion move over her, making those late nights worth it a million times over.

"I can't believe it! I won! Two VIP tickets!" She turns to me again, eyes wide and hopeful. "You *have* to come!"

"I don't—"

"We had a deal."

"It's really not necessary." Going would be incredibly irresponsible of me. So terribly stupid and irresponsible.

"I can't go alone," she insists.

"Bring Claire or Lainey or Sutton," I suggest, but she shakes her head.

"No, I'm bringing you. Lainey and Claire will be working because it's the Fourth of July weekend. Plus, we had a deal. Friends don't go back on deals." I open my mouth to protest. "And don't you dare tell me we're not friends, or I might cry."

She stares at me, glaring in a way I think she wants to be fierce, but really is just adorable.

"I know we're friends, June. Trust me." It's the truth, too. I'm painfully aware that June and I are friends, and that's all I can allow. Daily, it seems, I have to remind myself I'm her boss, that it would be far too complicated, and she can definitely do much better than a crotchety asshole like me.

June Taylor deserves someone as bright and joy-filled as she is, and that will never be me.

"Oh. Okay. So, you'll come with?" she asks, with a hesitant smile. I push my hand through my hair, unable to find a way out of this without disappointing her, before nodding.

"Yes, but only if you agree to let me pay for the hotel rooms." While I was having my late-night of entering contests on her behalf, it was the condition I set for myself, both for her safety and my sanity.

"No," she says with a shake of her head.

"Yes. The concert ends late, and traffic will be terrible on the way back. I'm not spending the entire day in the sun only to get into an accident with some drunk idiot who partied too hard for the weekend." I start filtering through options for how I can pay for a hotel stay if she refuses. Thankfully, that isn't necessary, because she sighs, then nods reluctantly.

"Fine," she says, her eyes narrowing at me, but then she rolls her eyes and sighs. "Whatever. But I'll buy the drinks."

I glare at her, but know I'll do anything to make June happy, so like a dozen times before, I agree, mentally planning some new scheme to handle it.

# TWENTY-THREE

# GRAHAM

June instructs me to get to her place at ten on Saturday morning before we make the ninety-minute drive to Wildwood. When I arrive, I text her that I'm out front, then wait for her to make her way outside. I remind myself I just need to make it through the drive there, the festival, and the drive back. We'll park in the hotel's lot, then leave our bags there until we check in after the concert. I was able to reserve two hotel rooms on opposite sides of the hotel, a fore-thought I'm grateful for when she steps out of her apartment building.

She's always gorgeous, but right now, casual and ready for a day in the sun, she's my own brand of cruel temptation.

Her lips are painted a bright red, and her hair is half up, half down, with two small pigtails on top of her head. There are a dozen colorful gems glued somehow to the top of her hair and along her eyes, making her look like a little disco ball. With the wide grin lighting her up from the inside, it's the perfect embodiment of the ray of sunshine that is June Taylor. She's in a red bathing suit top barely hidden beneath a loose-knit, white cover-up tee and a pair of frayed, tight jean shorts. As I step out of the car to grab her bag, I realize my plan of acting natural and just may just be a fool's errand. How the hell am I supposed to act natural when she looks like this?

She waves at me eagerly, as if she isn't completely blowing me away before starting to run toward me despite wearing a pair of flimsy-looking flip-flops. When she trips, I snap back into reality and step toward her, steadying her with a hand on her lower back.

"Jesus, June, don't run in those," I say, but she just giggles.

"Sorry, I'm just so excited!" I take the duffel bag from her and slide it into the trunk next to my small suitcase. When I slide into the front seat, she turns to me, beaming and nearly jumping in her seat. "Are you excited?"

I don't have any other choice.

I smile back, giving her something that is both a lie and the complete truth.

"Yeah, June."

"Can you take my picture?" June asks hours later as we walk past a colorful mural emblazoned with the festival's name. She chatted the entire drive, which was fine since it kept my mind occupied, but now that we're walking along the sand, bouncing around from stage to stage, it's impossible to ignore how fucking gorgeous she is. I welcome the distraction and the bit of space I'll earn and nod, taking her phone from her hands before she runs to the mural. I take a dozen photos as she effortlessly shifts poses and expressions before giving me a thumbs-up, my mission complete.

"Good?"

"Yeah, I think I got some," I say.

"Thank you! You're the best!" she says, moving to me and hugging me. It's her new go-to, and even though I've noticed she does it with everyone, I cherish each one, deluding myself into thinking it's something more, something precious.

"Do you two want me to take your picture together?" a woman

asks. I look over June's shoulder to see a group of three women, one in the front giving June a wide grin, her hand outstretched to take her phone.

"Oh, no, that's—" I start, but June untangles from me, stepping toward the woman with a nod.

"YES! Oh, my god, that would be amazing!" June says, handing over her phone before her small fingers wrap around my wrist, tugging me toward the mural. "Come on, Graham."

"June—"

"Friends take pictures to commemorate their outings together," she says, and who am I to argue? I'm incapable of saying no to her, it seems, especially when she's giving me that happy look. She settles me in front of the mural and stands beside me. On instinct, I slip a hand behind her, setting it on her back, and her arm moves around my shoulder.

"Try to look like you're not completely miserable to be here," she says, smiling and staring at the woman holding the camera, and I can't help but grin. After a moment, the stranger waves her hands closer together.

"Get closer! I'll get a few like that, too." My heart skips with nerves, but June is unfazed as always, instead shifting her body toward me, sliding her arm from my shoulders to my waist, and setting a hand on my chest. On instinct, my hand slides to her hip, pulling her into my side. "Cute!" the woman says.

"Try to look like you're not completely miserable to be here," I say low, and with my words, June's head tips back with a loud, full laugh. I smile down at her, enthralled by her joy, as always.

"That's the one! Oh my god, that was perfect!" the woman says.

"Thank you so much!" June says before she slips from my grip, moving across the sand to grab her phone. My arms feel empty without her, so I cross them over my chest, watching as June returns the favor, spending almost five minutes taking photos of the women, chattering on and laughing as she does. It's strange to see how quickly June can make friends of strangers.

"Can we sit in the sand? I want to post a few of these," she asks, and we do, finding a spot on the sand out of the way of foot traffic. She starts tapping her screen, then smiles at me and explains. "If you tag the festival, you're entered to win tickets for next year." I let out a loud laugh. I should probably feel nervous that she might be disappointed if she doesn't win, but something in my gut knows I'd do it again next year. The idea settles in me uncomfortably, since I don't know where I'll be then. I will probably be assigned some new location by then, and for the first time in my life, the thought settles sourly in my gut. I can't help but think I'd miss Seaside Point. Not even just because I'd miss June, either; the entire town is growing on me in a way I didn't expect.

I'm still lost in my thoughts when she shows me the photo on her phone, now in the company's tagged section. A shot of her and me is the most recent, but there have to be hu*ndreds* of tags for the last hour alone, all in front of that mural.

"Is that the point of that mural?" I ask, confused. "A marketing tool?"

She nods.

"It's a popular tactic, making a backdrop for an event or a city, then using it as a checkpoint for guests or tourists. It's kind of like the Hollywood sign or the Walk of Fame. People go just to take their pictures." I nod, understanding, and scroll endlessly. "Then people see it on their feeds and get it stuck in their mind that they *have* to go next year."

"It's smart," I say, handing her phone back.

"You know, that would be a really good idea for Daytrip," she says absentmindedly, now sending photos to her friends. My attention shifts back to the mural, watching as another group of girls stand in one spot and smile. There's a small line now winding along the art installation, people lined up for their shot. "A photo op. Or two, maybe?"

"Oh?" I ask, turning to her, intrigued.

"Yeah, imagine, a mural on the exterior of the building. You could have one inside, exclusive to guests, then another outside, maybe along the side of the building on the beach? Nearby, you could have some signage about more photo locations inside and pamphlets displaying the amenities, making it so people would want to grab a day pass to enjoy a luxurious beach day, and have the fun photos to share on socials." She bites her lip, lost in her thoughts as she stares off down the shoreline. "A temporary one would be perfect for the social media influencers. Or maybe a permanent one and then a seasonal one that changes, so there are reasons to come over and over?"

She looks a bit uncertain, but it makes perfect sense to me, though there's only one person I would trust with the project.

'Would you do it for me?" I ask. That gets her full attention, her head snapping to me with confusion written clearly across it.

"I'm sorry?"

"The murals. Would you paint them for me?"

Her face goes soft, apologetic almost.

"Oh, Graham, I didn't mean...I don't—"

"I've seen what you can do. If we commissioned someone, I would only want you to do it."

She shakes her head.

"You don't have to do this just because we're friends, Graham."

"This isn't because we're friends," I say, serious, but she's already flipped the switch, trying to deflect, a smile on her lips. I never know just what she's going to say when she gets like this, desperate to shift the attention off of her and her talent.

"Because we're more than friends?" she asks, and my brain short-circuits.

"June—"

"I'm just picking on you, Graham," she says, pushing my shoulder playfully. "Unless..." I wonder if it's being away from the office or the sun that has her wiggling her eyebrows at me sugges- tively, but either way, I don't know how to respond. After a moment, her head tips back, and a laugh leaves her lips, full and joy-filled, completely entertained.

She's joking with me.

I don't know if I should be relieved or disappointed, and that might be the most concerning part of all.

"Jesus, June–"

"Sorry, sorry, I'm out of the confines of the office, so I feel the need to push *all* of your buttons," she says, and I wonder if she knows just how much she *constantly* pushes my buttons, even when she's just sitting at her desk, chewing on the end of a pen, lost in her work.

"I'm serious," I say, after a moment. "I want you to think about it. Doing murals for Daytrip."

"Graham—"

"Just sit on it. We're not here for work, but on Monday, I'll be asking again." She pauses for a moment, but must see the firm look on my face, the fact that I absolutely will bug her about this next week, because she sighs and rolls her eyes dramatically.

"Next week, we'll talk about it."

I spend the rest of the afternoon successfully keeping a reasonable distance from her, making sure my skin never brushes against hers, and our conversation stays light and neutral. We see a ton of musical acts, which thankfully eats up any conversation time, but it also means I get to watch her dance around, carefree and happy—something that might be worse than talking with her.

By nine, we're almost home free, with just one more act to see before I can go to my separate hotel room and jack off while I think about her to relieve myself of this tension. Unfortunately, I didn't consider that June wouldn't want to simply watch from the available VIP balcony section. Instead, she wants to go to the VIP pit, to watch the show against the barricade in a sea of bodies, with very little space between us.

That's when I realized this entire scheme was a horrible fucking idea.

How the hell am I supposed to remain neutral and keep my shit together and not give in to the utter desire to make her mine? Every five seconds, her body sways to the loud music playing over the speakers while we wait for the band to come on, brushing against me while I stand behind her, trying to keep everyone else away from her.

I'm forced against her, forced to smell her light perfume and hear her magical laugh and get the full brunt of every small smile she tosses over her shoulder at me.

It forces me to come to terms with the fact that I want June Taylor.

So fucking bad.

When the kick drums start, she starts cheering, and relief moves through me. The band starting means I'm closer to the end of my own unique torture, but that relief is momentary. With the sounds, the entire crowd invigorates and shifts, pushing to the front of the stage, and the small gap I'd maintained between June and me is absolutely gone, my chest pressing against her back.

"I'm so sorry," I yell into her ear, frantic in my need to remain professional with her. "The crowd—"

"It's all good, Graham!" she shouts over the chords of a guitar. "It's the best part! Just go with it!"

Her hand reaches for mine, placing it on her hip and looking over her shoulder at me, beaming wide.

How am I supposed to argue with that look of utter happiness, with the music, with the closeness?

I can't.

So I don't.

Twenty minutes into the forty-minute set, I'm still plastered against June and trying my best not to think about the way her body moves and shifts, nearly grinding with her as she dances, sings, and screams to the songs. But when the chords change, going from rock to something soft, June stills.

"OH MY GOD!" she yells, eyes wide and fixated on the stage.

"We got a couple of requests to play an old song," Riggins Greene, the lead singer of the band, says with a grin. "Hell, we *all* got a couple of requests from one person, asking us to play this song."

"Begging," the bassist yells into his mic.

"Yeah, begging," Riggins laughs. "Even went so far as to reach out to Stell and Harper." My heart starts to pound with nerves. "He said this song was someone out there's favorite, and it would mean the world if we played it."

My panic only seems to heighten with each word.

*Please don't say my name. Please don't say my fucking name,* I think, over and over.

"So, if there's someone out there who was hoping for us to play this song, just know that someone tried really fucking hard to make all of your dreams come true," he says, then steps from the mic, leading into the song, and relief moves through me.

"It's my song!" an oblivious June shouts, turning in my arms and gripping my shirt in her hand excitedly as the intro continues to play. Her smile is so damn wide, so stunning, I know that it was worth it, despite the minor heart attack I just had. She mentioned the song a handful of times, saying it was an older tune they rarely play live, but she hoped they would. When I looked it up that night, I recognized it as the one she had me dance with her to at the Seabreeze and decided to send a few messages to request they play it for her.

To everyone in the band.

And their significant others.

And their agent.

And their publicist.

I didn't think it would work, but figured it couldn't hurt, just another opportunity to make June's whims come to fruition.

"It is," I say low, lifting a hand, and pushing some loose hair back. We're close; it wouldn't take much more than a couple of inches to graze my lips against hers.

"Pretty lucky!" she shouts, and I smile down at her.

I want to kiss her.

I've wanted to kiss her a dozen times today alone, each time, the urge to press my lips to hers becoming more and more insistent. But it's never been as fierce as it is right now, with her hand on my chest, her big eyes staring up into mine, cheeks flushed, and excitement written across her face.

Last week, when I gave in to that urge, it was the greatest idea and the absolute worst.

Part of me thought that maybe, just maybe, I was exaggerating how good we were together. A late night of hot sex and then insane tension between us for weeks could do that, right?

I was wrong.

It was not a fluke.

I also lied. Cece never stopped to look at us, never even hesitated as she walked away.

I just wanted to kiss her, to try and prove to myself that it was just that one time, that kissing June wasn't as explosive as my mind kept telling me.

Unfortunately, instead of sating that need, it just made my need for her a million times worse.

I convinced myself that all the moments of making her life easier, of making her small wishes and hopes for luck come true, were just because that's what friends do for each other. But after that kiss, I was forced to come to terms with the fact that I don't want to be just friends with her.

I want to be a whole fucking lot more with June Taylor.

Thankfully, before I can do something that I can't take back, the singing starts. June beams up at me, squealing before turning around and singing loudly.

And just like the last time we were together when this song played, I hold her close through the entire thing.

Eventually, the set ends, the crowd disperses, and I step away from June. As I do, my entire body feels cold. We move through the crowd, and at some point, June grabs my hand, twining her fingers through mine silently, not wanting to get separated, but even when we're off the beach and headed to our hotel, neither of us lets go.

It takes us about twenty minutes to walk the half mile to the hotel, and with the wild traffic on the street, I know I was right in insisting we stay the night in town. Relief moves through me as we walk into the lobby of the hotel. I'm eager to go to my hotel room, get some distance between us, and then try to wrap my mind around why I'm being so ridiculous and irrational right now.

I just need space.

That's what I keep telling myself.

Space will make this incessant need to kiss my assistant fade.

But when she stops before we can even make it to the front desk, grabbing my wrist with a wide, excited smile I've come to recognize well, I know I'm screwed.

"Make a wish!" she says, lifting her phone and closing her eyes even though we're stopped in the center of the lobby, people having to step around us.

"What?" She opens one eye as I watch her, confused, and she glares at me.

"Make a wish! It's 11:11!" Her eyes move to her phone again, the time displayed prominently on her screen. She closes her eyes once more.

"June, we have—"

I start to argue, but she opens both eyes this time, giving me one of her signature exaggerated sighs.

"My god, can't you ever just do one thing without making a whole stink about it? Close your eyes and make a damn wish."

She glares at me, and I bite back a smile. Instead, I give a sigh of my own, then, despite feeling stupid, I close my eyes and take in a deep breath.

I could fake it.

It would be easy. June is so superstitious, she would never ask what my wish was, but it would feel like a betrayal. That's why I find myself sifting through my thoughts until I land on one that shines bright. Before I can even stop, I mentally latch onto it.

*I wish I could have June Taylor.*

It's a wild thought, unruly and panic-inducing, but also, the second I think it, it feels right. I don't know if it's June's own superstitious ways or the endorphins from the night, or what, but I take in a deep breath and send the thought into the universe.

Because it's true.

*I wish I could have June Taylor all to myself.*

After, I open my eyes to see she's looking up at me, a soft, peaceful smile on her lips.

"Done," I say, and my voice sounds gruff to my own ears.

"Did you have fun tonight?" she asks, not moving from where we're stopped in the hotel entrance, her voice soft.

"Yeah," I admit instantly, because it's the truth. Her shoulders relax, and that smirk turns to a beaming grin.

"I really am lucky," she murmurs. I look at her, confused, but she explains without my asking. "That was my wish. That you would say you had fun with me tonight."

"What? Why?" Why would she waste a wish on *me?*

"Because we're friends, Graham," she says in a stage whisper before lifting her hands. "I know, I know. Scary stuff. Don't be alarmed. But friends care if the other has fun or not."

I laugh again, louder this time. After a moment, when I look back at her, her eyes are softer, the joking gone from them, though the smile still lingers.

"Yeah, my wish came true," she murmurs, voice low.

In that moment, I think I begin to realize just how screwed I am.

Because I don't think any distance would make me stop falling for June Taylor, not when I know that in some universe I can have her smiling softly at me like that.

# TWENTY-FOUR

# GRAHAM

In less than five minutes, I'm wondering if by some fucked twist of fate my own wish is trying to come true. I suppose that's the power of wishing and luck that June always talks about.

"I don't understand. My reservation was clearly for two separate rooms," I repeat for what feels like the tenth time. My pulse is pounding, and even though I know I look and sound like an asshole, I can't stop. Not when my reservation is currently fucked, not when it means my only option might just be spending the night in a hotel room with June.

"I understand that, Mr. Hawthorne. Unfortunately, something has gone wrong on the back-end system, and only one room was reserved," the receptionist says, genuine apology in the words. "And as I previously informed you, with the festival in town, we have no other rooms. We are fully booked."

"This is ridiculous," I grumble. "I would like to talk to your ma—"

I don't get the chance to finish my sentence, though, because June's hand covers my mouth before I can speak. I turn to glare at her, but she's smiling, sweet as pie, at the receptionist.

"I am so sorry, it's been a very long night, so we're both a bit tired.

I totally understand this is not your fault and also very out of your control, and we appreciate all you've done to try and help us. The room keys will be just fine. We can figure it out from here," June says. The receptionist stares between us, a mix of confusion and entertainment written across her face.

"No problem at all. Of course, we will be refunding the cost, since this was an error on our end." Her fingers move back to her clacking keyboard, and I open my mouth to say something once more, but June tightens her hand on me.

Despite the bubbling irritation, I find myself smiling beneath her hand. June feels it, inevitably, looking over at me and giving me one of her own beaming grins. The woman finishes checking us in, sliding two keycards our way before she finally lowers her hand. I open my mouth to say something, but June gives me a glare and points at me.

"Behave."

I have no option but to smile at her.

"Thank you so much," June says, taking the keycards. The receptionist points us toward the elevators and tells us the room number and floor before we're on our way. June reaches for the bags, her multicolored patchwork duffel sitting on top of my black rollerbag, but I glare at her, grab the handle, and go.

When we're closed into the elevator, all entertainment washes away with the memory of what happened the last time we were in an elevator together. Pressing her against the wall, kissing her, grinding into her. The need that rushed through me, the exhilaration that I was going to have her.

That same need thrums in my veins, and I wonder just how I'm going to survive the night. I'm silent, stuck in my thoughts as the elevator rises, then dings on our floor, and we make our way to our room.

"Is this really that miserable of a situation?" June asks, finally breaking the silence once the door closes behind us, shutting us into a luxury room. I don't have the opportunity to look it over as I always do when I'm in a competitor's hotel, stuck on the way the slamming door felt final, like the last nail in the coffin.

She's standing there, stunning and sun-kissed, most of the sparkles gone from her face and hair by now, her bathing suit top still the most tempting thing I've ever seen, and I know there's no way I can stay away.

What's the point, anyway?

"I'm sorry?"

"Is this really that miserable of a situation? Having to spend the night with me?" She moves to her bag, grabs it, and digs through to find something. "We've done it once before, and you survived just fine."

"That was different," I tell her, crossing my arms on my chest. "That was before you worked for me."

"Technically, it wasn't, but that's not the point, and you know it." I open my mouth, and she turns to me, standing straight with a firm look and a finger raised. "And don't even try some bullshit about against the rules and blah blah blah. Sutton told me it wasn't, and I double-checked to make sure. The only fraternization rule is that higher-ups must be informed."

I lift an eyebrow, fighting back a smile.

"You looked it up in the handbook?"

A blush moves over her cheeks, but her stern look doesn't falter.

"Hell yeah, I did. Strangely enough, I like this job. I also can't deny that I'm into you." I step closer to her, but she keeps going. "You're funny, if in a dry way. And you're smart. And you're insanely hot. You're also nice when you want to be, though you rarely do want to be. I like talking to you because you always make me think of things in a new way. I like the way you look at me when you don't think I'm watching. I like the way you entertain my idiosyncrasies rather than simply enduring them. I like the way you looked for four-leaf clovers with me, and the way you make wishes at 11:11 because I ask you to, and the way you protected me through a concert that you didn't even want to go to. I like the way you pretended to be my boyfriend because my bully was hitting on you, and the way you let me show you around my town simply because you know it's my favorite place on earth. But most of all, Graham, I like you. And I think you like me, too."

Silence hangs in the air between us, and my pulse races, but hers does, too, something I can see in her neck, where I desperately want to press my lips. Her breathing is heavy as she holds my gaze, reaching into her pocket for something.

"So, I think we should stop playing this stupid game and let luck decide what we do next." She opens her hand, holding it out to me, and a tiny copper circle sits in the palm of her hand.

"Is that—?" I start.

"The penny you gave me? Yeah. I keep it on me just in case I need to make an important decision." My pulse quickens.

"Important decision? What kind of important decision?" I ask, stepping a bit closer until there's barely a foot between us. She grins up at me.

"Heads you sleep on the floor. Tails, you admit that you want me, and then we see where that takes us."

My cock stiffens with the mere suggestion.

"June—"

"Come on, Graham. Let's let luck decide if this is meant to happen," she murmurs, eyes locked on mine as she takes the penny between pointer and thumb, holding it out for me.

I don't know why I do it.

But I put my hand out, and she drops the coin into the palm of my hand. It's warm from her touch, and I stare at the copper, trying to convince myself of all of the reasons this is a terrible fucking idea.

*I can't think of one.*

So I flip the coin and catch it in my hand, fingers curling around the warm metal and hiding it from view.

"If we do this, nothing changes," I say.

"Nothing at all," she says, her voice breezy and soft, though I hear the small shake in it, something so close to disappointment twining in the words. I pull her into me, the hand not holding the coin wrapping around her waist and tugging her in tight.

"But if we do *this*, everything changes." I drop the penny to the ground.

Her breathing hitches, her eyes going huge.

"Everything changes, because I'm not going back, June." I stare at her, and I let those words hang between us, heavy and weighted. "I'm not going back to pretending like I'm not absolutely gone for you."

She licks her lips and nods.

"Everything changes, Graham," she murmurs, her voice shaky.

I don't stop to look at the penny before closing the gap between us. I don't want fate or luck or the universe to decide this. I don't want there to ever be any kind of doubt in her mind somewhere down the road. I want June to know I'm all in and always have been.

I slide my fingers to the back of her hair and pull her face to mine.

# TWENTY-FIVE

For just a moment, I have the presence of mind to think I'd better get my penny back before we leave this hotel room, since I have become emotionally attached to that tiny piece of metal, but then Graham's lips are on mine, and I can't think about a single other thing.

Because Graham Hawthorne is kissing me.

Deep.

And hard.

It's not like the last kiss, either. This one is filled with pent-up emotions, need, lust, and want, and pining and yearning, and in some strange way, it's a comfort to know it hasn't been in my head; it hasn't been one-sided all along. The kiss tells me everything I need to know—Graham has been as into me as I have been to him; he's just *much* better at hiding it.

His hand is in my hair, and my chin is in the palm of the other one, his fingers spread along the side of my jaw. He uses his grasp to guide my face where he wants it, taking what he desires, and I let him.

"Graham," I murmur as his lips travel, licking down my neck and pulling my earring into his mouth, little dangling suns today, making me gasp.

"Mmm?" he says against my skin, and the sound travels straight between my legs.

"Are we, uh," I swallow, stumbling on my words. His fingers brush along the skin of my belly, gripping the bottom of my loose cover-up top, pulling it over my head, and tossing it to the side before his lips meet my skin again, pressing kisses to the bare skin at my shoulder. My breathing goes shaky as I try to hold onto a single thought. "Are we, uh, really doing this?"

He pulls back, a wide, happy grin on his lips, that dimple taunting me, and everything in me melts.

"I sure as fuck hope so," he murmurs. He looks so boyish like this, years younger, without the stress of work and what I now think may have been the stress of having to keep these pent-up emotions inside. Still, in a heartbeat, his face changes, eyebrows furrowing, his body stilling. "Unless—"

I shake my head fervently. "No, no, I very much want—" I start, but I'm stopped with another deep kiss, lips and tongues colliding in a preview of what's to come. Then his head dips again, pressing to my lips and nipping the bottom one before making the same trail down the other side of my neck. My hands roam his back, finding the bottom of his shirt and tugging weakly, my mind muddled with lust. Thankfully, he gets the hint, stripping it off before returning to his mission. His body moves, small, staggering steps toward the bed, moving me with him as his hand lifts to where the tie at the top of my bikini top is, tugging until my top comes loose. He pulls back for just a moment to watch the material fall, a deep, satisfying groan leaving his lips as a nipple is revealed.

"Fuck, your tits have been haunting me."

I giggle at the thought, but the sound melts into a moan when his hand lifts, cupping and rolling a nipple. My head falls back as his free hand tugs at the back string of my bikini, tossing the material aside, then slides down my belly to the button of my shorts. I slide my arms around his neck to pull him closer until we're chest to chest, skin to skin. His head lifts, moving back to my lips to kiss me as my fingers sift through his hair, taking a page out of his book to take what I want, to hold his head where I can devour his mouth as he gets my shorts undone. Soon, they're sliding down my legs with my underwear, and he's pushing me to the bed until I'm sprawled before him. He watches as I settle in, his hands moving to the button on his shorts, sliding them and his underwear down until he, too, is naked. His cock bobs free, and my mouth waters.

"What's this?" he asks, moving closer to the bed, his fingers grazing the small red and black tattoo on my hip. "I didn't see it last time."

"You were a bit preoccupied," I murmur. "It's a ladybug. She brings me good luck." His fingers run over the ink on my skin again, trailing in and down until he's inches from where I'm desperate for him. Chills run through me.

"My lady luck." His voice is so slow I almost miss it, but god, that name on his lips, I'm so fucking grateful I didn't. "What else did I miss?" he asks, and I bit my lip, lifting a shoulder.

"Not sure."

"I guess I should look every inch over, shouldn't I?" he asks.

"You can look later," I murmur. "I want you, Graham." A deep, needy groan leaves his lips, but he shakes his head all the same.

"No, no. I made that mistake last time, rushing through. I thought it would be enough, thought it would ease my mind, but it didn't." He bends, pressing his lips to the tiny ladybug on my hip. "It made it worse. It left me wondering every day."

"Wondering?" I say in a breath, watching as his tongue darts out to lick my skin before standing straight once more. "About what?"

"What your face would look like when I did this," he says, hand sliding up my belly, cupping my breast. "And this." His thumb and forefinger come together over my nipple, pinching and rolling and causing me to gasp. A smile spreads on his lips, and this, too, is different than last time.

The smiling. The teasing.

They've been coming easier, but tonight, it's like he gave up trying to keep them in, decided it wasn't worth the effort.

"Yeah, that's the look I was hoping for. Though it is much prettier in person," he says, then drops his head, circling his lips on my nipple and sucking. I thread my fingers through his hair, holding him to me, enjoying his skin on mine. His hard cock bobs, brushing my thigh, and I moan.

His hand slides down my belly as his lips continue to move on my nipple, and I gasp as his middle finger grazes over my clit. I'm wet and needy, more than ready for him.

It's just like the first time, and I know if I let him, my dominant man will have me writhing in just a moment.

But while Graham may have been daydreaming about the faces I'd make, my own mind has been preoccupied with what he would look like if he lost that tight grip on his control. It ignites something in me, hotter than the need to have relief of my own, and I sit up, then roll until I'm standing beside him.

"Is everything—" he starts, looking concerned, but I just grin.

"Sit," I order, pushing him toward the bed.

"What?"

"You had your fun last time. Now it's my turn."

"June, you—"

I glare at him.

"You told me next time, I'd get to suck you off. This is next time." His hand captures my jaw, tipping it to look at him, and my breathing hitches when I see the hot look in his eyes. He sits on the edge of the bed, and I grin in pleasure, but then squeal as his hand moves to my hips, pulling me into him. I let out a little shriek, my hands moving to his shoulders.

"Only if you touch yourself while you do. Only if you get yourself all nice and wet for me." He presses hot kisses all along my jaw to my ear, nipping the lobe and making me suck in a breath. He reaches for my hand, grabs it, then settles it over my center, making me cup my pussy. "Can you do that for me, June?" I nod fervently, then shift away, moving to my knees quickly, eager to make both of us feel good.

My hand, still between my legs, starts to wander, sliding over my clit as my mouth wraps around the tip of his cock. We both moan as I use my tongue to slide over it, then slowly lower my mouth onto him. His hands come to my hair, gathering it and pulling it away from my face. I slide a finger into myself as my lips hit the base, and I let out a heavy breath.

"Are you fingering yourself with a mouth full of my cock?" His voice is low, and I nod, sliding in another finger, my thumb grazing over my clit as I settle my free hand on his thigh to steady myself. "That's it. Ride those, lady luck. Get yourself nice and wet for me."

I moan around him, the sound muffled, and the combination has my pleasure ratcheting. His hand tightens in my hair just a bit, his other hand gripping his knee as if trying to restrain himself, and I feel the smallest jerk of his hips before he stops, letting me take the lead.

But that's not what I want.

I want him to use me.

With that in mind, I cover his hand on my head, pushing it deeper, then pulling it back, showing him what I want, what he can take. A deep groan leaves his lips, his head falling back as his cock throbs in my mouth. "Fuck, June, you want me to fuck your face?"

I nod as best I can, moaning as my hips speed up with the mere thought. I don't have to rely on my imagination for long, though, because Graham takes full advantage, and soon the room is filled with both of our pleasured sounds.

I'm on my knees before him, his hand in my hair, forcing me to look at him as he stares down at me between his spread legs, using the hand in my hair to fuck my face, and I have never felt hotter in my life. I've never felt more needed, never felt more desired, never felt more in control.

"You look so fucking pretty, your lips wrapped around my cock, eyes watering. Is your pussy soaked for me, June?" he asks after a minute of this. I take him in deeper and moan my answer. "Show me." My brows furrow as I suck on him, but he reaches for my arm, tugging on my bicep. "Show me your hand, June. Show me just how wet you are for me." I groan, sinking my fingers deeper to get even more wet from my center before pulling out and lifting my hand. His free hand wraps around my wrist and pulls it closer for inspection. The hand in my hair pulls me deeper until his cock hits the back of my throat, and he groans, though I don't know if it's from my hand or my mouth.

"God, you really are a wet girl, aren't you? Is this all for me?"

I don't answer, lost in the emotions, thoughts, and needs swirling through me, but his hand slows my descent, urging me until my eyes meet his. "Is your pussy drenched because of me? From the fact that your mouth is wrapped around my cock, that you're sucking your boss off, that he's liking it so much, it's taking everything in him not to blow right this fucking second?"

I nod the best I can, watching as his head dips, sliding my fingers into his mouth and groaning deep as he sucks them clean. I make another muffled moan, my hips rocking, my legs tightening around emptiness.

"I know, baby. You want something so bad, don't you? You want my cock inside your pretty wet cunt?" I moan and nod, and he drops my hand, smiling wide. "A little bit more. Take yourself a little closer." The next sound is far less pleasure and far more panic. I'm too close as it is, and he is far too entertained right now. He's not suffering or as gone as I clearly am, something I need to amend. I moan around him as I move my wet hand down, but instead of fingering myself some more, I run my fingers, wet from a mix of my pussy and his fingers, over his balls, tugging gently. His cock leaps in my mouth, and his hand tightens in my hair.

"You fucking tease," he grits out, but I know I won this battle when he pushes my head deeper onto his cock, hitting the back of my throat. He moans my name low and needy before he pulls back with a reluctant groan. I sit on my heels, watching him as I lick my lips, breathing heavy, my legs pressing together with unsated need.

"Fuck, June, you're so perfect," he murmurs before he bends, lifting me and laying me on the bed.

"I'm perfect, and I also desperately need to come," I whine, my fingers gently moving through my center, my entire body jolting with need. I'm teetering on the edge, and I know it would just take one hard press to shatter completely.

But that's not what I want.

Not right now.

I don't want an easy orgasm, I don't want the relief; I want the moment. I want to come with him deep inside of me, his hair falling into his face, his body against mine, breath coasting over my skin.

"Please fuck me," I say, slipping one finger inside of myself. He watches, enraptured, before he turns, fumbling for his shorts.

"Let me just...fuck," he says, a bit too unhappy for my liking, not the kind that's filled with desire, but instead panic. I shift to see he's holding his wallet and looking over my naked body, forlorn.

"Fuck? Yes, that's the goal, Graham." His jaw tightens.

"I don't have a condom," he says. "Do you?" I bite my lip and shake my head.

"As much as I'm a progressive woman who believes women should be fully in charge of their own sexual health, the mere idea of going into the drug store in my small town and having to ask someone to unlock the condom section makes me want to die a little," I admit.

"Fuck," he grins, pulling a hand through his hair. His cock is hard, the tip red and leaking precum, and suddenly, all I want is for him to stretch me, to fill me.

And I trust him. I know it deep in my chest, the same way I knew that very first night I was safe to go to his room with him.

"I have an IUD," I say without overthinking it, capturing his attention. "And despite that one night, I've never actually had a one-night stand. I was tested after, and I was all clear." His tongue darts out, wetting his lips, and he takes a slow step toward me. The need melts away for a moment, sincerity taking its place as his hand comes out, brushing my hair back as I prop myself on my elbows to look at him.

"You want to take me bare?"

The mere idea has my pussy tightening, but I attempt to stay focused.

"Is this..." I lick my lips, biting the bottom one, swollen from sucking him off. "Is this a one-time thing?" He pulls me into sitting, my legs over the bed as he kneels between them, his hands cupping my cheeks.

"It was never a one-time thing. I was just too stubborn to realize it." My pulse goes into overdrive, and it has nothing to do with how turned on I am and everything to do with his words and the way he's looking at me.

This is different.

This isn't a night of fun.

This isn't just getting lucky and moving on with our lives.

This isn't convenient, finding the closest person to scratch an itch.

This is a bubbling pot boiling over. This need has been simmering. This is a desire that turned into friendship and then into something more.

This isn't temporary.

This is the beginning of something big, something important, and with the way he's looking at me, I know it to be true.

"If you want, I can run out, grab a dozen condoms, and come back, fuck you into oblivion. If you want, I'll use my hands and my mouth to make you come again and again until we get back to Seaside Point tomorrow, then I'll fuck you for real with protection. If you want to wait a week, a month, if you want dates and assurance and doctor's printouts, I'll do it, just say the word, June. But none of those circumstances will change the fact that I'm tired of pretending you don't mean everything to me. I'm tired of pretending I'm not absolutely head over heels for you, that I've never felt this kind of pull for a woman, that I know somewhere deep down that you're going to be in my life for a long fucking time."

I reach up, covering his hand with mine on my cheek.

"You mean that, don't you?" I ask,

"That you're going to be in my life?" I nod. "June, you've taken up every waking moment of my life since you fell into it. How could you believe otherwise?" His words strike me with their sincerity, and with the need blooms again, more insistent than ever. I shift, lying back onto the bed, shimmying back until I'm on it completely.

"Fuck me, Graham," I mumble as he groans, putting a knee on the bed. His cock bobs before me, and I fight the urge to suck him off again, but I need him more. He moves, shifting onto the bed over me, planting his arms in the bed on either side of my head, covering me as he settles between my legs, and suddenly, everything changes.

The frantic energy is gone, replaced by a slower, headier need.

The look in his eyes goes from lust-filled to something fonder, sweeter.

Reaching between us, my hand wraps around his cock. His eyes flutter shut for just a moment, a jagged breath leaving his lips as I line the tip up with my entrance.

It's different this time. Utterly and completely and beautifully different, and we both know it. The truth of that glows in my chest, burning, flickering, and warming my entire being, and that same look is reflected on his face.

This is not a one-night thing.

This is something bigger, something better. This is giving in to whatever strange power has been continually pulling us together, a bond of luck and chance and fate bringing him to me.

"I'm so gone for you, June," he says before he slides into me, slow and steady, stretching and filling me until he's planted deep, making me feel whole for the first time since that night.

"Oh god," I moan, my eyes drifting shut with the overwhelming pleasure of having him inside me. His hand leaves the bed, shifting to grip my chin, to force my face to stare at him, and my eyes pop back open.

"No. Eyes on me, lady luck. You're going to let me watch it take over you. Watch what happens to the very first time I make you mine for good."

"Graham," I murmur as he slides out slow, then slams back in hard, filling me. I gasp, my legs widening to take him deeper, and a small smile plays on his lips, his dimple coming out. Like this, the smile feels almost sacred, something special and important, a look reserved just for me.

"I know, June. God, I fucking know. You feel so fucking good."

"I need—"

"You'll get it," he says before I can tell him what I need, not that I think I could put word to it. "Until then, you're going to be a good girl and take what I'm giving you." Another slow retreat and hard thrust. "Next time, we can be wild. Next time, I'll fuck you face down, slam into you, and watch that ass that's been teasing me shake with each thrust." I tighten around him at the mental image, and his own eyes flutter, not closing completely as if, just like me, he doesn't want to miss a moment.

"Okay," I breath as he slides out, then slams in. "Fuck!"

"God, you're so fucking wet, June. So fucking wet and tight and perfect. And mine. All fucking mine." My fingers dig into his ass, trying to get him deeper, to get more of his skin on mine as I gasp and writhe on the bed, pleasure deepening and growing in my belly.

"Yes, yes," I moan, the words coming out breathy and nearly incoherent. "Yours. Fuck, I'm yours." A deep groan leaves his chest with my words, his head falling into my neck as his hips start to move faster, fucking me harder than before, grunting with each movement.

"All mine. You're all mine, June. I'm never letting you go," he moans, and my orgasm starts to crest. I don't know if it's just the long build-up to this, or his words or the pace, or what, but I'm tipping the edge in moments, my nails digging into his back as I hold him close, trying to hold on, to savor every moment.

"Now," he groans, slamming in, head lifting to look at me. "Come with me."

That's what does it.

Or maybe it's the way his eyes lock on mine, the way his face goes somehow soft before the pleasure takes him, as if he wants to cement this moment in his mind, as if he really, truly believes that this is starting our own version of forever, everything and nothing at all changing in a moment.

Either way, I hold his gaze as long as I can before I scream, pleasure washing through me in intense waves as my head falls to the bed, my back arching as I come hard. Graham follows, bellowing my name as he slams in deep, staying there as we both shake with the force of our orgasms.

His body relaxes after a few moments, though he stays planted deep, and I tighten a bit as aftershocks move through me. A small groan leaves his lips before he peppers small kisses to my neck, his scruff scratching along my sensitive skin. My breathing is ragged, and I try to catch it, my heart so full I can't think straight. A hand lifts, and I brush my fingers through his hair, a small laugh leaving my lips. His head lifts, and he looks at me, a brow raised.

"I guess having only one bed really was lucky, wasn't it?" I ask, and that shit-eating grin spreads across his face.

"The luckiest," he says, before we both burst into loud, raucous laughter that, sooner than later, is replaced by soft moans and heavy breathing as we start everything all over again.

# TWENTY-SIX

# GRAHAM

Light streams into the room, pulling me from the deepest sleep I've had in some time. I'm warm and groggy and confused as I come back to the land of the living and even more so when I open my eyes, not recognizing the room. It's not the luxury long-term rental in Seaside Point I've been staying in for a few months.

That's when I realize the warmth is not the sun or even the summer weather, but a body.

Suddenly, the night comes back to me.

The concert, realizing I am into her in a way I couldn't ignore any longer, and then there being only one available hotel room. June handing me that coin to decide what we'd do next, then not even bothering to check the results of her game of chance before I pulled her into me and kissed her the way I've been dying to for weeks.

Now she's tucked against my side, feeling like she's always been there, always belonged there. I thought if I ever crossed the line with her, I'd feel panicked. I'd feel shame or embarrassment for my lack of control or be anxious about whether I made the wrong choice.

But instead, I simply feel this strange sense of belonging, something I've never really experienced anywhere. It's something that I have a feeling June brings with her everywhere she goes, but I never thought I would be so damned lucky to feel myself.

What feels even better is when her face moves, rubbing on my chest, a small mewl leaving her lips that has my cock instantly hardening.

Fuck, this woman is everything to me.

"Morning," I murmur tentatively, still unsure what her reaction will be. She was sober last night, but it was a long day, and for all I know, when she wakes up without the exhaustion from the sun, she might have a different perspective on what happened last night. She might want to forget what happened and move on completely. If so, I'll be disappointed, but like everything with June Taylor, I'll give her whatever she wants.

I hold my breath as she lifts her head, her eyes hazy as she blinks a few times, trying to wake up.

Then it happens.

Her lips spread, her eyes going warm, her body shifting until her entire chest is pressed against mine, her body lying on top of me.

"I kind of thought that was a dream," she says, voice croaky with sleep.

"A dream?"

"A good one. A great one."

I can't help it—I smile down at her, a hand lifting to push her hair back. At some point, we took a shower together, so it's smooth and free of the gems, but her hair is so thick that it's still a bit damp in some places.

"Does that happen often, you dreaming about me fucking you into the mattress?"

A blush burns across her cheeks, and it looks so fucking pretty.

"Maybe once or twice."

I groan, then move, rolling her beneath me and pressing my lips to hers before looking at her seriously.

"How are you feeling?" I ask.

"Good. Really good. You?"

"Fan-fucking-tastic. I woke up with you in my bed," I inform her.

"Not a bad way to wake up. We uh," she looks at me, her teeth sinking into her plush lower lip. "We should do it more often." I'm silent as I stare at her. "I mean, if you want, of course. I'm not sure—"

I dip my head, pressing my lips to hers to quiet her before pulling back. When I do, she's a bit dazed, but I don't hesitate to explain, not when this is so important.

"I told you, June. It changed everything for me. This has been a long time coming, and we both know it."

She hums contentedly, melting a bit, and my body eases with the sound, like even that small bit of making her happy heals something inside of me.

"Oh. Well, good," she says with a little smile. I laugh, shaking my head, then dip it to press my lips to her temple.

"It seems like I was right after all," I say, pressing kisses anywhere I can find. Her shoulder. Her cheek, her jaw, her eyelid. I want to taste her and feel her everywhere I can. It's not even really sexual. It's more like, now that I have her, I want to touch her, make sure she's real and not going anywhere, that she's mine.

"What were you right about?"

"We aren't friends," I say, pressing my lips against her ear. Her entire body stills, and I lift my head, looking into her eyes as my free hand lifts, pushing her hair back. "We are so, so much more than that."

She smiles then, wide and genuine.

"Oh, you're good at this, aren't you?"

"Only for you." It's not an agreement, but also not a denial, and I shift to my side, pulling her into me.

"So, you've been into me?" she asks after a moment, a smile on her lips.

"Don't be cute, June. You know I've been in you."

"I'm always cute, Graham," she counters, that wide, contagious grin on her lips.

I fought it for weeks, trying not to give in to her friendship and joy, to bite back smiles, desperate not to encourage her, but the day at the Seabreeze when she lit up, cheering just because I gave her a mere smile, I decided I couldn't do any longer.

"How long?"

"How long?"

"How long have you been in me? I mean, I know there was that one night at your place, but...after that you were so...cold."

I lift my hand, tucking her hair back behind her ear.

"I needed to be that to keep my sanity. I was losing it before you walked in for your first day, and I knew being around you nonstop would only make it worse. If I gave in then, I'd never get anything done."

She lifts her eyebrow, and I figure it won't hurt to tell her at least *some* of my secrets.

"You coming into Daytrips that day was the luckiest moment of my life, but I wasn't going to rely on luck to find you."

"Oh?" I smile, looking down at her and brushing my lips against her forehead.

"No way. I went into Seaside Coffee every single morning before work, after the convenience store. I spent two hours there for a week, pretending to work, waiting to see if you would walk in."

Her face melts, her jaw going slack.

"Is that why Mrs. Miller gave you that weird look?"

The reason Mrs. Miller gave me that weird look when we went to the cafe was that I've been buying her out of donuts to make sure June could get the one she wanted, but I don't plan to tell her *that*.

"Yeah. It was probably strange, seeing a stranger in the place for hours at a time, then not at all." *Lie, lie, lie*, my mind yells, and for the first time since I started this scheme to give June everything she wants, panic moves through me.

Because now I have her, and I won't be letting her go.

But now, there are lies between us. White lies, on white lies, and probably a few that she would argue are on the edge of the gray area, but lies all the same.

When I offered her a job, I never anticipated we'd be back here again.

When I got the donuts, moved the four-leaf clovers, and bought her art, I never thought we'd be in bed together, that in just a few weeks, she would become my whole world. I thought I'd fall for her from afar, and it would stay that way until I left town, which is another thing I don't want to think about too closely.

As I sit there, panic rushing through me, June's phone blares out with a new message.

Then another.

And another and another.

"Fuck," she groans, her head settling on my chest as the tone of another new message fills the room.

"Is everything okay?" I ask because if I were getting back-to-back messages like that on Sunday morning, something terrible would be happening. She lets out a loud sigh, then shakes her head before rolling away from me, leaving me cold as she reaches for her phone. I plugged it in last night after we showered, had a round two, and June promptly passed out.

"Yeah, my DND turns off at nine am on Sundays, and my friends know it. It's just Claire and Lainey." She bites her lip and looks up at me. I lift an eyebrow. "They're asking for details."

I stare at her expectantly, not understanding her reluctant look.

"Is that okay?" she asks nervously after a moment. My brow furrows, unsure of what she means.

"Is there a reason it wouldn't be?"

"Well, you know. You're...my boss. And Claire is Sutton's sister, and they don't know how to keep a secret to save their lives, so..."

I see where she's going with this and want to quash whatever worries are brewing in her pretty little mind before they get out of hand. I reach out once more, grab her, and pull her back into me.

"They're your friends, June. You can tell them whatever you want."

"It won't be a problem? I mean, Sutton told me that there are no non-fraternization rules or anything, but...."

"Will you get in trouble?" she asks, and I shake my head.

"There's no rule about people having relationships at Daydream, but if there's a power dynamic, everyone needs to be informed. I'll tell Rowan on Monday."

"Oh, you're right, of course. Are you...Are you okay with that? I mean, if you want —"

"Do you want this to be a secret?" I ask, cutting her off before she can finish her sentence. If that's what she wanted, I'd give it to her, but God, I hope it's not what she wants.

"Is that what *you* want?" she asks, and I see that same masked nervousness on her face, and I relax just a bit. What a pair we are.

"That's not what I asked, June. I asked if *you* want things to be a secret." She bites her lip and looks at her phone, where it seems messages keep coming through. "The truth, June. Not what you think I would want to hear."

"I would enjoy this not being a secret. I want to show you off. But I also understand—"

Before she can finish the sentence, I'm rolling her onto me. She lets out a tiny squeal, then a giggle, as I sit up and settle her into my lap, shifting so my back is to the headboard. I'm grateful I slid on a pair of boxer briefs before I went to bed and that June slid on my tee, not because I don't want to feel her naked body against mine, but because it would be so terribly distracting. I'd never be able to finish this important conversation.

"You could have absolutely anything you ask of me, June. I'm weak to the tornado that is you. I would like things between us to be out and open, so no, I don't want a secret. I just wanted to make sure we were doing what *you* wanted."

"You'd say yes to anything?" she asks, lifting an eyebrow, and it's the main clue I need to know she has absolutely *no* idea what I've been doing behind the scenes for her. If she did, she'd realize just how humorous that question is.

"Anything," I state simply.

"Even... a beach day?" There's nervousness in the words, though I have no idea why.

"You in a bikini? I don't think you have to twist my arm, June," I laugh.

"My friends will be there. Everyone's meeting at the beach behind the Seabreeze this afternoon to unwind after a busy weekend." Without meaning to, I know my face changes a bit, and she sees it. "You can say no," she starts, trying to cover quickly, though I don't miss the disappointment that flashes across her face.

"No, no," I start, shaking my head, trying to push away the discomfort in my chest. "I just...I don't want to get in the way of you spending time with friends."

She licks her lips, setting a hand to my shoulder, the other coming up to brush my hair back. I lean into her touch, and she smiles a bit.

"Is this...is this going somewhere?"

"I really hope so," I answer honestly and instantly, making her smile wider.

"Then you're going to become a part of the crew. You don't just get one friend when you're tied to me. You get a bunch." I stare at her, uneasy at the idea of friends, but her warm smile spreads wide, and I can't hold onto my hesitancy much longer. "So that means this afternoon we're all going to the bay behind the Seabreeze for a grill and hang out, and it's going to be so fun. The girls will grill me, of course, but otherwise it will be smooth sailing. Claire gets off at noon today, and Lainey's dad is taking over at the Seabreeze for the night. It's the perfect, low-key way to reintroduce you to everyone as my...." She hesitates, unsure.

"As your..." I encourage.

"I just realized I have no idea what we are. I know we...you know...but I shouldn't have assumed—"

I cut her off, pressing my lips to hers, hard, before settling my forehead to hers.

"You're mine, June."

"Okay," she says, her words trailing off, unsure. "But what does that mean to you?"

I brush my thumb over her cheek, collecting my thoughts before spilling them.

"It means if I see you flirting with another man, I'll lose my mind." She rolls her lips into her mouth and tries to fight. a smile. "It means as many nights as possible, I want you sleeping in my bed." Her breathing hitches, and my hand slips under the back of the tee she's wearing, gilding over her hip and to her waist. "It means that even if we're busy, you force me to take lunch with you. It means I'm probably going to pull you into my office a few times a day to kiss you, because I've got an empty well that I need to fill. It means I'm going to push you with your business, and you're going to push me to focus on anything other than work occasionally, because we care about each other. It means you're mine."

"I can work with that," she says, voice husky. Her hips tip, and I know that neither of us will be able to concentrate much longer. "So when people ask, I say you're my..."

I slide my hand up and down her waist, my thumb brushing along her ribs.

"Whatever you want to call me, lady luck."

A soft breath leaves her lips at the term of endearment, the same way it has the other handful of times, and it makes me aspire to use it even more.

"Boyfriend?" She barks out a laugh at what I can only assume is a sharp look of distaste that crosses my face. "Not a fan of boyfriend. Is that because..." she starts, but I finish.

"Because I'm a thirty-four-year-old man, not a boy." That fire returns, and she licks her lips.

"Man friend?" she suggests.

"That sounds like I've been hired." She lets out another laugh. "How about your man?"

"Like the sound of that," she says. I settle my arms to her hips, sliding her as close to me as I can, chest to chest, her lips brushing mine.

"Is it important to you?

"Important to me?"

"Me going to the beach today," I clarify.

"Oh, hum...." she says, looking away, but I lift a hand, keeping her face directed to mine.

"It's important to you. It's important to you, so I'm there." Her eyes light up, and I know it was the right decision.

"Easy as that?"

"Anything important to you is important to me, June. I might be new at this friend thing, but I'm a quick learner." She licks her lips then, hips canting to rub along where I'm hard for her.

"I'm kind of turned on by how nice you're being right now," she murmurs.

"Mmm, I can do it more," I say, my hand moving to her hips and rubbing her along my length.

"No, I like when you're an asshole, too." I let out a laugh, then move to slide the shirt she's wearing off.

"How long do we have before we have to get out of here to make it to this thing on time?" Her words are breathy when she responds.

"We should be out of here before ten," she murmurs, the words ending in a moan as her hips continue to rock against me. I note that it's already 9:15 when I look at the clock.

"Then we'd better make this fast," I say, moving her to her back and starting to kiss down her belly.

We do.

And it's glorious.

# TWENTY-SEVEN

# June

We park at the Seabreeze before walking over to the bay behind it, my hand in Graham's. While I'd planned to change and pack a beach bag before heading over, we ended up taking a bit too long to get out on the road and only had time to get Graham a change of clothes at his place and grab my bag. Thankfully, I'd brought about three different changes of clothes because I'm an over-packer, so it worked out just fine. I had enough time to run inside, grab a bag, some towels, and waters before making our way to the beach behind the Seabreeze. Said bag is now looped over Graham's shoulder, something he insisted on holding for me, and something I know Grant will appreciate even if he's inevitably going to hate that I'm dating my boss.

And I am.

I am dating Graham Hawthorne. Every time I think about that fact, it makes me a little bit giddy, and I have to swallow the happiness down.

"This is a terrible idea," he murmurs when we round the corner and see the large group on the beach of the bay behind the Seabreeze.

It's my second-favorite beach down the shore, second only to the state park ten minutes from Seaside Point. It's where, most often, if we're craving a day in the sand, we meet up to avoid tourists.

"It's a great idea. A Band-Aid, rip it off," I tell him, squeezing his hand.

"Why does meeting your friends have to be painful?"

"You already met them. Stop being dramatic."

His steps falter, and I glace over my shoulder to find he's staring at me with a thick eyebrow raised.

"Did you just call me dramatic?"

I grin.

"Yes, now smile and stop looking like I brought you here at gunpoint. Hey, Claire," I say, waving at my best friend, who is watching us approach with rapt attention. She's sitting in Miles' lap in one of the mismatched Adirondack chairs Benny keeps back here, a smile playing on her lips.

"How was the festival?"

"Amazing," I say.

"I can see that," Lainey says, barely hiding a smile of her own.

"Which part was better, the concert, or when Graham—" Claire starts.

"Okay, none of that. Let's get this over with. Yes, Graham and I are dating. No, I will not give anyone any details here," I direct that specifically to Claire, who pouts while Miles lets out a laugh. My brother is standing with his arms crossed on his chest, dark sunglasses perched on his nose, a scowl on his face. "And you, I don't want to hear anything from you. You might act like my dad, but you're not. Don't make this weird. None of you make this weird, okay?"

I expect an argument or at least some kind of snide remark, but I don't. Instead, Benny, Lainey's dad, takes out the pipe he pretends to smoke but really just blows bubbles with, and waves it around.

"Well, you heard the girl," he says. "Everyone skedaddle. Let the boy breathe *before* we give him the third degree." He directs his look to me, "But June, girl, you know just as well as I do, the kid's gonna get the third degree at some point."

"Did he just call me a kid?" Graham asks low.

"You get used to it,' I say, then pull him onto the sand where I kick off my shoes. "You can set the bag down over there," I say, tipping my chin. "But can you get me the sunscreen?"

"Here we go," Lainey grumbles, and I snap my head to her. She's in a beach chair, her fair skin complemented by a dark red bathing suit, and, if I know my best friend, she's not wearing any sunscreen, despite definitely needing it.

"Lainey, I know for some reason you love getting sunburned like, once a week, but some of us want to live to be a hundred and three."

Graham hands me the sunscreen, and I take off my cover-up, smearing the white stuff around my arms until it blends in.

"A hundred and three?" Graham asks, a bit alarmed, and I just smile.

"Yeah, I think that sounds like a good number."

"That means you'll have to live to…what?" Sutton asks, looking at Graham. "One hundred and eleven?" A look of horror crosses Graham's face. "You wouldn't want to leave poor June to be alone."

I look to the sky and groan.

"Sutton! Stop! I told you guys to be cool! You can't scare him this fast; we've only been together for a day!"

"And a month, if you count the time you guys fucked each other's brains out before you—" Claire starts.

"LA LA LA," I nearly scream, glaring at Claire as I glance at my brother. He's talking to Deck, and I pray to all that's good in the world he didn't hear. "I said no details!"

"You said no *asking* for details. I already knew those." I glare at her and her love of loopholes.

"How are we friends?" I ask, moving to my legs.

"We're not. We're best friends. There's a lot more room for being obnoxious when you're best friends." I roll my eyes, but I don't argue. She's right: best friends are basically sisters you choose for yourself, and from my understanding, sisters are supposed to be the most beloved and most irritating people on the planet. With a sigh, I turn to Graham, deciding to just move past it.

"Shirt off. Let me put sunscreen on you so you can live to be a hundred and eleven," I say, fighting back a smile. Lainey fails, a loud laugh leaving her lips, but it turns into a choked cough as Graham takes off his shirt.

Well, that's one way to shut them up.

"Oh my god," Claire says.

"I know," I respond, almost begrudgingly, because I know the magnificent hotness that is Graham without his shirt on. Slowly, I start spreading sunscreen on his back.

"But...how?" Lainey asks in a breath.

"No idea. It's wild, right?"

"Do you think Rowan is like this?" Sutton asks, seemingly half-alarmed and half intrigued, before she blinks and shakes her head with disgust. "Actually, no. I don't want to know. I wouldn't be able to work with him anymore."

I finish rubbing sunscreen into his back and hand him the bottle to do mine.

"Maybe Lainey should do it. I think I should—" Graham starts, looking over his shoulder, concerned, before moving to step away, but Sutton lifts her hands, and he halts in place.

"No," she says. "Stay there, don't move. Another five seconds. Actually..." She turns to me. "Do you have paper?"

"Absolutely not. That's enough for that." I take the sunscreen back and hand it to Lainey, who begrudgingly stands to lotion me.

"Draw him. I beg," Claire says, hands clasped before her, standing from where she's sitting.

Miles shakes his head and sighs before standing as well. "Wanna get a beer? Save you from all of...this?"

Graham looks from Miles to my friends, then back, and nods.

"Yes, please."

Miles looks to me with a solemn nod. "I'll make sure everyone plays nice."

"Please and thank you! I'll owe you if we make it out of here in one piece!"

He salutes me, and I laugh before turning to the girls.

"Okay, now tell me everything," Sutton says low, eyes eager as she cracks open a drink for me and she hands it over. I take a long chug, needing the courage to survive the next hour.

Then I tell my best friends everything.

The afternoon is great. Perfect, even, with everybody getting along and smiling and joking. At some point, Miles gets a football and starts tossing it with Graham, which is when we learn that his high school team went to States when he was a kid and that he was the quarterback.

"Oh, I need those pictures," I say low. "Do you have them?"

"No way," Graham says, not even bothering to look at me. "They're buried deep where you're never going to find them."

"That's probably what June said last night," Claire says, and Graham chokes, missing the ball Deck threw his way.

"Jesus, fuck, Claire, can you not?" Grant groans, turning a bit green. "I'm trying to be cool, but it's really hard."

"Also, what she—" Thankfully, Miles slams his hand on Claire's mouth, muffling her words. I'm sure he's going to get an earful later from her, but I'm grateful.

"Are they buried because you're so old and they didn't have technology back then?" I ask, trying to shift the focus.

"He's what, a year older than me?" Grant says, oddly and unexpectedly, sticking up for Graham. I knew they would eventually get along, since they are very similar in both personality and work ethic, but this came sooner than expected. Though I suppose that, with this crew being very much boys-versus-girls, another person on his team would be a relief.

"Exactly. Old." Lainey says deadpan. I really need to figure out what's going on there.

"Tomorrow I'll get Josie on it. If anyone can find them, she can," Sutton says.

"I'm so intrigued by this woman. A secret spy, apparently hot as shit, nailed down Rowan...I need to meet her. I think I want to be her when I grow up," Claire says.

"She'll be here with Rowan early next week," Graham says.

"Really?" I ask, clasping my hands together. I've heard a lot about Josie, the undercover PI who works for a super-secret firm that you can't just contact, but you have to know people who know people. They call her the Maneater because she's so hot and a huge flirt, and she has a personal skill for getting men to tell her whatever information she needs to solve a case. She met Rowan last year while undercover as a vacationer at the Keys location to figure out who was sabotaging it.

"Yeah, he'll be here Monday after the grand opening."

"How are you feeling about that?" Grant asks, and Graham shrugs.

"Opening day is different for each location, but I fully anticipate at least a few hiccups."

I knock on the wood table, a long, picnic-style table built years ago after our crew kept on growing. It could probably fit ten more people, and a part of me has always pictured Lainey and me sitting here with our partners and our kids when we're older, carrying on the tradition of summers behind the Seabreeze.

"Don't jinx it!" I say, and he puts an arm around me, pulling me into his side and pressing his lips to my hair.

"Not jinxing it. It's my job to prepare for anything."

I lift an eyebrow at him.

"Who's superstitious now?" I ask, and he smiles at me. My own melts off my face with Claire's words, though.

"Since we're talking about work stuff, how's the proposal coming?"

My entire body stills.

"Claire—"

"What proposal?" Graham asks.

"Nothing, I—" I start again, but Claire cuts me off.

"We want June to bid on the mural project."

Graham nods, and my jaw tightens.

"Oh, the one that bitch is doing?"

Grant chokes on a chip, letting out a loud laugh.

"I forgot you met Cecelia! Yes, her. I want June to beat her ass, not only because June is a million times more talented, but because I don't want that bitch to have anything good in her life. Wouldn't it be absolutely amazing to be able to shove that in her face?" Claire asks, but I have a counterargument, one I've been weighing for a while and, in my humble opinion, is a solid one.

"And would it not be terribly embarrassing if she were to get it instead of me?" I ask, but Lainey shakes her head.

"No, because she won't. She might have her dad voting for her, but he's the only one. You're just a big fat scaredy cat who's afraid of rejection."

"I am not!" I argue like a child, but when Graham reaches out under the table, twining his fingers with mine, I wonder if maybe I am, and even he knows it. "Wasn't me opening my shop enough?"

It sounds like a whine even to me.

"No," Claire says, bluntly.

"I don't even know how to make a proposal for something like that," I sigh, even though in moments of bravery, I've found and begun replicating other successful mural bids.

"Lucky for you, you're fucking a businessman."

"Jesus Christ, Claire, can you chill?" Grant asks, groaning and putting a hand over his ears.

"Oh, come on. Look at them. She's hot. He's hot. If they weren't fucking, I'd be concerned."

"I'm concerned that you feel the deep need to remind me of that every other moment."

Claire grins wide and I know what's coming next.

"I'm sure she felt the deep—"

"Okay, okay, enough," Lainey says, putting all of us out of our misery now. "Let's stop before we completely scare Graham off. What I think Claire was trying to say is that Graham probably knows how to put a great business plan together, so June has no excuse not to follow through."

"I'm more than happy to help. You know I think your art is fantastic," Graham says. "I was just telling her I want her to do a mural at Daytrip."

I bite my lip. "It's really not—"

"I actually think moving into murals is a good idea," Grant says, and I snap my head toward him.

"You do?"

"Well, yeah. I mean, your art business is going pretty well. It makes sense to do so a large contract. You could garner more interest in your business, and it would essentially be free advertising."

A familiar nervous energy churns in my gut.

"Yeah, but art is...art is just a hobby."

He looks at me oddly, reading my face, and my stomach tightens, unsure of what he's going to say, but before he can speak, a little bit of luck interrupts.

"A ladybug!" I call when the red and black beetle lands on my arm. "A ladybug!"

"Let me guess, it's good luck." Grant says, utter exhaustion in the word. I glare at my brother, but he just grins, immune to my laser eyes.

"My luck has been treating me very well thus far, thank you very much." Graham's hand tightens in mine, and I look at him, smiling.

"I think this means you should submit your proposal," Graham says, putting a hand on my thigh.

I glare at him.

"That is not what it means." I roll my eyes, then turn my attention to the bug.

"You found a four-leaf clover and made your shop live. This is basically the same thing."

I scrunch my nose but don't respond.

"You did that?" Claire asks, a mix of irritation and shock on her face.

"Maybe?" Graham says, rightfully hesitant.

"I'd been trying to get her to open that shop for years. One day, it's live, and she's selling prints out of nowhere. You're telling me all it took was a hot guy?" I shrug, grinning at my friend.

"A hot guy, a four-leaf clover, and a pep talk."

"Well, happy you're here, then, Graham. You're good for our girl." Graham looks at me, smiling.

"She's even better for me."

# TWENTY-EIGHT

# GRAHAM

We make it three days before I get the opportunity to bring the mural up to June. I'd been biding my time, trying not to scare or pressure her, but after doing some research on my own, I saw the deadline is in just two weeks, so I couldn't wait endlessly until the perfect moment. It doesn't help that we've both been terribly busy. She's been staying at my rental with me since it's closer to the office, only stopping home to get some things and bring them to mine. But on Wednesday morning, I got my opening when she asked if we could spend the night at her place so she could pack some orders.

"Do you mind if I take a quick shower?" she asks as we reach her door after walking four flights of stairs, since the elevator is broken. She pulls out a set of keys, a dozen colorful keychains on it, before unlocking her door and pushing it open. "I know you've never been here, but I feel so grimy from being outside sweating all day." We finally reach her door, and she pulls out a set of keys, a dozen colorful keychains on it, before unlocking her door and pushing it open.

"Of course," I say distractedly. My mind tumbles over thoughts and ideas, wondering just how much maneuvering I would have to do for June to hit another patch of luck in the form of her apartment implementing some new improvements.

"I think I can manage being alone in your place for thirty minutes."

"I don't know: you might have sensory overload. It's very different than your place," she says with a smile, but when I peek into her apartment, it's exactly how I expected.

Bright and colorful, a bit cluttered, not because she's messy but because she doesn't have space to display all of the things she loves, the things that bring her joy. Art and photos cover the walls, and all of her furniture is either brightly colored or covered in a blanket that is. No surface is bare, and somehow, without even asking, I know each and every print or tchotchke or art piece has some kind of meaning, intentionally chosen or created so some small part of June's soul can be on display for the world to see.

"I know, it's a lot," she murmurs, setting her bag down and then reaching to pull the clip from her hair. Her long waves tumble down, and with the backdrop of her home, her clear labor of love, she fits perfectly.

"It's great," I say honestly, looking around as I step to her. "It's very June." My eyes catch on a horseshoe overhead, and while she's told me a bit about her childhood, I don't remember horses being part of it. "Do you ride?" I ask, tipping my chin toward it.

She laughs, shaking her head.

"No, I've never ridden a horse. I live in Seaside Point; it's not exactly horse girl central."

"But you want to?" I ask, desperate to understand her. Something tells me I could do this all day, asking about everything here and learning all of her secrets, her wants, fears, and hopes.

"Also no," she says with a laugh, moving toward what I assume is her bedroom. I follow, and she explains. "Horses are terrifying. Have you ever seen how freaking big they are? They can jump over huge things, and they're super-fast and easily spooked. No, thank you."

I laugh, shaking my head and sitting on the edge of her bed, covered in a blue patchwork quilt, as she moves to her drawers, pulling out an oversized shirt and panties. I note with contentment that she does *not* pull out a pair of pants or shorts.

"Then what's with the horseshoe?" I ask.

She grins at me over her shoulder.

"It's good luck. You're supposed to hang one upside-down over your doorway like that to catch the luck."

"I should have known," I say, and she nods, then bites her lip.

"Do you need anything at all? I'm thinking we can just order in from the sandwich place down the road, if that works for you, because I do not want to leave this place until morning."

I nod, pulling out my phone to get the info.

"All good. Enjoy your shower. Just tell me what you want, and I'll order it while you're in there."

"You really are perfect, aren't you? Can you order the chicken Caesar salad wrap for me? It's my second favorite."

"Second favorite?"

She lifts a shoulder, grabbing her bundle of clothes.

"Sometimes they have this tomato and burrata sandwich that is what my actual dreams are made of, but it's a special, and they rarely have it. It's late, so even if they had it today, they're probably out."

"Got it. One chicken Caesar salad wrap, coming up," I say with a grin, standing and pulling her in to me to press my lips to hers before stepping away and ushering her off. "Now go; shower."

She does as I demand, and as soon as the shower starts, I lift the phone to my ear to make a call, wandering into the living room area just in case.

I should stop.

Now that we're more than coworkers and friends, I should absolutely stop this game of making the world work in her favor.

But it brings her so much damn joy, and I can't seem to find it in me to.

"Sandy Shore Sandwiches, how can I help you?" a bright and cheery female voice answers.

"Hey, I'm looking to place an order, but I was wondering if there's any way you can make a burrata and tomato panini? Just one. I'll pay as much as you need, triple the normal price, whatever you need."

Because if June Taylor wants something, I'm going to make sure she gets it.

"How's the business going?" I ask, closing my laptop later that night. When I told June that the shop just so happened to have one of her favorite sandwiches, she squealed with excitement, making the fact that it took an extra thirty minutes and four times the list price to get here completely worth it. Now she's finishing packaging her orders while I sent off a few emails.

"Amazing," she says with a laugh, disbelief still in the word. It cuts something in me, the fact that she's surprised her business is thriving when it's clear to everyone around her just how damn talented she is. "I can't believe it's growing so fast."

"I can," I say, and I mean it. I have one of her pieces hanging in my office at the Daydream headquarters in Hudson City, and, according to Sutton, at least five people have asked her where I got it. I hadn't intended to buy it, simply checking the morning after she told me about her plan to see if she had actually opened her shop. But when I saw the ocean landscape, I instantly knew it was Seaside Point, and I needed some small reminder of this town that has both given me intense headaches and made me feel more challenged and fulfilled than ever before. It's a shock, the tiny location I felt so annoyed to be assigned to, becoming my favorite project to date, but it's the truth all the same.

And even more of a shock that I never want to leave.

I get it, now, what June is always saying about this place being magical.

I'm thinking about that when I spot a sketchpad with *Welcome to*

*Seaside Point* drawn across the center. Instantly, I know that, despite her dismissal, this is one of her ideas for the mural Claire has been hounding her about.

"What is this?" I ask, and she turns to me, her hair in a messy bun on top of her head, her oversized Seaside Point High School shirt just barely covering her ass.

"Oh, that's nothing," she says with a quick shake of her head, reaching for the paper and trying to pull it away. I don't let her, though, grabbing her wrist, stopping her retreat. She lets out a deep sigh, explaining before I even have to ask a second time. "It's one of the sketches I have for the proposal."

"One of?" she rolls her eyes, tugging her arm back and crossing them on her chest.

"Don't tell Claire, but I *have* been trying to put something together. Just to see if I could," she justifies quickly, biting her lip. "I don't think I'm actually going to submit it."

"Can I see it?" I ask. I expect her to argue, to tell me no, and to make me get creative with how I move forward with this, but instead she sighs, moves to her old laptop on the kitchen table, and pulls it up. I sit in front of it and start scrolling, instantly shocked at how much she's actually accomplished on this.

It's not just her messing around in her downtime: she's almost finished the proposal, including three different fully colored variations of the mural.

"This is actually very good, June," I say, looking over the actual proposal, which includes the length of time, the cost of materials, and what other provisions she would need from the town. "The price is a bit low." I go back to the top and begin looking through the pages with a keen eye, as I would with any business proposal. "And you need to make sure you're including any local resources you might need to use."

"Local resources?" she asks, looking over my shoulder.

I turn, put my hands on her hips, pull her into my lap, then point to the map she included, showing where the mural is planned.

"That location is in a busy area—if people decide to stop and watch you, it's going to cause an issue with traffic. You might need an officer or two to be on standby or monitor traffic for you."

"I didn't think of that," she says, seeming embarrassed, but I shake my head.

"You wouldn't have," I say, with a shake of my head. "Most wouldn't, unless they've been doing this kind of thing for a while. I have, so I know. I don't think most others would include that, which might set you apart in the final decision process. Not that you need an edge, June. This design right here is the clear winner." I look over it again, awe in my words. It's colorful and vibrant, showcasing the community and some of the town's landmarks for locals and tourists alike. It perfectly encapsulates the town, and more importantly, the way June sees it. I smile when I spot a few of her lucky symbols tucked in there, as well—a rainbow and a ladybug. "If it's not chosen, you should sell prints. It's amazing, June."

"It's just a rough draft,' she murmurs, trying to downplay her ability as usual.

"No, it's not," I say firmly.

"Yes—"

"June, don't lie to me. Friends don't do that." I press my lips to her neck, and her breath hitches.

"And we're friends," she asks, voice going breathy, lifting a hand behind her and holding my head to her.

"We're so much more than friends, lady luck," I murmur, pulling the laptop closer. "Come on. Let's finish this."

"Finish?"

"You lied to your friends the other day—you already have the proposal done; you just haven't submitted it. You're going to finish it and submit it right now."

"Graham," she starts, but I shake my head.

"No. Because if you don't just do it, you're never going to. You're scared, but I'm right here to help you be brave."

There's a moment of hesitation before her words go soft, nervous. "I just don't think I know what I'm doing. I'm fully unqualified."

"That's not true, but even if it was, it would solely be the business aspect of it you're not well-versed in. And lucky for you, you have me. Now, let's finish it. Start with the pricing." My hand moves to her thigh, and I squeeze her bare skin. "Come on, June. The faster we do this, the faster I can get you in bed." She takes in a heavy breath, the sound shaky, not with nervous energy this time, but something different.

"Graham, let's do this later. We have better things to do." She wiggles her ass into my crotch to prove her point. I'm already growing hard for her, and I think she thinks she can tempt me into giving in, but I think she greatly underestimates just how long I've had to ignore the attraction always brewing in my gut for her.

"We do, and once we get this done, we can move on to those better things." I tighten my fingers around her lush, soft thigh.

"This isn't important," she starts, but I stop her.

"Nothing is more important than chasing your dream, June. Nothing. Now." My hand slides up, my thumb grazing along the center of her panties, over her center. "Be a good girl and show me what you've done on your proposal so far." Her breath catches, and a tiny mewl leaves her lips. The sound travels straight to my dick, making it jump, but I'm enjoying this game far too much, and I want to win.

"Graham—"

"Now, June." My thumb grazes over her clit, and I dip my head to press another kiss to her neck. "Pricing. We have to factor in the time and the cost of goods. What do you have for the projected expenses?"

She sighs, then opens a spreadsheet. I'm again impressed to see she has outlined it well, including the basic cost of materials, plus tiers for different levels of quality, her hourly rate, which should *absolutely* be higher, and the cost of the machinery she would need.

"This is good," I say, my hand sliding up, then down her thigh. "This is really good, baby." I cup her pussy in reward, and she lets out a breath, hips shifting forward into my hand. "You need to increase this number." I lift my free hand and point to her hourly rate as if I'm not pushing one finger against her entrance over her panties. "And add ten percent more materials than you think you need."

"I don't want to take advantage," she says, and somehow, her not brushing me off and going with this is even more of a turn on.

"And you also don't want to undershoot the cost and have to eat it. Trust me." She looks over her shoulder at me, a bit confused and unsure, before starting to do some calculations and adjusting the numbers. In response, my hand shifts, my thumb meeting her clit over her underwear and starting to rub there gently.

"Graham," she murmurs.

"Mmm."

"What are you doing?"

"Giving you some motivation."

"Graham—" she breathes, but my finger slides over her again, this time pressing harder on her clit, and she lets out a small moan.

"Now start taking those projected expenses and put them into your proposal. They look logical to me, and if I were the one hiring this out, it's around what I would expect for a project this large." She looks over her shoulder at me, and then I see it: the sparkle. The joy, the love of poking at me, of making my life complicated, of teasing and irritating me. Her desire to rise to my challenge and beat me at my own game.

She's all in now.

Her fingers move on the keyboard, editing and changing some things, seeking my encouragement and advice on others, comparing formatting to other successful bid applications she found online. She's a natural, and it makes sense, since these are things I've had her do in her day-to-day work over the last few weeks. It seems her day job has just been preparing her for her dream job.

"Next is the timeline," I say, and watch as she starts to organize her already-written outline for what the entire project would look like from start to finish, from priming the wall to sketching the design.

She's done with the hard work and over the hurdle of fighting me. Knowing that the rest is mostly formatting and finishing the actual proposal, I decide she deserves a reward.

Shifting, I lift her a bit, using a hand to tug her panties until they're a bundle at our feet. Then I settle us back down, lifting one of her legs and sliding it over my knee. I repeat the process until she's in my lap, spread wide across my legs.

"Graham—" she stutters,

"Be good, June, and I'll reward you." Sliding a hand up her inner thigh, I splay a hand over her center, the tip of my middle finger grazing her entrance, and groan into her neck at how soaked she already is.

"How am I supposed to—"

"Because you're a good girl and you do what you're told," I say, nipping her ear, sucking the dangling ladybug earring she wore today into my mouth. As I do, I slide that middle finger into her, letting it settle there. She tightens and groans, and I bite back one of my own, but I don't move anymore.

"Come on, June. Finish the timeline."

"You're just going to..." she starts, but I push the finger deeper, the heel of my palm pressing on her clit, and she lets out a real, unfiltered moan.

"Yes. Until you do as you're told, now finish up the timeline. The faster we do this, the faster I get to bend you over this table and fuck you into it." To my utter fucking delight, she does as I instruct. The work is almost completely done and just needs a few small tweaks I can help her make, and as she does, I slowly move my finger in and out of her. Her breathing is getting more and more ragged. We work for nearly ten minutes, and by the time she's just about done, she's soaked and panting. Her hips are rocking now, though any time she tries to get too much or gets too distracted, I tighten a hand on her hips, stopping her movement.

"How do I even know we're doing this right?" she asks, breathy.

"I've been getting my job done with the distraction of you for weeks, June. I'm basically an expert at this point." It's the truth, too. "And I'd never let you do anything that wouldn't guarantee you get the job you deserve."

"I don't—" I slide my finger out and then back in, adding a second one, harder and deeper than before, and she lets out a low moan, tightening around them. Thank god this torture is almost over.

"All done. Now export it and attach it to the email," I murmur, fingers deep inside of her, gliding over her G-spot. Her head falls back, her breathing ragged, her hips shifting. I've learned June's body well in just the few days we've been together, and I know that to come, she needs my thumb on her clit. Without giving that to her, I could have her teetering on this edge for some time.

"Graham, please."

"Do you want a reward, baby?" I murmur, pressing kisses to her neck. "Something to incentivize you to get the job done?"

"Yes," she breathes. "God, yes. Get the job done."

I know inherently the reward I'm going to give her is not what she's expecting, but that's what she gets for not being specific. In business, you have to know exactly what you want and ask for it explicitly. I take my wet hand from her, then move between us, shifting to slide my shorts down until my cock bobs free. Then I settle, using one hand on her hips to encourage her to lift, the other to my cock as I slowly guide her onto me. The moan that leaves her lips is full and loud, complete and utter delight and relief as I stretch her. I have to fight every instinct not to divert from my plan, not to push her face down into his table and fuck her into oblivion before she hits submit.

Instead, I take in a deep breath and bite back a moan as she tightens around me. Seated on my cock, my hand moves between her legs to play over her clit ever so gently and ever so slowly. It's swollen and needy, the result of twenty minutes of playing with her cunt, not letting her hit the peak she desperately craves. With each pass, she tightens over me, the sensation absolutely torturous, but I know it's still not enough to make her come.

"Attach the file to an email, June." My head drops, lips pressing against her neck. Her pulse throbbing, her breathing erratic, her hands slowly attaching the file to the email.

"Now write a short note," I say, forcing my voice to sound neutral despite the throbbing of my cock inside of her. It's not just June that's in the most blissful, hellish state: I'm right there with her.

"Graham, how the hell—"

"To Whom It May Concern," I say, my voice low even to my own ears. "I have attached my proposal for the Third Street mural to this email." I lift my hips, pushing myself a bit deeper into her.

"Graham!" she shouts, head snapping back, her own hips shifting. I take one hand and grip her jaw, tilting her head toward the screen.

"To Whom It May Concern," I repeat through gritted teeth. My other hand moves, gripping her hips and holding her in place, not trusting myself not to throw away the plan and fuck her without abandon until we both come. Before I can second-guess myself, though, her shaky hands began to move, tapping out my words. I guide her through writing a concise, curt email, and she types it out, signing off with her name.

In reward, I brush my fingers over her clit, enough to give her something, but not enough to make her come.

"You're doing so well, baby. Now hit send, June."

She groans.

"Are you blackmailing me with sex?"

"Sure, if that's what you want to call it. Either way, until you take this step and are brave, I'm not going to let you come."

"Graham," she says, hips grinding back into me, taking me just a bit deeper, and I try not to let out a noise, any kind of sign that I'm tipping closer to the edge. "This is ridiculous. Just fuck me."

"Hit send," I say. I slide a hand down, gripping her inner thigh hard, in a way that will probably leave a small bruise in the morning. She whimpers, but it must be the motivation she needed to slide the mouse down and hit send.

"That's my good girl," I say in a growl, then reach up, slamming her laptop shut and pushing the computer away from us.

Without warning, I lift her, then slam in deep. Her legs are still hooked over mine, so she's stretched over my lap and full of my cock. Her head flies back as she cries out, but it's not until I put my hand between her legs and start to stroke her clit as I fuck her from beneath her that she comes, tightening like a vise and then screaming out my name as she comes in just moments. It's glorious to hear, and even better to feel.

"Fuck!" she shouts, body quaking over mine as relieved moans leave her lips.

"Yeah, June. That's it, Fuck, you feel so good, coming around my cock," I grit out. I could come, too, but she deserves more than just one hard orgasm after that.

When she comes down from her high, she looks over her shoulder with hazy eyes and a smile.

"I can't believe you just did that," she murmurs. I grin, but don't have the brainpower to speak. Instead, I shift us, putting an arm around her waist and standing with her still attached to me. Sliding the computer out of the way, I lay her belly on the table, my cock still planted in her.

"Oh my god, ah!" she moans as I pull back nearly entirely and slam in hard and deep. "Fuck!"

"Fuck yeah," I groan, taking an ass cheek in each hand and gripping tight, using the hold to push and pull her on my throbbing cock. "Fuck yeah, June. God, you should see this." She tightens around me as she moans into the table. "You're gonna come again, aren't you?"

"Fuck, yes, yes, yes!" she cries, her fingers white as she grips the edge of the table. Her legs are barely touching the floor as I pound in, each thrust pulling another moan from her lips. A hand slides up her back, leaving her hip, and wraps her dark hair around my fist, tugging back until she's forced to look at me.

"Do you know how much you fucking turn me on? Everything you do, June, is absolute torture. So fucking smart, talented, and beautiful. Absolutely brilliant, the perfect woman for me." She starts to mutter incoherently, and when I know I can't hold it any longer, my hand moves from her hip, sliding down and around to strum her clit hard and fast, causing her to tighten instantly.

"That's it, lady luck. God, you look so good like this, taking everything I give you. Do you like it?"

"Oh fuck, yes, I love it!" she shouts, sending me closer. "Fuck me, Graham. Come in me, please."

"You first," I order, then pinch her clit. Her entire body tenses as she follows my command, and I can't hold back any longer, sinking in deep as she comes around me and filling her with my cum.

It's the most erotic moment of my life, something that will be burned onto my brain for eternity, but somehow, instinctively, I already know we're going to top it again and again for the rest of our lives.

She lies there, catching her breath, and I stay planted deep, not wanting to leave her warmth just yet. In a moment, I'll slide out, carry her to her bed, and then get a cloth to clean her, but first I need to get the oxygen back into my brain. After a moment, she looks over her shoulder with a goofy smile on her lips.

"Who knew business proposals would turn you on so much?" she says.

My head falls back as a deep, free laugh fills the room.

# TWENTY-NINE

# GRAHAM

"Oh, my fucking *god*," June shouts, taking me deep as I fuck her, ass lifted into the air, back arched deeply, and face to the mattress. My fingers dig into her thick hips, denting the flesh there as I groan through gritted teeth. She moves, thrusting back into me, and I let go of my hold, watching her ass move, taking my cock, taking me how she wants me.

"Fuck, yeah," I murmur, hands hovering as I watch her slap her ass against my thighs, taking me to the root each time. "You should see yourself, June. See how pretty you look fucking my cock like this."

She tightens, as she always does when I talk to her during sex, and I bite back a moan, knowing I won't last much longer.

"I need you to fucking get there, June," I groan, lifting a hand and sliding it down to between her legs, rubbing at her clit fast and hard.

"Yes!" she shouts, then tightens one last time before her entire body stills, her head snaps back, and her body quakes beneath mine as she comes. I groan into her neck, slamming in deep and filling her as I come. Eventually, I slide out of her, pulling a tiny moan from her as I do, then roll to my back beside where she has collapsed.

"What was that for?" I ask in a heavy breath. Her lips are spread wide with a smile, and she lifts a shoulder in a half-shrug.

"Wanted to start your day off on the right foot, a little bit of good luck."

"Yeah, I think that was definitely lucky," I say with a laugh. "It would be even luckier if I could convince you to take a shower with me." She gives a grin, wide and beaming, before shifting and sitting up, pressing her lips to mine.

"Your wish is my command," she says softly. I lift an eyebrow, and she laughs, shaking her head. "I don't think I can handle that again right now, but tonight, we can celebrate the perfect first day."

"Deal," I say, pressing my lips to hers before we get ready for opening day.

It turns out her plan didn't work; luck isn't on our side today. That much becomes clear the second we step foot into Daytrip. Callie, the GM we hired two weeks ago, comes up to us, a frantic look on her face, as we walk past the small photo-op spot June created this week. She's already made plans for a permanent mural on the side of the building along the sand, so both guests and tourists can take photos there, as well as one on the deck, exclusive to guests, but she wanted something fun for opening day.

"*It's not my best work,*" she said two days ago when she showed it to me after spending most of the day working on it while Sutton packed prize bags for the first one hundred guests who come in. "*But it will do.*"

I didn't bother to tell her that it was perfect, that I'd like to keep it and frame it once we're done with it, because I knew she wouldn't believe me, despite it being true. It's phenomenal, a mosaic of painted seashells and summer icons in an arch shape, with "I took a Daytrip" painted across the top in bright blue letters. The entire thing is bright and colorful, lighting up the space, with the social media information in the bottom corner, but even spotting that sunshine-y piece of art isn't enough to make me feel better about the look Callie is giving us.

"Jackson called out," she says, and I don't know who she's talking about, but June seems to, her eyes going wide.

"Oh no! What happened?"

"I don't know, but ten minutes later, Molly called in sick too. A stomach bug or something."

"Fuck," I say quick and sharp because I remember Molly to be the bartender. A handful were hired, but if I recall, Molly is the head bartender on today. Before I can say anything else, Callie's phone rings again, and her face goes pale as she lifts it.

"Hey, Lynn, how's—" She cuts off by someone speaking on the other end of the line, and her eyes close, a look of resignation coming over her face. "Oh no. Really? A stomach bug?" She pauses again. "Jackson and Molly are also sick." She pauses and then groans loudly. "Food poisoning? Shit, sorry, Lynn. No, no, I understand, there's nothing you can do." I want to argue, to tell her that they have to fucking come in because now we're three people down, but June tightens her hand in mine, bringing me back to reality. I can't take my stress out on the staff, not if I want things to work long term. "Feel better." She takes in a deep sigh before letting it out, and when she opens her eyes, desperation lies in the depths.

"So, that was Lynn," she says.

"Manager," June says in a stage whisper, leaning into my side.

"It seemed everyone went out to eat last night at Seawater Clams, and now everyone is sick."

"Why the fuck would they go there?" June asks with a groan. "Everyone here knows that place is a health inspector's nightmare."

"No idea, but they did, and now they're all sick."

Callie goes pale when her phone rings yet again. June groans. My pulse picks up, that gagging nervous energy turning into something much, much purer. "Hey, Liam. Oh, no, you, too?" My mind is reeling as I watch her accept another sick employee's excuses, and I barely notice June drop my hand, moving to her phone. When Callie hangs up, June is on a call.

"Call Trevor. I went to Molly's socials to see who they were with last night—four others were there. I'm calling Quinn now, but we need to know who won't be in today." I may be panciking, but June is clearly in figure-it-out mode. I watch, feeling utterly helpless as June and Callie make calls.

By the time they're done, seven of the nine employees they reach out to are sick and not coming in today. I'm beginning to spiral as Callie gets called off to something else, and June tells her we'll be in the office making plans, panic and misplaced anger rushing through me.

"We're fucked," I say, slamming the door to my office and beginning to pace. Unlike me, June is strangely calm.

"No, we're not," June says, moving to my computer without even asking, logging in, and then beginning to type. I'm not sure when or how she got my password, but she's friends with Sutton, and it seems they have nearly identical work styles.

"June, we have twenty people on today, and seven are sick, all of them higher up on the chain of command. We're fucked." She continues to type, biting her lip as she looks for something in her files before she grins, then stands. She reaches for me, stopping my pacing, and places a hand on each side of my face, and smiles at me. "We've got this, babe. We've got luck on our side."

It's times like these I realize my flaw in creating and faking her luck. She truly believes at this point that everything will work out in the end, while I'm much more based in reality.

"I think we're going to need a bit more than luck, June," I say, trying to be gentle despite the emotions bubbling inside me. I know this isn't anyone's fault, except for possibly a retaurant selling bad shellfish and still somehow in business.

"Well, good thing we also have friends," she says, so much optimism in her words. I look at her, confused, but before I can ask, she steps away, grabs her phone, making a call.

"Hey, babe, sorry, I know it's early for you, but is there any way you are off or could have Benny cover today?" She pauses, looking at her feet while she listens to the phone. "No, no, there's an emergency at Daytrip. Everyone is sick, and it's opening day. We need a bartender." Another moment of silence before her head lifts, her eyes locking on mine, a wide smile on her lips. "Oh, I could kiss you. You're the best!" Something akin to hope lights in my chest. "Let me call around, see what else we need, and I'll call you with a time. No earlier than noon, though, you can go back to sleep. Love you, thank you!" Then she hangs up and grins at me. "We've got a bartender."

"That's great, but we need a lot more," I say, trying to be realistic.

June just rolls her eyes. "And we've got a lot more friends, babe. Give me a sec."

*We've got friends.*

Her words roll through me, bringing a sweetness I'd never thought I'd actually experience myself, one I often feel when June is around. A mix of peace, hope, and satisfaction, I realize I've been reaching for for years, unsure how to attain it.

"They're not going to uproot their lives to help out. I can't expect that of them." Again, she gives me that soft smile, lifts to her toes to press a soft kiss to my lips, her hand on my cheek.

"The beauty of friends is you don't have to expect anything from them. When things hit the fan, they want to help. And I'm telling you, they'll want to help."

"June—"

"Give me ten minutes. If not, I'll call a temp agency. But I promise, this is all going to be fine, Graham."

I look at her skeptically, my anxiety not fully quelled, not when there's so much that could still go wrong.

"Do you trust me?"

The truth is, yes.

I trust June. I not only trust her with my career and what might be the most pivotal day in it, but I trust June Taylor with a whole lot more—like my heart.

"Yeah, June," I say low, stepping closer to her and pulling her into me. And when a wide, happy, beaming grin spreads across her face, I know it was the right choice.

Somehow, in four hours, June pulls it off.

I don't really understand how or why all of these people came to help, but they did. They dropped everything—Lainey and Benny and Miles and Mrs. Miller—all closing their own businesses for a bit to come, none of them expecting anything in return. However, I did inform June that, for safety and legal reasons, they would need to go through the quick process of being temporary hires for the day and would be paid accordingly. Strangely, everyone she pulled in tried to argue that fact, but Sutton reluctantly informed them it was procedure and unavoidable.

Every position is manned and then some, with June and Sutton running from zone to zone to go over quick protocols for each location.

Claire manages the beach aspect, bringing one of the Rec department's lifeguards with her. Lainey and Benny work as bartenders. Jonah and Decker handle the kids' club, Mrs. Miller mans the gift shop, and Grant, Sutton, and Miles help out wherever else we need. Claire and Sutton somehow even convinced their brother and his wife to help, since they were staying with Miles and Claire for the weekend.

Somehow, some way, the day is a success.

When the Mayor comes with his big scissors, June smiles, schmoozes him like a pro, and sets up the perfect shots for social media. Mayor Mosely insists I be in a few photos, and after two with just us, I pull June in, knowing she is the only reason this entire day wasn't a complete dumpster fire.

I've witnessed many opening-day catastrophes and employee issues. This is not the first time a large number of employees have gotten sick at the same time, though it's the first time this has happened on opening day. But this *is* the first time it's been resolved quickly, purely because people wanted to help out.

It's that Seaside Point magic at work once more.

It's after dinner when I finally let myself take in a deep breath. People are enjoying a meal on the deck or the beach, and Claire and her lifeguard are about to pack it in for the day. The second round of employees for the evening shift are here, as are a few who were sick but felt well enough to come in, though we told them they didn't have to.

It seems June is once again correct in that loyalty runs deep in this town.

They all want to help out, to see this place succeed. It's such a stark difference to the way I felt when I first arrived here, when all the locals murmured that this place was bad for the town, was just a cash grab that was going to hurt the locals. Now, just like June, they want it to succeed. June was right when she said we needed to get more involved in the town.

She must feel me watching her where she's running some crafts with the kids, because her head lifts, turning in my direction. When she sees me, she winks. I smile back, and her eyes go soft, but a kid runs at her, grabbing her hand and dragging her off before she can make her way to me. I watch her get pulled away laughing, completely enamored by her.

It sinks in fully then: I don't want to leave.

Ever.

I don't want to leave June or, strangely enough, Seaside Point. For the first time in my life, I belong somewhere and have this strange urge to root myself.

I want to spend every morning waking with June in my bed, and to go to bed every night hearing the waves crashing on the shore. I want to stay in Seaside Point for as long as this little town will have me.

I don't know what it means for my career or how Rowan will

react to the news when he comes next week, but I know in my gut it's the right choice. If I have to take a lower salary, commute to Hudson City, or find a new job altogether, I will.

I'm still mulling over this revelation, lost in my thoughts, when someone calling my name snaps me out of it. Decker and Grant are standing beside me, smiles on their faces. I wonder how long they've been there, watching me.

"Come on, have a beer with us," Decker says, tipping his head toward the bar where Lainey is laughing with a guest.

Surprising as it is, I don't want to leave this, either.

I wouldn't call these people my friends, but they're slowly becoming something more than mere acquaintances, even if Grant always looks at me with a healthy dose of skepticism. My night at the Seabreeze was enjoyable, and when we spent the afternoon at the bay, I liked chatting with the guys who consider themselves part of her crew, talking about nothing in particular. I don't think I've ever hung out with a group, talking about random shit without the conversation inevitably veering to work, opportunities, and, of course, as June loves to bring up, networking.

No one in Seaside Point seems to actually *want* anything from me,

Except for June, who, even if she won't say it just yet, I know wants everything.

And I'm more than happy to give that to her.

Being lost in thought must be taken as hesitation, because Grant throws an arm around my shoulder, steering me toward the bar. "A beer won't kill you," he says. At the bar, Lainey gets us each a beer before I lead them to a spot on the beach that's a bit more secluded and not overloaded with guests. From here, I can still see June, who, when she spotted me walking with her brother, gave me a huge grin and a thumbs up, the nut.

Once we sit, Decker forces us to cheers, something I'm pleased to see Grant and Miles roll their eyes at before we all sit back, taking in the scene before us. Guests mill about on the sand, chatting and laughing, some taking in the last few sun rays, others packing up. Every table in the outdoor seating for the restaurant is filled, and I know it's the same on the pool deck.

"This place is amazing," Miles says, looking around. "I've been the number one hater of this place, what with how sketchy the old company was with growing it, but this is perfect. Adds to the town without taking anything away, isn't too uptight, but also a bit of a nicer experience than just getting a beach badge."

"I couldn't have done it without June," I say, eyes still on her. She laughs, chasing a little girl who has escaped from the kids' area, then lifting them up and over her shoulder. The girl laughs, squealing as June brings her back to the group.

"You two work well together," Grant says, and I turn to him, he's taking me in with a skeptical older brother eye.

"Is this where I get the *if you hurt my sister,* talk?"

"No," Grant says, sitting back, casual as can be, sipping his beer.

I'm not buying it in the least.

"Because you don't want witnesses?" I ask, lifting an eyebrow.

"No. Because I don't have to give you that warning."

I look at him, a bit skeptical, but take it as a win all the same.

"Oh. Well. That's good, I suppose. June told me you were going to be a bit protective, but sometimes she likes to tell me shit just to—"

Grant's smile grows wider.

"I don't have to, because if you hurt her, there will be at least three other people ahead of me in line, so it won't even matter. I won't even get to you first. "

"I'm sorry?"

'Claire, for one," Miles says with a nod, already on the same page as his best friend. "Claire tells me regularly she wants to kick some-one's ass."

I look behind him at where the small blonde is chatting with some guests.

"And you could probably take Claire," Decker says, "But then you'd have to deal with Miles if you hurt Claire."

"Fair enough," I say with a nod.

"And then if there's anything left, you've got to deal with Nate."

I met Nate today, Claire's older brother, and it's clear he has a deep soft spot not just for his sisters, but whoever his sisters deem to be one of their people.

"Got it," I say with a nod. "Just don't let June find out, okay? She's under the impression we're all going to be friends."

The three men look at one another, a bit confused.

"We are," Decker says with a shrug. "Consider it a double-duty celebration. We're also celebrating you passing the vibe check. You're officially one of us."

"I'm sorry?"

"We all love June, but we wouldn't be here all day on a Friday if we didn't also like you, too," Grant says. "You're good for this place. If today crashed and burned, you'd probably have to high-tail it out of town, if you didn't get canned. So welcome to Seaside Point," he says, tipping his beer to me.

It's not the rousing endorsement of friendship that I think June wants for me, but it's good enough for me.

"Pleasure to be here," I say, reaching out to tap my bottle to the other men's.

Friends.

I guess it's not too bad after all.

I have to drag June out of Daytrip at eight when she yawns a dozen times in ten minutes, her bright smile no longer able to mask her exhaustion. It's been a long week and an even longer day, but since I know she will refuse to take tomorrow off, with it being the first official weekend open, I need her to get home and get some sleep before we do it all over again.

She nearly falls asleep in the car, and I just barely resist threatening to carry her through the lobby and into my place. Thankfully, she brought a bag of things there on Wednesday, so she has what she needs for bedtime. We shower together, not for any sexual reason, but because I'm afraid she might fall asleep. After we finish getting ready, we climb into bed, where I hold her as her breathing evens out. I think she's already fast asleep, so I'm surprised when she speaks.

"How do you feel?" she asks, low. "About today?"

"Good," I say.

She turns in my arms, a sleepy smile on her lips. "Good?"

"Yeah. I feel…. I've done this a bunch of times, been there for grand openings and been a huge part of it, but it's never felt as good as it did today. As satisfying and fulfilling."

She tips her chin at me. "Because it was your own project? You really did great, Graham."

I smile at her in the dim moonlight and shake my head, pushing her hair back behind her ear.

"No, June. Because I had people to celebrate it with. Every success has felt empty for years, and today I realized it wasn't because it wasn't impressive enough or because I wasn't the project lead. It was because I wasn't doing it with anyone. I had no one to celebrate with. Today, I had you and your…our…crew, and I finally felt… satisfied."

She smiles, her lip wavering and her eyes watering, though I'm sure it's mostly exhaustion making her emotional.

"Good thing I convinced you friends are better than networking and work opportunities, huh?" she says as I brush one of the tears away with my thumb.

"You're the luckiest thing that ever happened to me, June," I murmur, pressing my lips to her forehead. "Now go to sleep, lady luck, or I'm not letting you go in until noon tomorrow." She scrunches her nose, but instead of arguing, she tips her head, presses her lips to mine, and snuggles into my chest and falls asleep.

# THIRTY

# GRAHAM

I meet Rowan at his hotel bright and early Monday morning, a week after opening. According to Sutton, he arrived at the fancy hotel I was staying in late the night before. When he walks out of the hotel room, giving me a wide grin, I understand what Sutton was talking about. He's been dating Josie for about a year now, but I never really noticed the way he smiles more, the way he looks lighter and less stressed, something that, to my knowledge, is a testament to Josie.

I wonder if that's how I look these days, lighter and happier, thanks to June.

"Hey, Rowan," I say, smiling as I approach, offering a handshake. My boss wanted coffee and a Daytrip tour before the staff arrived. I agreed eagerly, telling him I'd pick him up, and we'd walk to Seaside Coffee together. As June would say, walking the boardwalk is the best way to experience Seaside Point, and although he's been here before, I want Rowan to love this town as much as I have started to.

"Graham! Good to see you," Rowan says.

"How was your flight?" I ask. He shrugs.

"It was a flight, but we got in late, so Josie's still out like a light." Josie had a mission in California, and she didn't get the intel she needed until the very last minute. I don't know much about what Josie does with the Mavens, mostly because I never felt it was my place to ask, since Rowan and I were coworkers, not friends, but something tells me that as soon as June meets the woman, she'll find out everything. "How are things here?"

Quickly, I fill him in on everything that's been going on over the last week. While I sent him a recap email on Monday after the opening, there's so much to expand upon, ideas and discoveries I believe will make Daytrip a runaway success. While my job is technically just to get a business going, I'm so motivated by this location. It could be the start of something amazing.

Eagerly, I tell him about the newest idea I've been turning over in my mind: transforming the interior into an event space in the winter, when we might need to get creative with income streams. While the outdoor areas will be relatively unusable in the cold winter, the giant windows facing the beach and ocean would make a gorgeous backdrop for weddings or other events. The idea came to mind when June mentioned in passing that the high school might need a location for its homecoming dance this fall, and I've been turning it around ever since.

"I'm thinking we can offer the school a discount. It's good publicity and lets the community know Daytrip will be available for events. Integrating with the community is vital, and it's working—this week, a quarter of our visits were from locals, trying to have a more relaxing beach day away from the rush of tourists."

"I'm impressed. Honestly, the more Sutton told me, the more worried I was this wouldn't be a sound investment, but you've identified the needs here and made it work seamlessly." I lick my lips, clearing my throat before continuing. It feels like I'm in the spotlight, an unexpected proposal of my own.

"I think it's all about tailoring it to what the town needs: during the summer, it needs revenue, and it needs somewhere more upscale to bring in a fresh set of tourists. At the same time, there has to be some kind of cohesion with the community. That's why we started the gift shop and why I sent you the email last week about offering a locals' discount." Rowan nods. "But in the fall and winter, this place doesn't need an exclusive club. I don't think that will be a successful venture, and I think we should consider pivoting."

The original plan was to turn Daytrip into a high-end nightclub during the fall and winter months, but the more time I spend here, the more I realize that's the wrong call.

"Seaside Point needs somewhere to continue to build community. Local events are huge here." He nods, seeming interested in the idea, and I spill out some numbers and figures as we walk. We pause our conversation when we get to Seaside Coffee, where I introduce Rowan to Mrs. Miller, telling him about how she's supplying the coffee beans. She chats with us as she makes our drinks and sends me off with an extra coffee for June, which I carry as we walk back to the office.

"You seem to know everyone here," Rowan says with a bit of surprise, grinning as he sips his coffee. I just shrug.

"It's a very small, close-knit town. June, my assistant, was born and raised here. *She* knows everyone, and she wants everyone else to know everyone, so I've met...well, everyone."

"June, the girlfriend?" he asks. I can't help but smile as I nod. "Yeah."

He studies me and, though I know it's not a problem, nerves slide through me. I called him after we got together to inform him I was dating my assistant, something he was fine with, but talking to Rowan about my love life still feels strange.

"Sutton's told me all about her, says she's a great woman. I'm happy for you." He grins, assessing me as we walk. "You seem settled here."

"I am, strangely enough," I say, waving to the landscaper, Mark, out in front of Daytrip.

"You were pissed when I sent you here," Rowan says as we step inside. He looks around, visibly impressed, and pride rushes through me as I lead him to the office area.

"Pissed is probably a strong word, but yes. I was disappointed to be assigned the Seaside Point project." I furrow my brows as I open my office door, holding it for him to enter, filtering through our conversations. "But I didn't think I told you that, though."

"You didn't, but you don't hide your feelings as well as you think."

I laugh, shaking my head. He sits in the visitor's chair, gesturing for me to sit in my desk chair.

"Okay, well, I think disappointed was the right word. I expected something bigger after the Aspen project. This seemed like a step down at the time," I say, and he nods in understanding. "But now I see it was the right move for me. I needed this challenge."

He leans back, sizing me up. "So, what's next?"

"What's next?"

"Yeah. For you. What's next for Graham Hawthorne?"

"I, uh..." I look over, spotting a colorful art piece June hung in the hall, and it gives me the confidence to speak honestly. "I want to stay here."

Rowan smirks, though it's not in a rude way, but in a knowing one I don't quite understand.

"You want to stay? Graham Hawthorne, who usually leaves right after opening? Always on to the next location, the next project?"

"I know it's not what you wanted, not what you hired me for, and if I need to take a pay or position cut, that's fine. But I want to stay here in Seaside Point, and see this project through."

Rowan stares at me, and unease slides through me.

I am so getting fucking fired today, aren't I? I'm telling him I don't want to work the position he gave me, that I want something altogether different. I wonder if this is how June felt in that convenience store, the panic of knowing you can have a sure, stable job, but realizing it's the last thing you want.

"I was hoping you'd say that," Rowan says, breaking into my messy thoughts.

"You... you were hoping I'd say that?" The shock is clear in my voice.

"Absolutely," he says. "You were made for Daytrip, Rowan. It's clear to me that this is the project you came to this company to lead, and you've done a fantastic job at it. Why wouldn't I want you to stay on, make sure it continues to succeed?" Relief moves through me rapidly, making me lightheaded, but he doesn't stop surprising me. "But I don't want you limited to just this location."

I raise an eyebrow, heart pounding as Annette walks into the office.

Now I understand why Rowan kept glancing at the door.

He was waiting for Annette. *But why is she here?*

"Is it my turn now?" she asks. Rowan rolls his eyes, clearly exasperated by the CEO of Daydream Resorts and his own mentor.

"Sure, Annette, come in and derail my conversation, why don't you?"

"I think you forgot this is my business," the gorgeous older blonde says, sitting down on the chair beside him primly.

"I'm sorry, what...what is going on here?"

"Annette loves drama," Rowan sighs. "Remember when she hired the Mavens to investigate The Keys without telling anyone?"

"Worked out pretty well for you, didn't it?" she deadpans, giving Rowan a narrow-eyed look. He rolls his eyes, then turns to me.

"We've been using Daytrip as a proof of concept, and you've been on an interview for the last few months, so to speak."

I blink at her. "I'm sorry?"

"We're looking to create a more accessible line of smaller Daydream resorts—The Daytrip line." Annette pulls a folder out of the bag she came in with, then slides it onto my desk. "And we want you to head it." My eyes are wide as I reach for it, and Rowan looks at me with a shit-eating grin.

"You know, Annette told me one day, I'd have some asshole in my office telling me he didn't want to worry about anything but work, and I'd understand why she was so worried about me. But she didn't tell me just how entertaining it would be to watch him fall in love and find a purpose," Rowan says, contemplatively.

"Told you," Annette beams. "It's fun, isn't it?"

"I'm sorry, what is happening?" I ask as I open the folder and see *"Daytrip by Daydream"* on the cover page. There's a business card pinned to the packet of papers that reads, *Graham Hawthorn, Managing Director of Daytrip by Daydream.*

"I hired you because I saw myself in you, Graham. Then I gave you this place because I knew you could handle it, this challenge you clearly needed. I knew you'd be pissed that you didn't have a traditional location, but I thought you could use something different. Something bigger and smaller at the same time."

I lift an eyebrow as pieces start to fall into place.

"So...you gave me a rundown business in a small shore town?"

"So I gave you an entire new branch of a business and hoped you'd rise to the challenge. Then Sutton told me there was a girl, and I knew the universe had pushed me in the right direction."

There's the damned universe again. It's a theme that seems to be following me around—fate and luck, and meant to be. My lady luck making everything fall into place.

"So if you want it, Graham, it's yours. You'll be the head of all Daytrip locations. We're scouting out a handful now, but I'd like your input before we secure any. Your headquarters could be here, since you already have an office here." My heart pounds. "Though you'd have to come to Hudson City a couple of times a month. All of the information is in that packet, so you can read it through before you give me an answer—"

"I'm in," I say, closing the folder. "I'm in."

Why wouldn't I be? It's everything I've always strived for and everything I didn't even know I wanted.

I can have it all now—the job, the constant challenge, the prestige. Seaside Point and the friends I've found here.

June.

Roots.

Rowan lets out a laugh, shaking his head. "As much as I am happy to hear that, I have to suggest looking at all that's involved, including expectations and the salary, before accepting." He and Annette are grinning widely, and I know I am, too. I open my mouth to tell him I don't care about the money or responsibilities, that I trust him, but the door creaks open, a distracted brunette popping in, her eyes on the ice coffee cup in her hands that she must have spotted in the fridge.

"Hey, is this for me— Oh! I'm so sorry," June says, her face going beet red. "I didn't even think, I—"

"This is her, isn't it?" Annette says as I stand, looking at me with a big smile. I step forward, pulling June into my side for a quick hug, unable to contain my joy and needing even the smallest outlet for it.

"Yeah. Rowan, Annette? This is June, my lucky charm for this entire project." Her blush deepens, but Annette's smile grows wider as she stands, stepping to June and pulling her in for a huge hug. June hesitates before returning it, giving me a confused look over the CEO's shoulders.

"Always an honor to meet a woman who can pull a grumpy asshole's head out of his ass," Annette says, and Rowan lets out a loud laugh.

"Don't let her become friendly with Annette," Rowan warns. "I made that mistake with Sutton, and now the two conspire against me. Add in Josie, and I have no hope at all."

He also stands, stepping over to June as Annette releases her. He doesn't hug June, though, instead shaking her hand.

"Don't tell him my secrets, Rowan," Annette stage whispers.

"Oh, don't worry, I already drive Graham crazy. There's no hope for him," June says.

Annette looks from me to June and back, a softer smile on her lips now.

"I can see that. Now, who is going to show me around this fabulous place?"

"The photo backdrop—whose idea was that?" Rowan asks as we show him around the resort. I look over at June, who is suddenly incredibly interested in her shoes.

"June," I say. "We saw something similar at a festival, and she said it might be a good idea here. She painted it herself." Rowan nods appreciatively.

"Smart. I really like it. Brings people over and gives them something to tag on social media."

"It's been doing great," Sutton adds. She arrived twenty minutes or so ago, her own Seaside Coffee in hand. "The tags for this location have been higher than any other new open."

June bites her lip, and I wonder if she'll keep it in, but her excitement wins out as expected.

"I was thinking we could even do a social media contest, so everyone who posts it is entered to win a day pass. Maybe pull a winner once a week or so? It would bring in revenue if they came in with someone and would promote the club by default."

Again, Rowan nods, interested.

"I like it. Sutton, do you think we do something like that?" he asks, and Sutton lifts a shoulder.

"I'd have to check with legal, but I don't see why not. It makes sense to me."

"Do you do this for a job?" Rowan asks, turning to June. "The murals?"

"It's just...something I do on the—"

She starts to downplay her work, and I sigh, cutting her off before Sutton gets the chance to.

"She's just starting, but she's building quicky. She's already booked out to the end of summer."

June pinches me because it's a lie, but I also know she won't call me out in front of my boss.

"I love this idea. Would you be interested in doing more?"

"More?" June squeaks.

I have to fight back a grin. God, she's fucking adorable.

"We're hoping to have more Daytrip by Daydream locations opening over the next few years, and I really think these would draw people to make it a must-see while in town. But I'd also love to add a few to some of our locations with celebrity clientele. A perfect backdrop for them to add to their vacation round-up posts." June's eyes are wide now. "It could be great exposure for you, as well."

"Oh, I—" she starts, and I'm relieved when Rowan continues, ending her argument before it starts, so I don't have to.

"Can you put together some proposals? Maybe tiered at one location, three, five, and ten?"

"A proposal?" she asks in awe. "Ten locations?"

"I could help you with the expected structure for it," I say in a low voice. That cuts through her shock, and she glares at me. I smile, remembering the last proposal I helped her with.

"We would cover your travel, of course. And the supplies. It would be separate from your work with the company, so it wouldn't be your hourly rate as an employee. And since it's corporate, you can charge more," Sutton says with a smile.

"You're not supposed to tell people that, Sutton," Rowan says, exasperated.

"Why, it's not going to come out of your pocket? Plus, she's already going to undercharge you because she doesn't know her worth, so really, I'm just making sure you don't get the opportunity to take advantage of a young, up-and-coming artist."

"Can we not assume that I'm going to take advantage of people?" he asks. "Much less state it aloud in the middle of the hotel I work for, loud enough that everyone can hear?"

Sutton rolls her eyes. "Oh, you are so dramatic; no one is even listening."

"Sutton, you're shouting," Rowan says.

They continue arguing, but I watch as June begins to panic.

"I actually," June says, biting her lip. "I need to go grab something from my desk. I'll be right back."

"I'll go with, I should check my email. You two can just... continue this or whatever," I say, then start following June.

"Ohh, someone's in trouble," Sutton says low enough that thankfully, I don't think June can hear. I look over my shoulder and try to shoot daggers at her, but fail miserably as they bounce off her Teflon exterior. I don't think anything gets under Sutton Donovan's skin.

I jog to catch up with June, then walk with her, but don't miss her tight jaw. I'm not completely sure what's wrong, but my own nerves start to brew, worrying that I may have accidentally upset her. When we reach the business area, I reach for her arm, but she turns to me before I can.

"Did you do that?" she snaps, a surprisingly angry look on her face. "Did you set me up in there?" I stare at her, confused, before she continues, poking me in the chest, and the *why* becomes clear. "Did you convince Rowan to ask if I could do the murals? Because we're dating and it would mean a lot to me and probably make me believe in myself or something like that?"

I shake my head, stepping closer to her, putting a hand to her chin to tip her face up and force her to look at me.

"No, June. I don't think anyone but Josie can convince Rowan to do anything. That was all you and your talent."

Her jaw goes tight, and I fight the urge to kiss her. She made it terribly clear last night that kissing her while Rowan was here was a no-go, wanting to maintain a semblance of professionalism.

But it takes a lot of effort, especially when she's looking at me like that, with a mix of irritation and hesitant excitement.

"I would never do that, June. I would do anything to make you smile, but I would never do something that would impact your career or your future. I think you know that."

Once more, that guilt for the piled-up lies and mistruths churns in my stomach, but it's still an honest statement. I would never do anything to impact June's real life, outside of giving her a job. I don't count buying her first piece of art in that, mostly because it was just one piece and has nothing to do with the dozens of pieces she has sold since then.

I know she values earning her successes just as much as I do, and I would never want her to doubt that.

With my words, her panic melts, leaving only happiness in its wake.

"So that was all Rowan's idea?" I nod and a grin spreads on her full lips. "I really am so lucky, and everything works out for me!" Her voice is pure excitement, but I need to set her straight before I join in.

"No," I say with a shake of my head, pulling her closer. "No. It's you. It's your talent and your mind, and it's been that all along. You're not lucky, you're just June, and that is what is making everything work out. It's the fact that you're hard-working and kind and creative. That's it."

"I really want to kiss you right now," she murmurs, her face soft, and I grin.

"Say the word, lady luck."

She bites her lip and smiles, but before she can make a decision, her face changes.

"Wait, how did things go with Rowan this morning? Why is the CEO here? Is it just to see the resort?"

"Oh, uh, it went well. They like the place a lot. This morning, Rowan and I talked a lot about Daytrip. Then he essentially told me this was a trial period."

Her face changes, something so subtle, if I weren't always so attuned to every tiny microexpression on her face, I might miss it. Apprehension is buried beneath that sunshine smile, trying to stay positive while gearing herself up to sound excited no matter what I say next.

That's when I realize June is just as wild for me as I am for her, in a way that means all she wants is for me to be happy and fulfilled. If I think about it, really, that's what she's always wanted. And right now, she doesn't want me to leave Seaside Point, but I know she would cheer me on if Daydream sent me to the other side of the world, so long as it made me happy.

Lucky for us, we both get to have exactly what we want.

"They're creating a new division of Daydream, small resorts under the Daytrip umbrella. This was a test to see whether it was feasible and whether there was an audience for it. They're impressed by the success and want me to be the head of it."

Her eyes widen, her smile becoming a bit less guarded, but when my next words spill out, whatever remaining nerves melt away, leaving nothing but unbridled joy in their wake.

"I'm going to be the managing director of Daytrip by Daydream. There's still a lot to figure out, but my main office will be here, in Seaside Point."

She gasps, a wide, beaming grin spreads across her face, lighting up the entire room in a way only June Taylor can do, before her kissing rule goes out the window. She puts her hands on my face and kisses me, hard and deep. When she breaks it, she begins peppering kisses all over my face, as if she can't help herself.

"Oh, my god! Graham! I'm so proud of you!"

Warmth settles in my chest.

She's not happy for me.

Not excited.

*Proud.*

And I realize then this is what I needed all along. This was the moment, this was what I was missing. Not a new job or a promotion to finally make me feel successful, though I'm grateful to have that, too.

But someone to share it with. Someone to be *proud* of me.

And I know then, with June Taylor placing kisses all over my face, joy shining through, that I'm the luckiest man in the world.

Because I have her to share my successes with.

# THIRTY-ONE

Graham isn't leaving Seaside Point.

He's not moving to a new job or location to keep trying to prove himself successful. He's staying here, in Seaside Point.

With me.

My heart is so full right now. Of course, I'm happy the man I'm falling for is going to stay in the town I could never leave, but even more, the look on his face tells me everything I need to know about how he feels about this update: he's both thrilled and at ease. The comfort between us settles warmly.

From what I understand, this type of ease has happened only a handful of times in his life, and I'm honored to experience it with him. I rest my forehead gently on his, my eyes watering while I soak up the quiet relief on his face.

"I'm so proud of you, Graham," I repeat. His eyes go melty at my words, a soft smile spreading on his lips as if that simple sentence means more to him than any promotion ever could. God, this man. Such a hard exterior, but so soft inside. Will he always keep his tough attitude, giving only me his sweet? Part of me likes being the only one who sees this side, but another part hopes he'll grow comfortable sharing it with others.

Our peaceful bubble pops as the door swings open, banging against the wall, and we part quickly. I step back and brush down my dress. My pulse pounds thinking Graham's boss just caught us in an unprofessional position, but relief rushes in when Sutton walks in instead. She has a shit-eating grin on her lips, and behind her, a tall, curvy brunette enters.

For a second, I just stare—she might be the hottest woman I've ever seen.

"Well, well, well, what do we have here?" Sutton teases.

"Sutton, how many times have I told you not to just barge into my office?" Graham demands.

"A million." Sutton turns to me, grabs my wrist to pull me from Graham, and spins me so I'm facing the other woman. "June, this is Josie."

My eyes go wide with excitement.

"Oh, my god, hi!" I say, feeling like I'm meeting a superhero. "I've heard so much about you. You're possibly the coolest person on earth. I want to be you when I grow up," I babble like an idiot, but her stunning smile puts me at ease.

"And I've heard so much about *you!*" she exclaims. "I bought one of your pieces last week. I was wondering if you could do a custom piece for me. I figured I'd wait until I was here to ask, but I have so many ideas. Rowan and I just moved in together, and his place is boring and needs some color. I also wanted to get a friend a gift to commemorate her stint as a monster car driver."

"A monster car driver?" I ask, eyes widening. Josie smiles.

"It's a long story—she's all rainbows and butterflies, drives a unicorn truck, and I think you could capture the vibe perfectly."

Instantly, ideas for the custom commission flash through my mind. It's such a fun concept, I'd do it for free, but I know everyone would yell if I even suggested it.

"Oh my god, yes! I need to hear all about these monster trucks.

An assignment?" I look at Josie. She nods eagerly. Rowan walks in next, and suddenly Graham's office feels tiny.

"Yeah, it's utter chaos. Let's do lunch, and I'll tell you all about it," she suggests, and I nod eagerly. Claire is going to be *so* jealous that I got to spend the afternoon with Josie.

"Didn't you want a beach day while you were here?" Sutton asks, then turns to me. "We should gather the crew. Claire's working, but we'll park by her stand."

"Yes! Please! I need a day in the sand desperately," Josie nearly claps.

"Actually, that would be great," Rowan begins. "Graham and I could scout locations for another—" Josie shoots him a fierce glare; Rowan only returns it, though his is already tinged in defeat.

"No, no, no, no. I was promised a beach day."

"Troublemaker—" he mutters. I smile at her fitting nickname. She stomps her foot, a move that is unexpectedly adorable on her.

"No! A beach day. Give me my beach day, Rowan Fischer, or I'm getting Annette."

"Oof," Graham sighs, but then Josie turns her iron will toward him, a finger pointed in his direction.

"I'll tell her that you also don't have a life, Graham Hawthorne," she says, and suddenly her ability to cut men down is clear as Graham's eyes go wide with alarm. She's kind of scary, if I'm honest.

"What did I do?" Graham asks, lifting his hands in resignation.

"Nothing, unless you block my beach day."

Rowan sighs, looks at me, then at his girlfriend, and shrugs.

"Looks like we're having a beach day. Josie gets what Josie wants."

By two, everyone is on the beach—not on the Daytrip property, but in front of the lifeguard stand where Claire is working for the afternoon. We did this a lot last summer while she was working, and it always worked out well. Since it's Monday, the Seabreeze is closed, so Lainey agreed instantly, in part because she also wanted to meet the cool, hot PI, Josie. Deck and Grant had no job today, so they tagged along, and Miles happily closed up the mechanic shop early, taking any excuse to join his girlfriend on the sand. Now, the guys are throwing a football, and we girls are sitting around Claire's chair, chatting and tanning.

It's the perfect summer day.

"Oh, I almost forgot," Josie says after a while. She slides her sunglasses onto her head, pushing back her dark brown locks, then digs through her bag before handing me an orange bend-clasp folder. "These are for you." I eye it skeptically, because I've heard of a PI handing over files in a folder like that, and it's typically bad news.

"For me?" I repeat as she grins wide and shakes the folder for me to grab.

"I heard you were hunting for information and found it. It was easy—I only flirted with one gross principal."

My emotions flip instantly.

"No way," I say, eagerly taking the envelope from her hands. "You got them?"

"Sutton told me they existed, and I couldn't resist." She leans back, arms crossed behind her head, and sighs blissfully. "My best friend, Rory, is a genius with records. I could've asked her to hack the school files, but that's no fun."

"Yeah, definitely," Sutton agrees, even though she seems lost as Josie rambles. "What's the fun indeed?" I want to tease my best friend's sister, but then I'm opening the clasp and sliding out the photos, and the words catch in my throat.

"Oh my god," I murmur as I move through the stack. There are a dozen photos of Graham at various ages playing football. He's in various uniforms, from elementary school to college. Through them, I get to see every stage of him growing up.

Unfortunately, it means I can't show Graham my own old cheer photos—he never had an awkward phase. He was always sure of himself, always put together, likely always the coolest guy at his school. It's a little sad, since I know he behaved that way as a curated defense mechanism. I watch him stumble in the sand. Decker laughs before offering him a hand up, and I smile.

I love that here, he doesn't feel the need to keep a facade up, no longer has to present only one, perfect, closed-off version of himself. He catches my eye, smiles, and gives me a wink before throwing the ball to Rowan, and I look back down at the photos again.

"Is it weird to think these are hot? He couldn't have been older than nineteen in this one," I say, voice low. In my defense, the shot is some kind of douchey photo he must have posted on some social media site, but my *god*, it seems the abs aren't a new development.

"No, they are hot," Lainey assures. Without our noticing, my brother appears beside us, scaring the shit out of me.

"What's hot?" Grant asks, brow raised.

"June's boyfriend," Claire answers from her perch above us. Grant's face scrunches up in confusion.

"Hey, so, that's a child," he says, a bit alarmed, and I let out a laugh. Lainey reaches over to grab one of the photos.

"It's *Graham* as a child, and in this one, he's of drinking age," she says. "I think it's okay to say he's hot here."

"What are we talking about?" Graham asks, walking over, and we all scramble to hide the photos, but one falls into the sand. He reaches to grab and inspect it before giving us a confused look. "Are those all pictures of me?"

"Yes," I say, smiling up at him. I have a sudden urge to explode with giggles, and Graham's partly annoyed, partly confused face only makes it worse. He looks at Josie and lets out a deep sigh before glancing over his shoulder to where Rowan is approaching.

"Rowan, your girlfriend is doing deep dives on me," he complains, but Rowan just shrugs.

"Welcome to my life," Rowan replies, and Graham blinks at him. Carefully, I take the photos from him and slide them back into the envelope for safekeeping.

"I'm hiding those," he says, glaring at the one on top, a photo of him in what had to be middle school, before I close up the envelope and slide it safely in my bag.

"I have them all saved on a digital drive. I'll email you the originals," Josie says with a smile, and I let out a loud laugh as Graham grimaces.

"So, you were always hot, huh?" Sutton asks, and a blush burns on Graham's cheeks. Hot and absolutely *adorable*. How on earth has no one ever cracked him, tried to win over this version of him?

Further proof that I'm lucky.

Sutton laughs at the look, then stands, brushing her hands off. "I'm going to the water. Anyone else want to come?"

"I'm stuck here for another ten," Claire says, looking at her watch, and Miles smiles up to her, not even bothering to say he won't be leaving her side.

"I'll stay, too. I'm in a good chapter," Lainey says from under the umbrella, lifting her Kindle. Grant settles in on a chair next to Decker, but Josie and I stand.

"I'll dip my toes in," Josie says.

"I'm gonna go wash off the sand," Graham says, and we walk to the water's edge. Rowan, Graham, and Sutton all head into the water, but I stay back with Josie, feet sinking into the wet sand.

"You're not going in?" she asks, and I shake my head.

"No, no. I've lived here all my life, so I know it's still too cold for me," I say, tipping my head to the water. "August is when it's warm enough to brave the water. I'm more of a sand girl, anyway." Josie nods, but we're both distracted when we watch Rowan get knocked over by an unexpected hard wave. Graham laughs, loud and happy, a free sound that if you'd told me I'd be hearing just a month ago, I'd tell you you'd lost it. But my magical small town has changed him in that short time. Rowan smiles as he wipes the water out of his face, then brushes his hair back before sending a large splash of water at Graham with his hands.

"They're a lot alike," Josie says, pulling me from my thoughts.

Her gaze is still out at the ocean, watching the two play like kids. "You know, before I added some spice to his life, Rowan was living for work, work, and more work. His only friends were workplace acquaintances," she says.

"Graham told me that friends are just networking opportunities when he got here."

I half expect the tall brunette to give me a face like Claire did when I told her that, but instead, her head tips back, a tinkling laugh leaving her.

"Yeah, that sounds about right," she says, shaking her head. Her lips settle into a soft smile as she watches Rowan, grinning and laughing as Sutton seems to tease both of the men. I wonder if she's seeing Rowan as he was when they first met, closed off and solely focused on work. "And now?"

"Now?" I ask, not expecting her question.

"He seems to have found some friends here."

Before I can respond, Graham shouts to the group behind us, beckoning Decker over as Sutton starts splashing both men. "Deck! Help us, Sutton's ganging up on us!" he yells, and Claire lets out a sparkling laugh.

"It's already two to one!" Sutton yells. "You guys are just big babies!"

"Two to one isn't fair odds. Donovan women are built differently, you know that, Sutt," Claire says.

"Amen to that," Miles says, part agreement, part resignation. Deck runs down the beach, holding the football they were playing with before.

"I told you I was getting *away* from you!" Sutton whines, but there's a small smile on her lips as he throws the ball to her and she catches it seamlessly. She throws it back, but the wind takes it, sending it off its target and nearly hitting Graham before he catches it, giving Deck shit about missing the catch. Deck lifts his hands in irritation, and Sutton lets out a loud laugh.

"Yeah, he's got some friends here," I say with a smile. Deck moves toward a smiling Sutton, who is still laughing, but starts waving her hands in defense.

"I'm sorry!" she says in a laugh. "I'm sorry, don't do it!" But it's a lost cause. She lets out a shriek as he puts a shoulder into her belly, lifting her over his shoulder before jumping into an oncoming wave. Despite her seeming constant irritation with Decker, it's more of a flirty kind that always makes me wonder. When they both surface from under the water, she tries to glare at him, but it's not very successful since a grin wins out.

When Deck hears Josie and me laughing, he turns in our direction. "Which one of you is next?" he asks with a grin. I step back away from the water, but Josie stays there, feet planted in place.

"Put me in that water, and I'll show you my taser," she says sweetly, fluttering her lashes at Decker, and his face goes white. "She's pink and bedazzled and named Betty."

"Jesus Christ, Troublemaker, can we not here?" Rowan says, with a sigh. "This is my place of work." Josie lifts a shoulder as if it's a non-issue.

"Your girlfriend is scary, but it's kind of hot," Deck says, looking at Josie, a bit awed.

"You're telling me," Rowan says, low.

"Decker has a thing for strong, empowered women. I think he's secretly into it when they're mean to him," Sutton says, and once again, Deck looks at her with heart eyes.

"Only for you."

"In your dreams, Decker."

"You would know, you're in them every night."

Sutton rolls her eyes, but again, that smile is still on her lips.

"I need to eat before dealing with your bullshit," she grumbles, stepping out of the water, hair slicked back and dripping before standing on the sand beside Josie and me. "Want to get boardwalk pizza? We need to introduce Josie to Jersey's finest." I nod, then Sutton looks over to her sister.

"Claire, is it your break yet? I want pizza!"

Claire looks at her watch and grins, then nods as we make our way to our little camp.

"Someone should be here to replace me any minute. Can we get fries, too?" Claire asks.

"Oh, god, yes, please," Lainey says, nearly whining.

"I want one of those big lemonades, too," Josie says, reaching for her cover-up.

"You know, I don't know if Graham has had *any* of this yet," I say thoughtfully. The girls all turn to where he, Rowan, and Deck are trailing behind us, and I hand him a dry, sand-free towel.

"Are you ready to have a true Seaside Point summer lunch?" I ask. "All the boardwalk classics."

He looks at me skeptically. "Why do I feel like I'm about to have a stomachache?"

I shrug, grinning and still floating in my happy state. "Because you are, but in that good way." Reaching for my own cover-up, I grab it and slide it over my head. "You know, I could go for one of those ice cream truck ice pops, with the hard as rocks bubblegum eyeballs?"

"You're disgusting, June," Claire says with a grimace, stepping down from her chair as one of the other guards takes her place. She lifts her sticker-covered water bottle and takes a contemplative sip. "But now I really want soft serve with sprinkles."

"We can get real ice cream after lunch," Miles says, turning to Graham. "Have you had Kohr's yet?" Graham looks at him, confused, then shakes his head.

"No, I don't believe so. But I'm in for whatever. My treat," Graham says, and I mourn the loss of his chest as he slides a T-shirt on. Grant, Miles, and Rowan all open their mouths to argue, but Decker slaps him on the shoulder.

"Sure thing, money bags. Make mine a triple, okay?"

Graham's head tips back with a laugh before grabbing my hand and leading me up the sand to the boardwalk.

# THIRTY-TWO

# June

Life settles into a new kind of normal in the following weeks.

Just a few days after Graham formally accepted his new position, he asked if I knew a realtor in town. I may have cried a bit when he asked me, something that thoroughly entertained him, but once I got myself together, I called Maggie, who called Leanne, the best realtor in town. She was at Daytrip the very next day, eager to find out exactly what Graham was looking for.

By some stroke of luck, he found a townhouse just a block from the ocean that was about to go to market, and was able to put in an offer before it was formally up. I refused to even ask about the offer, for fear the number would make my tummy hurt. He closed on the new home in just two weeks.

Since then, at Graham's insistence, I've spent most of my nights at his place. This unexpectedly created a bond between my boyfriend and brother, since both decided my apartment is a shithole and not up to their safety standards. I argue with both of them about it regularly, but the truth is, nights at Graham's *are* nicer, and about half of my things have found their way into his drawers and closets.

Most mornings, we go to work together, sometimes walking if the weather is nice, and other times driving together. Some mornings, he leaves well before me, the workaholic that he is, needing to get a few extra hours in, or doesn't end up going to the actual office at all, since he's currently scouting the next Daytrip location. They've got their eye on Ocean View as a second Jersey Shore location. Rowan's also been sending information for the Carolinas, Ocean City, Maryland, and Cape Cod, wanting to focus on the East Coast for the first few locations.

I spend my days bebopping around, helping wherever I'm needed, and keeping Graham's day running smoothly while also working on the two new murals for Daytrip. While I haven't heard back on the proposal I submitted to the town, I've already gotten approval from Rowan to do postcards for nearly every location. We're ironing out the final details for a mural at the Keys location this fall. My business is thriving, with orders for paintings and digital prints coming in every single day. With each one, I become more confident that I'm doing the right thing with my life. Going back to teaching hasn't even been on my radar for the last month, if I'm being honest.

I've never been happier.

Life has been so perfect, so I should have expected a bad day to hit eventually.

They don't happen too often, but I am human, after all. Usually, I can snap myself out of it pretty quickly, but I stayed up late at my place painting last night and woke up with my period, which means I woke up tired, alone, *and* with cramps. It's gloomy out, the sun not yet burning off the clouds from last night's storm. Even worse, when I tried to start my car this morning, nothing happened. I had to call Miles to tow it to his garage, and I know that later today or tomorrow I'm going to be stuck arguing with him about how much I owe him, because he's going to try to say it's on the house since I'm *like a sister to him.*

All this to say, when Graham walks in around ten, I'm grouchy and irritated and not feeling like my normal happy self.

"Morning, lady luck," he says as he walks over to my desk, a grin on his lips. He doesn't hide those anymore—not from me, and more often not from the world either. His laughter and smiles come freely now, something I normally love. But right now, I'm just not in the mood, especially as I try to find a spreadsheet I may or may not have accidentally wiped.

"Hey," I grumble, eyes moving back to the screen. Thankfully, I remember there's a button to recover previous editions, and with a sigh, I restore the file.

"What's wrong?" he asks instantly, brows furrowing.

I shake my head. "Nothing."

"June, you look like someone told you that they're never going to make rainbow sprinkles again." He stares at me. "And you didn't even give me shit about making an actual, real-life joke. Something's wrong. What is it?"

"Nothing," I say, shaking my head despite the irritation filling me once more. "I'm fine. I deleted a spreadsheet, but I fixed it."

His eyes narrow, but instead of letting it drop as I hoped, he reaches down, tugging me until I'm standing before him, a bit of my defenses melting away with the move.

"Tell me what's wrong? What's dulling your sunshine, June?"

"I hate that you notice things," I grumble, but he just smiles wider. When did our personalities swap?

"Well, you're stuck with it, so spill. What's wrong? Has your luck run out?" he asks with a small tilt of his lips, and my nose scrunches.

"No, I'm just having a bad day. Everyone has bad days, you know."

He smiles down at me, that small dimple coming out as he pushes a lock of loose hair behind my ear. "I bet that if you'd stayed at my place last night, it would have been a good day." I glower. "Why's it a bad day? Tell me so I can fix it." I open my mouth to argue, but he lifts an eyebrow, and I sigh before the word vomit starts.

"I got my period this morning, and I have cramps, and I'm starving, but nothing sounds good, so I haven't eaten yet today. My car finally crapped out, and Miles has it now, which means I'm going to argue with him about paying for it, and then tonight I'll probably have to argue with you about buying me a new one or something stupid. Claire keeps bugging me about my birthday, and I just erased my stupid spreadsheet, and I keep getting the most annoying spam calls. I still haven't heard from the town, which means they probably hated my mural proposal, and I'm the laughingstock of the chamber of commerce, and—" My throat starts to ache as the words spill out. Something drops to the ground, and he takes my jaws in both of his hands and cuts off my words with a soft kiss.

As annoying as it is, it eases a bit of the tension in my chest.

When he pulls back, he bends down, grabs the bag he dropped, and hands it to me. Spotting the Seaside Coffee logo on the side, I instinctively know it's a donut, and my eyes water.

Graham doesn't stop, though, instead grabbing me, setting my ass on my desk, and watching as I open the bag.

"Hungry for a donut?" he asks, and my lips wobble as I nod and reach into the bag, taking one of the two rainbow sprinkled donuts out. I chew a bite of the treat, the sugar hitting just right and making me sigh with contentment.

"Now. I'll try to deal with Claire and your birthday. You fixed the spreadsheet? If not, I can call IT, see if they can recover it."

I shake my head. "I got it."

"Do you need anything for your cramps or period? Medicine, tampons?"

I shake my head, though the idea of Graham getting tampons for me does perk up my mood a bit.

"I've got what I need."

"Now, the mural proposal."

My stomach drops again.

"They hate it. That's the only explanation," I murmur before taking another too-big bite, sating my self-pity with sugar and Red Dye 40. He rolls his eyes, stepping between my legs, dipping his head to kiss me again as if he can't help himself.

"I never thought I'd have to outshine you in the positivity department, but I guess there's a first time for everything," he mumbles against my lips. "June, the deadline has barely passed. You need to give it time."

"I can't stop thinking about it," I whine, even though I know he's right. He lifts an eyebrow, lips tipping in a smirk.

"I can give you something else to think about."

I glower at him.

"No, Graham, we're at work."

"I'm the boss. I can do what I want."

"I also have my period, and while some people are cool with that, I have never been into that."

"I could make you feel good," he says, hand moving up my thigh and making me shiver. "I don't have to get anything out of it. I hear orgasms help." For the briefest moment, I contemplate his offer before common sense kicks in.

"No, I'm good. But thank you."

"Okay, but the offer still stands." That almost pulls a smile from my lips.

Almost.

"Now, what's going on with the car? Something wrong with it?" I shrug.

"I don't know, Miles says it might be the starter. He towed it to the garage this morning to take a look."

"How'd you get here today?"

"I walked," I say with a sigh, and he glares at me.

"Why didn't you tell me? I would have come to pick you up."

"You were working," I murmur.

"Weren't you the one so intent on showing me there's more to life than work?" I bite my lip, looking away. "Working or not, all I ever want to do is share the sunshine that you radiate all day long, even when you're having a shit day. Next time, you call me." My lower lip wobbles.

"You're not allowed to make me emotional when I'm on my period, Graham. It's a rule."

"Oh, sorry, I didn't realize, my bad. I'm new to this whole boyfriend thing."

That alone makes me want to smile, but the dark cloud hanging overhead keeps me from doing so. He sees it, I think, because after a breath, he steps back, tipping his head to the front door.

"Let's go for a walk. The sun's out now," he says, but I shake my head, resigned to my doomed fate.

"No, I'll just wallow away in misery in here."

"Wow, when you're having a bad day, you really have a bad day, huh?"

"I only know extremes," I say. "Extreme joy, or extreme misery. There is no in-between."

"I thought you said some vitamin D would help out even the worst moods?"

I groan, balling up the now-empty bag, tossing it toward the trash, and missing. I glare at it, just another small bit of deceit.

"I think I'd need an entire day in the sun to turn this mood around."

"Then let's do it."

"What?"

"Let's spend the entire day in the sun, turn your mood around."

"We can't just cut out for the day," I say.

"I'm your boss. I say we can. Come on." He steps away, using his hand in mine to tug me off the edge of the desk. "I'll email Rowan now to tell him we're taking the day to explore and engage with the community. He won't care." He pauses, reaching out to push my hair back. "We'll chase rainbows, June. That's what your grandmother said to do, right?"

My heart melts at the mere idea that he remembers that small moment.

"We don't have bathing suits," I argue weakly. "We'll have to go back home." He shakes his head.

"Buy some in the gift shop. Go pick them out while I finish things up here." I stare at him, wide-eyed, but his face is serious. "Go, June. Now. That's an order."

And really, who am I to argue?

"Are you sure about these?" Graham asks as we walk to his car, tugging down the hem of the swim shorts I grabbed for him. They're a seafoam green color and just like I daydreamed about all those weeks ago, short as can be. The perfect slutty inseam for my man to show off his killer thighs.

And again, just as I daydreamed all those weeks ago, the man has thighs that should never be trapped in the crime that is dress pants. They don't do even *close* to the justice they deserve.

"Graham, I swear to god, I have never wanted to jump your bones more than right now."

He looks at me, confused, as we slip into his car.

"Really?"

"Oh yeah. Your thighs..." I look at them for long moments, then fan myself. "How do you even maintain those?" A small smirk tips his lips.

"Genetics, and I used to work out for ninety minutes a day." My eyes widen in awe.

"Over an *hour*? On purpose?"

I, of course, know he works out because he tends to do it while I paint, but it's definitely not ninety minutes.

"I never had anything else to work toward, no one else to spend my time with," he says, looking over at me and placing a hand on my thigh. He squeezes once, and I smile at him. My bad mood is already lifting, but if I tell him that I'll sacrifice our day out.

"But now you do?"

"Now I do."

He smiles at me as he opens the door for me, then walks around the car to the driver's side before taking us to the local deli to grab lunch to go.

"Okay, where to?" he asks once we have a feast inside the small cooler he also bought from the gift shop. With a smile, I direct him toward my favorite beach. It's not technically in Seaside Point, but a state park right outside of town, so it doesn't have all of the chaos that Seaside Point does, just the peaceful ocean and stretch of sand. We unpack the towels we brought and spend time lying in the sun or dipping our toes into the water.

It's the perfect day, perhaps even more perfect since we're here purely because I was having a shit one. It only gets better when I find a white circle sitting half-buried in the sand. Excitedly, I bend to pick it up, then gasp when I pull a perfect sand dollar out.

"What is it?" Graham asks, putting his hand on my lower back.

"It's a sand dollar!" I say excitedly, turning to him to show him the delicate discovery. "It's lucky to find a whole one. I can't believe it!" My eyes narrow. "Did you drop it?" I've lived in Seaside my entire life and have probably spent whole days and weeks wandering these shores without ever finding a whole sand dollar.

"What?" he asks, looking genuinely confused. "Why would I drop it?" I let out a laugh, then shake my head.

"Claire has always been in love with finding seashells, and when they first met, Miles started buying nice ones and dropping them when she wasn't looking. She thought she was just really good at finding seashells. Last summer, she found out he's been dropping them for her, long before they even started dating."

Graham's eyes widen, and his arm on me tightens, pulling me in closer.

"Was she mad when she found out he'd been dropping them all along?"

I think about that, never considering it because Miles and Claire are so deeply in love, then shake my head.

"No. She understood. It's a sweet thing between them now. He still does it."

He smiles then, something close to relief flashing over his face. I open my mouth to question it, but before I can, I'm distracted as the soft tones of an ice cream truck filter through the air.

"Is that the ice cream truck?" I ask, turning my head up the beach and toward the parking lot

"Sounds like it," he says.

"Oh, my god. I *need* an ice pop. I need to go grab my wallet!" I say, excited, but he grabs my wrist.

"No. I've got it," he says, pulling his own wallet out. I narrow my eyes at him, and something clicks, a memory from a few weeks ago when I said I was craving an ice pop.

"Did you do this?" I ask, tipping my head to the side.

"Do this?"

"The ice cream truck, did you do it?"

A tiny, mischievous smile tips on his lips.

"How would I have done that?" I don't buy his half-assed denial in the least.

"Oh, my god, you totally did. You totally had the ice cream truck come here just to make me happy, didn't you?"

A laugh leaves his lips as he takes my hand and leads me up the sand.

"You mentioned wanting one. I just sent them a message on social media when we got here. It was no big deal; they were already coming this way."

I stare at him in awe.

"Are you mad?"

"Why would I be mad?" I ask with a laugh, shaking my head. "Because you're the kindest, sweetest, most caring man alive? No, I'm not mad. Let's go before they drive off."

Then, Graham buys me a Powerpuff Girl ice pop, and I smile as I eat it. He gets a boring soft serve, but watches me in something close to horror.

"How are you eating that?" he asks eventually, and I just shrug.

"This is what I always get from the ice cream truck. You can get soft serve all over the island, but there are only a few places you can get a Bubbles ice pop."

He shakes his head but smiles all the same.

"You're a nut, you know that?"

"You like it though," I say, and he pulls me in close.

"I really do. I must be out of my mind, but I really do." Then he kisses me, long and deep, until a drip melts onto my hand. I pull back, licking the melted ice pop off. When I look up, he's watching me with rapt attention, and I giggle, not because of his teenage boy look, but at the fact that his face has pink and blue smeared on his lips.

And somehow, my day is completely better.

"What's the damage?" I ask as Miles meets me in the garage, a blue shop towel in his hands. He texted me while we were at the beach to tell me my car was ready, and Graham took me over to pick it up on the way back to his place. He gives me a wide, brotherly smile.

"A hundred," he says, and I stare at him before looking at him, annoyed. Graham lets out a little snicker, thoroughly entertained by this.

"Okay, and what's your not my brother's best fri*end and my best friend's boyfriend* price?"

"Hundred," he repeats, and I fight the urge not to stomp my foot.

"Miles Miller," I start. "Don't make me call Claire. Or worse, your mom. She knows how important it is for a woman to pay for things herself."

He lets out a laugh and shakes his head before lifting his hands in surrender.

"Serious, June. It wasn't too bad, just two minutes of tinkering. Then I recharged the air conditioning. That was like, five bucks, and I knew you wouldn't be down with that, so I changed your oil and refilled your windshield wiper fluid and changed the cabin air filter." I narrow my eyes.

"You're telling me the only thing wrong with that is that you needed to *tinker?*" He nods. "What about the starter? You said that might be an issue." He shakes his head.

"Something was loose." I narrow my eyes.

"An oil change alone is a hundred bucks, Miles."

"That's just because shops upcharge. I only charged you for materials. Those aren't that much, right Graham? Back me up on this," Miles says. Graham nods.

"Stop giving him a hard time. He's probably overcharging you for oil, too, if we're being honest, since he's afraid you'll do exactly this."

"I am! Thank you!" I look between the two of them, then roll my eyes.

"I'm sorry," I say with a sigh. "It just sounds...too good to be true. That car is older than me."

"It's a good car. You got lucky, June. It didn't need much."

There's that word again: lucky. My chest lightens, and I grin, because more and more, that seems to be the truth. Maybe it's finally my turn to have things work out for me, or maybe I really am manifesting my luck turning around, but either way, I try not to look at it too closely.

"Here's the keys, you're good to go," he says, and I glare at him.

"I have to pay," I remind him, and he grins, shaking his head before rolling his eyes.

"You're a pain, you know that?"

"It's pretty much my one job in life to make your and Grant's life a misery."

"And now Graham's," Miles adds. I look over my shoulder at the man in question.

"No, he likes it, trust me."

A loud laugh fills the garage, and it's not until I've paid and I'm following Graham back to his place in my car that's never run smoother that I realize Graham never argued my point.

# THIRTY-THREE

"Want to watch the fireworks?" Graham asks after a takeout dinner at his place. I'm in a pair of boy shorts underwear and one of his tees, and I hadn't planned on putting on real clothes again. Because of that, I look at him, then to the darkened sky, confused.

"Fireworks?" I ask, and he nods.

"Yeah, on the beach. They have them every other Thursday night." I knew this, of course, since planning that is in Claire's jurisdiction, but I rarely make the effort to see them. He looks at me for a moment before tipping his head, not to the front door, but to the stairs.

"Come on," he says, then stands, putting a hand out to me.

"I don't really want to get dressed and go out," I murmur, biting my lip. He laughs, twines his fingers through mine, then leads me up the stairs.

"Good thing we don't have to," he says, then opens a door I'd never been through, leading me to a rooftop patio. I look up at the night sky in awe, the boardwalk lit up, the stars bright over the ocean. It's enclosed with a railing and a couple of feet higher than the other rooftops, meaning nothing is impeding our view.

"This is all yours?" I ask, looking around in awe. I knew the place was tall, but I didn't realize *how* tall. Suddenly, I'm desperate to come up here first thing in the morning and watch the sun rise on the water with a cup of coffee and my sketchbook.

The wind blows gently, a cool breeze off the water, making me shiver a bit, and Graham pulls me to the edge of the railing with a waist-high bar table built in along the edge.

"I didn't want to share a private space," he says with a shrug. "I need to get outdoor furniture out here, though." He moves so his chest is to my back, holding me against him.

"Can I help?"

"I was hoping you'd do it for me. Shopping isn't my favorite."

I nearly squeal with excitement.

"Oh my god! This will be so much fun!"

He shakes his head before dropping his head to press his lips to my neck. My breath hitches, and my mind travels to things that could be done up here, both secluded and out in the open, and...

Since Graham and I have gotten together, my long-buried libido has been on overdrive, my body constantly filled with need and desire for this man. While I normally have no libido whatsoever during my period, it seems that changes when Graham is around.

With a shake of my head to clear it, I take a deep, steadying breath, then release it just as the first firework explodes over the ocean. It sends a colorful burst into the sky, with sparkles crackling as it falls. I'm captivated, unsure of the last time I actually watched fireworks, which is why I barely register when his hand starts to move. One stays planted, splayed over my belly, but the other travels lower to the edge of the tee. His thumb moves up, sliding along my bare skin.

"You look good in my tee, June," he murmurs, then his hands slide forward to my inner thigh. He tugs my thigh a bit, and I widen my stance without thought. His fingers slide in and up over my center. "But I like it even better because that's all you have on."

"Graham, we can't. I have my period," I murmur.

"Doesn't bother me in the least, but right now I'm only focused on you." His fingers slide up my center over my panties, making my breath hitch. "Orgasms are good for cramps," he repeats his refrain from earlier, and despite never being into this, my center throbs.

"You don't have to—" I start, but as another two fireworks burst into the night sky, his hand moves up then slides down into the front of my panties, his warm fingers settling over my now needy clit.

"I never do anything I don't very much want to do, June. Trust me. I know I don't have to."

*Why is that so hot?* The mere idea of his wanting nothing more than to please me? My body melts back into his, and a low groan leaves him at my acquiescence, vibrating against my back.

"Should we go inside?" I ask in a whisper.

"No," he says, before his fingers start making small, steady circles over my clit.

"Graham," I breath.

"I like you out here well enough." His hand on my belly slides up to my breast, cradling it and tweaking the nipple over the fabric. I let out a low moan, my breasts terribly sensitive right now, and start to writhe. I look around nervously, as it's dark but not pitch black. Relief glides through me as I note the rest of the neighboring rooftops are empty.

"Quiet, lady luck. You wouldn't want anyone to find out just how dirty you are," he says as if reading my thoughts. "Letting your boss rub your pretty pussy on the roof, where anyone could see." His words are a taunt, and instead of instilling fear, they make me want him more, make that pleasure heighten.

"Graham," I murmur. His fingers continue to work me. "I need you."

"After you come, I'm dragging you into the shower and fucking you," he groans into my neck.

"Okay," I mewl, my hips rocking against his hand, one hand lifting to hook around his neck and stop myself from falling if my knees give out. The loud booms are filling the air more and more frequently and pleasure builds seemingly in time with it, circling and twisting in my lower belly. I'm about to let out a breath, to come hard on his hand and beg him to take me inside for a hard fuck when a door opens, a couple coming out onto the rooftop of the building in front of us. Graham's hand slides from my breast to my belly once more.

No, no, no, *no!*

We're going to have to go inside and finish this, even if it's just in the stairwell, before we're actually inside. I don't think I can make it much further without self-imploding.

"Hey there," the man says, waving in our direction as he steps onto his own roof. Another firework goes off, lighting up the sky and taking his attention.

"Hey, how's it going?" Graham asks, voice so casual.

I start to pull away, disappointment flooding my system, but the hand that was on my breast slides under my tee, pressing to my bare belly and holding me in place. Then, slowly, meticulously, *torturously*, he begins sliding his fingers over my clit again. I bite back a moan, eyes wide and panicked but that need reigniting quickly.

"Stay quiet," he murmurs into my neck, and my breath hitches, my fingers tightening around the railing before us. There's a solid wall that starts at my waist, so they couldn't see anything if they wanted to.

"We almost forgot about this, but I'm glad we heard it and made our way up there," the man across the way says over his shoulder.

"Definitely wouldn't want to miss it," Graham says, pushing me further into him. His hard cock pokes my back, and the pleasure ratchets up, bringing me right back to that edge again. He grinds into me from behind, and my knees weaken, though he holds me upright.

"God, you feel so fucking good," he groans low into my neck, and I tighten further.

"Graham," I whisper, quiet and nearly inaudible over the loud boom of the fireworks.

"I know, baby. I know. It feels good, doesn't it? You're so wet. I can't wait to slide inside you." My breathing is ragged now, my hands shaky, and with spectacular timing, the finale begins.

Dozens of fireworks explode over the ocean, one after another, a near-deafening cacophony, and I let out a small moan as fireworks of my own burst behind my closed eyes, as Graham's fingers speed up, pressing harder and giving me exactly what I need to come.

And come.

And come.

The sky becomes silent just as I return to myself and I realize Graham is breathing heavy in my ear, his body still holding me up, his cock still hard as a rock. Clouds of smoke drift in the sky, but I can barely register anything other than the feel of Graham's hand still between my legs.

"Quite a show, right?" the man on the other balcony says. I let out a little laugh that almost ends in a moan as Graham's fingers continue to slide over my clit.

"Fantastic," Graham says, moving to cup my still sensitive pussy.

"Well, have a good night," the guy says with a wave before taking his partner back inside, but I can't respond, not when I'm swallowing another moan and letting my head fall back.

There is no reason why I should still be turned on, but god, I am. I buck my hips and let out a soft mewl of need as the door slams behind our neighbors.

"We should go inside," I murmur, feeling him hard beneath me and shimmying a bit. "Take that shower you offered."

"Yes," he says, his hand pulling out of my panties and leaving me cold. But before I can complain or step away, he points into the sky right above us.

"Look," he says, tipping his chin toward the sky, and I gasp.

"Is that—"

"A shooting star. Make a wish, June." My breath catches, completely and totally blown away by this stroke of luck, another thing I've never experienced. Closing my eyes, I take in a deep breath and try to think of something I want. But lately, it seems like every-thing is working out for me, and there's not much to wish for.

Except for the one thing hanging over my head.

*I wish I get the mural job.*

It's not that I need the money or even the notoriety. It's just that Seaside Point is my town. It's my grandparents' town, and it's my friends' town, and it's the place I love more than anywhere else in the world, and despite trying to play it cool, I want to leave my mark here. Maggie was right: it's what my grandmother would have wanted.

In a way, it would also be a way to prove to my parents and to myself that I can have it all: the creativity, the drive, and the desire to create for a living, and to be there for the people I love. I have my hometown, family, and friends, and in my own way, I can have it all: I just have to make it work for me.

I let the wish go with a soft sigh, settling into Graham, and a sense of peace falls over me, knowing that it's all in the hands of the universe, and that which will happen will happen.

"I've never seen a shooting star," I say, turning in his arms to face him. He dips his head and presses his lips to mine.

"No?"

I shake my head.

"I've always wanted to. Just like the four-leaf clovers." I let out a little laugh, shifting to press my lips to his cheeks. "I'm starting to think you're my own lucky charm. Everything really has worked out for me since you came into my life."

He lets out a small hum, and I lie back in his arms, content in the knowledge that everything really does work out for me before he takes me inside and fucks away the last of my bad day.

The next day is sunny, so I spend some time working on the mural on the beach. Since I'm a disaster and likely to get paint on *everything,*

I've taken to leaving my phone in the office while I paint. So it's not until Graham and I are getting ready to go to lunch together that I check my notifications.

That's when I notice a new email in my personal account. Thinking it's probably junk, I tap on it to clear my inbox, then freeze.

"Oh my god," I say low, staring at the small screen.

"June?" Graham asks, stepping out of his office and watching me with apprehension.

"Oh my *god!*" I shout, continuing to stare at the screen. I tap out, then back in to confirm I'm not imagining things.

"What is it?" Graham asks, sounding more nervous now.

"Oh my god, oh my god, oh my GOD!"

"June, if you don't explain, I'm going to—" Graham warns, voice low, but doesn't get the chance to finish his threat because I turn to him, eyes watering.

"I'm a finalist," I murmur, reading the email thanking me for applying to the Seaside Point mural project and asking if I'm available to present my proposed mural to the city council on Tuesday after Labor Day. "For the town's mural project. I have to present early next month," I whisper, my heart pounding.

"June! That's amazing!" he says, moving to me and pulling me into his arms.

Instead of the anxiety I expected to feel if and when I got to this point, there's just joy, plain and simple. I put my arms around him and hold tight, savoring this feeling before I pull back. Then, he presses his lips to mine, kissing me long and deep.

This is the reaction I secretly wanted when I sold my first painting, and I love that somehow, the universe is still letting me get my way. When he finally breaks the kiss, he presses his forehead to mine, and my chin wobbles a bit, overwhelmed by emotion.

"It was my wish," I say through a tight throat. "On the shooting star. I wished that I would get this job." My eyes are watering as I look up to Graham, who puts my hands to my face before pressing his lips to mine, soft and sweet.

"And you will, June," he says when he pulls back. "You'll get it, because everything works out for you. My lady luck, you're going to have the whole world."

And really, I must be the luckiest girl in the world to have a man in my life who gets me the way he does.

# THIRTY-FOUR

# GRAHAM

It took almost two weeks and some careful maneuvering to convince June to celebrate her birthday this year.

It started with a quiet mention to Sutton when she was at Daytrip, timed to when June was working on her mural. I told her I wanted to celebrate June's birthday, to take her somewhere and do something fun, but when I mentioned it, she shot it down.

*I don't want to make a fuss over it, Graham. It's just a birthday,* she told me.

But I'm pretty sure I was put on this earth to make a fuss over June Taylor.

Next, Sutton conspired with Claire and Lainey, who informed me the perfect way to celebrate would be to go to Atlantic City, something June has always wanted to do, and, despite living barely an hour from the casinos, has never been. According to Lainey, my lady luck spent all of high school talking about going on her twenty-first birthday, but that year, her grandparents were sick, and she didn't find the time.

Each year, she's made her own excuses, but according to Claire, it's always mostly boiled down to the fact that June doesn't want to inconvenience anyone.

I personally love when June inconveniences me, though, and I would be fine with inconveniencing the entire world to make her happy.

While she shot the idea down the moment *Claire* brought it up, we had planned for that. A week later, I offered her a challenge at the Seabreeze's trivia night a week later: if the boys win, June agrees we all go to Atlantic City and celebrate her birthday. She was in instantly, but didn't realize *everyone* was in on it. She got the hint right around when Sutton answered that hermit crabs are from Canada, giving me a burning glare across the bar. When the girls inevitably lost, Claire cheered, *We're going to AC, baby!* which definitely was the last straw. June stomped over to me then, Decker muttering an *oooh, you're in trouble* as she stood before me with her hands on her hips.

"You planned that, didn't you?" she asked, but thankfully, there was a smile in her eyes. I returned it.

"Maybe."

"And you got them in on it, too?"

"I want an excuse to go to Atlantic City, so I was always going to be in," Lainey said with a shrug. June glared at her.

"Can't go back on a deal, lady luck," I reminded her, pulling her in close.

"My god, you all suck," she said, pouting, but after a moment, she sighed. "Fine."

Which is how we find ourselves walking into a casino in Atlantic City, June, trying to hide her excitement as she looks around in awe. The smell of smoke is heavy in the air, cheering and bells ringing as I hold her hand in mine, her duffle bag balanced on my suitcase in the other, and guide her toward the front desk. June insisted on sitting beside me while I booked the hotel, knowing if she didn't, I would probably splurge on something June told me was *absolutely unneces-*

*sary.* I smile to myself as we check in, remembering the last time we went to a hotel together.

That one ended well enough.

"Okay, and I have you...oh, look at that," the receptionist says, giving June a wide grin. My nerves tick up, wondering how she's going to receive this. "You've been upgraded."

"Upgraded?" June asks, looking around. "Why?"

"It says here that you were randomly selected. There was an opening, and we put you in one of the high roller rooms. You also will have full access to the hotel buffet."

"Oh, I think you have it wrong," she says, and the woman shakes her head, turning the screen toward June. "Graham Hawthorne and June Taylor, correct? This is you?" June inspects it carefully, then a slow smile spreads across her lips. In plain text, it says *Selected for Upgrade.*

"No way. Really?"

The receptionist smiles and nods. "Really. Looks like your luck is starting a bit early."

"It looks like it," she says, happily, then turns to me, that light dimming. "This wasn't you, was it?"

I shake my head. "All you, lady luck."

She smiles the way she always does when I call her that, and my gut churns at the lie.

I told myself I would stop making things work in her favor, but I'm a selfish man. I will never be over the way she lights up when something lucky happens to her, and I desperately want to see it as often as possible. The look of her beaming grin makes whatever small bit of guilt melt away.

There isn't much I wouldn't do to get that smile on her face.

She spent the summer trying to make me smile, but she doesn't realize I've been doing the same.

We check in, quickly breaking into the bed in the huge suite before June disappears from our room to get ready with the girls. I offered to have them use our room, but June told me that while she loves her friends, she didn't want our room to become the default getting-ready zone, and that if they did, we'd get interrupted *"while you're balls deep because Claire needs her curling iron."* A little over an hour later, the buzz of the automated lock fills the space. I'm wearing an outfit June picked out, a pair of dress pants and a button-down shirt, this one in the lightest blue that she said she hoped wouldn't send me into anaphylactic shock from the color.

It turns out, while it's completely passed my notice, since I just wear and buy the easiest clothes for work, June noticed I *only* wear white and black, and is determined to add more color into my life.

As if that's not what she's been doing since the first day she stumbled into it.

"Graham?" Heels click on the marble entryway. "My god, this place is so huge," she grumbles under her breath, and I let out a laugh.

"In here," I call from the living area, closing my laptop and moving toward where her voice is coming from. I stop when she comes into sight.

"Jesus," I breathe, taking her in—the electric blue dress hugging her curves, high silver heels on her feet. Her dark hair is down and straightened down her back, her makeup bold and sexy, a nervous smile on her red-painted lips.

"Is it too much?" she says, a bit of nerves in her voice. "I told Claire it was too much, but she insisted. The dress is her gift to me."

I remind myself to send a huge thank you to Claire for this.

"No, no. It's perfect." I take her hand, letting her spin beneath my arm and watch in fascination as the shiny material glimmers in the low light, showing off all of her delectable curves. "Fuck, June."

I fight every urge to strip it off her, throw her on the giant bed, and fuck her senseless. Who needs to gamble when I have my own lady luck in my bed?

I check my watch, trying to gauge how much time until we have to be downstairs for our dinner reservation with the crew.

Not nearly enough, so instead, I lead her out for our night of fun.

After dinner, we stand together outside. The entire crew is here:

Claire, Miles, and Sutton, Decker, Lainey, and Grant, all managing to get the time needed off. June is completely ecstatic to have all of her people with her, celebrating, having a good time without the pressure of work hanging over them.

"What's next?" I ask, pulling her into my side. She wobbles, either from the two drinks she had or the high heels, but I hold her steady.

"Let's gamble!" Claire yells, putting her arm into the air and cheering. "Test our luck!"

"I don't know," Lainey says, looking a bit nervously toward the tables. "I don't even know how any of these games work. It sounds like a lot of counting and math, which is my nightmare."

"We'll hang out on the slots like little old ladies," Claire says with a grin, hip-checking Lainey, who smiles.

"Slots are a money suck," Grant says. Lainey glares at him, irritated, seemingly her normal response to him.

"Not if you have luck on your side," June says, hooking her arms through her friends and moving toward the casino.

That's when, for the first time, it hits me that maybe taking June to a casino wasn't my best plan, especially when I've spent the last few months making her think her lucky stars just always happen to be aligned.

The slot machines last a total of thirty minutes, Claire losing five dollars, and June making a hundred before they decide to try their hand at something new. They end up at the craps table, a game that none of them know and need Deck to explain before get going.

And going.

And going.

Somehow, June starts winning and winning, a small crowd gathering around her until she's turned a hundred dollars into a thousand.

"Maybe we should go to the club," Sutton says nervously, looking at June, who is nearly jumping with excitement.

"A thousand!" she yells, throwing her hands into the air. "Bet it all!"

"Hell yeah!" Claire yells, cheering her on, the biggest instigator of them all.

"Uh, June—" Grant starts with the same hesitation brewing my chest.

"I can't lose. I'm lucky! Everything works out for me!"

Guilt swirls in my chest, knowing the truth of her lucky streak has a lot more to do with my incessant need to make her happy than her inherent luck. I didn't think it would be a problem, but a birthday gambling trip *might* just be the stupidest idea I've ever had.

"Yeah, but—" I start.

"Let her live!" Claire yells, cutting me off as June slides all her chips in before grabbing the dice, shaking them, and throwing. Panic moves through me as the small dice moves along the felt. It's not a panic of her losing money, because I would happily replace every penny.

I just don't want her to be disappointed.

Unfortunately, I can manipulate a lot in her favor, but there are two things I can't touch: the New Jersey lottery and her career.

One, because it's illegal, and I can't take care of her from prison.

Two, because her career is all hers, and I never want her to think it's anything but.

I hold my breath as I watch the dice fall, and then stop, a three and a four.

"Oh my god!" she yells, jumping up and down and shouting. The room erupts with her, but she only has eyes for me as she jumps into my arms. "I am so lucky, and everything works out for me!"

"You really are," I murmur into her hair, relief rushing through me.

"Again!" Claire yells, but June looks over her shoulder and shakes her head. I let out the breath I'd been holding.

"I think that was enough testing my luck, even for me," she says, giving me a wide, happy grin. I nod eagerly, and Grant laughs from beside her. We cash out, then once more, I pull her into my side.

"Now what, birthday girl?" I ask, pulling her into me, pressing my lips to hers gently. When I pull back, her eyes are just a bit dazed, a happy soft smile on her lips.

"We could go back to the room," she murmurs, voice low and filled with implication.

I pick up on it and instantly want to live out those implications.

"We could," I say low, my hand tightening on her waist.

"Absolutely not," Claire says, moving closer and pushing us apart.

"Claire, babe, let them—" Miles starts, but she gives him a fierce look, and he stops, lifting his hands.

"No, we're here to party, and we are going to party." She turns to me. "You got that reservation, right?"

I bite back a groan, remembering that I did, in fact, reserve a party box at a club at Claire's request. I nod, knowing that regardless of my desire to take June back to our room, she'll have fun with what her best friends have planned.

"Let's go party, lover boy."

We're in the private room that Claire and Sutton helped me pick out for a total of five minutes, just long enough for the girls to ooh and ahh over the view and the luxury before the opening chords of some song I vaguely remember fill the club. June and Claire turn to one another and scream.

"It's our song!" Claire shouts, and then, as if there's some unspoken understanding I'm not privy to, June kisses me before all of the girls hustle down to the main dance floor. When the door shuts behind them, I stare at it for a moment before looking to Miles, who looks far less confused than I, an old pro at this, it seems.

"Do I want to know?" I ask.

"Would the idea of Claire and June dancing on a bar top scare the fuck out of you?" Miles counters. My eyes widen, and he grins, clapping a hand on my shoulder. "Yeah, you don't want to know. Might as well have a drink: it's gonna be a long night, my man."

We move to the bar, each of us grabbing a drink before settling into the barstools at the edge of the room. Part of the reason I chose this particular club was the ability to look out over the main dance floor from the private rooms, and I spot June dancing with the girls.

"How panicked were you out there?" Miles asks, and when I look to him, there's a wide grin on his lips that I don't quite understand.

"Panicked?"

"She put a grand on a craps table thinking she was lucky," he says. I stare for a moment, unsure of how to respond, before settling on ignorance, lifting my shoulder with nonchalance, and taking a sip of my beer.

"She is lucky."

"Sure, she is, but that luck isn't all natural," he says, his grin widening.

I should have known.

I should have known that stepping outside of my carefully laid plans and asking Miles to tell her that her car issues were just small fixes was a bad idea, but I couldn't help myself.

I should have known it would bite me in the ass.

"Not sure what you're talking about," I say.

"Can't bullshit a lovesick bullshitter, Hawthorne. I kept seashells in my pockets for six years for Claire, dropping them so she'd think it was some kind of luck. I know a grand gesture when I see one."

I sigh, realizing there's no use.

"Have you told Claire?" I ask, not bothering to defend myself. He shakes his head.

"No reason to." Relief washes through me. "Did you do that?" he asks. "At the casino?" I shake my head, then take a long sip of my beer.

"I might be lovesick, but I have no desire to go to prison."

"Smart man," he says, tipping his beer toward me.

"Who's going to prison?" Grant says, coming over to where we're sitting.

"No one," I say quickly.

"Graham, if he keeps his shenanigans up with June."

I snap my head toward Miles because that sounds way worse than it actually is. Instead of correcting himself, he starts laughing.

"I'm sorry?" Grant asks, his anger looking more and more palpable by the moment.

"It's not like that."

"Then what is it like?" he asks, crossing his arms on his chest and lifting an eyebrow. This is not good.

"I—" I hesitate, unsure what to say. Grant Taylor might be the most important person in June's life; making him angry could easily end things between us. Before I can answer, though, Decker speaks up.

"Is this about how you've been intervening with all of her shit to make her dreams come true or whatever?" Decker asks.

"What do you know about that?" I ask, then far too late realize it's an admission of guilt.

An entire summer of scheming successfully and three guys and a beer are going to be what brings me down, isn't it?

"Sutton's got a big mouth," he says. There are plenty of ways I could respond to that, and I'm sure June would have a field day decoding that sentence, but I don't touch any of them.

"I'm not explaining my relationship with June, because it isn't any of your business."

"Fine. I'll just call June up and,—" Grant starts, and I know I'm fucked.

It's all going to come tumbling down.

"Stop, stop. I'll tell you." Grant puts his phone away with a smile, and I realize the threat was empty. There's no point in avoiding the topic though: it would only look worse.

"I've been...setting things up for June."

"Setting things up?" Grant asks, and Decker lets out a snort of a laugh, clearly entertained. Miles sits, sipping his beer and smiling.

"Nothing bad. Just... She thinks she's lucky, right?" Grant nods, crossing his arms on his chest. "So I've coercing with things occasionally so that things go her way."

"Like?"

"He paid for the updates to her car," Miles says, looking at me assessingly. "He asked me not to tell her. Told me to say she just needed a cabin air filter and an oil change, but then had me fix her air conditioning, the starter, and any safety updates it needed."

"Why would you do that?" Grant asks.

"Because that car is a piece of shit and a death trap, but there's no world where she should have let me cover the updates needed or even pay for them all herself at once. So when I found out her car was in his shop, I asked Miles to do what needed to be done and bill me for it, and then tell her it was just a few things."

"I would have done it anyway," Miles says, a smile on his lips. "She's my best friend's little sister, but I figured I might as well make some money for the shop while I was at it."

Grant stares at me as if he's unsure if he approves or absolutely hates me. "What else have you done?" Might as well put it all out on the table.

"I got her favorite donuts every day the first week she worked at Daytrip." He nods, as if he noticed. "And I helped her find four-leaf clovers. I got her concert tickets." I decide *not* to tell him about the job, at least until Sutton spills it.

That can be a concern for another day.

"And she knows nothing about this?" I give him a tight look.

"Not unless one of you tells her." He stares at me for long moments, the room silent except for the booming bass. I become painfully aware that I'm the odd man out here, that we're in a room with all of his friends, and if he hit me, they would all defend him. Hell, they'd probably pitch in.

But he doesn't.

Instead, he surprises me.

"You're why she started leaning into art, aren't you?" he asks. I shake my head.

"That was Claire and Lainey," I say. He looks at me as if he doesn't buy it in the least.

"They've been trying to get her to open that shop for years. It never happened. It was you."

I sigh. "I made her feel lucky by making sure she found a four-leaf clover. She saw it as a sign that she should put her shop live. When I realized she actually did it, I also bought the first piece from her shop, which, I'll admit, I think made her believe in herself and start actually promoting it. But the rest was all her." Grant stares at me, then nods. His jaw goes firm, one final test, I think.

"The proposal for your boss—did you set that up?" I shake my head quickly.

"No. That was all her. Rowan saw potential because he has an eye for talent."

His face shifts, and he sighs. "You're good for her," Grant says, begrudgingly. "This summer has been good for her. When she quit, I was nervous because she was giving up everything she knew, every-thing she worked for, but I saw fast enough she was only teaching because she thought she was supposed to. She was always supposed to chase art, but I think I talked so much shit about it, she didn't even think of it as a real option. I feel bad for that. I don't know how much she's told you about our parents, but they weren't the best, and that fucked with me, but it isn't June's fault. I'm glad she has you helping her realize what she's meant to be doing, because burning herself out with teaching wasn't it."

I nod, relief rushing into me like cold water at what sounds almost like approval.

But then a smile spreads on his lips, and he tips his drink to me.

"But when she finds out, good luck. She's going to have your balls."

# THIRTY-FIVE

It's the best birthday ever.

I was never the type to daydream about big parties and celebrations, but if I had ever allowed myself to, this is what I would have imagined—chaos, luxury, life, luck, and all of my favorite people enjoying it with me. I can't stop smiling as the girls and I move to the center of the dance floor, Claire and I screaming along to the song that, in college, we determined was *our song*. The four of us dance to a handful of more songs, giggling and grinding on one another before Claire tugs my hand.

"Sutton's gotta use the bathroom," she yells, tipping her head toward the edge of the club. I nod, grabbing Lainey's hand, the four of us moving to the bathroom together in a line so as not to get separated. When we enter, the bathroom is surprisingly empty, a small blessing, and blissfully quieter once the door closes on us. Claire and I stand at the mirrors, waiting for Lainey and Sutton to be done.

"You having a good time?" Claire asks, giving me a wide smile.

"The best," I say, my eyes drifting shut, the liquor in my veins making me feel warm and light, the unfettered joy of being out with my favorite people only improving that.

"I don't know the last time I've seen you let go this much," she says with a laugh. "You seem...freer."

"I'm happy," I say, and I mean it. "Everything really is working out for me. Today's been amazing. I have the hottest boyfriend," I say, with a giggle. "And I'm figuring out what I want to do with my life."

"So you don't want to teach anymore?"

I lift a shoulder.

It's the first time I've actually thought about it in weeks, the fact that in a year, I'll have the option to go back to teaching. The thought of going back makes that dread creep back in, though. The liquor makes my tongue looser, confessing.

"I don't...think so. I haven't thought much about it or made any real decisions, but I like having art in my life. I never thought it would be a viable option, but here we are..."

"I mean, you're about to be a huge, famous artist with your big mural for the town." I don't argue with her even though I still have to present my idea next week. Instead, I grin.

"And my first big mural for Daydream," I say. "End of September, I'm spending a week at the Keys location. They also have four new Daytrip locations opening next year, and he wants to make them must-see destinations. I'm about to be a busy girl." I bite my lip as Claire's jaw drops.

"What?" Lainey asks, coming to the sinks to wash her hands, eyes wide. I nod, giving her an excited smile. "Why is this the first I'm hearing of this?"

"It's been a busy couple of weeks," I say with a laugh, even though the truth is it all feels a bit too good to be true, like if I start telling people before the ink dries, it might disappear. But yesterday I got the final contract back from Rowan, signed by all parties included, so now it's official.

I'm making a career out of art. The one thing I always swore I'd never do, the one thing I always swore was impossible after a lifetime of watching my parents chase it at the expense of thee people I love.

Lainey's eyes go wide, Claire's tear up, and my throat aches a bit at the sight of their utter joy and pride.

"It really is the luckiest summer ever," I say with a smile.

"Told you that you getting fired was lucky!" Claire says, grabbing a towel and dabbing at the corner of her eye. I glare at her. "Oh, come on. It might not have felt that way at the time, but now…I mean, it's obvious. Everything just… worked out so perfectly. Your career, your love life, everything."

"So, are you going to quit on Graham?" Lainey asks, and something churns in my gut. I hadn't actually thought of that.

"I…I don't know," I say, with a shrug. "We haven't talked about it, to be honest. Originally, he wasn't going to be here much longer after the season, moving on to bigger and better things, but now he's staying here, taking on the Daytrip branch…" I bite my lip as my words trail off.

"Why does everyone look so sad? We're supposed to be celebrating!" Sutton says as she walks toward us, joy in her words as she moves to wash her hands. "No pouting on a birthday Atlantic City Trip! Sad, drunk girl on her birthday does not actually have to be a real stereotype!"

"June just realized she doesn't know what she's going to do when she has to tell Graham that she doesn't want to be his assistant forever," Claire murmurs.

Quickly, before Sutton gets the wrong idea, I shake my head.

"It's not that I don't like the job—I do. I actually enjoy it so much more than I thought, but I don't want to be stuck in another job that I feel like I *should* stay in. But I also don't want to leave Graham high and dry."

Sutton looks to me, brows furrowing before she shakes her head.

"That won't be a problem," she says. "You could quit today, and he'd be fine."

I give her a look.

"I can't imagine him hiring anyone else for the position. He'd be mean and scare them off."

"It wouldn't be a non-issue because he'll get a new assistant. It will be a non-issue because Graham doesn't need an assistant," she says. Claire hands her a paper towel to dry her hands while I stare at her, lost.

"I'm sorry, I—"

She looks at me before her eyes go wide. "He didn't tell you."

My stomach drops to the floor. "Tell me what?"

The color starts to leave her face, and panic fills my veins.

"I really thought he told you," she murmurs.

"Told me *what*, Sutton?" I ask. She looks at me, both appeasing and nervous.

"It's really not a big deal, June. And it's kind of sweet, if you think about it."

"Hey, Sutton, babe, you gotta tell her before she has a coronary," Claire says to her sister, something I'm grateful for, but I'm too panicked to be able to express that.

Especially not when Sutton looks at me a bit drunk, her eyes apologetic, a tiny smile on her lips.

"I made this position for you."

"What the fuck," I say, eyes locked on Graham as I walk into the private room. It's quieter in here, above the rest of the party, and I'm grateful for that, though the cameras that are most definitely in here would work against me in case I actually *kill* Graham Hawthorne.

"June," Graham says, stepping over to me, an entertained look on his face. I want to slap it away.

"What the *fuck*, Graham?" I repeat, and his face goes from humorous and sweet to confused in an instant.

"What's going on?" Instinctively know it's my brother speaking, but I don't break eye contact with Graham.

"June's about to rip Graham a new asshole," Claire explains.

"She found out, didn't she?" Decker asks, and all eyes turn to him, including mine. "About Graham setting things up for her?"

His words settle, and I realize in a heartbeat it's not just the job. Tiny moments I thought were pure, unadulterated luck settle into place, confirmed only when Graham's face goes pale. I don't know how to feel right now, so I focus on an easier target.

"*You* knew?" I ask, my eyes wide.

Deck lifts his hands and shakes his head as if realizing his error. "I didn't know shit," he says, lifting his hands. "Not until like, ten minutes ago."

"Sure, convenient," I say with a roll of my eyes, returning my focus to Graham, but I'm distracted once more in a moment.

"I knew," Miles says, a grin on his lips.

"*You* knew?" Claire says, aghast. "And you didn't tell me?"

He gives her a deadpan look, then reaches over and pulls her into his side.

"Love you, but you have the biggest mouth on this planet, Claire. Of course I wouldn't tell you."

Her jaw goes tight, but she doesn't argue because we all know he has a good point.

"How did you know?" I ask, and his eyes go wide. I groan, covering my face. "My car. It was my car, wasn't it? I *knew* that you were undercharging. I can't believe you did that, Graham!" He opens his mouth to argue or defend or apologize, I'm not sure, but Grant speaks then.

"Cut him some slack, June; he was trying to help you out. It's not his fault that you're the most stubborn person on this planet." I snap my head to him, my anger suddenly having a new target. I feel untethered, confused, and unsure of where to focus my irritation. Or, a tiny part inside of me whispers, if that irritation is even valid at all.

"You're not supposed to be on his side! You're supposed to be on *my* side!" I say, stomping my foot and pointing to myself, but my brother just rolls his eyes, letting out a deep sigh.

"June, I am on your side," he says, looking a bit exasperated. I point to Graham.

"No, you're not, you're not kicking his ass," I argue.

Graham's eyes widen, and I get a small amount of joy, seeing his discomfort, even if I don't *actually* think I want Grant to get into a fight with him.

"For what?" Grant argues. "For making you happier than you have been in a long time? For giving you a job, something steady while you figure out what you want to do with your life? For making everything work out for you so you could live in a la-la-land of manifesting and woo-woo shit?" I blink at him, but he keeps going. "Everyone knew you were miserable. Getting the chance to safely do what you were made to do, to start your business and pursue art, is a gift, June, and you wouldn't have done it without him working in the background."

"You think I should pursue art?" I ask, confused. I came in here on a mission, anger fueled by liquor and the feeling like I was the last to know something about my life, but now that it's fading away, a glowing ember is all that's left. And that ember's warmth isn't angry at all. It's soft and sweet and hopeful.

"You gave me shit about it," I murmur.

Grant rolls his eyes and sighs.

"One of us has to be rational, June, and it's never been you." Without meaning to, I smile, just a bit, though a new wave of confusion filters in, my world set on its side once more with the understanding that Grant might not actually be as pessimistic about my art career as I've always assumed. I don't have time to dwell on that, though, because he's speaking again. "But none of that is relevant right now. I'm the first one to be skeptical of anyone who is wronging you, but I'm failing to see how trying to make things easier on you and—"

"He made me think I was lucky!" I say, throwing my hands into the air. "He let me think everything worked out for me."

"And that made you brave enough to try things you'd been too scared to do before," he countered. My mouth closes, unable to think of an argument.

"He's got a good point, June," Claire says, echoing my thoughts. When my attention shifts to her, she looks a bit apologetic, lifting a shoulder. "I mean, was it the best move? Not sure. But would you really have taken the whole lucky girl summer thing as seriously as you did if not?" My mouth purses, and I take in a deep breath, seeing her rationale.

"She's got a great point. You should definitely listen to Claire more," Graham says, making Claire smile.

"You're not off the hook, Graham Hawthorne," I snap, turning to him, that irritation igniting once more.

"Well aware, lady luck. I earned your ire. Now, can we go outside and talk about it somewhere quieter? I'll tell you everything you want to know."

"I don't know, I'm kind of enjoying the show," Decker says, a shit-eating grin on his face. I roll my eyes, but before I can argue with him, Grant hits him upside the head.

"Shut up and let them be," Grant says. "I think it's time for everyone to pack it in for the night."

"Excuse me—" Lainey starts, but Grant glares at her, and she sighs. "Yeah, you're so right. I'm actually a bit tired myself." Everyone murmurs their solemn agreements before we wish each other goodbye.

"Hear him out, June," Sutton says low as she hugs me. "The man is wild about you." I nod, then give everyone one last wave before leaving.

The walk to our hotel room takes about five minutes, and we're silent the whole way. When we get into the elevator, his hand brushes mine as if on instinct. He pulls away quickly, giving me a mumbled apology, but with a sigh, I reach over and twine my fingers with his.

I hate that the second I do, something in my chest eases.

I might be terribly annoyed, angry, and confused by him, but I still love having him close.

It's not until the hotel door closes us into our suite, a suite I'm now pretty sure Graham upgraded us to, that I slide my hand out of his, crossing my arms on my chest and facing him. I brooded over my thoughts, feelings, and emotions the entire way, but I have only one question that matters.

"Why did you do that?" I ask. My voice is low and even, but the hurt rings clear. "Why did you lie to me?"

His face softens with regret when I speak. "I didn't lie to you, June."

"So there was an assistant position?" He looks away, and my heart drops a little. "That's what I thought."

"That's a bad example,"

My brow furrows.

"A bad example?" Something crosses his face, stubbornness or frustration or embarrassment, I don't know, but either way, it's a tipping point. "A bad example, Graham? The entire summer, I thought I was lucky. I thought that the universe was pushing me in the right direction, giving me signs I was on the right path, only to find out it was you *manipulating* me."

"I wasn't—"

"You had my brother's best friend lie to me and pay for my car. You had my best friend's sister make up an entire job for me. You slept with me knowing damn well that the next day, I'd find out that I would be working for you. You—" I hesitate as something new hits me, my stomach churning with nerves, and his face goes blank. "Did you buy my art?" The words are faint even to my own ears, but when he closes his eyes and takes in a breath, I know he heard me.

"June, you have to understand—"

"You bought my art, didn't you? You were that first sale?" My mind is reeling now, nausea filling me with the thought that much, much more than just my luck has been fabricated.

Has the entirety of my success been fake?

"Just that first sale. I promise. It was partly because it was fucking beautiful, and partly because even after the Daytrip project was done and I was on to the next one, I wanted to have a piece of you and your sunshine and your luck with me at all times."

Relief moves through me at his reasoning, and even if it makes me an idiot, I buy it. It makes sense, and the thought that even when we were nothing, he wanted a piece of my art to remember me by warms me. Unfortunately, it's so buried by confusion and frustration that I can't let the issue go.

"So you let me just believe a stranger found my website and bought my painting?" He closes his eyes again, sighing defeated. "Why would you do that? Why would you lie to me like that? Why did you—"

"Because I'm in love with you!" he shouts, cutting me off, and the world goes quiet. Long moments span as he stands before me, running a hand through his tousled hair, looking at me with pleading eyes. Begging me to understand.

"You're what?" I ask in a whisper, and he throws his hands up.

"I'm in love with you, June. I have been since the day I met you. It's why I went to the coffee shop every day for a week, hoping I would bump into you." He did tell me that, at least. "It's why when you stumbled into my place of business, I couldn't give up my shot at getting to know you, even if I have never made time or put in energy for any kind of relationship in my entire life. It's why I took you to my hotel room, hoping I could get you out of my system, even if by then, I knew it would be impossible. Even if I *knew* the next day that you'd be walking into my office to become my assistant."

My heart is pounding, but he's oblivious to that as he continues his monologue.

"I'm in love with you, and I have been since that first day, when you smiled over your shoulder at me and apologized for eavesdropping on my call. It's why I told Sutton to give you a job, any job. It's why I did everything I could to avoid you in the beginning, and why your incessant need to be my friend worked: because I never needed convincing, June. I just needed to give myself the permission to love you. It's why I make sure there are always enough chocolate frosted donuts with sprinkles for you to get one. It's why I stayed up for *hours*, making a dozen emails and entering a million different contests to get you those goddamn tickets because I knew you'd never accept them from me."

My eyes widen as more pieces fall into place; his mission has been far more intricate than I realized.

"You what?" I ask, my voice barely a whisper, but instead of explaining, he continues.

"It's why I spent an hour outside to find your earring, which, just so you know, somehow flew like, fifteen feet away from where you were standing, and put it right where you'd spot it. It's why I upgraded our hotel room on your birthday and—"

"You fixed the craps game, didn't you? It's illegal to cheat in a casino, Graham," I say with wide eyes, panicked even though I think I'm supposed to be mad at him right now.

Even if I'm mad at him, I don't want him to go to *prison*.

A tiny smirk lifts his lips, and he shakes his head.

"That was all you, June. *That* was your luck. I'm not so far gone as to commit fraud in a casino." I smiled a bit, then my mind moved through moments over the summer, big and small.

"The hotel rooms in Wildwood. Did you plan on just one?" I ask.

"No. At that point, I just wanted you happy, but I didn't want to cross that line. It felt selfish."

I nod, understanding in a twisted way.

"The clovers?"

He looks away before letting out a sigh and running his hand through his hair.

"You were excited to find them, so I found one in another spot of the yard and transplanted it."

A new thought hits me, and panic comes with it. "Did you set up the proposal with Rowan?"

He instantly shakes his head. "No. No, I didn't. That was all you, and that was all Rowan. I drew the line at anything that had to do with your career."

I give him a deadpan look. "You had Sutton give me a job!" I say, throwing my hands in the air before running one through my hair. "Now my entire career is a lie!"

He gives me a knowing look, a hint of a smile on the edges of his lips. "Working as an executive assistant is not your career, June."

Crossing my arms on my chest, I glare at him, but there's not much indignation left. In fact, I'm slowly coming to terms with it and finding it all a bit endearing. This is the kind of thing that, if I heard it happening to someone else, I would swoon. Not that I'll be telling him that.

"It could be," I say, and even I know I sound petulant.

He shakes his head, taking a step closer, and I let him, staying where I am. "Not for you, and you know that. That was always a stop along the way, and you were always meant to do so much more. You and I both know as much."

God, how does he always know the right thing to say?

And why am I suddenly desperate for him to be closer?

"I don't know if that's insane or precious," I murmur, taking a step closer and letting him wrap me up in an embrace. I can process all of this much better in his arms.

"I'm hoping precious," he murmurs into my hair, and I let out a sigh, snuggling into him, that feeling of *home* moving through me again. His hand moves to tip my chin, and I'm forced to look at him. There's no shield or mask on, and I realize it's been that way for a while. There's also worry, nervousness, and regret.

But most of all, shining bright in a way I don't know how I didn't realize it sooner, is pure, unadulterated love.

God, this man loves me. So much so, he would work tirelessly behind the scenes to make sure all of my whims come true.

"Do you forgive me?" he asks, eyes hopeful.

"I can't believe you did all of that," I murmur.

"And I can't believe that even when I was the grumpiest asshole on this planet, you kept working at me, trying to make me like you, trying to get me to open up, to see the magic that is Seaside Point. I can't believe you made me want to stay in one place, and that you made me make actual, honest-to-God friends I look forward to spending time with. I can't believe I won you somehow, made you mine."

"You really think you won me, Hawthorne?" I ask, lifting an eyebrow. I'm no longer angry, and I'm sure I'll have a million questions after this, but I can't find it in me to be genuinely mad, not when he clearly has been tying himself in knots trying to do anything he can to just...what? Make me happy? See me smile? Make me believe that I really could have everything if I just wished on enough dandelions, four-leaf clovers, and lucky pennies?

"If I'm lucky," he says, voice low, and it settles in my chest.

Because despite everything, the truth is, I am lucky.

The luckiest girl in the world.

Not because I got a job when I needed it, or because I sold a painting, or I found a four-leaf clover, or even because I made two grand at a craps table.

But because I have everything I could want.

# THIRTY-SIX

# GRAHAM

I dip my head, kissing June, and when she returns it, relief moves through me.

Tonight could have gone so, so badly. Terribly even.

But somehow, she understands.

Somehow, I think she's going to forgive me.

I press her back to the door, and her hands begin to shift, tugging at my shirt, moving up under it, kissing me with the same need that's been simmering under my skin. It's part liquor and part relief and part pure endorphins that have both of us going crazy, I'm sure, but I don't inspect any of it too closely. My hand moves down her ass, gripping each cheek hard and pulling her into me, making her moan into my mouth. In her heels, she's a bit taller, easier to kiss, making me think about turning her around, hiking that tiny skirt up to her waist, and sinking in deep. Who needs a bed or even a couch? The entryway will do just fine.

But then I remember the plan.

The clock in the small kitchen reads 12:14, and I remember I have a plan. So instead of fucking her like I want, I begrudgingly and with a bit of pain, pull away.

"Get your pajamas, I have a surprise for you," I murmur, smiling at the pouty look on her face.

"Is it your dick?" she asks, and I let out a laugh, something I do a lot more often with June in my life. "Because that's what I really want right now." I hesitate for one long moment, contemplating throwing the plan aside, but my woman loves whimsy and magic, and I'll be damned if I don't give it to her on her most magical day of the year.

"Not yet," I say with a laugh, stepping further away to maintain my defenses.

"But it's my birthday," she whines.

"I know, lady luck. Now go get some comfies on. Wash your face. Give me..." I think, unsure before committing to a time. "Five minutes."

"Graham—" I pull her into me, pressing my lips to hers quickly to cut off her protest before stepping away again.

"June, please."

She grimaces, but must see something on my face, because she sighs and nods, then shuffles off to the bedroom, kicking off her heels as she goes.

Once the bedroom door clicks closed behind her, I move with a mission.

Quickly and quietly, I head for the kitchen and smile at the small heart-shaped cake in the fridge the hotel staff delivered while we were out. On the counter are matches, and I dig into the cabinet, pulling out the candles I brought. Three twisty rainbow ones, as bright and sunshiney as the birthday girl herself, as well as a glittering number 2 and 7. Pressing them into the cake, I grab it and move through the hotel room to the large coffee table, one of the main reasons I actually upgraded to this room, and set it on the center. I sit on one side of the coffee table awkwardly before calling her in.

"You can come in, June," I say. Instantly, I hear her bare feet padding on the floor, eager to see her surprise as I begin lighting the candles. I'm just finishing lighting the 7 when she stops in the doorway, eyes wide. I smile, warmth spreading through my chest at the look on her face. She's wearing a tiny light blue tank top with matching shorts, delicate lace along the edges, a sliver of her belly revealed, no bra, her hair up in a messy bun atop her head, and somehow, in the five minutes I was in here, she washed her face clean of makeup.

She's never looked more beautiful.

She's never looked more like June, *my* June.

"Happy birthday, lady luck," I murmur when she stays quiet. "Come, sit." I tip my chin to the other side of the low coffee table. Apprehensively, she moves into the living area, her eyes shifting from me to the cake, awe and shock written clear across her face. Somehow, it's even better than the excited face she gets when something lucky happens, which is a relief since I think I'll want to put this one on her face even more.

"Graham," she says, shaking her head. "My birthday is tomorrow." I smile.

"It's after midnight. It's your birthday." Her eyes go wide. "Sit."

"On the coffee table?" she asks, confused when I nod, but does as I ask all the same.

"Isn't that how it goes?"

There's a moment before her face goes soft, those brimming tears returning to her blue eyes, making them shine brighter.

"Are you *Sixteen Candles*-ing me?" she asks through a small laugh. I just smile at her, gesturing to the cake and shrugging.

"It's your favorite movie."

"What did I do to deserve you, Graham Hawthorne?" she asks.

"Maybe you're just lucky."

She lets out a loud, cheer-filled laugh before looking at the cake. "Must be."

"Make a wish, June," I say, watching the wax start to pool as it drips down.

"I can't believe you did all of this just for my birthday."

"I might play with fate a bit, but I promise I'll never forget your birthday." One of those tears drips, rolling down her cheek. "Blow out the candles, June. Make a wish," I whisper. More tears fall, and I reach over to brush one away, streaking the wet across the apple of her cheek. She gives me a watery smile before laughing and shaking her head. My brows furrow. "What's wrong?"

"I don't know what to wish for." She lets out a small, disbelieving laugh. "I have everything I ever wanted. I'm the luckiest girl in the world."

And for a moment, nothing else matters. Nothing but June and her sweet smile, her hair pulled into a messy knot on top of her head, the candles burning beneath her, the glow lighting up the angles of her face. So at ease, so content, so... everything. And I know she means it: she feels lucky, because she has everything. It has nothing to do with career, money, or things. Instead, it has everything to do with me, her friends, and her family. With her town and that settled feeling I too now feel when I'm there, when I'm home.

"I love you, June," I say low. She asked me once if I've ever been in love, and the answer was no, not that I told her at the time. I've never said that to a woman, never been close enough to make it something that even crossed my mind, but I've been biting my tongue for weeks now, trying to find the right time to confess this secret to June in a way she would find special and magical and whimsical.

I don't know if blurting it out while confessing all of the white lies I've told her over the past few months is the most romantic, but when her eyes soften, her hand covers mine, and she speaks, I know it's going to work out in the end.

"I love you too, Graham." I smile then, leaning in and pressing my lips to her softly before pulling back. "Best birthday ever," she says low, then finally pulls back and blows out the candles.

# THIRTY-SEVEN

# June

A week after the chaos that was my finding out that my boyfriend had been quietly working behind the scenes to make all of my wishes come true, I wake in Graham's arms, in Graham's bed.

It's been the best week of my life, if I'm being honest.

Once everything was out in the open, Graham seemed lighter, and I realized he must have been nervous about my finding out for some time. Part of me wonders if he would have held onto those secrets forever, but another part simply doesn't care. Nothing he did was manipulative in the way of making me have feelings for him: if anything, from what I understand, it was meant to be a way for him to make me happy from afar, though my incessant need to be friends with him threw a wrench in his plans.

But now, there's nothing between us, and I'm happier and more settled into my life than I ever have. Yesterday was Sunday, and we spent the night at the Seabreeze with the crew, Graham hanging with the guys; me and the girls gabbing while Lainey worked, and it felt so incredibly perfect, like where we were all supposed to be. This week, we'll be ironing out the dates and times for my heading down to the

Keys for my first big commission. Graham is heading down with me and has already convinced me to tack on a few days. When I objected, he said a weekend with me at a luxury resort is his dream. I reminded him I'll be there for work, and when he said that I needed a better work-life balance, I laughed until I couldn't breathe.

Oh, how the tables have turned.

"Morning," Graham says as I slowly enter the land of the living. His fingers move through my hair, pushing it back over my shoulder.

"Morning," I murmur into his chest, melting back into the bed. Maybe that third drink Sutton talked me into wasn't my best plan. Before I can fall into the depths of sleep once more, though, his voice enters my consciousness once more, knocking me straight into reality.

"Happy second birthday, June."

Everything stops.

My eyes open, blinking once, twice, three times as his hand continues to brush my hair back before I dare to look up at him. He's grinning down at me, a smile I have come to love so damned much, near-blinding. "Did you think I'd forget?" Hesitantly and nervously, I sit up, his tee pooling around my hips. My hair is a mess, I'm sure, but I watch intently as he reaches over to his bedside table, pulling out a flat square box wrapped in pink paper with a red ribbon.

"What is this?" I ask as he hands it to me.

"Your second birthday present," he says simply. I fumble the package with his words, letting it tumble to the bedspread. Everything stops: my breathing, my heart, my world.

"Second…" I start, the words clogging in my throat as my eyes water again. This seems to be happening a lot lately.

"Today is a week after your real birthday. It's your second birthday." For a moment, he looks confused and a bit nervous. "That's what you told me, right? One week after your birthday and…"

His words trail off, and I watch in awe before letting him out of his misery.

"Yeah. Yes, Graham. It's….this is it. But you didn't have to do this," I say with a shake of my head.

"Yes, I did," he says, lifting the package once more and handing it over. This time, I don't drop it, even if my hands are shaking.

Instead, I gently tug on the ribbon, already thinking of ways to use it, to add some color to his place. My apartment lease is up in two months, and while we haven't had the formal conversation yet, Graham has made it clear that he wants me to move in with him rather than renew my lease. As much as I plan to fight him on it, it's mostly for the thrill of it, because I like fighting with Graham. We both know I'll be moving in with him. Hell, I've already been working on adding my touch to every inch of the place.

But all thoughts of decorations and moving in are gone from my mind as I open the box and find a shiny gold bracelet lying inside. Dainty links make a chain big enough for my wrist, and along the edges are three different charms.

A paintbrush.

A sand dollar.

A four-leaf clover.

"A lucky charm," he says, watching as I run a careful finger over the little clover. "Now you'll always have something lucky with you." My eyes water at the gesture, my throat tightening with emotion. " June, don't—"

"Do not tell me not to cry, Graham Hawthorne, not when you're doing sweet things for me." He grins, and I take in a deep breath, putting a hand out to him. "Put it on me." He gives me the soft, entertained smile I get from him a lot lately, the one I now realize is intertwined with love, before he puts the gold chain around my wrist. It's cold but warms quickly, and as his fingers slide over my skin, that warmth travels through my veins, settling in my chest. I stare at it as he finishes with the clasp, touching the dangling charms.

I can't believe this.

I can't believe him.

I can't believe I'm somehow so damned lucky to have found a man whom I mentioned something to one time, in passing, and he made it happen.

"I thought I could add one every second birthday," he says low, and the implication of what he means by that, that he plans to be here for every second birthday from now on, is not lost on me.

"God, you're so fucking good, aren't you?" I say, turning my wrist and hearing the happy jingle the charms make. I always wanted a charm bracelet as a kid, though I never told Graham that. Just further proof he was made for me, that he knows me better than anyone ever has tried to know me before.

"I'm learning." A soft smile plays on his lips, and I slide my arms over his shoulders, pulling him close to press a kiss to his lips.

"You're doing great," I say, then shift until I'm straddling him. "Now, I think it's time I showed my appreciation."

And then he lets me.

And he shows me some back.

And we're both fifteen minutes late to work.

# THIRTY-EIGHT

The Tuesday after Labor Day, I wake with a pit in my stomach. I ignore it throughout the day, going to work with a smile and pretending I'm not an absolute nervous wreck. Graham notices, obviously, and takes me out to lunch, trying to distract me, but it doesn't help, not really. The girls text me a few times throughout the day, asking how I'm feeling, telling me they know I'm going to do great, and asking whether I want them to meet me outside City Hall or just go in when they arrive.

Today is the big day for the presentation.

At quarter to six, I arrive at City Hall, driven by Graham because there was no way I would be able to drive myself, and walking in the late summer humidity would have had me stressing about my hair. At the end of today's City Council meeting, which starts at six, Cece and I will present our proposals. While I know my proposal is solid and I've practiced my presentation so many times, in front of so many different people, I could probably do it in my sleep, I can't seem to stop total and utter panic from creeping in. And now, sitting in the car in our super close parking spot outside of City Hall—something

Graham proclaimed to be lucky—I am rethinking every life choice I've ever made that led me here.

"Ready to go in?' Graham asks, shutting the car off and turning to face me. I stare at the building, lightheaded. After a moment, he speaks again, concern lacing the word. "June?"

My head snaps to him. "Let's go home."

"Home?"

"Yeah. Mine, yours, whatever. Let's go. Just...let's go. Turn the car back on."

I reach for the keys in his hand as if I'm going to start the car and force him to drive off, but he moves them out of my reach, a small smile tipping his lips.

Stupid fucking dimples. Why did I work so hard to see them? I don't need their handsomeness when I'm having a full-blown panic attack.

"We're not leaving."

"Well, I'm not going in," I say, knowing I sound childish but beyond caring as I cross my arms on my chest. Instead of looking entertained, his face shifts, looking concerned.

"June, baby, what's going on?" His hand reaches for mine, twining out fingers and pulling me a bit toward him. The charms on my bracelet make a pretty sound, and it eases something in my chest just enough to speak.

"I can't do it!" I say, shaking my head. "I can't go in there. I'm going to make a fool of myself. I'm unqualified. I have no idea what I'm doing, and I'm going to just...ask them to give me thousands of dollars? What was I thinking?"

"You were thinking that you're the only one who loves this place enough to create a mural to adequately represent Seaside Point. You were thinking you're talented and an amazing artist and that by being the one chosen to do this mural, you'll be continuing your grandmother's legacy in a way you can feel proud of."

A lump grows in my throat with his soft, steady words.

"Well, past me was an idiot, and current me is a realist who wants to go home."

He lets out a small laugh, shaking his head. "What happened to the June I fell for, the one with boundless confidence?"

My chest lightens just a bit with his words, but it's swallowed when another wave of reality comes crushing in.

"She was delusional! She thought she could manifest her way into the life of her dreams! She thought she was lucky, but it was really just you!"

His face goes serious then, and he lets go of my hand before undoing my seatbelt, then using his strong grip to turn me in my seat toward him. Then he grabs my face, pulling me close and pressing his forehead to mine.

"No. You don't get it. Or you do, but you're too nervous right now to admit it. You were right. You are lucky. You're lucky because we make our own luck, June. You want to live a life that makes you feel happy and fulfilled every single moment, and you made it happen. You helped me realize that, helped me find my own luck, my own happiness. Now it's your turn." My throat tightens with his words, and I sniff.

"You can't make me emotional when I'm already mid-freakout, Graham. It's poor boyfriend behavior."

He smiles then, leaning in and pressing my lips to his.

"Sorry, I told you; I'm new at this. How am I doing on the pep-talk side of things?"

The joking and banter ease my nerves in a way I don't think anything else could, and I realize that's the true stroke of luck: having Graham when I need him most, and more importantly, him knowing exactly *what* I need.

"Pretty good," I grumble.

"You sound disappointed in that," he says with a laugh, and I can't help but return it, even if it's weak.

I take in a deep breath, knowing the truth in his words because he's right: I *am* lucky. Finding Graham was lucky. Finding someone who would do absolutely anything to make my every whim a reality was beyond lucky. Getting laid off was lucky, and winning that scratch-off was lucky. Walking into Daytrip that day was lucky, even if getting the job was all Graham. Being talented isn't lucky; it's genetics and innate skill, something I'm still trying to remind myself of daily, but having friends who pushed me to take a scary leap? Lucky as can be.

There are a million different lucky moments that led me to this one, and with that reminder, I nod, take in a deep breath, and smile at Graham.

"I am, mostly because it means you're right. I've gotta do this, and I'm going to kick ass when I do. Now let's go before I lose my nerve."

He grins but doesn't say anything. Instead, he leans in to kiss me, whispers, *stay there*, then walks around the car to help me out before we walk hand in hand into City Hall.

That confidence lasts for another thirty minutes, until about ten minutes into the meeting, when I need to step out for some fresh air and calm my rising nerves.

"I'll be right back," I murmur, then start to stand from where we're sitting along the side of the room. Graham looks to me, a bit confused, but I give him as confident a smile as I can muster. "Bathroom." He isn't buying it, but nods all the same, squeezing my hand. Claire catches my eye as I step away and mouths a question, asking if I want her to come, but I shake my head.

I just need air, space, and a bit of alone time to panic.

But this is Seaside Point, so I should have known I wouldn't get it.

"Hey, June bug," a familiar voice says as I pace the hall outside the city council meeting.

"Oh, hey," I say with a sigh as the door closes behind my brother. "I was just... getting some air. I can only listen to them arguing about things for so long." Grant doesn't buy it, but nods just the same, walking over to me with his hands in his pockets.

"How do you feel?"

"Like I'm gonna barf," I say, and Grant laughs, shaking his head.

"You're gonna do great. You're going to get this job, June. Trust me. I know these things." I bite my lip, looking away, then deciding that maybe one more thing off my chest would help.

"Even if I don't get this, I'm not going back to teaching." I bite my lip, taking in a deep breath before confessing what I did this morning. "I already sent Mrs. Jones an email, telling her as much." She replied near instantly, seeming relieved and telling me Mrs. Evans was planning on delaying her retirement, so all's well that ends well, I suppose.

I guess it really was the universe guiding me along after all. If there was even a shot that my job wouldn't be there next fall, I never would have taken a leave. But god, I'm so glad I did. Even if in this moment, it means my stomach is completely tied up in knots.

Grant nods, but doesn't speak, and I try to fill in the silence.

"I know you're disappointed—" I start, but his brows furrow, confused, before he finally speaks.

"Disappointed? Why would I be disappointed?"

I blink at him, unsure. "Because I'm turning into Mom. Because I'm chasing art instead of something practical. Because—"

He shakes his head, quickly stopping me in my tracks. "June bug, I would never think that."

"You wouldn't?" He takes a step closer to me, concern on his face. "You're not Mom, June. And not for nothing, Graham isn't Dad." Well, *that* much is true. The mere idea makes a small smile spread on my lips, and his own tip up as well. "What I mean is, you're responsible. You didn't jump from teaching to art in a heartbeat." I lift an eyebrow, and he laughs, his own sounding freer than mine. "Okay, well, you kind of did, but you had a backup to your backup. And pretty soon, you found a job, made your life stable, and *then* built an art career from the sidelines. And that was after years of hemming and hawing, planning to do just that. You also didn't quit your job and move to Paris the moment you sold a single painting. Did you really think I would be disappointed if you didn't go back to teaching?" I shrug, picking at the nails I painted last night, summer sky blue, Graham's favorite color.

"You sacrificed a lot for me, and I'll always be grateful for that. You could have gone away to school, could have left mom and dad's house long before I was able to, but you stayed in Seaside Point to keep an eye on me. I know that."

Something crosses his face, and I wonder if he thinks I didn't know that, if he thought I was living blissfully unaware.

But instead, he shocks me.

"June, I was never going to go to a traditional college. I was always going to head into some kind of trade." I blink at him, confused. "You may have gotten the creativity gene, but I got the working with my hands part of it and the resistance to authority. Do you really think I could have been wearing a tie and listening to some asshole tell me a report was due at ten?"

"I—" I start, but the mere thought of it makes me laugh, and if I'm being honest, even though I wasn't even a teenager when he graduated high school, even then it wouldn't have fit his style.

"I always want to work with my hands. I'm lucky that Miles' dad took me in, showed me what he could before he passed, but this is what I was meant to do. I thought you knew that."

"I mean, now that I'm being logical, I do."

"And now that I'm being logical, I see that you weren't."

'What?"

"Doing what you wanted to do."

Guilt wracks through me. "I like—"

"I know. I know, June. You like teaching. I know that. But you don't live for it. You live for making art. I'm worry that I talked so much shit about Mom and Dad and their lifestyle, I didn't make you feel safe in pursuing it. I should have been more mindful and—"

"No, no," I say, shaking my head and wiping a tear away. "We're both idiots. Probably some kind of stilted emotional growth we can blame on our emotionally immature parents."

Grant lets out a loud laugh, then shakes his head before pulling me in for a big hug. Wrapped in my brother's arms in the same way I have been a million times over the years, my nerves melt away.

"Now, that was enough sappiness for a decade, at least. Go in there and kick some ass, June. You're going to get the job; we all know it. But make it really hurt for those Stevens assholes, will you?" I pull back and smile, but his face goes soft. "It's what Grandma and Grandpa would have wanted."

"I thought you said no more sappiness," I say, eyes welling once more. He grins, then steps back.

"I'm your big brother. It's my job to be an asshole to you." I roll my eyes, then go to say something in argument, as is a little sister's way, but the door opens, and Maggie is in the doorway. She smiles wide at us before tipping her head inside.

"Come on, you two. Cece is about to present."

My stomach flip-flops, and I hesitate, contemplating running, but Grant is behind me, pushing me inside.

"You've got this, June. You don't need luck, or fate, or destiny. You've got talent. That's all you need today."

I nod, but when I walk in to see our entire crew looking at me, wide grins and thumbs up directed my way, I know he's wrong.

Because all I really need is this crew believing in me.

Cece does well: even I have to admit it. She would make a fantastic politician's wife, full of hair flips and wide smiles, her perfectly straight, shiny blonde locks gleaming in the fluorescent lighting. Her presentation itself is fine, I suppose, though she has way overshot the cost and, unless she's ridiculously fast, she undershot how long it will take to complete the project. Her concept is simple: a beachscape with the town's name front and center. It would be fine, would get the job done, and would be pretty enough.

It's fine.

It would be a fine mural for a generic tourist-trap town.

Unfortunately, Seaside Point isn't just some little tourist trap for a town. It's a year-round community, not just a place for visitors from Memorial Day to Labor Day. It's my home, it's the place I've always felt I belonged, and I know there are so many people who feel the same. Yes, it's a tourist destination with a beach, but that's not all it is. And *that* is what I am bringing to the table.

Instead of feeling resigned after her presentation, I'm invigorated, knowing even if I don't get the job, my mural is better.

I reach into my pocket, rubbing my thumb over the lucky penny there, but as my eyes move across the room to the corner where everyone I love most is sitting, I know I don't need the luck.

I am enough.

I always have been; I just needed the reminder. I guess at the end of the day, that's what my lucky girl summer was about. Everything worked out for me—not because I'm lucky, but because I work hard, and I deserve it.

The universe, and, of course, Graham, may have been moving me along, making things more obvious, but it was so I could end up here.

With my brother smiling at me, proud.

With Claire and Lainey giving me grins and thumbs up, full confidence that I'm going to knock this out of the park.

With Graham, leaning into the Decker to listen to something he's saying, then tipping his head back with a laugh, happy and at ease.

Who needs luck when you have the whole world?

So when I approach the stand, the PowerPoint that the girls helped me finalize behind me, I already know I have won.

Afterward, the council talks quietly amongst themselves, and each time Chet's face gets redder, my heart soars. He throws his hands up in the air a couple of times, and twice I look over at Cece, who is sitting, arms crossed on her chest, a smug look on her face as if she already knows the result.

But for the first time, I don't care. I don't care she's some town princess who always gets her way or that she's smug and a bitch. I don't care because I know this time, I'm going to get *my* way.

I'm going to land this job. I know it when I look around the room and see Seaside Point residents giving me waves and thumbs up. I know it when I looked around the room as I presented and saw them nodding and giving me encouraging smiles. I knew it when Mayor Mosley shook my hand eagerly after I presented, telling me I did a fantastic job.

But most of all, I know it when Benny stands after their deliberation and smiles in my direction. My hand tightens in Graham's and Grant's, the two most important men in my life sitting on either side of me, supporting me, and I hold my breath as he speaks.

"The city council has voted, and due to its unique way of capturing the love both tourists and locals have for our small town, we're awarding June Taylor the Third Street mural project," Benny's loud voice booms. Cheers erupt around me, my friends and family excited as I drop my head into my hand and let out a deep, relieved breath. I only get that one second to let it sink in before Graham bends, picks me up, and spins me around. I let out a laugh, tears rolling down my cheeks as he peppers kisses across my lips and cheeks,

"You did it," he murmurs when he sets me down. "God, I'm so proud of you, June."

"I guess I did," I say with a laugh, the joy bubbling over now, washing out the nervous energy from before.

"How do you feel?"

I pause, then look at Graham, feeling only one thing.

"Pretty damn lucky."

# ACKNOWLEDGMENTS

HAPPY ACKNOWLEDGEMENTS TIME FRIENDS!

If you're new to the Morganverse, this is where. I wax poetic about my favorite people on this planet. As a very codependent person with raging ADHD and crippling anxiety (I know, I know, I need to talk to a professional about that, but do you know what gives me anxiety? Doctor's appointments. And phone calls), it's important for me to. Make sure I give praise to the people who made this story a reality, since without them, this book would MOST DEFINITELY never exist. Like, At all.

So here we go!

First and foremost, always. and forever, Alex. Thank you for being the best person on this planet, and the first person to ever really get me. The steadfast, stoic Graham, who handles all of the realities of life, to my floaty, head-in-the-clouds June. There's a line in here that says she loves how he entertains her. idiosyncrasies rather than enduring them, and that's you. You've never made me feel weird for any of the things i do to make myself happy, be it tapping on the roof while you go through a yellow light or making everyone stop to wish at 11:11. If I didn't know any better, I'd think I wrote you up, my own personal book boyfriend. I love you forever.

To Ryan, Owen, and Ella, thank you for being the best kids ever and for letting me be your mom. I'm so honored to get the opportunity to watch you all grow up into the coolest humans. Also, if you're reading this, you're in so much trouble.

To Rae, the best PA a girl could ask for, my best friend, and possibly the funniest person I've ever met. Thank you for always enduring my meltdowns, for holding my hand when I need it, and for always being there. I scream I APPRECIATE YOU probably four times a week to the point where you probably don't even believe it anymore, but truly, I could not do this at all without you. I love you, and you're never allowed to leave me.

To Ashleigh, thank you for always being the best comic relief when I need it and for always yapping with me about old lady crafts and gardening. Love you so much, and I miss you like crazy, sorry I always have to actually work instead of yapping(blech)

To Taj, the best agent a girl could ask for. Thank you for always championing me and making my biggest dreams come true!!

Thank you to Becca and Lori for helping to make this book what it is!

Thank you to Cat for making the most AMAZING cover, always.

Thank you, Kylie, Marlee, and April, for alpha reading and assuring me this isn't a complete dumpster fire when I'm in the depths of writing and sure it is, in fact, a dumpster fire.

To Kayla for being the biggest help with keeping my social media running smoothly and getting the word out!

Thank you to my ARC and content team for being absolutely amazing. I love each and every one of you, and I can never fully tell you what your love and support mean to me. I know that the success of this book is in huge part due to all of you, and I can't possibly thank you enough.

Finally, thank you, dear Reader. I once thought being an author was a pipe dream, but you all told me I could make it a reality, and I'll never be able to thank you enough for that. Thank you, thank you, thank you. I love you all forever.

Passenger Princess

If This Was a Movie

Never Been Worse

**Down the Shore Series**

Tourist Trap

Lucky Girl Summer

**Mavens Series**

Maneater

**Holly Ridge Series**

The Bright Side of Christmas

The Promise of Forever

The Lie of Having It All

**The Mastermind Duet**

Ivory Tower

Diamonress

**All My Love**

www.ingramcontent.com/pod-product-compliance
Lightning Source LLC
Chambersburg PA
CBHW071730150726
47998CB00005B/1577